THE CAPITAL

ROBERT MENASSE

THE
CAPITAL

Translated from the German by
Jamie Bulloch

MACLEHOSE PRESS
QUERCUS · LONDON

First published in the German language as
Die Hauptstadt by Suhrkamp Verlag in 2017

First published in Great Britain in 2019 by MacLehose Press.

This paperback edition published in 2020 by

MacLehose Press
An imprint of Quercus Publishing Ltd
Carmelite House
50 Victoria Embankment
London EC4Y 0DZ

An Hachette UK company

The translation of this work was supported by
a grant from the Goethe-Institut and from the
Austrian Federal Ministry of Education, Arts and Culture

ISBN (MMP) 978 0 85705 864 5
ISBN (Ebook) 978 0 85705 861 4

1 3 5 7 9 10 8 6 4 2

Designed and typeset in Minion by Patty Rennie
Printed and bound in Great Britain by Clays Ltd, Elcograf S.p.A.

"Rêver, c'est le bonheur;
attendre, c'est la vie."
VICTOR HUGO

Prologue

THERE'S A PIG on the loose! David de Vriend caught sight of it when he opened his sitting-room window for one last glance at the square before leaving this apartment for good. He wasn't a sentimental man. He had lived here for sixty years, looked out onto this square for sixty years and was now bringing it to an end. That's all. It was his favourite phrase; whenever he had something to say, report, attest, he would utter two or three sentences, followed by, "That's all." For David de Vriend this phrase was the only legitimate résumé of each moment or chapter in his life. The removal firm had been to fetch the few personal effects he was taking to his new home. Effects – a strange word, but it had no effect on him. Then the men came to clear out everything else, including those things that were screwed and nailed down, and the screws and nails too. They yanked it out, dismantled it and took it all away until the apartment was "as clean as a whistle", as people say. De Vriend had made himself a coffee while his cooker and moka pot were still there, watching the men, taking care not to get in their way, and he had held on to his empty cup for a long moment before dropping it into a rubbish bag. Then the men were gone and the apartment was empty. As clean as a whistle. One last glance out of the window. There was nothing there he did not know, and now he had to move out because another time had come – but there it was:

3

down below was . . . a real pig! In Sainte-Catherine, the centre of Brussels. It must have come from rue de la Braie, it trotted along the construction hoarding in front of the building, de Vriend leaned out of the window and saw the pig turn right at the corner into rue du Vieux Marché aux Grains, avoiding a few passers-by and almost running under a taxi.

Kai-Uwe Frigge, thrown forwards by the emergency stop, fell back into the seat. He grimaced. Frigge was late, he was stressed. What was wrong now? He wasn't *really* late, but he liked to get to his appointments ten minutes early, especially when it was raining, so he could tidy himself up a bit in the loo – his soaked hair, fogged-up glasses – before the person he was meeting arrived —

A pig! Did you see that, Monsieur? the taxi driver exclaimed. It almost leaped into my car! He was bent right over his steering wheel: There! There! Can you see it?

Now Kai-Uwe Frigge did see it. He wiped the window with the back of his hand and caught the pig trotting off sideways, its wet body glistening a dirty pink in the glow of the streetlamps.

Here we are, Monsieur! I can't drive any closer. Fancy that! Almost went slap bang into a pig. What a road hog! But I saved his bacon, didn't I, eh?

In Menelas, Fenia Xenopoulou sat at the first table by the large window with a view of the square. It annoyed her that she had got there so early. To be waiting in the restaurant when he arrived didn't convey self-confidence. She was nervous. She had worried that the rain might make the traffic worse and had left herself too much time. She was already on her second ouzo. The waiter buzzed around her like an irritating wasp. Fenia stared at the glass and told herself not to touch it. The waiter brought a carafe of fresh water. Then he came with a small dish of olives – and said, A pig!

What? Looking up, she saw that the waiter was staring out at the square, mesmerised, and now she could see it too: the pig was making a dash for the restaurant, a ridiculous sight as its short legs flitted back and forth beneath its solid, round body. At first glance she thought it was a dog, one of those revolting creatures overfed by widows, but no – it really was a pig! It could have been straight out of a picture book. She saw the snout and the ears as lines, contours, that's how you would draw a pig for a child, but this one seemed to have sprung from a children's horror story. It wasn't a wild boar, it was a filthy, but unquestionably pink domestic pig, with something mad, something menacing about it. The rain continued to pour down the window and, in a blur, Fenia Xenopoulou saw the pig screech to a halt as it encountered some passers-by. The creature's legs were at full stretch, it skidded, threw itself to one side, jack-knifed, gained traction again and galloped back, now in the direction of Hotel Atlas. At that moment Ryszard Oświecki was leaving the hotel. He had already pulled the hood of his coat over his head on his way through the hotel lobby. Now he stepped out into the rain, briskly, but not in too much of a hurry; he didn't want to attract attention. The rain was a boon; in the circumstances both his hood and lively pace were perfectly normal and inconspicuous. Later, nobody would be able to say that they had seen a man running away – about this old, roughly this tall, and yes, of course they remembered the colour of the coat . . . Turning smartly to his right, he heard animated cries, a scream and a bizarre panting mixed with squeals. He gasped and looked back. Now he spotted the pig. He couldn't believe his eyes. There, between two of the wrought-iron poles that lined the hotel forecourt, was a pig. It stood, head lowered, like a bull about to launch an attack. There was something both preposterous and menacing about this creature. It was a total mystery: where had the pig come from and why was it there? Ryszard Oświecki got the impression that all life in this square – at least as far as he could see – had stiffened, frozen, the animal's tiny eyes reflected the neon light from the hotel's façade. Oświecki started to run! He ran to the right, glanced back, the pig yanked up its head with a snort, took a few steps backwards, turned around, then ran right across the square to the row of trees outside the Flemish Cultural Centre, De Markten. The passers-by witnessing the scene kept their eyes on the pig rather than the man in the hood, and now Martin Susman saw the creature too. He lived in a building next to Hotel Atlas and was just opening the window to let in some fresh air. Susman couldn't believe his eyes: that looked like a pig! He had just been contemplating his life, thinking about the coincidences that had led him, the son of Austrian farmers, to be living and working in Brussels. In his present mood everything seemed crazy and alien, but a pig on the loose in the square below, that was just *too* crazy, it must be his mind playing tricks on him, a projection of his memory! He scanned the square but the pig had vanished.

The creature sprinted across rue Sainte-Catherine, keeping left to avoid the tourists coming out of the church, and raced on past to the quai au Briques. The tourists laughed, no doubt thinking that this stressed pig on the verge of collapse was a Brussels tradition, a local phenomenon. Some of them would later check their guidebooks for an explanation. Weren't bulls driven through the streets of Pamplona in Spain to mark some holiday? Maybe they did the same in Brussels, but with pigs? If you encounter the incomprehensible in a place where you don't expect to understand everything, then life can be very amusing indeed.

At that moment Gouda Mustafa turned the corner and almost walked straight into the pig. Almost? Hadn't it in fact touched him, brushed his leg? A pig? Leaping aside in panic, Gouda Mustafa lost his balance and fell. Now he was lying in a puddle, which made the whole thing even worse. It wasn't the grime of the gutter that made him feel defiled, but contact – if there *had* been contact – with the unclean animal.

Then Mustafa saw a hand reaching down to him, he saw the face of an elderly gentleman, a sad, troubled, rain-sodden face; the old man seemed to be crying. It was Professor Alois Erhart. Gouda Mustafa couldn't understand what he was saying, all he grasped was the word "O.K."

O.K.! O.K.! Mustafa said.

Professor Erhart kept talking, said in English that he'd had a fall today too, but he was so confused that he said "fail" instead of "fall". Gouda Mustafa didn't understand him and said O.K. again.

The blue lights had arrived. Emergency services. Police. The entire square rotated, flickered, twitched in the blue light. The emergency vehicles sped howling towards Hotel Atlas. The sky above Brussels played its part: the rain fell. Now it appeared to be raining blue, twinkling drops. A strong gust of wind joined in, tugging at several umbrellas and wrenching them inside out. Gouda Mustafa took Professor Erhart's hand and allowed himself to be helped up. His father had warned him about Europe.

One

*Connections need not really exist, but without them
everything would fall apart.*

WHO INVENTED MUSTARD? Not a great beginning for a novel. Having said that, there can be no good beginning because, whether good or not so good, there is no beginning. For every conceivable opening sentence is already an end – even if things continue afterwards. It sits at the end of thousands upon thousands of pages which were never written: the prehistory.

When you embark on the reading of a novel you ought to be able to leaf back after the very first sentence. Such was Martin Susman's dream, it's what he had really wanted to be: a teller of prehistories. He had abandoned an archaeology degree and only then – well, it doesn't matter, it's part of the prehistory that has to be edited out of the opening to every novel, because otherwise in the end we would never get to the beginning.

Martin Susman sat at his desk – he had pushed his laptop to one side – squeezing mustard from two different tubes onto a plate, a hot English mustard and a sweet German one, and wondering who had invented mustard. Who had hit upon the quirky idea of creating a paste that entirely masks the flavour of a dish without itself tasting good? And how was it possible that this had become a successful mass-produced item? It is, he thought, a product like Coca-Cola. A product that nobody would miss if it didn't exist. On the way home Martin Susman had stopped at the branch of Delhaize on boulevard Anspach to buy two bottles of wine, a bunch of yellow tulips, a bratwurst and of course mustard, two tubes, because he couldn't decide between sweet and hot.

The bratwurst was now bouncing and hissing in the pan, the gas was too high, the fat was burning, the sausage charring, but Martin wasn't paying any attention. He just sat there staring at the somewhat lighter yellow ring of mustard on the white plate and beside it the dark-brown one – miniature sculptures of dogshit. The specialist literature has yet to describe staring at mustard on a plate while a sausage burns in the frying pan as a clear and typical symptom of depression, but we may interpret it as such.

The mustard on the plate. The open window, the curtain of rain. The musty air, the stench of carbonised meat, the sizzle of burst intestine and burning fat, the shit sculptures on the china plate – then Martin Susman heard the shot.

He didn't even jump. It sounded like a champagne bottle being opened nearby. But there was no apartment on the other side of the curiously thin wall. Next door stood Hotel Atlas – what a euphemistic name for this slight building which chiefly housed hunched lobbyists pulling wheelie suitcases in their wake. Time and again, without thinking any more of it, Martin Susman would hear things through the wall that he didn't especially wish to hear. Reality T.V. or – who knows? – just reality, snoring or moaning.

The rain grew heavier. Martin felt like leaving his apartment. He was well kitted out for Brussels. At his goodbye party in Vienna people had given him pointed presents in preparation for Brussels, including nine umbrellas, from the classic British "long" and German "telescopic" models to the Italian mini in three Benetton colours, plus two cycling ponchos.

He sat motionless in front of his plate, staring at the mustard. Later he was able to tell the police exactly when the shot had been fired, because what he imagined to be the popping of a champagne cork had encouraged him to open a bottle of wine himself. Every day he postponed the first glass for as long as possible. He never drank before seven. He checked the time: it was 19.35. Martin went to the fridge, took out the bottle, turned off the gas, tossed the sausage into the bin, put the frying pan in the sink and turned on the tap. The hiss of water on the hot metal. Stop gawking! his mother would hiss whenever he sat there with a book, staring into space, instead of feeding the pigs or helping muck out the shed.

Dr Martin Susman sat there in front of the plate with mustard and poured himself a glass of wine, then another. The window was open, from time to time he got up and went to peer out of it, then sat down at the table again. On the third glass a blue light swept the walls of his room. The tulips in the vase on the fireplace pulsed a bluish colour. The telephone rang. He didn't pick up. Let it ring a few more times. From the display Martin Susman saw who the caller was. He didn't pick up.

Prehistory. It's so significant and yet it flickers unremarkably, like the eternal flame in the church of Sainte-Catherine at the other end of place Vieux Marché aux Grains, where Martin Susman lived.

In the church a few people had taken shelter from the rain, they stood around indecisively or wandered down the nave, tourists skimmed their guidebooks and followed the itinerary of sights: "Black Madonna, 14th century", "Portrait of Saint Catherine", "Typical Flemish pulpit, thought to be from Mechelen", "Tombstone of Gilles-Lambert Godecharle" . . .

The occasional camera flash.

The man sitting alone in a pew appeared to be praying. Elbows propped up, chin on his interlaced hands, rounded back. He wore a black jacket with a hood which was pulled over his head, and if "Guinness" hadn't been emblazoned on his back he could have been mistaken at first glance for a monk in a cowl.

The Brussels rain probably accounted for the jacket with the hood, but the impression he gave wearing it also betrayed something fundamental about this man. In his own way he was a monk. He regarded the monastic existence, or whatever he understood by this – asceticism, meditation, retreat – as the saving grace of a life under constant threat of chaos and distraction. For him this wasn't associated with any order or monastery, nor did it imply detachment from the world. Every man, irrespective of his job or function, could – *must* – be a monk in his field, the servant of a higher power, focused on his task.

He loved to gaze at the tortured man on the cross and think of death. Each time he found it purified his feelings, concentrated his thoughts and refreshed his energies.

This was Mateusz Oświecki. His baptismal name, however, and the one in his passport, was Ryszard. Oświecki first became Mateusz in the seminary of the Lubrański Academy in Poznań, where every "enlightened pupil" was given one of the eleven apostles' names. He had been re-baptised and anointed as "Matthew, the tax collector". Even though he had left the seminary, he kept Mateusz as his *nom de guerre*. Where he needed to show his passport at border crossings he was Ryszard. From statements given by former contacts he was known to intelligence services as Matek, a diminutive form of Mateusz. That's what his comrades-in-arms called him. He undertook his missions as Mateusz, was a wanted man as Matek, and slipped through the cracks as Ryszard.

Oświecki didn't pray. He didn't formulate sentences in his head which began with "Lord" and were only ever requests, "Give me strength . . ." to do this or that, "Bless . . ." this or that . . . There was nothing to be wished for from an absolute spirit who remained silent. He gazed at the man nailed to the cross. The experience that this man had undergone and ultimately put into words for the sake of mankind was that of complete abandonment at the moment of confrontation with the absolute: when the mortal coil is slashed, lacerated, gashed, pierced and torn open, when the agonising screams of a life fade to a whimper and finally to silence. Only in silence is life close to the almighty spirit, who on an inscrutable whim has discharged from his self the very opposite of his being: time. Starting at the point of their birth, a person can think back, back and back further, back into eternity, but they will never arrive at a beginning, and with their foolish concept of time will grasp only one thing: before they existed, for an eternity they did not exist. And they can think ahead, from the moment of their death to as far as they wish in the future, never reaching an end, but only this realisation: they will be no more for all eternity. And the interlude between eternity and eternity is time – the clamour, the hubbub, the stamping of machines, the drone of engines, the crash and bang of weapons, the chorales of the furious and happily betrayed masses, the rumble of thunder and terrified panting in the microscopic terrarium of the earth.

Mateusz Oświecki gazed at the tortured man.

Rather than folding his hands he had interlocked them, and now dug his fingernails into the backs of his hands until his knuckles cracked and the skin stung. He felt a pain older than himself, a pain he could urgently recall at any time. In early 1940 his grandfather, Ryszard, had gone underground to fight in the Polish Resistance under General Stefan Rowecki against the Germans. In April of that year he was betrayed, arrested, tortured and then publicly shot in Lublin as a partisan. Mateusz's grandmother was eight months pregnant at the time, her child was born in Kielce in

May 1940 and was given his father's name. To avoid the boy being punished by association, he was taken to the family of a great-uncle in Poznań, where he grew up, and witnessed the uprising when he was sixteen. The young schoolboy joined Major Franczak's group to fight in the anti-communist resistance. He was used for acts of sabotage and later to abduct people working as informers for the S.B., the Polish secret police. In 1964 he was betrayed by a comrade for 6,000 zlotys. Ryszard was arrested in a safe house and tortured to death in an S.B. cellar. At the time his wife, Marija, was pregnant, their child was born in February 1965 in the village of Kozice Górne and christened with the same name as his grandfather and father. Another son who never knew his father, about whom his mother spoke little. Once she said, We would meet in fields or in the woods. He would turn up to our rendezvous with a pistol and hand grenades.

An eternally silent grandfather. An eternally silent father. The Poles, Matek concluded, had always fought for Europe's freedom. Everyone who joined the struggle had grown up in silence and then fought until they passed away into silence.

His mother took him to see the priests, sought advocates, bought letters of recommendation, she put her faith in the protection that the Church could guarantee. In the end she placed him with the Brothers in Poznań, where he learned for himself the vulnerability of the human body: blood is a lubricant to help get inside the mortal coil, skin merely damp parchment, the mouth and throat a black hole that is stuffed until the last sound fades to nothing, after which silently it sucks up what life ought to bestow. And there too he encountered an entirely new concept of "underground". When the pupils were assigned their apostolic names, they were led into the magnificent cathedral of Poznań, into the secret underground vaults and sepulchres, via stone steps that

16

shimmered and glinted in the flames of the torches, down into the deepest underground, through a final roughcast tunnel and into a chamber that turned out to be a sunken chapel of death and eternal life. A barrel-vaulted room, hewn in the tenth century from stone one hundred feet below the blood-soaked earth of Poland. On the far side of this room was a monumental crucifix with a terrifyingly naturalistic Christ figure, behind it reliefs of angels protruding from the stone or seeming to pass into and through it, horrifyingly animated in the flicker of the flames. In front of the crucifix a Madonna, the like of which young Ryszard had never seen before, not in any church, nor in any picture in his books. She was completely covered up! The Madonna wore a cloak that she had arranged over her brow, nose and mouth in such a way that only her eyes were visible through a narrow slit, eye sockets so deep and so dead as they could only be after a thousand years of weeping. All of this, the altar too, had been sculpted and shaped from the stone and marl clay of the geological layer breached at this depth. Benches of cold stone on which sat eleven monks in black habits, their backs turned to Ryszard and the other pupils entering the room, and their bowed heads covered with cowls.

The pupils were led forward along the aisle between the praying monks to the Christ figure, where they crossed themselves and were then instructed to turn around. Looking back, Ryszard could now see that beneath the cowls glistened skulls, while the rosaries in the monks' hands hung from bones – these monks were skeletons.

Beneath the earth one is closer to God than on the mountaintops.

Mateusz Oświecki tapped his forehead several times with the tips of his fingers. His own flesh felt heavy and rotten. And in his abdomen – beneath the navel and to the left – he sensed a burning. He realised that death was burning there. But rather than frighten him it took the fear away.

These skeletons in habits were the bones of the missionary bishop Jordan and the members of the founding college of the Archdiocese of Poznań. For almost one thousand years they had sat there in eternal silent prayer. In the presence of these eleven skeletons each pupil was assigned one of eleven apostle names. Eleven? No Judas? Yes, there was. But to give a pupil the name of Peter, God's primary vicar on earth, would have been insolent. He who is chosen can, as John or Paul, become Peter too.

Mateusz Oświecki pressed his palms to his ears. So many voices inside his head. He closed his eyes. Too many images. This wasn't memory, it wasn't prehistory. This, here, was now, now as he was sitting before the crucified Christ. With the burning in his stomach. He wasn't afraid, just felt that numbness you get before an important test or difficult task. The most difficult test is the one you can take only once. He opened his eyes, looked up and stared at the wound in the Redeemer's side.

Mateusz Oświecki actually envied his victims. They had it all behind them.

He got up, stepped out of the stone of the church, cast a brief glance at the blue light dancing outside Hotel Atlas and walked, head bowed and hood pulled down, slowly through the rain towards Sainte-Catherine Metro station.

When Alois Erhart returned to Hotel Atlas he was initially barred from entering. Or at least he interpreted the policeman's out-stretched hand as an order to stay where he was. Unable to speak good French, he couldn't understand what the policeman was saying.

When from a distance he'd glimpsed the rotating blue lights his first thought had been suicide. As he approached the hotel, the feeling that had assailed him at lunchtime was back: as if the nothingness into which everyone plunges sooner or later were spreading – suddenly, like an announcement or even an invitation – through his chest and abdomen. It had left him numb and breathless, this miracle that a growing emptiness can unfurl within the finite mantle of the human body, infinitely. The soul as a black hole, sucking up all the experiences he'd had in a lifetime and making them disappear until all that was left was the nothingness, the absolute emptiness, utterly black, but without the mildness of a starless night.

Now he stood by the hotel steps, his bones aching and his muscles burning with tiredness, a few onlookers behind him, and explained in English that he was a guest at the hotel, he had a room here – which failed to elicit any laxity in the outstretched arm. He found the situation so surreal that he would not have been surprised if he were now arrested. But he wasn't just the old man whose body was irrevocably beginning to let him down, he was also Professor Emeritus Dr Erhart, who had been an authority for half his life. A tourist, he said determinedly, he was a tourist. Here! In this hotel. And he wished to go to his room. The officer accompanied him into the lobby and led him over to a man in his mid-fifties, almost two metres tall and wearing a grey suit that was too tight, who asked him for his I.D.

Why was the professor standing with his head bowed? He saw the inflated, gassy belly of this gigantic man – and was seized by pity. There are some who, with their massive physical presence, appear eternally strong, always fit, never ailing until suddenly, as if struck by lightning, they're lying there dead at an age where people say, That's no age at all. Ever proud of their constitution, they've regarded themselves as immortal so long as they've been able to publicly hone their body, thrust it in the faces of others. These people have never been confronted with the question of what they'll do when they're old and chronically ill, an invalid in the foreseeable future. On the inside this man was rotten and brittle, his decline was imminent, only he didn't know it.

Professor Erhart showed him his passport.

When had he arrived? *Parlez-vous français?* No? English? When had he left the hotel? Had he been at the hotel between 7.00 and 8.00 p.m.?

Why these questions?

Homicide squad. A man had been shot in one of the hotel bedrooms.

His right arm was painful. It crossed Professor Erhart's mind that people might soon begin to notice that he kept stroking, pressing, kneading his arm.

He took his digital camera from the side pocket of his raincoat and switched it on. He could show them where he'd been. Each photograph was tagged with the time it was taken.

The man smiled and browsed the photos. An afternoon in the European Quarter, rond-point Schuman. The Berlaymont and Justus Lipsius buildings. A road sign that read "rue Joseph II". Why that road sign?

I'm Austrian!

I see.

The "Dream of Europe" sculpture in rue de la Loi. The bronze figure of a blind (or sleepwalking?) man taking a step from the plinth into the void. The things tourists take pictures of! There. 19.15: Grande Place. Several photos there until 19.28. Then the last photograph: 20.04, Sainte-Catherine, the nave. The man pressed again and was back at the first picture. He pressed the back button.

Christ, the altar, and before it a man sitting in a pew with "Guinness" on the back of his jacket.

He grinned and returned the camera to Erhart.

Up in his room, the professor went over to the window, looked out at the rain, ran his hand through his wet hair and listened to his inner voice. He couldn't hear anything. On arrival that lunchtime he had immediately opened the window and leaned out a fair way to get a better view of the square; he'd leaned too far, almost losing his balance, his feet no longer on the ground, he saw the asphalt rushing towards him, it all happened so quickly, he pushed himself back, fell to the floor beside the window knocking his right forearm against the radiator, and found himself sitting in an absurdly contorted position. Erhart felt as if he were in the freefall he had avoided by a whisker, a feeling you might get in the moment before death. He had then pulled himself onto the bed and sat there panting, and a sudden wave of euphoria washed over him: he was free. Still. He could decide for himself. And he would make the decision. Not now, but at the right time. Suicide *victim* – what a silly term! An autonomous and free individual, rather! He knew he had to – and now he knew that he was able to. Now he realised that death was as banal, trifling and inevitable as the "A.O.B." at the bottom of an agenda. The moment when there was nothing else. He had to leapfrog dying. Leap.

He didn't want to die like his wife had. So helpless at the end, so reliant on him . . .

Erhart picked up the remote control and turned on the T.V. He took off his shirt and examined the bruise on his right arm. He pressed the remote: keep going! He took off his trousers, keep going! Socks, keep going! Pants, keep going! He ended up with the Arte channel, where a film was just beginning, a classic: "From Here to Eternity". He hadn't seen it for decades. He stretched out on the bed. "This film is presented by parship.de, the leading partner agency," announced a voice.

It was no coincidence that Fenia Xenopoulou had been thinking about rescue at the very moment the ambulance turned into the square and the sirens wailed. For days she had been thinking of nothing else; it had become an obsession and that's why she was thinking of it now: rescue! He's got to rescue me!

She was having dinner at Menelas, opposite Hotel Atlas, with Kai-Uwe Frigge, who she had privately called Fridsch since a brief fling a couple of years before, although it was teasingly unclear whether she was bastardising his name to "Fritz" because he was German, or as a nod to "fridge", because in his fondness for factual accuracy he came across as so cold. Frigge, a lanky, agile man in his mid-forties, originally from Hamburg and now in Brussels for ten years, had been lucky (or had perhaps not relied on his luck) in the trench warfare, intrigues and bartering that inherently precede the formation of a new European Commission private office, and made an impressive career leap. Now he was principal private secretary in the Directorate-General for Trade, and thus the influential section head for one of the most powerful commissioners within the Union.

It had not been Fenia Xenopoulou's wish that the two of them should meet in a fairly mediocre Greek eatery in this city full of first-class restaurants. She wasn't homesick and felt no longing for the aromas and flavours of her native cuisine. Kai-Uwe Frigge had suggested the place. He had wanted to give his Greek colleague a sign of solidarity now that, following Greece's near bankruptcy and the fourth outrageously expensive E.U. bailout, "the Greeks" were very much out of favour amongst colleagues and the general public. He had felt sure he'd win Brownie points when he suggested via e-mail that they meet at "Menelas? On Vieux Marché aux Grains, Sainte-Catherine, supposed to be a very good Greek!" and she had replied, O.K. Fenia really couldn't care less. She had been living and working too long in Brussels to be interested in patriotism. What she wanted was her own personal bailout.

Calling the fund intended to avert Greek bankruptcy a rescue umbrella was unintentionally funny, Frigge said. You know it's the luck of the draw when it comes to metaphors in our business!

Fenia Xenopoulou didn't find it in the least bit amusing and had no idea what he was trying to say, but she beamed at him. It was like a mask and she didn't know whether or not people could tell it was affected. In the past she had always been able to rely on her masterful deployment of facial muscles, timing, blindingly white teeth and warm eyes to emit an irresistible genuineness. Even for the artificial you need a natural talent, but because of her career setback – at her age! She was turning forty! – Fenia was so distraught that she could no longer be sure of her natural talent for consciously appealing to people. In her mind, self-doubt had covered her face like psoriasis.

Kai-Uwe had ordered a farmer's salad and Fenia's first impulse was to say, I'll have the same. But then she heard herself ordering *giouvetsi*! It was lukewarm and dripping with fat. Why was she no longer in control of herself? She was beginning to come apart at the seams. She had to watch out. The waiter poured wine. She peered at the glass and thought, another eighty calories. Taking a sip of water and pressing the glass to her bottom lips with both hands, she summoned all her strength and looked at Kai-Uwe, trying to assume an expression at once complicit and seductive. Inside she was cursing to herself. What was wrong with her?

Rettungsschirm – rescue umbrella! Kai-Uwe said. German lends itself to neologisms like that. It only has to appear three times in the *Frankfurter Allgemeine Zeitung* for every educated person to consider it perfectly normal. After that there's no escaping it. The boss utters this word into every camera. The translators have worked up a nice sweat. English and French have their equivalent of a *Rettungsring* – lifebelt, and *Regenschirm* – umbrella. But what, they asked us politely, is a *Rettungschirm*? The French began by translating it as "parachute", but then there were objections from the Élysée Palace that a parachute only slows down a fall rather than stopping it altogether, this was sending out the wrong signal, so could the Germans please . . .

When he ate an olive and put the stone on his plate it seemed to Fenia as if he were ingesting only the taste of the olive, and sending the calories back to the kitchen.

Then the sirens began to wail, followed by the blue light, blue blue blue blue . . .

Fridsch?

Yes?

You've got to – she was about say it – rescue me. But that was impossible. She corrected herself: help me! No, she had to appear competent, not needy.

Yes? He peered at Hotel Atlas through the window of the restaurant. He saw a stretcher being carried out of the ambulance and men hurrying with it into the hotel. Though Menelas was very close to Atlas, the distance was still too great for death to cross his mind. For him it was mere choreography, people moving to light and sound.

She'd already said, You've got to, now she wanted to unsay those words, but that was no longer possible. You've got to . . . understand . . . but I know you do! I know you understand that I . . .

Yes? He looked at her.

The police sirens.

Fenia Xenopoulou had started off in the Directorate-General for Competition. The commissioner, a Spaniard, had been clueless. But each commissioner is as good as their office and she had stood out as an outstanding element of a perfectly functioning office. She got divorced. She had neither the time nor inclination to have a man sitting in her Brussels apartment every second – or later every third or fourth – weekend, or to visit him in Athens and listen to him gossip about the intimacies of Athenian society and puff on cigarettes like a caricature of a nouveau riche. She had married a star lawyer and ended up throwing a provincial solicitor out of her apartment! Then she climbed a rung higher and entered the private office of the commissioner for Trade. In Trade you earn merit by trampling down trade barriers. She no longer had a private life, nor shackles, there was only free trade. She really believed that the career she saw as her future would be the reward for her contribution to making the world a better place. To her mind, "fair trade" was a tautology. Surely trade was the prerequisite for global fairness. The commissioner, a Dutchman, had scruples; he was so unbelievably punctilious. Fenia worked hard to calculate how many guilders his scruples cost. The man still crunched numbers in guilders! The credit he got each time Fenia had persuaded him of something was worth its weight in gold! Now it was time for the next rung on the ladder. She expected it to happen after the European elections, when the Commission was reconstituted. And she was, in fact, promoted. She was given a department. What was the problem? In Fenia's eyes, this promotion was a demotion, a career slump, a rejection. She became head of Directorate C ("Communication") in the Directorate-General for Culture!

Culture!

She had studied Economics at L.S.E., done her postgrad at Stanford University, passed the E.U. *concours* and now she was stuck in the D.-G. for culture! It was about as pointless as sitting around playing Monopoly! Culture was a meaningless ministry without a budget or any weight in the Commission, without influence or power. Colleagues called Culture an alibi ministry – if only it were that! Alibis are important; every crime requires an alibi! But Culture wasn't even window-dressing, because nobody bothered to look at what was being dressed up. If the commissioner for Trade or Energy – even the commissioner for Catching Fish – needed the loo during a Commission meeting, the discussion was paused and they waited until he or she came back. But when the Culture commissioner had to pop out, they went on talking unperturbed; in fact nobody really noticed whether she was sitting at the negotiating table or on the loo.

Fenia Xenopoulou felt as though she was in lift that had gone up, but had got stuck, unnoticed, between two floors.

I need to get out! she said. When she came back from the toilet she saw that he was on his mobile. He hadn't waited.

Fridsch and Fenia gazed through the large window at the hotel, silent like an elderly couple delighted to have something to talk about at last.

What's going on over there?

No idea! Perhaps one of the hotel guests had a heart attack, Fridsch said.

But the police don't turn up if someone's had a heart attack!

You're right, he said. And after a brief pause he almost said, Talking of heart, how's your love life? But he bit his lip.

Something's weighing on your mind, isn't it? he said.

Yes!

You can tell me everything!

He listened, nodded and nodded again, uttering the odd, drawn-out "O.K.", to show that he was listening, and in the end he said, So how can I help?

You've got to ask for me. Can you . . . request me? I want to come back to Trade. Or could you have a word with Queneau? You get on well with him. He listens to you. Maybe he can do something. I *have* to get out of Culture. I'm suffocating!

Yes, he said. All of a sudden he was scared. Perhaps that's too strong a word. He felt a trepidation he could not explain. He never thought about his life. He *had* thought about his life back in the past – a long time ago when he'd had no life experience. They had been fantasies, dreams, he'd confused dreams with contemplation. It couldn't be said that he had pursued his dreams. Just as a traveller heads to a particular platform at the station, so Kai-Uwe had made for the starting point of a journey to a particular destination, and ever since he had been on track. Deep down he knew that it was often simply luck that stopped you being derailed. As long as you were on track there was nothing else you had to think about. Life. Either it functions or it doesn't. If it functions, then the "it" becomes replaced by "you". You function. He didn't think all this through; it just seemed clear to him. He confused this clarity with solid ground on which he was walking without having to think at every step. But now it felt slightly crumbly underfoot. Why? He didn't ask himself the question, he merely felt a faint trepidation. I need to pop to the loo!

He washed his hands and looked at himself in the mirror. He didn't feel like a stranger, but that isn't the same as feeling familiar. Frigge slipped a Viagra tablet from his wallet. He always had one on him. He crunched it between his teeth, took a sip of water, then washed his hands again.

He knew that, like him, Fenia had to get up very early the next morning. Which meant they would have to go to bed soon. They had to function.

They took a taxi to his apartment in Ixelles. He faked desire for her; she faked an orgasm. The chemistry was right. The blue light of Bar Le Cerf Bleu's neon sign on the other side of the road flashed through the window. Kai-Uwe Frigge got up to draw the curtain.

Was there a man at the window? Zorro. The Phantom. Batman. It looked like a comic-strip character painted on the wall of the abandoned house. All the windows of this building, diagonally opposite Hotel Atlas at the corner of rue de la Braie, were dark, and the display window of the shop was nailed up with boards on which fluttered the shreds of torn posters. On the wall beside it were graffiti, illegible words, – a secret script, symbols. In front of the building a construction hoarding bore the sign of the demo- lition firm De Meuter. Inspector Brunfaut knew that this black figure, framed by the window on the first floor of the dead house, was obviously not a graffito. But that was what it looked like. In all the nooks and crannies of this city the façades of buildings and firewalls were painted right up to the roofs with comic-book images, copies of, and variations on, drawings by Hergé or Morris, animals by Bonom or works by younger artists who regarded themselves as the heirs to these legends. If Brussels was an open book, it was a graphic novel.

Inspector Brunfaut had emerged from Hotel Atlas to instruct his colleagues in the van to do the rounds of the neighbouring houses, to ask if anyone might have seen anything from their window at the time in question.

It's a good start to the year, Inspector!

Every day starts well, Brunfaut said. The rain had let up, the inspector stood with his legs apart, hitched up his trousers and let his gaze wander along the fronts of the buildings opposite as he spoke to the men. And then he saw it: the shadowy figure framed by the window.

There *was* a man standing at the window. Of a house under demolition. The inspector stared up at him. The man didn't stir. Was it a real person up there? Or a dummy? Why would a dummy be standing at the window? Or was it a shadow, its contours deceiving him? Or a graffito after all? The inspector grinned. Not a real grin, of course, but an internal one. No, that was a man there! Was he looking down? Could he see the inspector peering up at him? What had he seen?

Right then! Inspector Brunfaut said. To work! You take this house, you that one! And you . . .

This derelict building too? But it's empty!

Yes, this one too – look up there!

But the shadow man had vanished.

He stepped back from the window. Where were his cigarettes? In his coat, perhaps. His coat was on the kitchen chair, the only item of furniture left in the apartment. David de Vriend went into the kitchen and picked up the coat. What did he want? The coat. Why? He stood there indecisively. It was time to go. Yes. Here there was nothing left. To do. The apartment had been completely cleared out. He looked at a rectangular mark on the wall. A picture had hung there. "The Forest at Boortmeerbeek", an idyllic landscape. He could remember putting it up. There it had remained for an entire life until he no longer saw it. And now it was an empty space to show that something had been on that wall which was no longer there. A life story: an empty outline on a length of wallpaper that itself had been pasted over a prehistory. Below it he could see the outline of the cupboard that had stood here. What had he kept in that cupboard? The sorts of things that accumulate over a lifetime. The filth behind it! Balls of fluff, streaks of greasy, sooty, mouldy grime. You can clean all your life, indeed, spend all your life cleaning, but in the end, when everything's cleared out, a layer of filth remains. Behind every surface that you clean, behind every veneer that you polish. When you're young don't imagine there'll be nothing rotting, mouldy or putrid when the time comes for your life to be cleared out. Perhaps you *are* young and think that you've had nothing yet of life, or too little. But the filth that lurks behind is still the filth of an entire life. All that remains is the filth because you are filth and you end up in filth. If you get old: lucky you! But you have deluded yourself because even if you've spent your entire given life cleaning – in the end everything is cleared out and what's left to see? Filth. It's behind everything, beneath everything, it's the basis of everything you've been cleaning. A clean life. That's what you had. Until the filth appears. That's where the sink was. He washed up continually. He never possessed a dishwasher. He washed up every plate, every cup, straight after having used it. Whenever he drank a coffee alone – and he was alone, he was almost always alone – he drank it standing up beside the sink so he could wash the cup straight away, take the last sip of coffee and turn on the tap, it was always one and the same thing, wash out, dry up and wipe till it shone, then replace the cup so that everything was clean, this was always important to him, a clean life, and now . . . what's visible where the sink was? Mildew, mould, grease, grime. Even in the darkness or the gloom you could see the filth. Nothing was there anymore, everything had been cleared out, but that was still there, that was still visible: the streaks of filth behind the cleaned life.

He put his coat down over the chair. He wanted to . . . what? He looked around. Why wasn't he leaving? He ought to go. This was no longer the apartment he had lived in. These were just rooms in which a past life had existed. One more look around? Why? To stare at empty rooms? He went into the bedroom. The wooden floor was lighter where the bed had stood; in the dim light the faded rectangle looked like a large trapdoor. He walked past it to the window; why didn't he walk across it, why, in this empty room, did he walk around it, as if fearful that this rectangle might really open up and devour him? He wasn't afraid. The bed had always stood here, and he went from the door to the window as he had all his life: around the bed. He looked out: the fire escape of the next-door building, a school, was almost within arm's reach. Once a year there was a fire drill. A siren would wail and the pupils would come down the fire escape in an orderly fashion. How often David de Vriend had stood at this window and watched. The escape. An exercise. Within arm's reach – that's what it's called. The fire escape had been within arm's reach when he moved in here. It was also one of the reasons why he took the apartment. It's a well-located apartment, the vendor had said, and de Vriend had looked out of this window at the fire escape and agreed with him. Yes, the location is excellent! It had occurred to him that if necessary he would be able to leap onto the fire escape from this window and disappear while fists were still hammering on the front door. He'd reckoned he could do it, yes, back then there had been no doubt. But now? – inconceivable. Now the fire escape was out of arm's reach. For half a century the children practising their escape had remained the same age, always children, only he had grown older, too old in the end, weak and fragile, and out of practice. As he peered out of the window he no longer saw an arm's reach. He realised he wanted to smoke. He ought to go, finally disappear. He walked across the hallway, not into the kitchen where the coat and his cigarettes were, but into the sitting room. He stood there uncertainly, looking around as if searching for something. An empty room. He wanted to . . . what did he still want to do here? He went to the window. That was it: he wanted to take in this view one more time, the view across the square on which he'd lived all his given life and tried to find his "place".

He looked down at the blue light, thinking nothing. He froze. He knew why. Mentally he didn't process the fact that that he knew or that this wasn't worth another thought. Old knowledge was embedded in him; he didn't need to formulate it in his head. Standing absolutely still, he stared at the police cars, his heart contracted, then expanded again – a shrug of the soul.

When he was a teacher it was something he had always tried to banish from his pupils' essays – these blah-blah-blah-comma-he-thought sentences.

But he couldn't stop them. Children really believed that when people are alone their heads are full of he-thought/she-thought sentences. And then these he-thought/she-thought heads came together to produce he-thought/she-thought sentences. In truth, it is so unbelievably silent beneath this godless firmament, all the way into people's heads. Our verbiage is merely the echo of this silence. His heart contracted coldly and expanded again. He breathed in, he breathed out. That blue light really was pulsating!

He heard the bell, then a fist thumping at the front door. He went into the kitchen and put on his coat. He went into the bedroom, and the pounding continued. Again David de Vriend walked around the non-existent bed as he made for the window. He looked out. Not within arm's reach. He sat on the floor and lit a cigarette. The pounding. The thumping.

Two

Ideas interfere with things that wouldn't exist without them.

YOU NEED TO be able to allow yourself a bout of depression. Martin Susman would survive. He worked on "Noah's Ark". He was an official at the European Commission, Directorate-General for "Culture and Education", assigned to Directorate C, "Communication", and ran the EAC-C-2 department: "Cultural Programme and Measures".

Internally, colleagues simply referred to their ministry as "Noah's Ark" or simply "the Ark". Why? An ark has no destination. It rolls across the currents, pitching and tossing on the waves, defying the storms and with only one aim: to save itself and whatever it is carrying on board.

It didn't take Martin Susman long to realise this. To begin with he was delighted and proud to have nabbed this job, particularly as he hadn't been sent to Brussels as an "E.N.D." (Expert National Détaché) by an Austrian political party or authority, but had applied directly to the Commission and passed the *concours*. He truly was a European official, without any obligation or duty to his country! Before long he had to conclude that the "Culture and Education" ministry had zero profile within the European Commission; others gently mocked it. Within the organisation people simply referred to this Directorate-General as "Culture", dropping the "Education" despite the remarkable successes chalked up in this sphere, such as the development and implementation of the Erasmus Scheme. And when people said "Culture" there was always an undertone, it sounded like Wall Street brokers saying "numismatics", the hobby of a cranky relative. But even amongst the public, insofar as they were at all interested, the image of "European culture" was a poor one. Martin Susman had only been in his job for a short while and he was still reading the newspapers from back home – the usual beginner's mistake – when outrage erupted in Austria because, as the papers said, the Austrians were being threatened with "Culture". Each E.U. Member State had the right to a commissioner's post; that country's government nominated an individual and the president of the Commission assigned them a ministry. When the ministries were reshuffled following the European elections the rumour emerged that the commissioner nominated by Austria would be getting "Culture". The coalition government in Austria began squabbling because the party of the designated commissioner suspected intrigue on the part of its coalition partner. There was protest, the Austrian newspapers kicked up a fuss and they could rely on the acute indignation of their readers. "We're being threatened with culture!" Or, "Austria's being fobbed off with culture!"

Quite an astonishing reaction when you consider that Austria has eagerly, if not "regarded", then at least described itself as a "cultural nation". However, the response tallied with the profile and significance that "culture" held within the European power structure. The profile and significance of a ministry depended on the size of the budget it was able to distribute, and the influence it commanded over political and business elites. "Culture" was poorly endowed in both. Ultimately the Austrian commissioner didn't get the Culture ministry, but Regional Policy, which led to celebration in this cultural nation: "We," the Austrian newspapers now trumpeted, "have a budget of 337 billion!"

"Culture" went to Greece, which seemed wholly appropriate when you think of Ancient Greece as the fundament of European culture – or thoughtfully cynical, if you wish to correlate the decline of democracy in Europe with the slave-owning society in Ancient Greece. In any event it was quite simple: because of its now endless financial and budgetary crisis, Greece was out of credit, which left it defenceless and obliged to take what it was given. The least-esteemed ministry. This was no mission, it was a punishment: those who are bad with money better not be given any, and thus are assigned the ministry without a budget. The Greek commissioner, a dedicated woman, fought to get a strong team she could trust and which might afford her some political weight in the Commission after all. To fill the key positions in her ministry she succeeded in requesting compatriots with prior experience in the Commission apparatus, who were well connected to other directorates-general and enjoyed excellent reputations. Thus Fenia Xenopoulou had been removed from Trade and promoted to head of that director-ate in "the Ark", where Martin Susman worked.

Fenia had not been able turn down the promotion. If you wanted to make it to the top of the Commission apparatus, you needed to demonstrate your mobility. Anybody who failed to show the requisite willingness and spurned an offer to change domains was out of the frame. And so she had relocated to the Ark with the intention of demonstrating her mobility more than ever. This she would accomplish by immediately striving for her next move, paying particular attention to her visibility. Being visible, working in a way that got you regularly noticed, was just as crucial for rising up the system.

Fenia knew what hardship was. She had experienced it. She

possessed that intense energy common to those whose souls burn incessantly with the hardship of their early life. No matter how far they have come they can never detach themselves from this adversity because their soul always accompanies them. From the beginning she had proved time and again that she was ready to grasp every opportunity. Whenever she was shown a door and told, Find the key and you'll pass through this door to the outside, she would meticulously search for that key, and was even prepared to spend ages patiently filing down all possible keys until one fitted, but at some point she simply grabbed an axe and smashed the door down. The axe became her skeleton key.

Martin Susman could not stand Fenia. Ever since she'd entered the Ark the atmosphere in the ministry had deteriorated. It was obvious that she despised the work that needed to be done here, but at the same time she was trying insufferably hard to ensure she was more visible.

Fenia Xenopoulou slept well. For her, sleep was all part of bodily control, self-discipline. She plugged into sleep as into a charging unit. She drew in her arms and legs, rounded her back and pressed her chin into her chest, thereby loading energy for the next day's battle. But she never had any dreams.

Did I snore? Fridsch had asked her early that morning.

No. I slept well!

Like a child.

Yes.

No, more like an embryo.

An embryo?

Yes, the way you lay there reminded me of photos of embryos! Fancy some coffee?

No, thanks. I've got to be off! She was about to give him a goodbye kiss and say, "Think of me!" but instead she just nodded and said, I've got to . . .

Martin Susman had got the latest information on the way to the office. Whenever the weather permitted, that's to say, when it wasn't raining, he cycled to work. It gave him a bit of exercise, but this wasn't the principal reason. The Metro made him sad. Tired, grey faces, even in the morning. People with their wheelie suitcases and briefcases, and their willingness to look dynamic, competent and competitive. Ill-fitting masks beneath which their true faces festered. The gazing into space when beggars got on with their accordions, played a tune and then held out a yoghurt pot for a few coins. What were these songs? Martin couldn't have said, perhaps hits from the twenties and thirties, the pre-war era. Alighting. The mechanically moving streams of people trudging onto escalators that were out of order, dragging themselves along the dirty corridors of the underground, a permanent building site boarded up with plywood, past the sliced-pizza and kebab shacks, the smell of bodily excretions and decay, then the wind tunnel on the way up to street level, up into a daylight that can no longer penetrate the sombre soul. Martin preferred cycling. He very soon became a member of the E.U. Cycling Group, which provided a personal trainer for every E.U. official who joined, to teach them the basics – for example, how to get across le square Montgomery alive. The trainer worked out the safest route from home to their work place, then they would spend a few days practising this route together and members would also learn how to slap "You're in the way!" stickers onto cars parked in cycle lanes. The stickers didn't damage the cars, they were easily removable. The E.U. Cycling Group was a great success, its rapidly increasing membership leading to a doubling of the number of cyclists on Brussels roads within a few years.

What Martin liked most of all about his ride from home to the office were the spontaneous communities that formed along the way. By the time he got to boulevard Anspach he would have bumped into his first colleague, then the second, until by the end they would often have grown to a bunch of eight or ten. The German officials would accelerate past them on racing bikes, riding to work in functional clothing, as if bent on winning a circuit race. The showers in the office basement, therefore, were used almost exclusively by Germans before the working day began. The Dutch officials were relaxed on their "granny bikes", as were their colleagues from the Latin countries, who cycled sedately in their suits without breaking into a sweat. They would ride side by side, chatting, learning more than they would in the canteen – the latest rumours, intrigues and career leaps. These cycle-lane conversations were more important than reading the *European Voice* and at least as important as scrutinising the *Financial Times* to keep abreast of affairs.

On rue de l'Écuyer, Bohumil Szmekal, his friend and colleague from C-1 ("Cultural Policy and Intercultural Dialogue") had joined the peloton, while a couple of hundred metres further on they heard the cry of Kassándra Mercouri, Fenia Xenopoulou's section head. Bohumil and Martin let the rest of the group go ahead as they slowed down to wait for Kassándra, then the three of them cycled on together.

Have you had any ideas yet? Bohumil asked, before shouting "Watch out!" and pointing to a car parked up ahead in the cycle lane. As quick as a flash he whipped out a sticker from his shoulder bag, peeled off the back as he continued to pedal hands-free and slapped the sticker on the side window of the car as he swept past. A chorus of horns resounded.

Bingo! Got'im! he said in triumph.

You and your stickers are a greater danger than the cars themselves, Kassándra said. She was a plump woman in her mid-thirties whose expression was always either anxious or affectionate. Beside her, short, delicate Bohumil looked like a naughty boy, even though he was a few years older. He grinned. Hey, have you come up with the great idea? The entire directorate's work is blocked because nobody's yet . . .

What sort of idea? I don't know what you're talking about!

The Big Jubilee Project! You haven't replied to the round-robin e-mail. I haven't either, by the way.

The Big Jubilee Project? I didn't think we were expected to reply!

Indeed. Everyone's playing dead. Nothing's coming. Nobody thinks it's important. Not a surprise, really, when I think back to the damp squib five years ago.

I wasn't here then.

What do you mean damp squib? That ceremony with the children in Parliament was very moving! Children from all over Europe! Expressing their wishes for the future, peace and . . .

Sándra, *please*! Child ambassadors!? That was child abuse! Thank God the public didn't notice anything! Well, my idea is . . . Watch it! He yanked his bike, forcing Martin into the middle of the road and already had another sticker in his hand, but then dropped it. Martin nudged him back into the cycle lane and cried, You're mad!

Well, the way I see it is this. Learning from history means never repeating it. It mustn't happen again. No more jubilee! It's expensive and embarrassing! I can't understand why Xeno's taking it so seriously!

All the directorates-general are involved. If she commits to the project she could really distinguish herself.

She's certainly piling on the pressure. The meeting's at eleven this morning. She wants to hear our ideas.

I understood it quite differently, Martin said. I thought . . .

The meeting might be postponed. It's not yet confirmed, but the boss is hoping for a last-minute appointment with the president today. By the way, do you want to know what she's reading at the moment?

I couldn't be less interested!

You mean, as in a book? Xeno reads? Come off it, Sándra, you're fantasising!

Yes, a book. And I'm not fantasising. I had to get a copy for her especially. You won't believe what it is!

Tell us!

Watch out!

Careful!

O.K. For several days now the boss has been preparing with military precision for her meeting with the president. She wants to know everything about him, from all his networks to his favourite food, everything, even his favourite book. It could come in handy for small talk. She's most fastidious about this.

The president's got a favourite book?

I bet it's *The Man without Qualities*, Martin said.

The Man without Qualities? What an excellent title for an autobiography!

Children, please! Listen to me! She found it out through private channels. The president really does have a favourite book, a novel! It's not public knowledge. And he must have several copies because he's always reading it. One's beside his bed, one's on the desk in his office. I expect there's another in his girlfriend's apartment! Kassándra's face glistened. A thin film of sweat? Pleasure? Anyway, she said, I had to get a copy of the book and now the boss is reading it!

Xeno is reading literature, Martin thought in astonishment, a novel! For the sake of her career she's even prepared to read a novel.

Fenia Xenopoulou sat at her desk, reading. What she was reading left her bewildered. She was able to read at high speed; she had learned to scan pages and immediately file away the information in compartments in her head, from where she could retrieve it at lightning speed. But this was a novel. She didn't have a scheme for this; what was it about? What information from it might prove useful, what in God's name should she commit to memory? It told the life story of a man, that was all well and good, but what did this complete stranger have to do with her? And he'd lived in a completely different time, too; people don't think and act like that anymore. More importantly, was he a real person or was the book pure invention? According to Google this man did actually exist and was said to have played a significant role in his time, influencing the political order of the continent and ultimately the entire world. But he couldn't have been *that* important, or she would have heard about him at school. He was more a subject for the experts, and ultimately even they couldn't agree as to the role this man had played.

She continued leafing through the book impatiently, skipping a chapter. She didn't understand. Up till now, at least, the book had been about love rather than political decision-making. The entire thing was written from the perspective of a woman who loved this man. But the name of the woman didn't appear in his Wikipedia entry. Nor was it clear whether she really loved him, or at least it wasn't yet apparent. At any rate, she felt it was her duty to attract his attention and gain influence over him. But if this woman was an invention of the author's, what was the point of reading about how she, a fictitious character, tried to gain power over a man who in historical times had actually been in power himself? If the author wanted to show how a woman can gain power over powerful men, why hadn't she written a self-help book instead? There were intrigues and mischievous little games, battles with political rivals, but ultimately – Fenia skimmed a few pages, read a bit, ever more impatient, read a page, skipped the next ten – ultimately it boiled down to love or to how insignificant political power was compared to the power of love. Could you really say that? That was crazy. Novels are crazy!

Fenia leaned back. Was this really the president's favourite book? The president was crazy! All these thoughts! What she thought, what he thought – how did the author know all this? If this man did really exist then there must be sources in archives, documents, contracts, certificates, but thoughts!? Thoughts are never – nor ever were – set down in documents. Surely anyone in their right mind would avoid doing anything that might allow their thoughts to be read.

She closed her eyes and thought of the previous evening with Fridsch, the night. Had she really thought that he ... Had he thought that she ...

She sat there quite still, although she fancied she was swaying. Fenia wrenched open her eyes, pulled herself together, and at that moment saw on her computer screen a new message from Kassándra Mercouri. "Unfortunately meeting with president not possible today. President's office will suggest alternatives in the next few days."

She shut the book and pushed it to one side.

To: B. Szmekal ("Intercultural Dialogue"); M. Susman ("Cultural Measures"); H. Athanasiadis ("Valorisation"); C. Pinheiro da Silva ("Language Diversity"); A. Klein ("Media Expertise")

– Fenia paused briefly, then deleted Helene Athanasiadis –

Subject: Jubilee Project

Meeting confirmed for 11 a.m., conference room. I'll be expecting suggestions.

The telephone rang, Martin Susman glanced at the display and saw it was an unknown local number. He took the call and regretted it at once. His brother.

It's me.

Yes. Hello, Florian!

You knew I was coming to Brussels, didn't you?

Yes.

I've been trying to get hold of you for days. You're not answering.

. . .

I must have tried at least ten times yesterday evening. Why do you never pick up, or call back?

Yesterday evening? There was a problem.

You've always got problems. I've got problems too, that's why —

There was —

Anyway, I've arrived. I'm already at the hotel. The Marriott. I'm about to go to my first meeting. Do you want to meet for dinner? When do you finish work?

Around seven, half seven.

O.K., then, pick me up at half past eight.

From the hotel?

Of course. Then you can take me to a restaurant where I can smoke.

You can't smoke anywhere.

45

I don't believe that. Right then, half past eight. And don't be late, little brother!

The Big Jubilee Project. In fact it was Mrs Atkinson who'd had the idea. She was the new director-general of D.-G. COMM, the communication service of the European Commission, also responsible for its corporate image which, as the last Eurobarometer poll had shown, had plummeted. She had realised at the outset that she needed to run the directorate-general differently from her predecessors. Good press work, a routine spokesperson's service and formal coordination of the dozy information offices in the Member States would not suffice. Not only were the figures the worst they'd been since 1973, when regular opinion polls were beginning to be held in E.E.C. countries, the current results had to be regarded as an unmitigated disaster. Half a year earlier around 49 per cent of E.U. citizens had viewed the Commission's work as basically positive, and even this result had been described as a "historical low"; it was unimaginable that it could ever fall short of this. Now the figure – after applying all possible embellishments – stood at barely 40 per cent, representing the most drastic fall in the history of the Eurobarometer, more drastic even than the 1999 collapse in the approval rating when the Commission was forced to resign *en bloc* following a corruption scandal. At the time, the slump from 67 to 59 per cent was seen as catastrophic – so what could you call this? And what was responsible for it?

Mrs Atkinson studied the papers, tables, percentage calculations, graphs, statistics and wondered how this dramatic loss in confidence in the institution could have come about. Much advance praise had been heaped on the new Commission president in the best European papers, and yet it wasn't the Commission that profited from this but the European Parliament, whose standing rose by almost five percentage points. For the first time in history the president had succeeded in satisfying the female quota, and not only amongst the members of the Commission – twelve of the twenty-eight were now women – but also at management level in the directorates-general, where the proportion of women was now 40 per cent. She herself had benefited from the policy, and – as she said – she could openly admit this without putting into question her qualification for the job. On the contrary, it was thanks to the consistent implementation of the quota system that Mrs Atkinson wasn't working under the totally unqualified careerist, George Morland, that pig of a man who'd initially been considered for the position and who was now running around painting a caricature of her as a prime example of the idiocy of the quota system. She'd heard on the grapevine that he was telling all and sundry she was such a cold woman that she suffered from freezing hands, which was why she always sat at her desk wearing an enormous muff. Women, eh?

Such a fantasy said everything about this schemer. The fact that he associated her with an enormous muff clearly demonstrated the upper-class British male horror of the vagina.

Mrs Atkinson had studied Marketing and Management at the European Business School in London, finishing her degree with a brilliant thesis "on counter-inductive marketing". To take the wind out of the sails of Mr Morland's intrigues, she contemplated an offensive tack: flipping the story in her favour and turning the muff into her trademark, a huge, outsized muff. Not only would this render Morland's caricature harmless, it would strengthen her own brand. But that wasn't what was occupying her just then. She wondered why this E.U. Commission success, the female quota, the clear indication of opportunities for women on this continent, had not improved the Commission's image. The proportion of women in the European Parliament was only 35 per cent, but Parliament's reputation was growing, including amongst women voters of all age groups, which was fine, but the Commission's was plummeting, and that was puzzling, *that* was the problem. And it was now her task to put a stop to this trend and reverse it. What were the criticisms, what was the reason for the Commission's poor image? Clichés. Prejudice. Always the same. A lack of democratic legitimacy, growing bureaucracy, obsessive regulation. She found it telling that there was no criticism of the *actual tasks* of the Commission; clearly the public knew nothing of these. Fifty-nine per cent of respondents thought the Commission "meddles in issues that would be better dealt with at national level", but only 5 per cent agreed that it "performs its functions poorly". They needed to understand this contradiction. She wondered why none of her predecessors had criticised the Eurobarometer methodology and implemented a change. If you give people the option of putting a cross beside "meddles in issues that would be better dealt with at national level" then a certain percentage will do precisely that. These Yes-it's-true types, those That's-what-I-always-say idiots! But if you were to propose a statement to the effect that the Commission protects citizens from injustices that arise from the differences between national legal systems, the result would be quite different.

She understood that it couldn't be her mission to improve the image of the "E.U."; she had to focus on the profile of the European Commission. And the idea of how she might succeed in this came to her an hour later, exhilarated on Charlemagne Brut champagne. For at that moment the door to her office swung open and she saw Catherine, her secretary, enter carrying a cake decorated with sparklers. Beyond the smoke and star-shaped sparks she could see . . . yes, it really was . . . the president, and behind him more and more bodies made their way into the room – her commissioner, managers, advisors, her entire office – and sang "Happy Birthday".

It was a big birthday. Oh yes. But she hadn't attached any importance to it. Her husband was in London, her daughter in New York. Both had called briefly. And she didn't yet have friends here in Brussels she would have wanted to celebrate with. Now she was the centre of attention. Surprise! The president spoke. Just a few words. Nothing formal, all very personal, including a minor reference to her image that gave way to general laughter. People she knew only to say hello to, second, third, fourth floor, laughed, champagne flutes bubbled over, clinked as they toasted her, she was kissed on the cheek, her arm squeezed, her shoulder clapped, people who knew nothing or only very little about her showed sympathy, or a willingness to sympathise, the commissioner raised his glass, said how pleased he was to have this marvellous and competent colleague on his team, in this position, how excellent it was that the female quota was in place, he himself was in favour of a 99 per cent quota, of course he didn't want to lose his own job, but otherwise he'd be delighted to have just women . . . Whistling from the men, cries of Macho! Macho! Macho! from the women, everything gave way to laughter and Mrs Atkinson cut the cake which was now sitting on top of the Eurobarometer file on her desk, crumbs and cream on the statistics, sparkler ash on the grave of European morale.

And then she was alone again, everybody had gone back to work and she was standing at the large window in her office, looking down at rue de la Loi, at the line of dark cars crawling past, glistening in the soft rain. She rubbed her hands, stroking with one the back of the other, massaged and kneaded her fingers, which were long and delicate, and tended to lose their colour quite suddenly, becoming white and numb. She sat down at her desk, something was at work inside her and she waited for it to become clearer. There was half a glass of champagne left, she took a sip, thought for a moment, then downed the rest. She kneaded her fingers, then Googled "European Commission foundation". When, in actual fact, was the Commission's birthday? Was there something like a birthday for the Commission? The day of its founding? And this was the idea: it wasn't enough to sell the day-to-day work of the Commission as positively as possible; it had to be honoured, people had to be encouraged to celebrate the very fact of its existence, they shouldn't simply be begging for acceptance, or rectifying clichés, or challenging rumours and myths. For once the Commission should be placed in the spotlight, not talked about in abstract and general terms as "the E.U.". What was the E.U., anyway? Various institutions all pursuing their own agenda, but if there was any point to the whole thing then it was down to the existence of the Commission, which stood for the whole thing, didn't it? That was how she saw it. They had to create a situation in which the Commission was standing jauntily in the middle, the birthday girl being congratulated. So did the Commission have a birthday? It wasn't that simple to determine. Was it the founding day of the E.E.C. Commission? Or the date of the foundation of the European Commission in its current form, following the Merger Treaty? In the first instance the Commission would be sixty in three years' time, in the second fifty in two years. She preferred fifty. Half a century. Easier to sell. And translated into human years it was an age when you were still full of beans, experienced and not yet ready for the scrap heap. Moreover, two years represented the ideal time span for preparation, whereas three might end up being too long: too much could get out of hand in three years.

She did some more research. Had there been jubilees in the

past? Yes. Awkward, half-hearted celebrations with lofty speeches, acknowledgements of predecessors, a little incense for the precursors of the E.U., fifty years of the Treaties of Rome, sixty years of the European Steel and Coal Community – but who would have been interested in that? Nobody. And what line did they imagine they would spin when trying to convince E.U. sceptics and opponents about how marvellous the foundation of the European Steel and Coal Community had been? Like congratulating a grandfather suffering from dementia on the time when he still had all his marbles, while his underwhelmed grandchildren had long since been doing everything very differently.

On the glass table by the group of chairs Grace Atkinson spotted an open bottle of champagne. There was still a little left, so she helped herself. She was in high spirits by the time she sent an e-mail to a few departments from which she fancied she might get some support and interest in her plan. Before she could begin the formal procedure she first of all needed to win over some allies. A big birthday party to mark the upcoming fiftieth anniversary of the foundation of the European Commission, she wrote, seemed to her to be an opportunity to put the work and achievements of this institution in the public spotlight, strengthen its corporate identity, improve its image, afford it a wholehearted celebration and thus sally forth from their defensive position.

She deleted the word "wholehearted" then put it back again, nodding; that was, after all, what it was all about. She rubbed her hands and then went the whole hog. In the subject line she wrote, "Big Jubilee Project – no more whining".

It had been Mrs Atkinson's idea. Fenia Xenopoulou was the first to react – and swiftly appropriated the project. It belonged in the Culture ministry, Fenia thought, no question. It was the opportunity she'd been waiting for to give herself visibility. And she made Martin Susman her Sherpa – *he* would shoulder the burden of the project.

In the beginning Grace Atkinson was pleased to have found such an enthusiastic ally so swiftly. And in the end she was delighted, because the emphatic commitment to this project by the ill-fated Culture ministry meant everyone forgot that it was she who had dreamed up this ultimately disastrous idea in the first place.

I'm waiting for suggestions, Fenia Xenopoulou had said, her voice tinged with agitation, it's incredibly important and I know that you . . . She looked around the room and uttered, far too stridently, a few sentences with big and theatrical adjectives. She probably regarded this as encouraging, this corporal discourse to the troops, and Martin had lowered his eyes to avoid her gaze, which is why he now saw a headless Fenia, only the skin-tight top, the close-fitting skirt, the legs in opaque tights, and he thought: This woman's wearing a corset, a suit of armour that's holding her together. The skirt was of the finest cloth, but to Martin it looked as if it would shatter if you struck it. You couldn't take it off, you had to smash it and . . .

So, what are we going to do?

Once again Bohumil was sarcastically counterproductive. Let's start by asking, he said, what we're *not* going to do. We must absolutely avoid everything that's been done for previous jubilees: sheer embarrassment mitigated by the general exclusion of the public. Glossy brochures for the recycling bins. Sunday sermons on workdays.

Martin?

He hadn't seen Fenia's reaction to Bohumil's statement, he was staring at her feet, at the little bulges at the openings of her too-tight shoes.

What Martin really wanted to say was: I'm not interested in the project. But he decided to agree with everyone else to avoid going out on a limb.

In view of the importance of this matter, he said in Fenia's direction, it was clear – and now towards Bohumil – that the mistakes of the past must not be repeated. Bohumil was right when recalling that . . . but Fenia was absolutely right too, of course, in expecting that . . . What had been the mistakes of previous jubilees? There had been no other ideas save that of celebrating a jubilee because an anniversary had come around. But the anniversary was not an idea in itself. It was all well and good to say that an institution had been around for so and so many years, but what is the *idea*? What idea do you put at the heart of it? It must be convincing, people must be so fired up that they really want to celebrate this occasion.

And thus Martin Susman fell into the trap. After a brief discussion Fenia Xenopoulou said, That's enough, evidently the only person who's given this subject any thought is Martin. What he said is perfectly logical. Having a key idea is essential. She assigned Martin the task of developing the idea and drafting a paper on it. How much time did he reckon it would take?

Two months? It needed proper thinking through and discussion with colleagues from other directorates-general.

One week, Fenia said.

Impossible. He was on a trip next week, which needed preparing for too and . . .

Alright then, two weeks, a few bullet points, surely you can manage that! And we won't start discussing it with colleagues until we've presented the paper. Understood? We *will* present it!

Martin Susman was exasperated and furious when he rode home at around six o'clock, having dealt with the day's business. Halfway there it began to rain. His poncho was in his pannier, but he'd left his pannier in the office. He arrived home soaking and freezing, and immediately took a shower. But the water wasn't particularly hot, and the shower curtain, clung cold to his back as if magnetised. He swatted it away angrily, ripping half of it from the pole. First thing tomorrow he had to get this stupid curtain replaced by a shower door, but he knew that this was just another of those ideas he would never put into action. He slipped on his dressing gown, fetched a bottle of Jupiler from the fridge and sat in the armchair in front of the open fireplace. He needed to calm down, breathe in and breathe out, relax. He stared at the books in the fireplace.

When Martin Susman first moved in here he couldn't believe his eyes. The fireplace had never been used since central heating had been installed in the apartment. His landlord had fixed two planks across it and put books on them. Which presumably he thought was nice and homely. Later Martin had seen the same thing in other period apartments of friends and acquaintances in Brussels: books in disused fireplaces.

In Martin's fireplace were a selection of Brussels guidebooks, tatty editions no doubt left behind by previous tenants; a few volumes of an encyclopaedia from 1914; three atlases, one from 1910, one from 1943 and the third from 1955; and a good dozen volumes from the 1960s series "Classics of World Literature", published by the Flemish Book Club – "Each volume contains four classic works, abridged for a contemporary readership." When Martin was leafing through the books one evening he was shocked – no, that is too strong a word – he was unpleasantly moved. Was this supposed to be progress? Not burning books any more, but merely putting them, "abridged for a contemporary readership", into a cold hearth?

Now he was staring at the spines of these books, drinking his beer and smoking a few cigarettes. The paper for the Jubilee Project – that was an imposition. As if he were a copywriter trying to sell the E.U. Commission product! He glanced over at his desk, on top of which still sat the plate with the encrusted mustard. What *is* the idea behind mustard? We put it on the side. Brilliant. A persuasive television ad: gorgeous young people laughing as they blissfully squeeze mustard onto plates and gleefully sing: Bursting with pride, we put it on the side! They're wetting themselves with delight, and the coils of mustard on their plates spiral upwards, they begin to dance rhythmically as if to the pipe of a snake-charmer: Bursting with pride, we put it on the side! That was . . . he pulled himself together, got dressed and set off for the Marriott, opting for the classic "long", which offered protection for two people in the rain.

It had stopped raining. The wet tarmac, the façades of buildings and the passers-by shimmered in the light of the streetlamps and the neon of the chip stand, as if a Flemish master had just applied the varnish to this scene. By now Martin had experienced this evening atmosphere that followed a rainy day in Brussels so often that it gave him a kind of homely feeling. Yes, he was at home here. He bought cigarettes from the Indian man in the 24-hour shop on the corner of rue Sainte-Catherine. After he paid the Indian always said, "*Dank u wel,*" if Martin spoke French, and "*Merci, monsieur*" if Martin had asked for his cigarettes in Flemish. You could read something into that, but perhaps there wasn't anything to it, perhaps it was what it was, eventually becoming another of those details that merely added to Martin's impression of being at home here, between many worlds.

Although the wind was not strong, it was cold. Martin walked rapidly and so arrived far too early at the Marriott, but his brother was already waiting in the lobby wearing a stern and self-righteous expression that said, Having always followed God's commandments, surely I can expect that . . .

Martin knew this face only too well. Whenever he met his brother he saw his father in him.

They greeted each other with a hug that turned out more awkwardly than usual because Florian was clutching a briefcase.

Shall we get a taxi?

No. I've booked a table at Belga Queen. It's a five-minute walk.

They set off in silence. Eventually Martin asked:

How's Renate?

Fine.

And the children?

Studious, thank God.

Martin wasn't ashamed of his background. But he didn't know whether it bothered him more that he had become so estranged from it, or that even though he'd become so estranged from it, it kept catching up with him. His father had died eighteen years ago on November 2, All Souls' Day. Far too prematurely and so horribly tragically. When Martin lived in Austria he had to endure the trauma of every November 2. When he read the paper, watched T.V. or even left the house, the reminder came days prior to November 2: All Souls' is coming, the day of father's death. And of course he had to go home, there was no excuse, because it was a national holiday, a day of morbid remembrance for everyone. In Brussels, November 2 was not a holiday. Here you were able to suppress your own private story, or might be able to, but when his brother turned up it instantly became All Souls' Day. Their father had got caught in the machine. People kept saying he'd got caught in the machine. As if they'd had only one machine. It was the granulator. However it might have happened, his arm got caught in the grinder, the machine absolutely devoured him and he bled to death. He screamed like a pig. That was the phrase: He screamed like a pig. Later there were people who claimed to have heard it. But why hadn't anyone come running to help? Because on the farm, the screaming of pigs was perfectly natural, normal, routine. With around twelve hundred pigs and slaughters daily, you didn't single out one scream. That's what Felber, the head slaughterman, said. "Single out," he said. So how does anyone know that he screamed like a pig? He must have screamed – everyone said that. He must have screamed like mad. But only briefly. You lose consciousness very quickly. That's how it must have been. It happens so quickly. Of course the pigs get wind that something's up when they . . . but before you know it they've been stunned. And the machine's already eating them. Their father had been such an industrious man that he made use of idle moments to crush any animal waste that was lying around. At the time the business had already grown enormously, but logistically it wasn't as well organised as now. Their mother went to call the doctor, but of course she was out of her senses and rang Dr Lamm, the vet. It was all too late anyway. A few days later, sixteen-year-old Martin giggled as he told his schoolfriends that his mother had called Dr Lamm, and when nobody laughed he repeated it: Lamm, for the pig farmer. Then he was silent for days before eventually confessing to the priest so he could receive absolution for having made a joke about his father's death.

His brother, older by four years, then took over the running of the farm, the crown prince, it had all been agreed and planned anyway, though not for so soon, while he, Martin, the second born, the "fool", the clumsy one ("No surprise, seeing how all he does is read!") was allowed to go off and study. This had always been clear too: he could study what he wanted, and "what he wanted" meant that the family didn't care what he did so long as he didn't make any demands and didn't become a burden. Archaeology.

When the Susman brothers entered the Belga Queen restaurant, Florian walked slowly into the middle of the room, ignoring the waiter who stood in his way, and called out, Hey! What is this? A cathedral?

Martin told the waiter they had booked a table in the name of Dr Susman, and said to Florian, No, it used to be a bank. The most beautiful art deco. We'll eat here in what used to be the banking hall, then we'll go downstairs into the basement, the vault, which is now a smoking lounge.

Martin was compensated when Florian took complete ownership of the farm and his mother retired. He was paid off with a sum of money which was put in trust until he came of age, and which he had never questioned or talked about. This money had enabled him to study in comfort and then, without feeling under any pressure, look around to see what sort of career he might like to follow. Considering the value of the farm, it can't have been an equitable arrangement, but Martin didn't mind; it had been enough to open up opportunities, and he'd been able to take advantage of these. But now it was being made out that the family had allowed Martin to study and procured him some kind of superjob in the European Commission, so that he could exploit this role to lobby on behalf of his brother's commercial interests. And so Martin always worried when Florian got in touch and said he wanted to meet him in Brussels. Even during their father's lifetime the farm had been a handsome operation, but Florian had turned it into the largest pig-production business in Austria, indeed one of the largest in

Europe. He had long stopped calling it a "farm", as his father had done; it was a "concern", and Florian thought there was nothing more absurd than E.U. policy with regard to pig production and trade. In his opinion there must be incompetents or madmen at work, being bribed, blackmailed or ideologically blinded by the animal-protection mafia and the vegetarian lobby. There was no point discussing this with him, he meant it in all seriousness, he could see how it was going, he knew how it worked. He had his experiences. He began to get involved politically, gaining senior positions in lobbying groups, which was why he kept coming to Brussels for negotiations. Recently he'd been elected president of "The European Pig Producers", a network of the continent's leading pig farmers. In this role and also as federal guild master of the Austrian pig farmers' association, Florian had held a number of meetings that day with members of the European Parliament and officials from the Commission.

Look at that! Florian said when he studied the menu. Pork goulash in cherry beer. Interesting. If it tastes any good, I'll get the recipe and put it on our website.

Martin ordered *moules-frites*. And a bottle of wine. Then he said, How was your day? It was a silly question, and he had made no effort to sound particularly interested. He knew he was triggering an avalanche, but that's why they were here and Martin wanted to get it over with.

How was my day? What do *you* think? I've been dealing with cretins. That's how my day was! They don't understand a thing. They're not able to change their policies, but today they're demanding from me a change of name!

A change of name? Why should you change your name?

Not me. Let me explain. First you need to know this: obviously every pig producer wants access to the Chinese market. China is

59

the leading global importer of pork. The demand from China is massive – that's the growth market.

That's good, isn't it?

Yes, it would be. But the E.U. isn't capable of negotiating an appropriate trade agreement with China. The Chinese don't deal with the E.U., but only with each country individually. And each country believes it can conclude a fantastic bilateral deal on its own, outdoing the others, and making a greater profit. But in reality China is just playing everyone off against everyone else. What's more, no single country can produce the numbers we're talking about. Not in years. Let me give you an example. Recently at the association, I got a call asking how many pigs' ears Austria can deliver.

Pigs' ears?

Yes, pigs' ears. It was someone from the Chinese ministry of trade. I say, We slaughter around five million pigs a year in Austria, so that makes ten million ears. Too few, he says, then hangs up after a polite goodbye. Do you get me? If China needs – let's say – one hundred million pigs' ears and there were an E.U. treaty with China, then we could supply 10 per cent of the amount. But what's the situation? Austria doesn't yet have a bilateral treaty with China, there's no common treaty of E.U. states being negotiated, and I can throw away my pigs' ears – in Austria they're slaughterhouse waste. But in China they're a delicacy, there's an insane demand for them, and yet we just chuck them away, or we're happy if a cat food factory comes along to collect them for free.

But even if treaties were in place, you can't just produce pigs' ears, you've got to have the whole pig. I mean, you can't rear those quantities of whole pigs just because of the demand for ears. What do you do with the rest?

Are you thick, or what? This means there'll be no wastage.

We've already got the leftover bits. Slaughterhouse waste. Pigs' ears are just one example. The Chinese don't just take ham, fillet, bacon, shoulder – that anyway – but also the ears, heads, tails, they eat everything, they take everything. What we call slaughterhouse waste they buy at the price of fillet. In other words, a trade agreement for pork products with China would mean a 20 per cent increase in revenue per pig and, on the basis of current demand, a 100 per cent growth in the medium term, i.e. a doubling of European pig production. Do you see? That's the growth market. No industrial sector has prognoses like that.

I understand, Martin said, and it was no good, that bored, affectedly patient, poor attempt at a polite "I understand!" The look his brother shot him made Martin start. Hurriedly he said, I don't understand. If this opportunity exists and the demand in China is so great, then why . . .

Because your colleagues are mad. Utterly clueless. Instead of forcing the Member States to give the Commission the authority to conclude an E.U. trade treaty with China – and also finance the expansion of pig production with subsidies – they sit there watching China play divide and rule, and at the same time take measures to reduce pig production in Europe. The Commission believes there are too many pigs in Europe, which leads to falling prices and so on. So what do they do? Provide less support. Introduce set-aside premiums even. Which means that now in Europe the situation is as follows: overproduction for the internal market, causing a drop in prices, combined with a block on access to a market we can't produce enough for. Measures that will decrease production further, but no measures to allow us access to the market where we could sell twice as much.

By now their food had arrived.

How's the pork in cherry beer?

What? Oh. Yes, it's fine. Anyway, what we need now is investment on a scale that no concern could afford on its own. Subsidies,
not cutbacks. Subsidies, an aggressive growth policy. Do you
understand? Instead we're getting constraints. Animal protection.
A ban on sow stalls, obligatory air ducts with diffusers. H.d.t.-
system . . .

I'm not even going to ask what that is.

It's expensive. It hoovers up your profits. Here, let me show you
something. He opened his briefcase, leafed through some papers
and took one out.

Here: E.U. pig price statistics for the last half year. 15 July: down
18 per cent in Europe. 22 July: rock bottom – if only! 19 August:
little movement on the markets. 9 September: down 21 per cent.
16 September: sharp downward trend. 21 October: pig prices fall
by 14 per cent. Shall I go on?

No.

Downward trend, drop in prices, rock bottom, another drop.
And no response from the E.U. Since the beginning of the year –
look at this! Here! It says it right here! – since the beginning of
the year, an average of forty-eight pig farmers per day have shut
the barn door for the very last time. And thousands of others who
have tried to hang on in there are facing bankruptcy proceedings.
But with a 20 per cent higher purchasing price for a whole pig we
could produce twice as much. We just need coordinated investment in the necessary infrastructure, and to talk to China. But try
telling that to Herr Frigge. He tells me that unfortunately the E.U.
has a different agenda for pig production. And at the same time
they're forbidding the Member States from handing out subsidies
because that would be a distortion of competition. Do you know
this Frigge guy?

No.

I don't believe that. He's a colleague of yours. I can't see what he's playing at. Listen, you've got to have a word in his ear, just amongst yourselves you've got to make it clear to him that . . .

Florian! The Commission doesn't work like the Austrian Farmers' Association!

Don't give me that! What's the point of having you on the inside?

There's one thing I don't get. You were saying something about a change of name? What did Herr Frigge want, what name are you supposed to change?

No, that wasn't Frigge. That was the gentlemen from the parliament. Not a woman amongst them. I might have been able to work my charm on a woman, but it was just men, and they were uncompromising in their stupidity. From the European People's Party grouping, do you get it?

No.

The European People's Party. I'd imagined it would be a home game for me, I mean, I'm a member of the Austrian People's Party. Here in the European Parliament it's called the E.P.P.

So?

Well, I'm here in Brussels as the president of the European Pig Producers, which is also E.P.P. Do you see? I had a mandate to negotiate on two points: subsidies for expanding pig production and coordinating European pork exports. We didn't discuss either of these for a second. The M.E.P.s said that first we had to change our name and logo. It wasn't right that when people Google the European People's Party, the E.P.P., the first thing they see is pigs. Don't laugh! I said it was difficult. We're a transnational organisation, officially registered in every single one of the Member States. That's a huge task. Do you know what they suggested? Seeing as our name is The European Pig Producers we should include

63

the "The" in our acronym, then we'd be called T.E.P.P. It's outrageous, so cynical!

But weren't you talking in German?

No, there wasn't a German amongst them.

Then it wasn't cynical. How are they meant to know that "*Tepp*" is German for "moron"?

Florian mopped up the last of his goulash with some bread, just like he used to do as a child. Their mother had always said that she didn't need to wash up Florian's plate after dinner.

A little bit sweet, that cherry beer sauce. Did you say something about being able to smoke in the vault? Show me! I could really do with a cigarette now.

They walked home like brothers, arm in arm, teetering and tottering on the Brussels cobblestones. They had drunk gin and tonics and, seduced by the selection, smoked cigars. The effect was noticeable when they stood up from the club armchairs, and even more so when they came up into the fresh air. After Martin dropped his brother off at the hotel it began to rain again and he realised that he'd left his umbrella at Belga Queen. He arrived home soaked through, took off his jacket and trousers, opened the fridge and hesitated briefly before taking a bottle of Jupiler and sitting by the fireplace. His brother had given him a magazine ("Look what I brought you! I'm on the cover!") which he now flicked through rather than read: "THINK PIG! The E.P.P. information bulletin".

Three

Ultimately death is just the beginning of after-effects.

ON THE WAY from Gare Centrale to police headquarters in rue Marché au Charbon, Émile Brunfaut always stopped and looked around, letting his gaze wander across the fronts of the buildings, watching people go about their tasks or making for their destinations, as if putting the city into operation. He loved the early mornings in Brussels as the city was waking up. He took a few deep breaths, sighed, but then noted uneasily that these were not sighs of happiness. As he crossed the Grande Place he stopped again to look: such splendour! Truly, the square only displayed its beauty at this early hour, before it became occupied by masses of tourists. He hated tourists, those barbarians that hunted down confirmation of the clichés they carried around in their heads, people who had replaced their eyes with tablets and cameras, who stood in the way, turning the living city into a museum and those who worked here into extras, museum attendants and lackeys. Brussels was already a polyglot, multicultural city before these masses, who had no business being here, arrived from countries all over the world. Taking another deep breath, he pressed his briefcase to his stomach and tried to expand his chest as far as possible. He gaped. Like a tourist. How beautiful! How beautiful this square was! But rather than happiness, he felt a worrying melancholy, a sense of grief. Back in 1914, his grandfather had said,

Brussels was the richest and most beautiful city in the world – then they came three times, twice in their boots with rifles, the third time in their trainers with cameras. We were thrust into a prison and released as servants. Émile Brunfaut had never liked his grandfather. He had respected him, yes, and even come to admire him in the end, but he wasn't able to love him during his lifetime, that bitter, old man. Now he was growing old himself. Far too prematurely. He loved Brussels early in the morning – had he ever felt this when he was younger? No, he had merely strolled across the square to work. Now he looked at Brussels as if he were saying goodbye. Why? He had no intention of . . . He walked on, quickly, he wanted to have his coffee and prepare for the 8.00 a.m. briefing. He wasn't sure that this sort of thing – prescience – really existed. He was an inspector. He had little time for hunches, speculation, flights of fancy. As his grandfather had always said, Dreaming of beer slakes no thirst. The inspector took a similar line and this would not have changed had he plumped for a different career.

The day would surely come when he would have to take his leave. He thought it would be his stomach. His large potbelly was pressing against his lungs, forcing them together. That was what it felt like and he supposed it was the reason for his breathlessness, which sounded again and again like a sigh.

It was an ice-cold January morning beneath a low, steel-grey sky. The earth a gravedigger would have to break up today was as hard as the cobbles on this magnificent square.

At the 8.00 a.m. briefing Brunfaut had to report that they had no leads in the "Atlas murder" case, not a sausage. He kept wiping his hands on his tummy, having just eaten a croissant with his coffee; its fatty crumbs stuck to his shirt. He talked and wiped, talked more and wiped more, it looked like a tic. They had a male corpse, identity unknown. The man had checked into the hotel under a false name. Ostensibly he was a Hungarian from Budapest, but his passport was forged. The receptionist had said he spoke English with a strong accent, but she couldn't tell whether the accent was Hungarian. The men from the laboratory had worked rapidly and thoroughly, but neither the dactyloscopy nor the forensic odontology and serology tests had given any clues, while there were no matches in the Police Fédérale database. The ballistic analysis of the lethal bullet had likewise produced no results. Something might still turn up from Europol. The obduction report merely corroborated the evidence: it was an assassination, a shot to the neck from close up. The killer didn't appear to have been looking for anything in the room and hadn't stolen anything. The victim's personal belongings offered no clue to his real identity, or even to a possible motive. There was nothing remarkable apart from the pig. Yes, a pig. Several people they had questioned who'd been in the vicinity of Hotel Atlas around the time of the murder, such as a neighbour, had stated that they'd seen a pig running loose in the streets around the hotel. A complete mystery, Inspector Brunfaut said. After all the investigation and questioning in this case we have but one single lead: a pig – and we don't even know whether this pig has anything to do with the case. He wiped his chest again, then placed both hands on his stomach, pressed in and took a deep breath. Gentlemen!

None of the officers said a word, but Émile Brunfaut didn't think that they might be keeping something from him, or that they were withholding some idea that hadn't occurred to him. He stood up and asked the men from his team to join him in the small meeting room.

As things stand, there's nothing we can do apart from the following, he said. First, we wait to see whether we get an answer from Europol. Second, the pig. We don't know the identity of the victim, but we may be able to find out the identity of the pig. He gave a forced laugh. A creature like that doesn't jump on a plane to Brussels as a tourist and go for a wander in the city centre. It must have an owner it escaped from, or someone who's abandoned it. So let's check out all the pig farmers in the Brussels region. Third, and most importantly, I want to know who that man was at the window of the condemned building. He might have seen something. Perhaps he was the owner of the apartment, or of the entire house. We should be able find that out very quickly. I want the information by the time I'm back here at 1 p.m. Now I have to go to the cemetery.

Only graveyards have gravity these days.

The room was overheated and David de Vriend went to open the window straight away. He discovered that it could only be tilted open, with a gap so narrow that you couldn't even stick your arm through it. Peering down at the gravestones, which stood upright in rank and file beneath the low, grey sky, he asked whether the window locks could be changed, or better still, removed.

Madame Joséphine made it plain that de Vriend shouldn't call her "nurse" because this was a retirement home after all, not a hospital. Alright, Monsieur de Vriend?

She talked far too loudly, she was practically yelling. After years of dealing with residents who were hard of hearing this had become second nature. David de Vriend closed his eyes as if this might allow him to close his ears too. The window, ". . . for your own safety . . .", he heard her shout or bellow – he just wanted this woman to disappear now. Her parade-ground tone was as objectionable as her mask-like friendliness, her mouth tensed into a permanent smile. He knew he was being unfair, but if life were fair then he would have been spared all this. Now she was standing beside him, shouting into his ear: Alright? Lovely view from this window, isn't it? All that green! He turned away, took off his jacket and tossed it onto the bed. She and her team were always here for him, alright? she said. If he ever needed help or had a problem, all he had to do was call, using the internal telephone here, or the bell beside the bed. Alright, Monsieur de Vriend? Looking around with an expression of glee, as if this tiny apartment were a luxury suite, she opened her arms and yelled, So this is your little realm! You're going to feel at home here!

That was an order. To his astonishment he saw that she was now offering him her hand. It took a while for him to react. She was just about to pull it back when finally he held out his. There was a bit of a kerfuffle before the handshake took place. I wish you all the best here, she said, then noticed the number tattooed on his forearm. Alright? she added softly, before leaving the room. De Vriend contemplated his little realm and was surprised that he hadn't noticed this before when visiting various old people's homes and opting for this one: everything in the room was fixed and screwed down tight. There wasn't one piece of furniture you could shift and set in a different place. Not just the bed with its table and the cupboard – half wardrobe, half cabinet with glass doors – but also the coffee table and L-shaped sofa were built in, the television was screwed to the wall and even the picture above the bed – a pseudo-impressionist Venice in the rain – was fixed so you couldn't take it down. Why Venice? And why in the rain? Was it supposed to be of comfort to the burghers of Brussels in their twilight years that it rained even in the most beautiful places on earth? A small built-in kitchenette. There was nothing you could move, change, arrange differently. Not even a chair. Everything was unalterable and permanent. He went to the cupboard, where the few books he had brought with him were behind glass, wedged between a pair of ceramic bookends – two reading pigs. A present from his final class of school-leavers before retirement. He wanted to take out some books, put them here and there, on the table, on the bed, they would be the only moveable things in this room. He opened the cupboard door, his eyes scanned the spines, then again, and he felt unsure. What did he want to do? Read? Had he wanted to read? No. He stood there, staring at the books, then closed the cupboard again. He wanted – what did he want? To get out? He wanted to get out. He went to the window. Brussels city cemetery. There was nothing within reach, but plenty in sight. He dressed warmly.

It was a short hop from the Maison Hansens retirement home in rue de l'Arbre Unique to the main cemetery gate. The icy cold. The grey sky. The wrought-iron gate. He found it reassuring to see birds – crows and sparrows. And so many molehills between the graves, he couldn't recall ever having seen so many molehills in a cemetery. In fact he couldn't recall ever having seen even one in a cemetery before. And fungi growing everywhere amongst the creeping ivy, vast numbers of fungi, that was . . . that was . . . he couldn't remember the name. He knew them, what did it matter? They were inedible. That's all. And here was an upside-down tomb, literally, turned upside down by the thick roots of an enormous tree. Beside it gravestones broken by fallen trees or branches. Moss on the shattered stones. Young, newly planted trees next to the old ones that had fallen or been felled, and which lay decaying between the graves. Even the trees perished on this field of death and sank into the earth. Small plaster wreaths hung on old gravestones. Sometimes two or three, and a few of these wreaths lay in front of the headstones or beside the graves. As if morbid children had been playing hoops.

He stopped by several graves, read the names and looked at the enamel photographs. He liked strolling through cemeteries, how lovely it was that people had graves with their names marked on them. People you could visit after they had died. He saw the graves of children, of people who had died young as a result of illness, an accident, or who had been murdered – tragic destinies, but at least they had a grave. So long as cemeteries existed, there was the promise of civilisation. His parents, his brother, his grandparents – their graves were in the air. No place you could visit, care for, where you could place a stone. No resting place. Just a persistent restlessness which could never find a place of peace. In the memory that would die with him, only one image of his family remained, captured with a final glance – and that glance was merely an assertion. He hadn't seen his mother's face, just her hand holding on to his sleeve until he tore himself away. He had no image of his father, just a memory of him shouting "Stay!", shouting "Stay there! You're leaping to your doom!" And his brother? Faceless, just the child's back pressed tight to his mother. What else? Memories that felt stolen from other people's stock of memories: father–mother–child memories, all-purpose memories, the happiest. As black as the ashes of burnt photographs.

His father had liked *tarte au riz*. That was a memory. He didn't have an image to go with it. Such as the family sitting around the table and Father, his face beaming with delight, saying, "Mmm, at last we're having *tarte au riz* again!" and Mother placing the tart on the table and Father exhorting the children to behave, saying, "Stop it! Calm down!" and Mother saying, "First a nice slice for your father," and . . . all wrong! Of this there was no image in his memory, no film in his head, he couldn't picture himself sitting at the table with his family, with a *tarte au riz*. There were only the words: "Father loved *tarte au riz*!" But why? Why these words?

And where did they come from? These words as the memory of a life? And at the same time dead words, buried inside his head. Then he saw a gravestone on which was chiselled:

TOUT PASSE
TOUT S'EFFACE
HORS DU SOUVENIR

He stopped and gazed at this inscription for a long while. Then he bent down, picked up a pebble and placed it on top of the grave.

So many ruined graves. The vandalism of nature. Headstones levered out by tree roots, slabs shattered by broken branches and fallen trees, stones swallowed by rampant plants. The decomposing memorials to human rivalry, the eagerness for representation. Dilapidated, mouldy mausoleums designed as monumental testimony to a family's power and wealth, but now derelict and manifesting only this: transience. Signs in front of them erected by the cemetery management: "The lease for this plot expires at the end of the year."

Without money, even the graves die.

He was tired and wondered fleetingly whether it might not be best to go back. But no, he wanted to make a thorough exploration of the neighbourhood in which he now lived.

He took a left turn without looking at the signpost – "*Deutscher Soldatenfriedhof*", "Commonwealth War Graves", "*Nederlandse Oorlogsgraven*" – and here began the neatly ordered rows of identical headstones, which in their endless uniformity provided peace and a dramatic beauty after the animated, almost howling chaos of the civilian part of the cemetery, the perfect redemption for lives stolen, in an aesthetic of dignity.

At the age of 24 years – died for the Fatherland.
At the age of 20 years – died for the Fatherland.
At the age of 26 years – died for the Fatherland.
At the age of 19 years – died for the Fatherland.
At the age of 23 years – died for the Fatherland.
At the age of 23 years – died for the Fatherland.
At the age of 22 years – died for the Fatherland.
At the age of 31 years – died for the Fatherland.
At the age of 24 years – died for the Fatherland.
At the age of 39 years – died for the Fatherland.
At the age of 21 years – died for the Fatherland.

Mort pour la patrie, for the glory of the nation, *slachtoffers van den plicht*.

Whoever walked along here inspected the rows like a general would an army of the dead, or a president might a military formation at a state reception in Hades. He closed his eyes. And at that very moment somebody addressed him. A gentleman who asked if he spoke German or English.

A little German.

Did he know where the mausoleum of unconditional love was?

I'm sorry?

The man said he'd read about it in his guidebook, did he understand? Yes? Good. So, in his guidebook . . . it must be somewhere here. The mausoleum of unconditional love. Don't you know —?

De Vriend didn't know.

Professor Erhart thanked him and continued on his way. At the end of the avenue he saw a building with a few people standing outside – maybe he'd find out more from them. He still had time. Most of the participants of the "New Pact for Europe" Reflection Group were only arriving this morning, which was why today's first meeting was scheduled for 1 p.m. He, however, had come a couple of days earlier. He wanted to see something of the city too, rather than spending the whole time in an airtight, air-conditioned room. Back in Vienna he had no commitments and no family. In this respect he was in the most awful situation you could find yourself in at his age: he was free. It was thanks to his excellent academic reputation that he still received the occasional invitation, such as this one; he always accepted and prepared meticulously, even though – or perhaps *because* – he felt increasingly that he was no longer presenting discussion papers, but offering readings from his testament. Maybe that was his role now: explaining to his successors that a legacy existed that was beyond the zeitgeist, and it was their task to take possession of it.

First of all Alois Erhart had visited the grave of Armand Moens, once a much-discussed and now forgotten economist, a professor at the University of Leuven, who already in the 1960s had developed a theory of post-national economics, from which he had inferred the necessity of establishing a United European Republic. The growing interlinking and interdependence of economies, the ever-expanding power of multinationals and the increasing significance of international financial markets would no longer allow national democracies to fulfil their essential tasks: intervening to shape the conditions in which people had to live their lives, and generally ensuring distributive justice. "Shut down the national parliaments!" – this was the battle cry of a true democrat, who wished to reinvent democracy taking into account the historical framework. The only reason his thesis had not been dismissed as scandalous or wildly utopian at the time was that the era had been so free-spirited, and this was also the reason why, ultimately, Moens was not able to prevail over the national economists, "the ruminants" (as he called them): "At first the wacky academic licence helped us, but in the end it consolidated the power of the really wacky ones," he wrote in his memoirs.

Forty-five years earlier Erhart, then a budding student, had heard a guest lecture Armand Moens gave in Alpach, and ever since he had regarded himself as Moens disciple. He had faithfully read all his publications. By the time Erhart published his own first work and sent it to his teacher, Moens was already terminally ill. He responded with a letter, but that was the end of their exchange, for Moens died a few days later. Now an emotional Erhart stood by the grave:

ARMAND JOSEPH MOENS
1910–1972

In front of the gravestone and to the side was a small enamel sign on which was written:

"Toen hij het meest nodig was,
werd hij vergeten"
Studenten werkgroep "Moens eed"
aan de Katholieke Universiteit Leuven

On the grave there were fresh flowers and a bottle of schnapps. And good luck pigs in various sizes and materials: plastic, fur fabric, wood, ceramic – Alois Erhart couldn't explain the pigs. He took a photograph. Then a second one, this time of the headstone and the sign without the pigs.

While researching the location of Professor Moens' grave he had stumbled upon a reference to another tourist attraction in the city cemetery: the mausoleum of unconditional love. Which he was now looking for. A Brussels baron – Erhart had forgotten the name – who had made his fortune from mining in the Belgian Congo, had fallen desperately in love with a woman on a trip to the colony. He brought the woman back to Brussels to marry her – "A negress!" This led not only to his ostracism from Brussels society, but also to some legal problems, which he ultimately overcame after a lengthy battle, partly by paying out considerable sums of money, and partly through the assistance of the best lawyers. The baron's love weathered all storms. "I'd rather be rejected with this woman than respected without her!" When the wedding was finally permitted to take place, none of the guests turned up save for mad old Countess Adolphine Marat, who after the ceremony invited the couple back for tea in her palais. The witnesses were two workers repairing a manhole cover in the road outside the registry office, and who were willing to interrupt their work for a quarter of an hour for fifty francs apiece. Countess Marat, who received a hostile reaction for having welcomed the newly-weds into her house, justified herself with the legendary words: "If he is prepared to give that woman his name, then the least I can do is give her a cup of tea!"

This woman, whose name was Libelulle (Professor Erhart had remembered this, it meant "little dragonfly") died soon afterwards in 1910, in childbirth. Their son had been stillborn, strangled by the umbilical cord. Racked with grief, the Baron – oh yes, he was called Caspers, Victor Caspers – commissioned a French architect to build a magnificent mausoleum in the Cimetière de la Ville for his beloved, a prayer room in the roof of which was an aperture, precisely calculated and designed so that each year, on the day and hour of her death, a patch of light in the shape of a heart would fall onto her sarcophagus.

This is what Professor Erhart had come to see. He had expected to find notices and signposts, but there was nothing of the sort. Were there several Brussels cemeteries? Was he in the wrong one?

He had reached the building he'd seen from a distance and where a largish group of people had now gathered.

He was nonplussed when he spotted a large and unmistakable figure standing amongst those assembled: it was the policeman who had questioned him in the hotel, he was absolutely sure it was the overweight inspector. The professor stopped and stared, their eyes met. Erhart wasn't sure if the inspector recognised him, and in any case the policeman's attention was drawn elsewhere when two men who had approached at speed greeted him and exchanged a few words before entering the building which, as Erhart now saw, was the crematorium chapel.

It was not Inspector Brunfaut's job to be present at the cremation of a murder victim. Nor was there any reason relevant to the case for him to be there. Following a murder the body is impounded and given a forensic autopsy. After that it is released for burial or cremation. If the victim's identity is known and there are relatives, they organise the funeral. If the identity is not known, a cremation is carried out within forty-eight hours of the autopsy, by order of the city. A municipal official turns up, checks the paperwork, confirms that the corpse is reference number X or Y, gives a five-minute speech about the transience of life and eternal peace to satisfy the minimum level of dignity as stipulated by E.U. funeral guidelines, then the coffin sinks into the combustor. Later the ashes are scattered on the lawn beside the crematorium – which effectively means they're tipped out – and a plaque with the name of the dead person or, if this is unknown, their police reference number is affixed to a column. It was highly unlikely that a suspect, let alone the perpetrator themselves, would turn up to this ceremony, given that nobody apart from the officials involved were aware of the time and place. But there were always members of the public, people who regularly went for walks in the cemetery, pensioners, widows, local mothers pushing prams, who would stop out of respect or curiosity.

Inspector Brunfaut had not come because of the case he was working on, but because this was the anniversary of his grandfather's death. Many years ago an impressive number of people, which got ever smaller as the years rolled on, had gathered at his grandfather's grave each year to pay their respects to this hero of the Belgian Resistance. Stories were told, schnapps was drunk, songs were sung. And to round it off, the Brabançonne. When they got to "*Les peuples libres sont amis!*" the geriatrics sounded like a bunch of madmen, so ardently were they singing, bawling even. At the line "*Le Roi, la Loi, la Liberté!*" there was always one who, like a conductor, would stop the choir abruptly with a swish of his hand and cry: We can't have everything! What could we do without? And the rest would reply: The king! And what can't we do without? Tutti: Justice and freedom!

As a boy Émile Brunfaut had found this ritual fairly intimidating, the graveside frenzy embarrassing, and believed the mothball smell of the old men's suits came from gunpowder. Later, after his parents had died, he began to feel respect and admiration for the man who had so terrified him as a child, and . . . yes, even pride! Later still, when tears were ready to spring from the ever-larger bags beneath his eyes, and he would have liked to embrace those who had gathered at this grave year in, year out, there was nobody left, no living soul who could remember his grandfather and his heroic deeds. Nonetheless, every year on this day he came to spend an hour in solitary contemplation by the grave. And because this was the way things had turned out today, he went afterwards to the crematorium, where his "case" was in the process of being incinerated. Not having anticipated that his presence there would bring him any further in his investigation, he was all the more astonished to spot a man he had spoken to during the initial questioning at the crime scene. To begin with the man had looked only vaguely familiar, and it had taken him a good ten minutes to work out where he knew him from. He ran at once out of the crematorium chapel, but the man was no longer there. Brunfaut hurried down a few tree-lined paths, but was unable to find him.

He left the cemetery. Right opposite the gate was Le Rustique, a restaurant he always went to after visiting his grandfather's grave. Brunfaut wondered why the windows in the first floor of the restaurant were bricked up. It was inconceivable that somebody living here objected to the view of the cemetery. Nobody bricks their windows up just because they find the view out of them depressing. Someone like that wouldn't have moved in here in the first place. What mystery was hidden behind these bricked-up windows?

As ever, Brunfaut ordered *stoemp*, his grandfather's favourite dish and for himself a sentimental taste of childhood. *Stoemp* is *stoemp*, his grandfather had always said, and the most important thing, of course, was the quality of the sausage: it should burst when you stick the fork in. Which meant the skin had to be made of natural casings rather than artificial plastic, as was increasingly being used, a dramatic symptom of the death of Belgian working-class culture. Here in Le Rustique the *stoemp* was still authentic. Simple, genuine, perfect. Washed down with a draught Stella Artois and a small jenever to finish. Émile Brunfaut sighed, then drove back to police headquarters.

When Émile Brunfaut arrived at the "*mine de charbon*" the duty officer said that the superintendent was already waiting for him and Brunfaut should go directly to his office.

Brunfaut had explained he was going to the cemetery and would be back at 1 p.m. Everybody had nodded. It was now 1.05. Was the boss going to throw his weight around again? Brunfaut anticipated a reprimand because there was no justifiable reason for his having taken a stroll around the cemetery, and then to come back late as well. He shrugged – not really, of course, but in his mind – and waited patiently for the lift, then walked sedately down the corridor to the boss' office, knocked on the door and immediately went in.

A topsy-turvy world, he thought. He had just come from the cemetery, but to his mind the burial was taking place here. To the superintendent's left sat the examining magistrate, to his right the public prosecutor, and all three wore a deadly serious expression.

Please sit down, Inspector Brunfaut.

Brunfaut wasn't particularly surprised that the examining magistrate was breathing down the superintendent's neck. He was the actual boss, after all; it was he who kept issuing instructions and demanding regular updates on how investigations were proceeding. The presence of the public prosecutor, however, immediately put Brunfaut on red alert: this signalled a political intervention.

What use was being on red alert if the alarm bells didn't ring until the consequences of the threat were already an irrevocable fact?

It was indeed a burial taking place in this room. The burial of the "Atlas case".

Well, said Superintendent Maigret, before falling silent. Brunfaut was convinced that this fool owed his career to the coincidence of having been born with this name, a highly unfortunate coincidence for the city. He said nothing, watching impassively as Maigret searched for the right words. Then Brunfaut looked expectantly at Maigret, who turned for help to the examining magistrate, and the examining magistrate turned to the public prosecutor, who finally said, Thank you very much, Inspector Brunfaut, for your time. We've just been discussing the murder case at Hotel Atlas, which, if I'm correctly informed, you . . .

Yes, Brunfaut said.

Well, Superintendent Maigret said.

There are new developments, said the examining magistrate, Monsieur de Rohan. The only thing about this vain man that Brunfaut found interesting was his wife. He'd met her once at a Christmas party, a young, very slight woman with large, black-rimmed eyes. Every time she opened her mouth to say something she was stifled by a smiling de Rohan with the words, "And you, *ma chérie*, need to keep quiet now!" Brunfaut had wanted to sleep with her at once. He couldn't tell whether this really was lust, or merely the desire to humiliate her husband. He had been drunk enough to whisper it into her ear – very directly, very stupidly. She stared at him wide-eyed, he was instantly ashamed, and she replied, Not tonight. Call me tomorrow!

With a narcissistic movement of the hand, de Rohan touched his perfectly blow-dried hair and invited Superintendent Maigret to fill Inspector Brunfaut in with the latest developments. Brunfaut sensed that the public prosecutor was disgusted by the policeman's ineptitude, that he was merely waiting for some straight talking so he could leave and turn his attention to more important matters.

Well, Superintendent Maigret said. The situation was as follows: there were compelling reasons for no longer investigating this case.

Do you understand?

No, Brunfaut said, I do not. Does this mean that we won't

investigate any longer, or I won't investigate any longer, or nobody will investigate any longer?

This was the third time in the past five years that he had been summoned to a crime scene and stood beside a body that no longer existed the following day. Are these the compelling reasons? That Brussels is the city of the Day of Judgment? Of the resurrection of the dead? Had the dead man's soul been reunited with his body, and where there was no body there was no case? Had this been confirmed by Forensics?

Well, Maigret said, I understand . . .

Brunfaut shot this fool an angry look. His ridiculous spiky hair. Twisted into shape with gel. As if the tight knot of his tie was making it stand on end.

I understand that you, well, that you don't understand, but . . .

The matter is quite simple, de Rohan chimed in, perfectly straightforward. We are going to have nothing more to do with this case, not you, not us, not anybody here. And what I'm about to tell you is strictly confidential. You never heard it, O.K.? Right then. There is one institution powerful enough to take a case like this away from us, that can make it disappear and resolve it in its own way. And the reason why this institution is so powerful is that in reality, and here I mean officially, it doesn't exist. It's intangible, you see? It snaffles cases like this one, but as an entity it is intangible. There are interests, which . . .

Interests, Brunfaut said.

Precisely. We understand each other.

The public prosecutor looked in silence from one man to the other, then nodded.

This will remain between us, Brunfaut said, and the public prosecutor nodded once more. Yes, Brunfaut said, this will remain between us, just like in a T.V. crime series.

I'm sorry?

An order from the very top, Brunfaut said, a political intervention to obstruct the investigation, mysterious intimations, otherwise silence. It's such a dreadful cliché, but of course the cliché has to be followed to its conclusion: by an inspector who feels compelled to strike out on his own . . .

Surely you don't intend . . .

And who ends up as the hero . . .

You are *not* going to do anything off your own bat, the state prosecutor said. That is an order. And I've just learned that your request for leave has been granted.

But I didn't put in any request for leave!

Well, this is a little misunderstanding, Maigret said. What I said was that Inspector Brunfaut still has quite a lot of holiday to take.

Brunfaut felt sharp pangs of anxiety and took a deep breath.

That's perfect, de Rohan said, you can use up your holiday allowance and spend some time relaxing. I know you've been under a huge amount of stress and . . .

The public prosecutor got to his feet, Maigret and de Rohan leaped out of their chairs, while Brunfaut stood up slowly, this two-metre-tall man who towered over everyone else in the room. He felt a twinge in his chest and fell back into his chair. Looking down at him the public prosecutor said, Gentlemen!

Émile Brunfaut went to his office and realised that the "Atlas" file containing the operation report, the initial interrogation records, the crime-scene photographs and the autopsy findings had disappeared from his desk. He had, however, saved everything on his computer. He entered his password, but the folder in question had vanished from the desktop of his monitor too. He opened the recycle bin: the folder was nowhere to be seen amongst all his deleted files. The activity log, everything relating to this case – the notification to go to Hotel Atlas, which patrol cars were at the crime scene, which officers were on duty, the first forensics report – everything was gone. The entire case had vanished into thin air.

He wheezed, pressed his stomach downwards to relieve his lungs, took a deep breath, and undid his belt and the top button of his trousers. He stared at the screen. For how long? A minute? Ten minutes? He realised that he wasn't looking at the monitor anymore, but at himself. How would he react? He didn't know. He saw himself sitting there like a corpse slumped in a chair. Then his fingers were tapping away at the keyboard and he Googled: What did the press report about the murder in Hotel Atlas? Nothing. No matter how he phrased it, there was nothing, no result. There hadn't been a single report in any paper. The murder never happened.

He looked up and noticed only now that his flipchart had been expurgated too. The sheet of paper on which at the last meeting he'd written *HOTEL ATLAS → PIG?????* had been ripped off.

Brunfaut had a strange thought: was this the moment at which he finally had to become the grandson?

The grandson of the famous resistance fighter.

He picked up the telephone and summoned his team. He was gung-ho, he could sense it.

The sergeant, the deputy inspector and three constables came in, Inspector Brunfaut switched off the computer, looked up, gazed into these men's faces and he knew at once: these men were abreast of the situation and had already come to terms with it. It was hopeless. He stood up and told them he just wanted to say goodbye, because he was . . . his trousers were falling down, so he grabbed them and yanked them up . . . because he was taking some holiday and . . . not wishing to do himself up in front of the men, he shouted, Get out, the lot of you!

Now these dutiful conformists and opportunists would have a good gossip about what a ridiculous figure their inspector cut. Misty-eyed, he went over to the flipchart, took a marker and wrote: *La Loi, la Liberté!* Then, recalling an inscription he'd seen on a grave in the cemetery that afternoon, he wrote in block capitals:

TOUT PASSE

TOUT S'EFFACE

HORS DU SOUVENIR

He picked up his briefcase, which was empty, and left.

The algorithm that filters everything imaginable and which has ordered our story until now is, of course, mad, but more importantly it is reassuring. The world is confetti, but the algorithm allows us to experience it as a mosaic.

Was it because of Brunfaut's visit to the crematorium that the following connection was now made?

New mail: "Subject: Auschwitz – Your visit".

Martin Susman was freezing. Because of the rain, he'd taken the Metro rather than cycle to work. The subterranean wind in the shafts and tunnels was different, harsher and more aggressive than the airflow on a bike. And the steaming heat from the herds in the jammed carriages brought no relief; he felt anxious about infectious diseases, but most of all he was worried about becoming infected by the apathy and submission that always seizes people on trains.

Dear Herr Susman, I look forward very much to pleasure of welcoming you soon in Auschwitz!

He'd got a mug of tea from the canteen and was now checking e-mails at his desk.

> Naturally, I pick you up from Kraków Airport and drive you
> personally to the camp. You recognise me by sign I hold with
> your name on it.

Susman put his tea down in disgust. He had chosen tea because he felt he was coming down with something, but it was making him ill just drinking it.

His official trip. Essentially all the preparations had been made. The Research Service and the Museum of the German Extermination Camp Auschwitz–Birkenau were subsidised by the E.U.; each year representatives from the E.U. Commission attended the ceremony on 27 January to celebrate the camp's liberation. This year the Directorate-General of Culture was sending Martin Susman, who was also responsible for administering the funding and monitoring how it was put to use.

> And if you would permit me to offer good advice for your trip,
> bring warm underwear. Bitter cold is Auschwitz at this time
> of year. We would on no account wish you to become ill
> in Auschwitz!
> On my last visit to Berlin I bought underwear in department
> store, the best underwear I have ever had. I do not know name
> of brand, but please go to shop and ask for German underwear!
> I always say German underwear because I bought it in Berlin
> and is definitely made in Germany. Will be known in Brussels.
> German underwear! I advise you to buy. German underwear
> is best underwear for Auschwitz!

Martin Susman clicked "Reply", wrote three friendly sentences, opened the next e-mail, got up, left his office and popped in to see Bohumil Szmekal, who was hurriedly typing something. Susman held up a packet of cigarettes, Szmekal nodded, and they went out onto the fire escape for a smoke.

Mrzne jak v ruským filmu, Bohumil said. Martin didn't understand, of course, but he agreed with him: Yes, we need German underwear!

David de Vriend left the cemetery. He was freezing. He shrugged it off, he had experienced harsher cold than this, and without the sort of coat he was wearing now. He decided to go to Le Rustique, the restaurant across the road, for a bite to eat and something warming to drink, a glass of red wine, perhaps. He found a seat by the window to the left. The waitress brought him the menu and asked, Are you from the Maison Hanssens, the old people's home? You'll have to show me your coupons before I draw up your bill.

Coupons?

For the discount!

No, no, de Vriend said – he didn't know anything about coupons, or at least Madame Joséphine hadn't mentioned it – I'm normal, I mean, I'm a normal guest.

Alright then, she said, handing him the menu. He ordered a glass of red wine, yes the house red, and asked, What would you recommend to eat? I just want something small.

Well, we've got the normal things, she said, tapping the menu, and then we have our daily *Anti-Crise* menu.

Anti-Crise menu?

Yes. Something hearty to begin with, followed by something very sweet. It's terribly popular here. Today we've got *choucroute à l'Ancienne*, then *mousse au chocolat*. Eighteen euros without coupons. And if you want the *duo de fondue* to start with, cheeses and prawns, that'll be twenty-five euros.

He looked at this cheerful woman and wondered what it did to a person, dealing every day with mourners, not the dead, but those who'd been left behind.

Alright, then, the *Anti-Crise* menu, but without the fondue.

And without coupons. *D'accord!*

As de Vriend waited he stared out of the window at the cemetery. Only now, from a distance and from this aspect, did it occur to him that the cemetery gates bore a certain resemblance to the gates at Birkenau.

His red wine came.

A wrought-iron gate always has similarities with a wrought-iron gate. And the towers on either side? What else should there be either side of a wrought-iron gate? Like the people in the camp – they were people, what else could they be? And yet it was crazy to think there were similarities. There weren't. That's all.

Four

If we could travel into the future
we'd have more detachment.

IT WAS MARTIN Susman's intention to survive his official trip to Poland with as little damage to his body and soul as possible. He could never have imagined that this visit would give him the idea for – nay, obsession with – the "Big Jubilee Project" and end up almost turning his life upside down.

But for now his preparations for the trip were causing him trouble.

He was taken aback when the sales assistant immediately interrupted his stammering. *Bien sûr*, of course she knew about German underwear, she trotted out a few brand names and naturally they stocked this – she smiled – quality German product.

Martin had asked Kassándra Mercouri if she knew of a specialist shop for underwear and she'd suggested he go to Ixelles, to the Galerie Toison d'Or, where there was a shop with a huge selection, the shop was called Tollé, no, it was called Fronde, yes, definitely Fronde. At any rate there was a large sign saying "Underwear" above the entrance, and he would recognise the shop at once from its display. They had everything. She herself bought all her underwear there.

When Martin found the shop, "Fronde Dessous", and peered at the display, he suddenly saw the maternal Kassándra with different eyes. This was where she bought her underwear? He can't have expressed himself with sufficient clarity, he thought, this must be a misunderstanding. He was gazing at beautiful, well, underwear – top-quality, really attractive *dessous*, but for him? And . . . for Auschwitz?

Looking around he spied an "Adventure Shop" opposite, where you could buy everything you needed to climb Mount Everest. Perhaps he ought to look there for his frost protection gear. Had those words really come to mind? Frost protection gear? The whole thing was so ridiculous. He couldn't decide which was the greater challenge: going to see the tanned, adventure-seeking machos across the road, or . . . no, Kassándra had recommended the Fronde shop to him and so he went in on the spur of the moment.

As Martin tried to explain to the sales assistant what he wanted, he felt like a seventeen-year-old from the provinces, attempting to speak to a girl at his first disco in the big city. When he said, "I mean, there's a special warm underwear, from a German manufacturer I think, I don't know if you understand what I'm getting at, anyway, it's particularly warm," he closed his eyes as if terrified that this woman would read in them that in his imagination he was picturing her in the very *dessous* that the mannequins were wearing in the window.

Bien sûr! Behind her was a cupboard full of drawers, of the sort he recognised from pharmacies. She opened one drawer, slid it back in, opened another and took out a few cellophane packages that she spread out on the counter before him. Did you mean this sort of thing? she said. Vest, long johns, tights, and these are arm warmers. One hundred per cent angora. And look here: it says, "German Quality". I tell you, these things are hotter than hell.

She laughed. Or let's say hotter than a sauna! Are you going abroad?

Yes, he said, to . . . Poland.

Oh. I don't know Poland myself. But I can imagine you might need this there, I mean, it's practically Siberia. She laughed, tore open a packet, unfolded a pair of long johns in front of him, stroked the material and said: Go on! Touch them! Can you feel how soft and warm they are? They're made from the fur of that rabbit, angora, you see? But from Germany, which means there's no animal cruelty – guaranteed. And look here, the certificate. These long johns already comply with the new E.U. guidelines for underwear.

What?

Yes, Monsieur. I was surprised too. We had the rep in recently, he explained it to us. It's to do with the flammability of the underwear, it's all regulated now.

You mean – Martin gave a fake laugh – the underwear is so hot that it's in danger of igniting?

The girl smiled. No, but the point is it mustn't be flammable. I don't know why. And angora is actually, well it *is* rabbit fur. Which of course is extremely flammable. But not any more. Now it has to be impregnated. The E.U., you understand? Maybe because it's mainly smokers who buy this underwear, they always have to stand outside in the cold. And now there's this E.U. guideline to prevent smokers from setting fire to themselves! She laughed. Or in bed.

In bed?

Yes, when smokers go to bed with a cigarette and fall asleep. Then it's the bed that burns.

Yes, but not this underwear. It's regulated now! Look at this: "Underwear flammability corresponds to E.U. guidelines . . ."

I don't believe it, Mademoiselle.

Nor do I, she said.

The first thing that Kai-Uwe Frigge did that Monday morning was to skim the "*Valise Voyage à Doha*" list that his secretary, Madeleine, had placed on his desk for him to sign. This was something Frigge had instituted: every Monday Madeleine gave him a list detailing his dress code for each day, from Tuesday to the following Monday, corresponding to his various appointments and engagements. Usually Frigge would sign the list, which Madeleine would then e-mail to Dubravka, his housekeeper. Then early every morning Dubravka would lay out his clothes as per the list, or pack them into a suitcase if he was travelling.

This routine was common knowledge in the office and there were some who laughed about it or made sarcastic comments, but it did no harm to Frigge's reputation. On the contrary, his quirky procedure showed that he was a hard-core pragmatist down to the finest detail, who possessed the talent of being able to come up with original solutions to make him less sweaty when tagging along, and less wet when going with the flow. Within bureaucracies a reputation like that is comparable to the highest peerage.

There is a telling anecdote from Frigge's student days recounted by Frauke Diestel from the Directorate-General for Energy. She was a fellow student of Frigge's at the University of Hamburg and was for a time in the same flat-share. One day, she said, Kai-Uwe gave away all his coloured and patterned shirts and bought ten identical white ones cheaply in a sale at the Shopping Center Hamburger Meile. His explanation for this had been that he would save himself time every morning by not having to deliberate over which shirt went with which jacket or jumper. No matter what he put on, a white shirt was always fine. Now in the mornings he could take the shirt from the top of the pile in the wardrobe without thinking about it, and when he wore the eighth shirt he knew it was time to take the dirty ones to the laundry, and then pick them up when he put on the tenth shirt, allowing him to start with the first one again the following day. Somehow it was madness, but there was a logic to it, Frauke said. He had been able to buy the white shirts cheaply because they were old-fashioned and unsellable, and you had to insert stiffeners into the collars. But he was delighted with his purchases, insisting that they themselves were a bit of culture. The sleeves were too long, but at the flea market he managed to find some old sleeve garters that he wore on his upper arms to adjust the sleeve length. For him, this too was "old culture". He loved gentlemen's accessories. At the time a number of American gangster and mafia films were released in which all the men wore these sleeve garters, so they became fashionable, and all of a sudden Kai-Uwe, with his oddly pragmatic approach to life and a total lack of interest in fads, had become a sort of trendsetter! Even if Kai-Uwe is misunderstood, Frauke said, it's safe to assume that it only adds to his reputation.

Kai-Uwe Frigge was annoyed when he surveyed the list. Once again Madeleine had forgotten what he had told her so many times now: on trips to hot countries he didn't need airy and thin clothes, on the contrary; in warm countries especially he needed warm items. They could be light, absolutely, but they had to be warm, for example fine cashmere cardigans, and definitely some vests. The thing was, in meetings and at mealtimes you sat continuously in air-conditioned rooms where the temperature was turned down brutally low. Nowhere did you freeze as miserably as when you were with these desert sheikhs, where the cold was viewed as a luxury and luxury as a *raison d'être*. Unless you were walking the streets in Doha – but who does that, and why would you need to? – it was colder there than on a park bench in northern Finland.

He called Madeleine in and instructed her to redo the list.

Forget all these linen and silk things, they're fine for Strasbourg in summer, but never for Doha. Wool, cashmere, O.K.? Cardigans and vests. Cravat and scarf. And under miscellaneous please put charging lead for mobile and tablet, as well as shoe polish. So that Dubra remembers to pack them.

Madeleine nodded and went to the door.

Madeleine!

Yes, Monsieur?

Just one more thing. Please put the blue turban on the list too.

No.

Yes. You never know. At some point we just might have to – he coughed – step outside.

Kai-Uwe Frigge checked the time. Now he had to deal with the "pig's ear", as he called it.

Mateusz Oświecki wanted to pray before his flight. He had to compose himself. It tortured him that he had executed the wrong man.

In front of security he saw protesters handing out leaflets, a good dozen young men and women all wearing the same yellow T-shirt with a slogan on the chest he could not read. Three police officers stood uncertainly to one side, while a fourth policeman talked to one of the activists. Another was speaking into a radio.

Mateusz slackened his pace to work out what was going on, then speeded up, a passenger in a hurry, not wishing to miss his flight. With a show of impatience he tried to worm his way through, and was almost at the barrier when a protester stood in his way. Excuse me, Sir, may I . . . he didn't respond and attempted to get past her. Do you speak English, Sir? Sir? He ignored her and steered his trolley past. *Parlez-vous français? Volez-vous vers la Pologne?* Are you going to Poland? Sir? It is important, *een vraag, mijnheer* . . . He bowed his head, noticed out of the corner of his eye that a policeman was looking over at him, and felt safe. This was almost comical – he was going to escape with the help of a policeman who would have to intervene if a passenger was being harassed. But Mateusz didn't want it come to that, he had no desire to become embroiled in anything that would involve the police. The woman held out a flyer that showed the picture of a man; it looked like a mugshot. Was this a wanted poster? Mateusz placed his ticket on the reader of the gate, a red light came on, what was wrong? Sir, please, are you flying with Polish Airlines? Flight LO 236? We have some important information. He knew that it was pointless, that it would make everything more difficult to now say, Sorry, I'm in a hurry! For that would be a conversation opener, she would say she'd only take up a minute of his time, he would have to respond again . . . no, he put his ticket on the reader a second time and once more it lit up red. He rubbed it back and forth a few times – why the hell wasn't it working? Finally the green light came on, the glass doors slid open and he was through. Mateusz joined the queue edging its way forwards to the baggage scanners. He saw a few people reading the flyer. Once through the scanner he looked for signs to the prayer room. He still had more than an hour until boarding. He pushed his trolley past the shops, moving ever quicker, and then he was already at the gates. Where was the airport chapel? He retraced his steps but couldn't see any sign of one. He wanted to pray. After reading the last set of instructions he had received, Mateusz realised that he must have shot the wrong man. Finally he spotted a pictogram of a person kneeling in prayer, beside it an arrow pointing to a side corridor. There he saw the praying figure with the arrow again, pointing to some steps.

As he followed the arrows he was reminded of Saint Sebastian, whose chest was shot through with arrows. Only a few days previously, on January 20, the feast day of Sebastian – patron saint of soldiers and those who fought the enemies of the Church – he had beseeched him for protection and success in his Brussels mission. But something had gone wrong and he couldn't work out what. The arrows led into a corridor monitored by video cameras. He continued on his way, head bowed, and wiped his brow with a handkerchief as if mopping away sweat, to prevent the cameras from capturing his face. He knew that he was being excessively cautious; these C.C.T.V. cameras were outdated. Was it snowing in here? Of course not. But the images from the cameras, which would be stored for the next forty-eight hours, were of such a low resolution that all they would show was a shadowy man apparently trudging through a blizzard. Pot plants on either side. Literally – they were hemp. But plastic. These were plastic hemp plants, no question. Who had dreamed up the idea of placing plastic hemp plants in the corridor to the chapels? And what could they have been thinking? Now he had arrived at the prayer rooms, one for every major religious community: Catholic, Protestant, Jewish, Islamic and Orthodox. All were empty, but more than that: they looked as if nobody had ever stepped into them before.

Mateusz felt a sharp pain when he entered the Catholic prayer room, an unbelievably ugly space. Unbelievable – more grotesqueness in a place of worship. Feeling an intense burning beneath his navel, he took a few steps forward, pushed away the trolley, removed the handkerchief from his trouser pocket and wiped away the sweat while the other hand pressed against his stomach. The trolley tipped over and made a crashing sound as Mateusz stood before Jesus Christ, the sweat-soaked cloth in his hand. The far end of the room was panelled with a few wooden slats on which the Crucified hung, but without a cross. As if the Son of God had been nailed to a fence rather than a crucifix. A spotlight on the ceiling shone a harsh white beam onto Jesus Christ, as if he were being forced to undergo a final interrogation after being nailed to the fence. In front of him was a small wooden altar, but it looked more like one of those radiograms that many Poles had brought back from visits to the West in the late 1970s, and which until the fall of Communism had pride of place in Polish living rooms as a permanent memento of much-longed-for modernity. On the side wall hung a triptych, oil on canvas, a piece that dithered strangely between the abstract and the figurative. In the left-hand picture he could make out a setting sun, or at least a red ball dropping onto a crowd of people or hovering above them. The people could be cardinals in purple robes, but then again they might not be cardinals at all, just reflections of the red setting sun, or flames, or plants. The centre panel depicted something that looked like a skewered U.F.O., but it might just as easily be a waste incineration plant. The picture on the right was the clearest: a pool of blood beneath a blazing white light and a white cross standing out against it. Beside the cross were the words: "*UBI LUX IBI BLUT*". He knew Latin, he had learned it in the seminary, of course, but he couldn't understand this. What did "*BLUT*" mean? What sort of a word was it? "Where there is light, there is . . ." He went closer to see whether he had misread it, then tried to decipher this mysterious word: "*BLUT*". Only now did he see that it was probably, no, definitely "*DEUS*", painted so feebly and unclearly as if it were trying to retreat into the background shadows of the image. Beside the triptych stood two large carved wooden figures that reminded him of shepherd boys from a nativity scene, and even more of seminary pupils in nightshirts.

Mateusz had stood there in his nightshirt, bare-footed on the cold stone floor. This was called "composure", when after evening prayers a pupil was ordered to stand to attention in the cloister, beside the statue of the saint assigned to him, looking down into the inner courtyard and up at the starry sky, to think about the "three questions". Then they would be summoned by the Pater Prior to give their answers, sometimes after two or three hours, sometimes not until the following day, before morning prayers. How great is the doubt in the strength of your belief? How certain are you that you can overcome this doubt? By which deeds will you prove the strength of your belief?

When he felt the cold smoothness of the stone beneath the soles of his feet, Mateusz had been struck by a peculiar tingling, not just general excitement or fear, but arousal, a sexual or erotic energy, as he felt the cold rising up from his feet, stiffening his muscles, his tissues, while at the same time the smooth surface of the stone felt like the skin of a body, a skin on marble, a saint's skin, a mother-of-God's skin, which he was caressing, snuggling up to, with which he was fusing. He had been forced to stand next to the figure of Saint Sebastian, not knowing whether it was coincidence or a carefully considered decision by the Pater Prior to make him undertake his composure here.

Mateusz had sought the conversation with the Pater, not because he doubted his belief, but because he harboured doubts as to how he was going to live out his belief. He was ready for the struggle, but he wished to bring a son into the world like his father and grandfather before they had embarked on the struggle.

You want your name to live on? Your blood? Something of you? When you die you will live for ever, but you want to go on living here on earth?

Mateusz had now become Ryszard again and was unable to give an answer.

Composure. He had been found before morning prayers sprawled in the passageway, as if he'd been trying to make as much skin contact with the stone as possible. He was seriously hypothermic and ran a high temperature for days. Afterwards he answered the three questions. Most convincingly and to the prior's satisfaction. But he couldn't stay at the seminary.

The burning pain. Mateusz turned away from the nativity figures and looked around. He had intended to pray, but he couldn't do it here. He put a hand on his diaphragm, groaned and wiped the sweat from his brow. There wasn't much time left. He breathed in deeply, then out, left the chapel and went to the gate.

The original plan was to fly back to Warsaw after completing his mission. But overnight an envelope had arrived for him at the hotel, which he was handed by reception in the morning. Inside he found a plane ticket to Istanbul as well as the confirmation of a reservation at an Istanbul hotel. Mateusz knew this wasn't a new assignment, it couldn't be. Each new mission opened with a dossier about the target, and was planned and prepared down to the minutest detail. And no soldier had ever been given a new assignment only a day after completing another. The return to base afterwards was just as crucial for the security of any operation as the meticulous planning beforehand. The only explanation he could muster was that the target had slipped away to Istanbul, but this also meant that he had shot the wrong man. Or it was a trap. If they wanted to get rid of him, then this was the simplest way: he had sworn unconditional obedience. An animal needed to be lured into a trap. A soldier just had to be given his marching orders to walk into one.

Something about it wasn't right. They had specialists for operations outside the Schengen Zone. Although Mateusz had confidence in his passport, which he was certain had been forged to perfection, controls at the Schengen border were stricter and he didn't want to have to rely on his passport passing this test too.

When he arrived at the airport he had tried to check in with his original ticket to Warsaw, but the woman at the counter told him that the booking had been cancelled.

No.

Yes. You're no longer on the passenger list, Monsieur. You cancelled yesterday evening.

It must be a misunderstanding! I want that flight.

I'm sorry, but I cannot issue you with a boarding card. You no longer have a ticket for this flight.

But I paid!

The woman typed something into her computer, looked, typed, looked and said, The price of the ticket minus the cancellation fee has been recredited to your credit card.

My credit card? I don't have credit . . . fine! I want new ticket. I buy new ticket.

I'm terribly sorry, Monsieur, but the flight is fully booked.

But I must go back to Poland. Today.

Are you Polish, Monsieur? We can speak Polish too, *drogi Panie*. My father's Polish. He came to Brussels as a plumber. Met my mother here. We'll find a solution. *Gdy zaleje woda, trzeba wymienić rurę.*

There was one seat on the flight to Kraków in two hours' time. Or there was a flight to Frankfurt an hour later with a connection to Warsaw. He took the Kraków flight; he wanted to get back to Poland as quickly as possible.

And thus it was that he found himself on the same plane as Martin Susman. But what significance do interrelationships, entanglements and connections have if those concerned know nothing of them?

*

Martin Susman was kicking himself for his crackpot idea of putting on his warm underwear for the journey so he wouldn't freeze when he got to Kraków. He was already sweating like a pig on the taxi journey to the airport. Unsurprisingly the taxi was heated, overheated probably, and in his rabbit fur he felt feverish. Why did people say "sweat like a pig"? As the son of a pig farmer he knew, of course, that pigs didn't sweat, they couldn't perspire through their skin. As a child he had come out with this phrase once. Why? Because it was what people said. His father had put him right. Pigs don't sweat. And you don't have to do everything other people do; if other people talk nonsense you don't have to talk nonsense too!

But why do people say it?

Because a lot of people have a problem with blood. In the past, when pigs used to be slaughtered at home and they saw how profusely the creatures bled, they called the blood sweat. It's a euphemism, do you see? It doesn't sound so bad. In the German-speaking world hunters still refer to animal blood as sweat, and the dog that seeks and captures a shot and bleeding creature is called a "sweat-dog", whereas in English they say bloodhound.

But we say blood sausage, not "sweat sausage".

That's enough, his father had said. Go inside and help your mother!

Susman hadn't used this cliché since that day, but now all of a sudden, in the taxi to the airport, it was back in his head, alongside the memory that it actually referred to blood, bloodshed, streams of blood, a bloodbath.

By the time he arrived at the airport Martin Susman had used an entire packet of tissues to soak up the sweat, and when he got out of the taxi he had a clump of them in his hand. With no tissues left he wiped his face with his sleeve, but it was hopeless: he sweated and sweated. Blood. He went to look for more tissues, he wandered back and forth, which just made him sweat more. In the end he decided to go straight to the gate, as slowly as possible, and take a seat there. Maybe if he wasn't moving he'd stop sweating. He was furious with himself; he ought to have realised that it was completely absurd to wear the underwear unless it was freezing cold. He would be picked up from the airport at Kraków, taken in a heated taxi to a heated hotel, where he'd be able to change. He could have put on the underwear there, before the drive to the camp, but now it was doubtful whether the sweat-drenched items would dry in time. They would probably be drying in his room while he was at the mercy of the vicious cold in the camp, underwear-less.

His blood was boiling. He was thirty-eight years of age and still incapable of dressing himself appropriately for a given situation and its demands. The term "life skills" came to mind – how often had he heard this! That child lacks life skills! No life skills! Thank goodness we have Florian too!

From "life skills" it wasn't a huge leap to "will to live". He knew, or thought he did, how they were related. They are inseparable. They spur each other on or bring each other down. In individuals, in families and social groups, in entire societies. He was lucky. His lack of life skills didn't result in a rapid end to his life; his will to live might break, but he was able to go through life broken for lengthy periods. Martin did, however, feel anxious when those life coaches kept popping up in the media, bandying about their platitudes: "You need to be able to let go", "You have to learn to unwind". . . They didn't have a clue what they were talking about. You could see this from the four archaeological layers in excavations – it was always possible to put a precise date on when it had begun, the letting go, the unwinding, the death preached by life coaches. The third layer.

Right by the entrance to the queue for security he was presented with a bizarre and baffling scene. Amongst the stream of passengers there appeared to be two teams facing each other, one wearing yellow, the other in blue. Was this a game, a competition? Not a game, but definitely a competition of some sort. A young woman in yellow spoke to him: Excuse me, Sir, are you flying to Poland?

Yes, he said. As she looked at him he felt embarrassed. What must she think as she noticed his wet face and red eyes? She smiled and went on talking quickly. She was an activist from the human rights organisation Stop Deportation and . . .

I'm sorry?

Stop Deportation, she said, pointing to the slogan on her T-shirt.

NO BORDER

NO NATION

STOP DEPORTATION

We're here because there's a man about to be deported, he . . .

Now someone from the blue team came over, a policeman, and said, "Is this woman harassing you, Sir? Just for your information, this protest has been officially registered and approved, but we can terminate it if passengers feel harassed.

No, no, Martin Susman said, it's O.K., it's O.K. I'm not being harassed.

He wiped the sweat from his brow into his hair several times.

The policeman nodded, moved away and spoke to another passenger who'd been drawn into conversation by an activist.

Susman learned that the man due to be deported was a Chechen who had been persecuted and tortured in his own country. He'd arrived in the E.U. via Poland. Now he was due to be sent back to Poland, from where they would extradite him to Russia.

107

The authorities considered Russia to be a safe country for Chechens. That was pure cynicism. There was plenty of evidence to suggest that Chechens deported to Russia had disappeared into torture chambers. The woman gave him a flyer. That's the man, she said, Aslan Akhmatov. He's traumatised and faces further torture and death. This is a human rights scandal, Monsieur, don't you agree? Here it says what you can do as a passenger to prevent the deportation if you see this man on the plane. Demand to speak to the pilot and ask him to abort the deportation for humanitarian reasons and for reasons of aviation security. He has authority on board, he can refuse to transport passengers who are flying against their will.

As he read the flyer she talked ever more rapidly.

It's all here! Refuse to take your seat or fasten your belt, alert the other passengers to the fact that this isn't just a normal case of transport, but an act of violence and . . .

Excuse me, Martin said, but it says here that the flight in question is LO 236 to Warsaw. I'm going to Kraków.

Oh! I'm sorry! I thought . . . Thank you. Thank you for your patience, your understanding. Please keep the flyer for general information. I mean, deportations are taking place all the time and . . . Thanks! And have a good day!

She turned away and he watched her briefly as she spoke to another passenger. On the back of her T-shirt it said "Resistance is Possible".

When all passengers had taken their seats and boarding had closed, a woman stood up and walked to the front of the plane, glancing left and right at the rows of seats. When she arrived at business class a stewardess stood in her way.

Are you looking for the toilets, Madame? They're at the back of the plane. But you can't use them now, Madame. Please sit back down and fasten your belt.

I don't need the toilet, she said, then she raised her voice: I'd like to speak to the captain! Apparently there's a passenger on this plane who is here against his will. And I want to know —

Please! You must —

We have to know whether he really is on this plane against his will. Please call the captain!

She turned and walked back down the aisle. Mesdames, Messieurs, on this plane there's a man who's due to be deported. Please help stop this happening —

Please, Madame! You have to sit down and —

The woman continued undeterred, passing the row in which Susman was sitting.

— we must help him get off this plane.

Martin Susman's neighbour stared at his newspaper, the woman on the other side of the aisle closed her eyes, while the man in the window seat beside her swiped away relentlessly at his smartphone.

Martin Susman stood up to get a better view of what was happening. A flight attendant was beside him at once, asking him to sit down and fasten his seat belt immediately.

Yes, he said, hang on a sec! I just wanted ... He opened the overhead locker to fetch a pack of nicotine gum from his bag. The woman now stopped in the aisle, turned to a passenger and asked, Are you Mr Akhmatov?

The man did not respond. He had pulled a hood over his head and his chin down to his chest.

Do you speak English, Sir? Are you Mr Akhmatov?

Mateusz Oświecki glanced up and shook his head. The woman hesitated; at first she was unsure whether he was indicating that he didn't speak English, or that he wasn't the man she was after. They looked at each other. Mateusz hadn't understood exactly what all this was about, but he realised that this woman was delaying their take-off and he hated her for it. He looked at her face, their eyes met, and . . .

At that moment something happened. In his diaphragm, where the pain was sitting. It felt as if an artery had burst and warm, sweet blood were oozing throughout his stomach. His head was devoid of thoughts, no words formed in his mind. All of a sudden his eyelids were incredibly heavy, he struggled to keep them open to see how this woman was looking at him, he wanted to linger a while in this gaze, savour a longing he had never known, as well as the feeling of security that he had once known but forgotten. Now it was back as a memory: he was a child with a high temperature, peering as if through a fog at his mother bent smiling over his bed. This image of his mother as an apparition in the fog had taken away all his fear, even the fear of dying were he to give in and close his eyes. This was soppy. He wasn't a child any longer, he had been forced to toughen up and he despised mawkishness. What he felt now was unclear, as hazy as the image in his memory. The longing for a secure childhood, either because you'd had one or hadn't had one, was shared by everyone, terrorists as well as pacifists. He just wanted to . . . her eyes . . . but the woman was on her way again. She apologised for the inconvenience of their delayed departure and asked for help in stopping the deportation. Martin Susman watched her, the passengers didn't stir, they sat there motionless. From the expressions of some he thought they probably sympathised with the woman, others closed their eyes and bowed their heads. Now a steward was standing next to him: You've got to sit down now, please sit and fasten your seatbelt! The steward gently placed a hand on Martin's shoulder, then increased the pressure. When Martin fell into his seat he heard a man's voice saying, Just shut up and sit down!

Another voice: Would you stop delaying our take-off? You're on the wrong plane! The man's on the flight to Warsaw! That's what it says on the flyer!

The woman: He was rebooked onto this flight. Because of the protest against his deportation. I got a text saying that he's on this plane now. To whisk him off to Poland unnoticed.

Now a young man right in front of Martin Susman got to his feet and shouted: No deportation! Further up the plane a woman's voice said, *Solidarité!*

Martin Susman leaned out to look back down the aisle. Now the woman was in the last row; he saw her bending over a passenger. The way he was twisted caused a sharp pain all the way up his back, from the lumbar vertebrae to his neck. He ought to stand up, he thought, but he didn't want to run any risk – what risk? He stood up, stretched, pressed his hands into his back, the young man in front of him sat down again, the steward and stewardess had vanished, and he heard the woman say to a passenger in the back row, Mr Akhmatov? Are you Mr Akhmatov?

Yes!

The man got up. Was that really him? He wasn't handcuffed, nor did he have a police escort. But he looked numb, as if he'd been sedated.

The woman showed him the flyer with his photograph to make sure. He said, Yes!

It's all over, the woman said. Don't you worry, stay on your feet, just stay on your feet and we will get off the plane.

The man started to cry. He put his hands up to his face, his wrists pressed together as if he were shackled.

Police officers came on board and accompanied the two of

them off. Passengers applauded. Why? Because of the woman's show of bravery? Or because the authorities had weighed in? Or because the plane could finally take off? Everybody had their reason.

It was four hours until Frigge's flight. Dubra packed his suitcase. And he still had a meeting with George Morland, his colleague from the D.-G. AGRI. Conflicts and squabbles over who had authority for what had always existed between AGRI and TRADE, it was tradition. In fact it was a very old game indeed. But now the conflict had escalated and the disagreements couldn't be laughed off any longer, they couldn't forge compromises on a case-by-case basis, then go and have a beer together or – if the chemistry with the organic farmers wasn't right – politely decline a drink for lack of time. Now it was war; you had to be armed, and seek arbitration. The issue that had led to the escalation was pigs. It was what Frigge called the "pig's ear"; others in the Commission referred to the conflict between TRADE and AGRI as "Sow Wars". AGRI was looking to reduce pig production by cutting subsidies, and thus halt the fall in pork prices on the European market. TRADE, on the other hand, wanted to substantially boost pig production because it saw major opportunities for growth in foreign trade, especially with China. For this reason TRADE was seeking a mandate to orient European pig production to demand on world markets, in order to negotiate and implement the export of pork products to third countries for Europe as a whole. AGRI, however, sought to regulate only the internal market and implement common standards, but this was complicated by the fact that veterinary standards fell under the jurisdiction of the Directorate-General for Health and Food Safety. And both wanted to leave the export treaties in the sovereign hands of the individual countries.

The result of these squabbles, however, was that each European country undertook their very own bilateral negotiations with China; Europe was divided, and this competition between European states gave rise to an even more pronounced price slump, both on the internal market and for export, while no country alone could satisfy the international demand because at the same time pig farmers were being urged to quit agriculture. Frigge thought the whole thing completely insane. And this Morland drove him round the bend. But why, in fact? Frigge wondered. Why was he getting so worked up? For now, the Commission had no mandate to negotiate for all Member States. The Member States were content to be able to exploit the situation to their own advantage and extract the maximum benefits for themselves alone. It was a fallacy, of course, and at some point they would realise this, but just now there was nothing he could do to change it. All he could do was let things wander across his desk, look on impassively, avoid getting on anybody's nerves and at some point move upwards again. But no! He found the situation so irrational that he couldn't remain impassive. So wherever he could he blocked the "business as usual" to force a decision.

The quarrel over jurisdiction was based on the fact that the pig was a transdepartmental good: the live pig in its pen "belonged" to the D.-G. AGRI; after slaughter as ham, ribs, schnitzel or sausage – in short, as a "processed agricultural good" – it was the responsibility of the D.-G. GROW; and only when it left Europe, for example as a pig in a cargo ship or lorry did it belong to the D.-G. TRADE. The problem was that you couldn't negotiate over a pig in a container if you were unable to make decisions about the pig in its stall. In this matter the D.-G. GROW wasn't hostile. They dealt with the regulations for listing ingredients, determining the maximum permissible levels of pharmaceuticals and chemicals, and quality criteria. They didn't give a fig about the pig so long as it was properly labelled. The match had to be decided between AGRI and TRADE.

George Morland had been avoiding a conversation with Frigge for weeks. He'd answered e-mails with empty promises: let's speak about it soon, when all the facts are on the table. But he responded to proposed appointments with clichéd references to his especially busy diary. The commissioners were holding back. They were new and they wanted to learn the ropes first. But time was pressing. The Dutch, German and Austrian governments had progressed furthest in their negotiations with China. Over the course of the past calendar year the German chancellor had been to China eight times. Next week the Austrian president was due to fly to Beijing with a plane full of ministers and representatives from industry, trade and agriculture. At the very top of the agenda: trade in pigs. And the Dutch had announced that they were visiting again straight afterwards. If one of these countries succeeded in concluding a substantial bilateral treaty with China, from a political perspective it was unlikely that the E.U. would get a mandate for negotiations. And then the serious contest would begin, the undercutting, the attempt to oust one's neighbour. Instead of proceeding jointly, they would destroy each other and in their desire for national growth they would precipitate a European crisis. It was as sure as eggs are eggs, to put it in Kai-Uwe's words. Of course Morland knew that Kai-Uwe Frigge was going on a work trip that day. And it was insidious of him to suggest this time for a meeting, three hours before Frigge was due to board.

Frigge had remained cool and agreed to the meeting. And now he was sitting face to face with this pig. A cheap association maybe, but Frigge couldn't help it. He couldn't stand Morland, he thought him devious, cynical and irresponsible. That in itself was enough to justify the unflattering comparison. But then there was Morland's appearance: his round, pink face and in the middle of it his little, broad nose, like a plug. He was in his mid-thirties but looked much younger, this scion of the British upper classes, as if he had only just started shaving, which was why his cheeks always glowed with such rawness. He had thick red hair, which he kept trimmed in a crew cut. Bristles, Frigge thought.

Frigge was from a family of teachers in Hamburg. Hanseatic internationalism, an understanding of historic German guilt, a major abstract expectation of peace and justice in the world, personal application and decency, a mistrust of fashions and the mainstream – these were the pegs his parents had hammered in to mark out the field in which he grew up. He knew he was being unfair to Morland. But he also knew that he had bloody good reason to be.

Morland stared at his fingernails and explained his perspective on things. Frigge closed his eyes, not wanting to witness the pomposity. Morland was right on every count. Yes, that's how it was, that was the situation. But the distinction wasn't that Frigge saw things differently; it was that Morland thought the situation a reasonable one and defended it, while Frigge wanted to extricate himself from it entirely.

O.K., George, Frigge said, just imagine you're a serf.

Why on earth —

It's just an idea to play around with. Anyway —

I don't want to play around with an idea like that!

Fine. Once upon a time there was serfdom. Right? You're aware of that? Now, imagine a peasant going up to his master and saying he needs to talk to him.

Were slaves allowed to talk to their masters just like that?

I don't know and it doesn't matter. All that matters is what he says – the serf, not the slave – anyway, he says, Master, I think serf-dom is a very bad thing, it's degrading, it goes against what the Bible says—

This story is in the Bible? I didn't know.

In the Bible it says that all men are equal before God, and that was the serf's argument, so —

Was he actually able to read? And *Latin*? To my knowledge the Bible was only available in Latin in the Middle Ages and most people were illiterate.

O.K. Forget the Bible. At any rate the peasant disagrees with serfdom. And using some rational arguments he suggests his master sets him free. What do you think his master's response is?

I imagine you'll tell me.

He tells the peasant that he's a serf because his father was a serf and his grandfather was a serf at the time his own grandfather was master. The world is as it is, and has been thus for generations, from the year dot, and surely there must be a purpose to it all.

I'd call that a reasonable argument. Or what do you think?

O.K., George, now tell me: does serfdom still exist?

I don't know. Anywhere in the world?

George! Once again! Somewhere in Europe a peasant complains and —

In the Middle Ages I imagine he'd sooner have been hanged, drawn and quartered than demand his freedom.

Precisely. And the master says it has always been so. But now let me ask you again. Does serfdom still exist? Do you see what I'm getting at? Everything you've said is right, absolutely correct – but only "inside the box". Objectively, however, it's absurd, and in the medium to long term it's completely untenable. Time and again we see things disappear that we thought would last for ever and —

Are you taking about the E.U.?

No, I'm talking about national interests. Surely it's absurd that the European states form a common market but can't act together when it comes to foreign trade. That each pig which leaves Europe can only enter the global market with a visa from its nation state. O.K., that's the situation at present, but at some point it will be different because things change. In fact we could organise it more rationally right now.

I'll have a think about your serfdom story, although I'm not convinced it's what we'd call a terribly useful example.

Kai-Uwe Frigge knew, of course, why Morland was resisting any further development of Community policy: first and foremost he was a Brit, not a European, and within the Commission he wasn't a European official, but a British official in the European civil service. And it was Great Britain's iron policy to prevent further transfer of national sovereignty to Brussels, however minor. With E.U. money they restored Manchester, which had fallen into total disrepair, but rather than express their gratitude they see the spruced-up façades of the city as proof that Manchester Capitalism will henceforth vanquish all competitors. This bloated, perfumed pig no doubt began his day by singing "Rule Britannia!" with his early-morning tea, and ... Frigge took a deep breath, then stood up and said, Well, I must be off to the airport. Let's talk again next week!

Anytime, Morland said.

Frigge had prepared a powerful departure. As he put on his coat he said, By the way, I assume you know that in the next few weeks the German government will be concluding a bilateral trade treaty with China? Well, it's only for pigs, which isn't so important for the United Kingdom, is it?

Is that confirmed?

Yes, it's a done deal.

Frigge buttoned up his coat and put the documents in his briefcase.

It's exclusive, to all intents and purposes a gateway for German business to the Chinese market. And it's not just about export statistics.

He offered Morland his hand.

The major investors will know how to interpret it, the financial markets will respond accordingly. The City of London will decline in importance as a financial centre while the Frankfurt stock exchange will be the dramatic winner.

Frigge clapped Morland on the shoulder.

Funny, isn't it? Misery for Britain, and all because of German pigs. O.K., I've got to go. Call me next week, we need to continue this conversation. I'm sure we'll find a way to work it out more sensibly, more equitably. But the Commission must be united. Frigge opened the door and glanced back at Morland. Pigs! he said with a shake of his head, and then he laughed. He was still grinning in the taxi on the way to the airport.

Forty-one forty-two forty-three four five six seven eight nine fifty! Breathe! Fifty-one fifty-two three four . . .

He was walking in the middle of the street, stamping at each step, panting as he counted his paces: seven, eight, fifty-nine, sixty! Breathe! Sixty-one, two, three – why was he counting? He wanted to know how many paces it was from the main gate to the end, from the entry to the end until the exit from the end; he wanted to grasp the dimensions of this place, this camp thoroughfare that seemed infinitely long, the road to infinity. The road lay snow-white and innocent before him, the entire vast area snow-white and innocent; why do we associate white with innocence, even here, in this place, the colour of murderous cold beneath the deathly light of the winter sun. Breath steaming from the mouth with each counted step, six seven eight sixty-nine seventy! Icy wind blew into his face.

Martin Susman felt a gentle pressure on his shoulder, seventy-one, seventy-two, seventy . . . a hand on his shoulder: Please fasten your seatbelt!

He gave a start and opened his eyes. Yes, he said, of course!

The return flight from Kraków to Brussels. Was he panting? He was breathing heavily. He fastened his belt, reached for the air vent nozzle and turned it on full. His eyes closed again, he felt cold sweat on his forehead and shivered. Of course he had caught a cold. He had worried about this trip; only with great reluctance and caution had he readied himself for his visit to the memorial site and museum, for fear of the shock of seeing the indescribable. But death is destroyed when it becomes a museum piece, while familiarity precludes the shock of recognition. The vending machines selling warm drinks or chocolate bars for ten zloty had shocked him more than the heaps of hair, shoes and spectacles he had seen so often in photographs and documentaries. Worst of all was the cold. It got everywhere, into his skin, into his bones, the icy gusts in the long corridor of history. In the Auschwitz marquee it had been just about bearable, but Birkenau was merciless; never before in his life had he been so cold. His grandmother had always worn multiple layers and said, "Those who stay warm stay alive!" Even in the stalls, with the warmth of the animals, she would stand there wearing all those layers. And when it was freezing she used to say, "You could catch your death of cold in this!" On the trip home to his heated Brussels apartment Susman felt embarrassed by this memory, as if he'd said aloud to the person next to him: I caught my death of cold in Birkenau. Absolutely freezing, it was! What can I say? I caught my death of cold.

He sniffed. His nose was blocked. He yawned – a kind of a greedy gasp for air – then began to doze again. He had the aisle seat in a row of three. He heard the voices of the two women next to him as if from a distance, as if from his memory. They were speaking German, cheerfully and excitedly.

He saw himself making his way along the camp road once more, panting, counting his paces as if obsessed, bracing himself against the wind, bent forwards, clouds closing the sky like heavy eyelids, the vast expanse of white turning ash grey. He sensed everything inside him giving in, he didn't resist the feeling, his head sank to his chest. Then he felt an upwind, he felt as if he were being carried upwards, losing the ground beneath his feet, he was flying. He was surprised that he could fly, but he also had an odd confidence, somehow it was logical and quite natural to rise so easily, disembodied, into the air. Was anybody watching? He wished the whole world were looking up and watching him as he flew skywards, circling and rocking in the air currents as he rose up to the clouds. He heard the German voices, so near, so far, talking about something completely different, art, literature, books, and he saw open books ascending like birds, their song filled the air as he gazed down at the large expanse. From above – this was first semester archaeology – you could see beneath the surface of the earth, you saw into a depth you didn't notice when you walked across the earth. When you walk and look around you, you see a snow-covered expanse. If you fly over it, you see structures, areas marked off from each other, the expanse breaks up into a grid of fields. The surface reacts differently, depending on what lies beneath it – untouched earth, or the interred debris of civilisations, bodies, stones from sunken buildings, water courses or ancient cellars and canal systems, or buried septic tanks and latrines – the vegetation grows more lushly, or sparsely. The more history there is, the more differentiated is each field from a bird's eye perspective. In the thin layer of earth over the stones of sunken civilisations, vegetation grows less luxuriantly than over a mass grave, where grass sprouts as you would expect it to: grass grows over it quickly! But even across an expanse of snow, differences become visible: with untouched earth the ground temperature is different from that of a thin layer of soil lying on top of stones or decayed wood or over a mass grave. For decades the decomposition process of dead bodies warms the earth, meaning that there the snow is icy, here it is crusted, and right over there it is translucent and already thawing. Anyone flying over it can see these grids and knows where to dig.

In his mind he saw Professor Krinzinger, his former teacher, saying, Modern archaeology begins with flying, not digging!

And then the professor was flying at his side, shouting something to him. What? The droning in the air was so loud that Martin couldn't understand him at first. He saw the professor pointing downwards and shouting something.

What?

Down! Down!

Now he understood: Come down! We have another task. We archaeologists have to excavate civilisation, not crimes!

But —

We're on shaky ground, but we'll tread firmly in our boots, we'll stamp the ground until it's firm, even at a gentle pace each step is a pounding, all that matters is that our feet are warm. Martin saw boots, warm boots everywhere – and now he heard more clearly the women's voices that had been in his ear the whole time.

I thought it was quite a good novel, but the dream sequences got on my nerves.

It's a classic.

Yes, and that's why I wanted to read it. But I don't like dreams in novels. She keeps dreaming something, which is then described in the minutest detail, it's completely surreal. But it's supposed to be poetic. For me, what a character sees and experiences I can understand. But dreams —

But in the novel they're living under fascism. It's only natural they should have nightmares.

Look, whenever there's a dream in a book I just want to go straight to sleep myself.

Martin saw all these boots, warm and comfy, a class of German schoolchildren on an excursion to Auschwitz. A teacher: Thorsten! What's wrong with you? Wake up! Come over and join the rest of us!

Two young people are speaking Turkish. A teacher asks them not to speak Turkish here, one of them replies, What, do you expect us to speak German? Here?

Martin felt giddy. It was as if he were spinning around, faster and faster, everything around him blurred, just occasionally an image flashed up, he heard a sentence, someone said something about coke, a pupil asked, What kind of coke?

An announcement. This is your captain speaking. Please fasten your belts as we're encountering some turbulence.

Martin Susman is standing outside the crematorium at Auschwitz I. He has seen the gas chambers, the incineration ovens, everything looks exactly like it does in the photographs he knows, black-and-white photographs, and what he has seen here for real is actually in black and white. He felt . . . how? He couldn't say, he couldn't find the word for it, because "shocked" was no longer a German word, it was a sort of sticking plaster for the German soul. This was an idea, but in his dream he could see it with his own eyes. He was standing outside the building, lighting a cigarette. All of a sudden two uniformed men hurried over to him, one slapped the hand holding his cigarette and the other said something in Polish, then in English: No smoking here!

A badge dangled from Martin's chest: "GUEST OF HONOUR / *GOSC HONOROWY* / *EHRENGAST* in Auschwitz". He held out the badge to the men in uniform, then Mr Żeromski came running over and called out, Herr Doktor, Herr Doktor, we have to go into the marquee! The ceremony is about to begin.

He woke up because the aircraft was shaking, dipping and shuddering. A child screamed.

The following day he called in sick. He stayed at home for five days. For three of these he had a fever. On the fifth day he jotted down his idea and drew up a preliminary plan for the Jubilee Project.

Five

Memories are no less reliable than
anything else we conceive.

LOVE IS A fiction. Fenia Xenopoulou had never understood the fuss people made over love. She regarded this feeling as an unproven phenomenon in another world, like water on Mars. People read about it in those colourful magazines such as *Xrisi Kardia* or *Loipón* – the love affairs of Hollywood actors and pop-stars, the dream marriages of princesses. Some thought love possible because they had longed for it, but everybody Fenia knew had surrendered at some point. Once at the hairdresser her mother had said of the luckless Lady Diana, "What she never got, I never got much more cheaply!"

As far as she knew, no-one in Fenia's family had ever been in love. In the emphatic sense that an abundance of emotion had resulted in a wedding, or that unrequited feelings had been the cause of a tragedy. All except for Uncle Kostas, her father's elder brother, who she had never met, but who lived on in family stories as the madman who met his death because of his undying love for a woman. This contradiction had greatly troubled Fenia as a child: death from undying love. In hindsight, he probably hadn't fea-tured as prominently in conversation as she had thought, but what she'd heard must have particularly fired her imagination, and ter-rified her. Uncle Kostas had fallen in love to the point of obsession, and because he couldn't win over the object of his veneration he went to join the resistance. At the word "veneration", young Fenia couldn't help thinking of the Virgin Mary and religious ecstasy; perhaps that wasn't so wide of the mark. But at the time she had been more interested in the word "resistance". She didn't know which war or civil war had been raging then, it was before she was born, and so for her it was as distant as the Peloponnesian War she was learning about around that time at school or soon afterwards. Uncle Kostas, it was said, "hadn't come back". In her imagination the "uncle in the resistance" was in an underworld where the dead – there because of their undying love – fought against this disaster called love and veneration. She had pictured this underworld as a dark place, very muggy and damp, and dangerous in an indeterminate way – certainly not a place she was in a hurry to visit, however desperate she was to escape her sun-scorched Cypriot village and that stony, barren land with its miserable olive trees, their silvery shimmer a mere deception, a fraudulent beauty for other people, for delighted tourists whose money allowed the village to survive, because it could no longer survive on the olives themselves. The tourists came to be led up to the "Baths of Aphrodite". The water from this spring supposedly gave those who bathed in it eternal youth. Here was where the Goddess of Love had frolicked with Adonis. This visitor attraction was no more than an unassuming natural pool in the cliffs above the village. It was almost always dried up, and beside it was a large wooden sign that read:

NON-POTABLE WATER

PLEASE DO NOT SWIM

The tourists would photograph the dry pool with the sign, and laugh. So those were the disciples of the Goddess of Love. After school Fenia sold them mineral water she had hauled up the mountain in two cooler bags. She saved up. She wanted out.

It was years before she realised that her uncle really had been dead for ages, had fallen as a partisan and was buried somewhere. Partisans, she now thought, were people who refused to acknowledge reality. In that respect they had much in common with those who were in love. She thought it crazy, completely crazy, to fight as a Greek man against Greek generals instead of retaliating against the Turks who had occupied half the island.

Fenia had a different idea of happiness, and of the battle she would fight in order to gain it. She wanted to get away. Far away. As a Greek Cypriot with the corresponding papers she had the opportunity to study in Greece. She wanted to go to Athens. With her meagre savings, Fenia's mother facilitated her plan. Did Fenia love her mother? She knew that ultimately it was all about interest, and interest on the interest: about the money she would send home after successfully completing her studies. The entire family flexed their muscles. This was the definition of love that Fenia understood. With small gifts and a good deal of pig-headedness her father called on people he knew, who themselves knew other people, and managed to arrange for Fenia passage on a ship from Limassol to Lavrio. It was a cargo ship that didn't take passengers. The captain agreed to have Fenia on board, tolerated as a kind of stowaway. The ferry would have been too expensive and a flight was entirely out of the question. She then had to make her own way from Lavrio to Athens. It wasn't hard, as there was one lorry after another on this stretch of road. You'll have to pay with sex, a friend had predicted. Fenia didn't pay. The drivers let a pretty young girl into their cabs, but then found a redoubtable, icy woman on the passenger seat beside them. In Athens she stayed with distant relatives. The price of family solidarity increased with distance. Her relatives asked for too high a "contribution to her board", far more than previously agreed by letter. Her budget, hers and her mother's savings, melted away too quickly. She wasn't allowed to take anything from the fridge that she had not bought herself, even though she was paying a contribution to her board. If the family were having meat in the evenings she only got vegetables and potatoes, and eventually the lamb bone, if there was anything left on it. She felt humiliated, but was too proud to relay this home. She kept her rucksack packed and looked around. A fellow student took her to "Spilia tou Platona", the fashionable haunt of the Chrysi Neolaia, Athens' "gilded youth".

Isn't it expensive?

Yes, but we'll invest only in one drink! And then the men are bound to pay! All the most interesting men hang out at the Spilia!

There she met a lawyer, Dr Jorgos Boutopoulos, and she was soon calling him Booty. It was never clear whether this was just her pet version of his surname, or an allusion to the Nazi sweethearts branded "German booty" back in the day. Jorgos Boutopolous had inherited the law practice his grandfather had taken over during the Nazi occupation, after the Jewish lawyer it belonged to was deported. But Fenia knew nothing of this. And she overestimated Jorgos. She fetched her rucksack and moved in with him. In her eyes he was a man of the world, a true sophisticate. Fifteen years her senior, generous, a man who could discuss French wines with waiters in expensive restaurants. She came very close to believing that fairy-tale love did exist after all. They got married. At the wedding Fenia had to laugh when in his speech Booty talked of "eternal love". It sounded like a schmaltzy feature straight out of *Xrisi Kardia*, the "Golden Romance" rag. And he did, in fact, sell the wedding photographs to the magazine, but all that appeared was a short article – half a page with a couple of pictures. Later it emerged that "sold" was not quite accurate; he had paid for the coverage!

How proud Fenia's parents were. But they began to worry when soon afterwards they discovered she was unhappy. They weren't so concerned for Fenia herself, rather for her marriage. The magic of this union was fading all too soon. When she surrendered herself to Booty in the jacuzzi in his apartment, it struck her with unbearable clarity how insipid the whole thing was. He was so proud of his jacuzzi, but rather than enjoy the luxury he had managed to secure for himself, he preferred being able to impress with it. He revelled in the symbols of a privileged life, but not in the life itself, he was delighted that he – *he* – possessed this beautiful young woman, he was in love with himself, and Fenia soon felt that she was interchangeable. He believed he was "making love", a phrase she found more ridiculous than every one of its vulgar variations, but he was making love only to himself.

Through him she gained entry to different social circles where she realised that, rather than the big shot he had first made himself out to be, he was an anxious conformist, a bootlicker who smarmed up to the seriously rich, in effect a shyster who earned enough from the foul fish he landed to believe he was one step away from serious money and power.

When Fenia began to shut herself off from him, Booty realised that he did love her after all. He demonstrated this with passionate remonstrations, a neurotic separation anxiety that he regarded as proof of his love, and by an emotional upheaval so tempestuous it could have been mistaken for a murderous rage. Fenia was particularly livid that he should demand her gratitude. That was madness: demanding gratitude from other people after you've satisfied yourself!

It was true that, financially, he had made her student life more comfortable, but she would have managed without him, whereas without Fenia he would have had less fun and certainly less kudos in his circle of acquaintances, the way he had dolled her up and paraded her about. As a student of economics, she found this balance sheet didn't add up. And even without his help she had secured the grant for England, which was her escape. She wanted to get out, go far away.

Theirs became a weekend marriage, with ever increasing intervals, first in London and then in Brussels. The last time she saw him in her bed, when she woke up to his sweaty grey locks, his face bloated by alcohol, she thought: He's more of a stranger to me today than when I first met him.

A good definition of the end, she thought. Time to boot him out of her life.

Fenia was buoyed by such thoughts. At breakfast that morning she was happier and more relaxed than she'd been in ages. Because everything was now perfectly clear. And this was the moment when even Booty showed a touch of class. He didn't misread the situation, he seemed liberated too, in a witty mood, and as he exited her apartment with his wheelie suitcase he said, Love is a fiction.

Yes.

All the best!

You too!

How crazy it was, totally crazy, that Fenia was now sitting at her desk, unable to work because she was waiting longingly, as longingly as a lover, for Fridsch's call. He'd come back from his trip to Doha the day before, and that morning had been in a meeting with Queneau at which he was going to drop Fenia's request casually into the conversation, to sound out the chances of extricating her from Culture. He had promised to call straight afterwards. She sat there, staring at the telephone. She picked up the receiver and put it back. No, she wasn't going to call him – he should ring her. She picked up her smartphone to check for messages or missed calls, but no. Fenia put it beside the keyboard, checked her e-mails, forty-seven unread messages, but none of them from him, she picked up her smartphone again, yes, of course the reception was good, she put it back on the desk. She felt a puzzling indifference to whatever Fridsch might report back from the meeting, whether or not Queneau had given any hint of a willingness to support her wish to move, in the spirit of mobility – she just wanted to hear Fridsch's voice. Irrespective of what he had to say. Just his voice. She felt like . . . well, how *did* she feel? It was madness: she was longing to hear his voice.

Martin Susman arrived at the Ark at 8.00 a.m. The aroma of freshly baked croissants wafted into the foyer. Normally he was unable to resist it, but today it reminded him of a chemical factory; this he took as a sign that he wasn't well. By the lift he met two young men from the Ukraine Task Force working on the sixth floor. Bohumil Szmekal had christened them "the salamanders", an expression which had now become common currency in the Ark. This allowed them to talk disparagingly or ironically about "the salamanders" even if they were sitting at a neighbouring table in the canteen. This is the new generation here, Bohumil had said, they're not Europeans, just careerists in European institutions. They're like salamanders: you can toss them on the fire but they don't burn. Their chief characteristic is their indestructability.

These were young men in smart, skinny-fit suits with large tie knots and pomaded hair, offering even at a visual level the sharpest contrast to the staff in Culture. They were smooth, flexible and emphatically polite in a way that Kassándra called "devastating" –

five minutes of small talk with the salamanders and I'm feeling depressed!

What is your task? Bohumil had asked a salamander when the Ukraine Task Force was housed here above their heads. He learned that it was their job to develop aid programmes for Ukraine to support the democratic movement following the Maidan Revolution. The challenge they faced was to allocate money they didn't have. They hadn't been given a new budget of their own, so their task was one of classic repackaging – if you don't have anything new, you repackage something old. And thus they repackaged old, long-existing aid programmes with new titles and new conditions in new combinations to make new aid packages, generating new conflicts of resource allocation with old budgets that gave rise to new statistics in which new percentages and graphic curves showed new dynamics. This assignment was the ideal baptism of fire for these young careerists: ultimately there was nothing to be gained save their own survival in the present circumstances, or the continuation of old arrangements with improved prospects for the future.

Martin Susman's mood was not improved by the fact that he was now waiting for the lift with the two salamanders.

How was he? The right answer was "Excellent!", of course, but feeling obstreperous Martin said "Crap!" and added, I've got a bad cold!

Oh, I'm very sorry!

Very sorry! the second salamander echoed.

And now Martin went the whole hog: It was sodding cold in Ukraine!

Oh, you were in Ukraine?

Yes, I was! And it's no surprise my immune system has collapsed! The people there are so frustrated, so disappointed in us, in the E.U. They feel they've been left in the lurch and . . .

The salamanders beamed: Oh yes, we know all about it, you're absolutely right, we . . .

Absolutely right!

We know, we have to . . .

The lift arrived, the door opened.

Third floor?

Yes, Martin said.

The salamander pressed 3 and 6, and said, We have to improve our communication. You're absolutely right! That's why we're now concentrating our efforts on communication!

The Commission needs to market itself better and we . . .

The lift stopped, the door opened. *Market* itself! If only they knew what they were saying! Martin thought. Goodbye!

Have a nice day!

Have a nice day and get better soon!

The lift door slid closed behind Martin, he took a deep breath – through his mouth; his nose was blocked. He'd arrived at work too early again, but on the other hand he urgently had to finish his paper on the Jubilee Project so he could e-mail it to Xeno. He could have done this from home too, but knowing her as he did, she would at once summon him into the conference room to discuss the paper with other colleagues from the department. So he had to be there and be ready.

He walked past her office, the door was closed. He walked past Bohumil's office, the door was open and Bohumil was standing on a stepladder in the middle of the room. When he saw Martin he called out, *Ahoj!*

Ahoj!

Martin's mind was so sluggish that it wasn't until he was in his own office that it occurred to him he ought to have asked Bohumil what he was doing on the ladder. For about an hour that seemed like an eternity he cleaned up his bullet points before sending them to Xeno. Then he worked his way through his e-mails. Most answered themselves or had been resolved during his sick leave. There was a message from Florian: "Dear brother, you parasite! Next week I'm flying to Beijing as part of a business delegation with His Highness the Austrian president and the pres. of the Austrian chamber of commerce. As things look now, according to info from the Aus. trade delegates in Beijing, the forthcoming negotiations will be a success . . . which would be a disaster. The pres. is clueless, the treaty he's going to sign will leave us open to blackmail. I'm wondering who the bastards are in all this . . . You really have to . . ." Martin Susman stood up and stretched. He wanted a cigarette, he was desperate for a smoke. He must be feeling better. Still no response from Xeno. He peered over to Bohumil's office but there was no sign of him, nor of the ladder. Martin stepped onto the fire escape and froze as he smoked two cigarettes, then went back into his office. He wrote a report of his official trip, calculated his expenses and took care of some admin – filled out some tables, in other words. Then he worked through some enquiries from students. There were two looking for internships, and he passed those requests on. One student was doing a Ph.D. in European Studies at the University of Passau, focusing on European cultural policy, based on a quotation by Jean Monnet: "If I were to do it again from scratch, I would start with culture." Martin Susman had no idea why, but he got about two e-mails like this each week. The student was asking for the European Commission's Directorate-General of Culture to give their position on this quotation. The answer was straightforward: there was no proof that Monnet actually uttered these words or published them anywhere. And even if he had, without further elucidation it was not at all clear what he meant specifically by "start with culture". Be sure to sing "Ode to Joy" before establishing the European Coal and Steel Community? Culture was inherently universal, it had always generated solidarity and affinity between people, a unity which ultimately must be realised at the political level too. And the exchange of regional culture, which had proved to be eminently important for Europe's integration, had only increased in intensity thanks to the political accomplishments of the European project: the elimination of borders, freedom of movement and settlement, and free trade in a common market.

He paused. Were these clichés? On the other hand, was there any single truth that could be repeated a hundred times over without becoming a cliché? His blocked nose was bothering him, he was anxious that his cold might develop into sinusitis, he felt a worrying throbbing in his forehead. Why was he taking so long over this e-mail to the student? His paper for the Jubilee Project – what he had written for that was anything but cliché. Still no answer from Xeno though, which surprised him. He checked the time. One o'clock. And Xeno wasn't responding. Why wasn't she responding?

He went out of his office, out of his work cell. In the corridor he bumped into Bohumil.

Are you sick?

Yes.

Lovesick?

What makes you think that?

The way you look: totally confused.

David de Vriend stood in the middle of his room and wondered what he was doing there. He'd been about to do something . . . but what? No, he wasn't going to ask himself that question now. He looked around as if trying to find something to do or – he noticed the telephone – as if he were waiting for something, yes, as if he were waiting for a call. He sat in his armchair, his gaze fixed on the telephone. Forgotten! He felt as if he'd been forgotten, completely forgotten by everyone and even by death. But who was left to remember him?

The January light, a silvery-grey surface in the window frame, like the door to a locker or a safe. The keys lost, the combination forgotten. Or the iron door to a bunker, beyond it the dark tunnel leading to death.

He stood up again and went to the window. Down below was the cemetery. Who should remember him? They were all lying there, beneath the stones under the grey mist.

No, not all of them.

He had become a solitary figure as those closest to him died, one by one. Their children had already struck out on their own paths that led them far away into a world with greater happiness or a quite different sort of unhappiness. Towards the end of his time in Sainte-Catherine he had still been greeted occasionally in the street – who was that? A former pupil, he's going grey himself now! And an astonished de Vriend had returned the greeting. That's all. Now he sat alone in the Maison Hanssens retirement home and was supposed to share common areas with people of his generation, but they had never been his contemporaries because they hadn't been obliged to share his experiences. Their misfortune was old age, his was life. No, there was nothing to share apart from odours, the odours of the mothballs that protected their clothes, of urine, sweat, decaying body cells. Only tears have no smell. He had wanted to forget, but this had only resulted in himself being forgotten.

He sat at the table and spotted a biro. He got to his feet again, his notepad must be lying around somewhere. Where was his notepad? A few days ago a doctor had been to see him, a psychologist from the municipal authority responsible for the old people's home. She had come for a so-called "accommodation chat" – a what? A chat about his care. She had brought a large notepad. As she explained, she had come to ease his passage into his twilight years and to provide assistance in structuring those twilight years, but most of all to dispel any worries he might have about his twilight years – she kept saying twilight years until David de Vriend interrupted her: it would be just as illusory, but a little nicer somehow if she could just call it "the next stage of his life" rather than "his twilight years". He was well aware that it was the last, but even so, it might bring some sunny days rather than merely exist as a perpetual dusk. The psychologist endeavoured to be empathetic. What de Vriend found especially intolerable was that this slender woman had shaved her head – why? Was this the fashion these days? Recently he'd been seeing more and more bald heads on the streets, young people with no hair and tattoos. Did they know what they were doing, what they were expressing, what associations they were evoking? He had wanted to forget the shorn heads and skeletons, and now they sent this woman to him. It made him aggressive. Go! You're insulting me – and he became melodramatic: You're insulting the world's memory!

The psychologist was empathetic. She probed further and eventually explained that she had just finished a course of chemotherapy. For breast cancer. But she was keen to keep working because . . .

De Vriend felt ashamed. And said nothing. He said nothing and allowed her to talk, no more misplaced accusations, the occasional nod, and he nodded when she took this notepad from her bag, placed it on the table and said, I brought this for you. Some advice: jot down your thoughts and plans. Believe me, I know what it's like. You have an idea and then you forget it. But if you write it down straight away you can always check. Have I done what I said I was going to do? Getting used to writing everything down is good practice against forgetfulness.

Where was the notepad? There, next to the bed.

He sat at the table and picked up the biro. It was a large pad, at the top was a strip of cardboard from which you could detach the sheets of paper. On this strip, beside the crest of the Brussels region, it read: "*Bruxelles ne vous oublie pas! / Brussel zal u niet te vergeten!*"

He wanted to draw up a list, write down the names of all those who had survived alongside him and who he knew to be still alive; he hadn't received notification of their deaths, at least. Why? He had memories, they thrust themselves forwards. Names would flash up in his mind, he saw faces, heard voices, peered into dark eyes, saw gestures and movements, and he felt the hunger, this chaff cutter of life that devours the body fat, then pulps the muscles and then the soul, which you first discover – if at all – when hunger becomes a metaphor: the hunger for life. He felt this hunger now, not as intensely, but he felt it all the same and he wanted to draw up the list, write down the names of those with whom he had shared the hunger and . . . he looked up. Hunger was the wrong word, hunger described the feeling of the well-nourished when they skipped a meal. It had nothing to do with the hunger he had survived. It was purely by chance that those who had simply lived and those who had survived spoke the same language, giving rise to a perpetual misunderstanding when they used the same terms.

He was going to write "Survivors". That's what he wanted to call his list, it was his idea. Who still alive spoke the same language as he did? The telephone rang. He paused, then began to write, but the telephone irritated him so he put down the biro and picked up the receiver.

It was Joséphine. Why hadn't he come to lunch? Had he forgotten it was lunchtime? We have to eat something, don't we, Monsieur de Vriend? She was bellowing down the phone. We don't want to go hungry, do we?

He was the only mobile resident who hadn't appeared in the dining room and —

The only what?

There's fish with rice and vegetables. It's wholesome and healthy, and —

Yes, yes, I forgot the time. I'll be down shortly.

David de Vriend put on a tie and jacket and took the lift down to the dining room. He looked about to see whether there was anywhere he could sit on his own. No. Joséphine hurried over and took him to a table. She said how pleased she was that he'd come; she'd been worried about him. We don't want you feeling faint all of a sudden, do we, Monsieur de Vriend?

At the table sat two men and a woman and Joséphine introduced them: a retired judge, an emeritus professor of history and a former registrar, all three of them widowed. They were very friendly and de Vriend found them immediately repellent. They were so – de Vriend searched for a word – so . . . entrenched in this life. All had been here for some years, they knew the system, the structures, the customs, they had their contacts with the management and staff, they knew their way around and had made themselves at home. What was more, they could be of assistance to a new arrival, but they could also make life difficult for him. This became clear after a few minutes. Then came the question: So, what did you do in life?

De Vriend understood of course that all they wanted to know was his profession, but he choked on his soup and started coughing, now his fish was arriving and his fellow diners were already on their pudding: *crème de lait*. De Vriend pushed away the soup and began to eat the fish, he ate quickly, not to catch up with the others, but because he wanted to get this meal over with as quickly as possible and leave. He wolfed down the fish and felt a bone slip down his windpipe and stick there. He took a few deep breaths to try to loosen it, but only felt it dig in more tenaciously, he panicked, he panted, clearing his throat and taking deep breaths, then exhaling forcefully. He leaped up, bent over, tried in turn to swallow the bone or bring it up, but it was stuck fast in his windpipe, choking him. He hit his chest, blew out as hard as he could, everything went red and he screamed. First a croaky Aaaaa that gradually got louder, then a curse, the professor and the registrar jumped to their feet, people at other tables were gaping in horror, Joséphine came running. The professor slapped him on the back and said, Breathe! He kept saying, Breathe! Breathe! The registrar tried to give him a glass of water, Joséphine stood behind him, threw her arms around his chest, pressed and shook him, but he pushed her away with his elbows and wheezed.

The registrar tried to get her fingers into his mouth, de Vriend swatted her away, she toppled and fell onto a chair.

He was screaming hysterically, this couldn't be happening, he had survived concentration camp and now he was choking to death on a fish bone . . . until all of a sudden he stopped because now he could only feel a slight irritation, he couldn't even say whether the bone was, in fact, still stuck in his gullet. Saliva oozed from his mouth, he sat down, took some deep breaths and said, It's fine. It's fine.

Everything O.K.?

Yes.

Are you sure?

Yes.

Do you need a doctor?

No.

A few moments later de Vriend apologised and went back to his room.

He lay on the bed, but felt so anxious that he had to get up again and sat at the table. There was the notepad, on it in his handwriting: "Survive". He had intended to write "Survivors" and draw up his list, but then the telephone had rung . . . Why "Survive"? He lit a cigarette and closed his eyes.

Of all people, it was a gravedigger who knew the way to Eternal Love. In the end Professor Erhart had asked him where the mausoleum of unconditional love was, and this man knew. It's called the mausoleum of *Eternal* Love, not unconditional love, he said, leaning on his shovel, I don't know whether unconditional love exists. Eternal love, certainly. You mean the mausoleum with the heart of light on the sarcophagus, right? Well, then. You're at the wrong cemetery here, see? The mausoleum of Eternal Love is at Laeken.

Where?

Laeken cemetery. North of the city centre.

He took a taxi, nodded off during a journey that took longer than anticipated, and found himself in a peculiar kind of trance when he arrived at Laeken. His bruised arm was aching, but now, in his almost somnambulistic state, he felt this pain as no more than a gentle and pleasant pressure, as if his late wife had linked arms with him, he felt her on his arm as if she were walking beside him, and with every step he seemed to adjust better to her rhythm and pace. This was all madness, of course. He shook his head, literally, and told himself not to be so silly. Now the pain in his arm was stronger, as was the unpleasant numbness in his swollen feet, which he carefully placed one in front of the other as if they were unfamiliar prostheses.

Just beyond the gate leading into the cemetery was the management office. There he obtained a map on which were marked the graves of famous people, as well as monuments and memorials of historical interest. The official also marked with an "X" the location of the Mausoleum of Eternal Love. The professor wondered why the official looked so sad as he gave him the information, and so dismayed as he handed him the map. What was it about this mausoleum that produced such a reaction? Some sort of occupational hazard, perhaps. The man worked in a graveyard and at some point his face must have turned into a mask of commiseration. And so for him even eternal love – in the form of a mausoleum – was nothing but a bereavement.

Professor Erhart had yet to get over the death of his wife. He wondered whether he still had enough of that time which supposedly heals all wounds and, if so, whether this was a desirable state of affairs. The pain that he had felt since that ghastly process of dying and ultimately the death of his wife reminded him so . . . yes, so vividly of the immense late happiness he had enjoyed with her, and he was sure that this memory would dwindle to a mere phrase if the wound did in fact heal.

He walked with the map down the gravel path, surprised not to hear any crunching underfoot. In all films and novels, gravel crunched underfoot. He stopped. It was so quiet. The boughs of the trees rocked silently in the wind, the crows flapped their wings without a sound. Ahead in the distance a few people crossed the avenue like shadows, gliding as inaudibly as the grey clouds in the sky. He kept going and . . . yes, as if there were a layer of cotton wool over the gravel he could now hear his footsteps very faintly.

Then he was standing in front of the tomb. He checked several times that this was indeed the Mausoleum of Eternal Love, but there could be no doubt. It was sad. What had he been expecting? Not the Taj Mahal, obviously, but certainly something impressive, something in the most beautiful human proportions that would give architectural expression to the idea and experience of an unending love, eternity in the material of eternity: stone. But this here was a ruin. The roof, with its famous and precisely measured aperture through which a heart of sunlight should fall on the sarcophagus, had caved in, while the left side of the mausoleum had subsided, causing shifts and cracks between the stone blocks from which weeds grew. The iron door decorated with two flaming hearts was rusted and locked with a chain, one door panel hung crookedly from its hinges, leaving a gap through which you could peer inside, but there was no sign of the sarcophagus, only rubbish, even plastic waste – how had that got in there?

To the left of the mausoleum a primitive, wooden sign – skewed, rotten and covered in moss – said that the lease for this plot had expired in August 1990 and requested any descendants to contact the cemetery management. Beside it was an enamel plaque in a wrought-iron frame that identified the mausoleum as a cultural monument.

Alois Erhart had been fascinated by the concept of an eternal love which takes eternity so literally that it makes sure of its posterity. But so long as eternity was just a human construct rather than an absolute, a relationship between people, in effect a negotiation, it would, like any human construct, come to an end at some point, both rapidly and mercilessly.

He ought to have known this. It had taken a small eternity –

until he was sixty, that's to say, forty years of marriage – before he had experienced this profound feeling of eternal love himself. And he had said to her, I will love you for ever!

How histrionic! And indeed he had been shocked to hear himself utter the phrase. At the time he'd felt he had arrived. And later he was surprised not to have realised straight away that there could be no for ever: it's nothing but a short stop on the journey of history. I know I will love you for ever, he'd said, and two years later his wife had died. And irrespective of whether there is life after death, i.e. eternal life, his declaration of eternal love, just like the feeling that had generated it, was now no more than a memory, history.

Such pathos! The truth of the matter was that Alois Erhart had reached the age of sixty before discovering that there was such a thing as good sex.

In all his born days he had never understood the proliferation in discourse of the term "good sex". Had those words really come to mind, "all his born days"? They could have come from his father, who had often come out with such expressions. At any rate he regarded "good sex" as nonsense, the dubious attempt to endow a human drive with an ideology, which, unlike the question of "good cooking" with respect to the human eating drive, could not be clearly substantiated or explained. Alois Erhart was one of the "you eat what gets put in front of you" contingent. You're grateful and make the sign of the cross before a meal. He was a post-war child, a child of reconstruction, he knew what need was, and although he swiftly understood that people's demands grew as prosperity increased, he couldn't comprehend why good and free sex should be a demand, something that had to be discussed in political arenas and fought for, as if it were a social benefit everyone was entitled to, such as free university access or the right to a pension. That was in the sixties and seventies, it was his generation who had proclaimed the "sexual revolution", but he had not been part of it.

His father had owned a sports shop on the Mariahilfer Strasse, one of the major shopping streets in Vienna. It was a good location, but what use was that if nobody had any money to buy things? Fired up by the "new era", and bursting with euphoria and enterprise, his father had opened the shop as a young man in 1937, so still just about in the inter-war period. Why a sports shop? His father was a fanatical gymnast and, as a member of the Jahn Gymnastic Association in Vienna, he referred to himself as one of the "Gym Brothers". He was also a footballer, playing for Wacker Wien, and soon securing a place in the first team as replacement for Josef Mahal, who was sold to Austria Wien. "With his greed, the Jew Mahal brought me great fortune," his father said. "He moved to Austria Wien for ten shillings a game, which meant I was in the team, more than content with my five shillings!"

He opened his business. But business went badly. At a time of mass unemployment and hyperinflation, who was going to buy football boots when they didn't even have the money for normal shoes? At the time many children went barefoot in the street. His father polished bicycles in the shop, selling the odd "Jahn vest" – also known colloquially for whatever reason as a "Ruder-Leiberl" – and fending off bankruptcy. In 1939 he was given fresh hope when via his contacts he succeeded in selling a large batch of tents and mess tins to the Vienna Hitler Youth and its division for younger boys, but he closed down the following year. In 1944 the house in Zollerstrasse, where his parents lived, was bombed; they survived in the air-raid shelter and camped in the storeroom of the shop, which was still standing. This was where Alois Erhart was born. "You're a camp child," his mother liked to say, and he found this phrase as normal as "times were bad then". It wasn't until he became a student that he realised how unbelievably cynical it was, and at the top of his voice he forbade her from saying it ever again. It took him years to understand that his mother was far too naive to be guilty, or that her guilt was a result of her naivety, thus discharging her of all blame. For Frau Erhart to call her "Loisl" a "camp child" was just playing with words familiar to her because they were in the air somehow, a desperate bit of fun in the desperate misery she had lived through. She was a "German mother", whose big heart and capacity for empathy towards people close to her had been abused without her knowing. The Nazis had forged their conception of womanhood and motherhood into an ideal, and this ideal, even if she didn't have another to turn to, couldn't be invalidated by defeat in a war. It was timeless in times that were bad, and even more convincing in times that were better. "Willing to make sacrifices" was a term in a similar vein, which described her accurately when her son started university, and so she cried when the haughty student came home and insulted her, calling her an old Nazi witch. Now she used sentences that began, "When I'm no longer here . . ." – he'd miss her then. Then he'd realise all she'd done for him. Then he'd feel sorry for having been so mean to her. Then he'd see that. Then he'd see what. Then he'd see how. When she was no longer here. She, who in the eyes of her son was stuck in the past, anticipated justice in the afterlife, where eternities would collide in her soul: the eternal past and the eternal afterlife. Alois increasingly avoided his mother, her gaze when he studied at the kitchen table, the conversations, the arguments, the tears, and he would walk to the shop in Mariahilfer Strasse and sit in the storeroom with his lecture notes. This wasn't a regression, however, no return to being the "camp child". It was an escape forwards, into a future that was now emerging. The economic upturn was evident; his father's business was going from strength to strength. Ever since the 1954 World Cup, to have football boots with the new type of studs had been the most ardent desire of all athletic boys, and now, at the beginning of the sixties, most fathers could afford to make their sons' wish come true. And genuine leather footballs. And genuine jerseys. Everything had to be "genuine", no more substitutes, no more fakes, no more making do with "what was there" because somehow you still had it despite the shortages. Now "what was there" was on display in the shop windows and on the shelves of the supermarkets, and you could buy these things – you could afford them. So, for example, his mother now bought Fru Fru instead of stirring a spoonful of homemade jam into a glass of soured milk. Anything homemade was the substitute, anything bought was genuine. Now his father employed a sales assistant, Herr Schramek, an acquaintance from his gymnastic association days, and then he also hired an apprentice, Trude.

Trude. She was sixteen and had a sinewy body which moved lithely between the shelves. Like a noble beast, Alois thought, suspecting that this simile might be rather silly. She had a "pixie cut", a short hairstyle then fashionable amongst young women and which Alois found remarkably bold. The flimsy material of her blue work coat looked almost diaphanous when she crossed the shafts of light that fell into the room through the windows, allowing him to see the contours of her body as if he had X-ray vision. She was a most serious girl, but occasionally when he said something she would laugh with such innocent glee that Alois was bowled over, and instead of studying he would ponder how he might make her laugh the next time. He noticed that with greater regularity she found an excuse to look for something in the storeroom behind the shop. But she didn't laugh at his pre-prepared jokes.

A year later they married. Alois needed a declaration of consent from his father; as a war orphan, Trudi was already deemed to be of legal age.

The escape forwards: moving out of home. Alois Erhart's father knew a fellow party member from years before who now worked in Vienna municipality's social housing division. And so the young couple obtained a cheap flat in the 11th district's Friedrich-Engels-Hof, in the very same year that the red lettering on the front of this communal housing complex was restored and replaced. The "Friedrich" and the "s" of Engels had been chipped off by the Nazis, and so during the National Socialist era the apartment block had to bear the name "Engel-Hof".

In the now renovated Friedrich-Engels-Hof, in their small council apartment, Alois Erhart was about as far as he could be from the house-shares and communes in which the sexual revolution was being discussed at the time.

Forty years later he discovered what "good sex" was. That such a sensation really did exist.

They had stayed together long after love and desire had parted company. They had stayed together after both love and desire had moved out. Respect and solidarity had moved in to share their home. Alois Erhart was alone among his friends and acquaintances in still being married. It's a good marriage, he said.

It was a Sunday, they had slept in, but for some reason didn't do their usual thing of getting out of bed straight away. A sunny day, light poured onto their bed through the two windows. He looked at her. His back was aching. She laid a hand on his back. He blinked in the light and then . . . why did he do it all of a sudden? He sat up and threw back the covers. He pushed up her nightie and felt a brief stabbing pain in the small of his back, like an electric shock. He moaned, she took off the nightie. She smiled. Surprised?

Intrigued? He looked at her body, studied it, reading every wrinkle, every blue or red blood vessel and every roll of fat like a map on which a long common path was marked out, a life's path with peaks and troughs, and he pressed up against her in his excitement, cried, pressed, the light, the X-ray vision and suddenly, at the height of his excitement, he felt it: a melting in which their souls touched.

And she laughed. Trudi. Their souls touched. That was the secret, Alois Erhart thought, this – touching a body so that your souls touched – was the "good sex" that gave him a hitherto unimagined pleasure, and which kept triggering the desire and lust, again and again.

Two years later Trudi was dead. Eternal love. How short eternity was.

Ciggy break?

O.K.

No, wait! Not the fire escape, Bohumil said. Far too cold and you're unwell as it is. Come to my office!

But the . . . Martin pointed up at the ceiling, he didn't know the English for smoke alarm. Bohumil understood:

I took the battery out earlier. It's dead.

Bohumil sat down at his desk, put a cigarette between his lips and grinned like a cheeky little boy. Martin Susman sat on the visitor's chair opposite and stared at the ceiling.

And just to make sure, I stuck a plaster over the sensor. Light?

Martin lit his cigarette.

I'm a civil servant, Bohumil said. I'm used to meticulous tasks. Taping up a dead alarm – now that's a metaphor for our work! At least we're not freezing. But tell me, what were you doing in Ukraine?

Me? In Ukraine? What gave you that idea?

That's what I heard. A salamander said you were in Ukraine and that you gave him some very useful information —

Rubbish! What made them think that? I was in Poland. Auschwitz. You know that!

Well, it did make me wonder. What does that say about our in-house Task Force? Do the salamanders think Auschwitz is in Ukraine?

What if they're right? Auschwitz is everywhere.

You've got a temperature.

Yes.

Why don't you go home and have a lie down?

I'm waiting for Xeno. I need to talk to her.

As Martin took out his smartphone his fingers got caught up in the ribbon of his Auschwitz lanyard, which was still in his jacket pocket. He checked to see whether he had a message from Xeno; at that very same moment Fenia Xenopoulou was peering at her Blackberry a couple of rooms down the corridor to see if Fridsch had finally texted her. This simultaneity is not contrived and nor was it a coincidence, for Fenia was checking her mobile every minute.

Martin took the lanyard out of his pocket and put away his telephone.

So, how was Auschwitz?

Look! Martin said, handing Bohumil the badge.

Guest of Honour in Auschwitz, Bohumil said. Cool.

Turn it over and see what it says.

Please do not lose this card. If the card is lost you are no longer permitted to stay in the camp . . . Is that . . . is it – Bohumil turned the lanyard over and over – real? Did you really get this badge in Auschwitz? And have it dangling from your neck? Seriously?

Yes, it's deadly serious. On the anniversary of the liberation of

Auschwitz the camp is closed to tourists, and that's when the heads of state, high-level representatives and diplomats come from all over the world. Of course there are security measures, I mean, I can understand that, but —

But this badge is like a bad joke, it's a parody that —

Yes, all those things. When I lit a cigarette on the camp thoroughfare, just by the ruins of the crematorium, a man in uniform appeared and said, No smoking in Auschwitz.

Bohumil shook his head, blew out smoke and said, Hitler was a non-smoker.

It was grotesque. Just like the machines where you can get hot drinks. The vending-machine company is called "Enjoy!" It was so horribly cold in Auschwitz that I was glad get a hot coffee. But maybe we're just shocked by normality where we least expect it. I mean, this lanyard isn't a cynical parody, it's perfectly normal. It's only in Auschwitz that we think it grotesque, that it ought to be worded differently, styled differently. Just as everything ought to be different there. But if we turned it around, if we saw everything that is normal or usual in that light . . . Do you see what I'm saying? That's why I said: Auschwitz is everywhere. It's just that we don't see it. If we could see it, we would understand the bizarreness and cynicism of a normality that here in Europe ought to be a response to Auschwitz, a lesson drawn from this history. Don't get me wrong, we're not talking about more sensitively worded badges or more reverent coffee machines, I mean fundamentally . . .

Yes, O.K.

Bohumil stubbed out his cigarette. The conversation was becoming too philosophical for his liking. He was of a cheerful disposition, and it was his belief that a small dose of irony was all that was needed to be a more critical citizen. He had no fixed career plans, but nor did he have any desire to put at risk what he had, let alone what he might achieve. He liked Martin, but sometimes found his melancholy tedious. He gazed pensively at his ashtray. It was a cast-iron figure of an African man with huge lips, frizzy hair and a grass skirt, his palms formed into a bowl to hold the ash. The figure sat on a plinth that read: "*Le Congo reçoit la civilisation belge*". He'd bought this ashtray years ago, at the flea market on place du Jeu de Balle.

You know what? Martin began.

What? Bohumil said.

At that moment Kassándra appeared, and when she saw the billowing smoke she faltered, Martin stubbed out his cigarette in the ashtray that he noticed only now, Bohumil cried, We're on fire! Help! The files! The files! Call the fire brigade! Then he laughed, stood up and opened the window. Don't worry, he said, I killed the smoke alarm.

You're such kids, Kassándra said. Martin, you're needed! Xeno wants a word!

The pig became a media star overnight. To begin with there was just a short piece in *Metro*, the free newspaper, reporting that some passers-by in Sainte-Catherine had seen a pig on the loose. The article was written ironically, as if it were about an alleged U.F.O. sighting, and was illustrated with a stock photograph of some cute piglet and the caption: "Anybody recognise this pig?" Afterwards many more people called the editorial office or sent e-mails to say that they'd seen the pig too and swore they had reported it to the police, but their sightings hadn't been taken seriously, and that the tone of the article along with the accompanying picture had played down the incident and deceived the public, because it was a much larger and more aggressive animal, perhaps even a wild boar. At any rate it was a danger to the public.

Recognising the story's potential, *Metro* followed up with a title-page story. They had questioned residents of Sainte-Catherine, "worried residents" who felt left high and dry and didn't know whether to allow their children to walk to school unescorted, or if women could still go out alone while there was a possibly rabid wild sow on the rampage through the streets. One Madame Eloise Fourier asked the *Metro* editorial team whether a pepper spray might be advisable to protect against wild boar, to which Professor Kurt van der Koot, from Vrije Universiteit Brussel, replied in the negative, in response to a request from *Metro*. A pepper spray might only exacerbate the unpredictability of a *Sus scrofa*, as the animal was known scientifically. Pepper, he continued, and incidentally salt and caraway too, was only to be recommended for roast pork. This lame joke by the professor, a figure until then unknown to the wider public and who, as people learned, was a behavioural scientist specialising in wolves, unleashed a shitstorm on social media which led to other papers taking up the story. *Le Soir* ran an interview with the chief superintendent of the Centre Ville police station, a Fleming who had long been on the paper's hit list. *Le Soir*'s desire to crucify this man combined with the naivety with which he committed hara-kiri ("What precautions have you taken?" "I've instructed the municipal dog-catchers to arrest this pig on sight." "Why the dog-catchers?" "We have many stray dogs. That's why the city has dog-catchers. But we don't have any pig-catchers." "The plan is as perfect as his French," the newspaper commented.) More and more eye-witnesses got in touch and now *De Morgen* was printing a new map of the Brussels region every day, with flags to mark where and when the pig had been spotted. It was soon evident that the pig had become omnipresent. One day, for example, it was sighted in Anderlecht, soon afterwards in Uccla and then in Molenbeek again.

In an effort to restore his reputation, Professor Kurt van der Koot published a consciously sober opinion piece in *De Morgen* in which he correlated the maximum velocity a pig could attain at full pelt with the distances it must have covered, thus proving empirically that there could be only two possibilities. Either – hypothesis one – we were not talking about a single pig here, but several, for according to a path–time diagram it was absolutely impossible that one pig could be in every place eye-witnesses claimed to have seen it. Or – hypothesis two – there was no pig, merely the fiction of a pig in the minds of a population irresponsibly unnerved by the affair, that is to say, a hysterical collective projection. Historically there had been a number of authenticated cases of such collective hysteria, such as the sighting of a unicorn in 1221, mentioned in the Nuremberg city chronicle. He, however, was sceptical that the Brussels pig represented a similar phenomenon, for all the historical cases referred to mythical creatures, not domesticated ones. Moreover, since the end of the Middle Ages there had been no more sightings and descriptions of mythical creatures with supernatural powers, such as omnipresence. In this case, he thus concluded, they were dealing with neither an imaginary pig nor a single one, but with a horde of pigs that had been sighted in various places around Brussels at the same time.

A horde! And what was the chief of police doing?

Six

Can you plan a comeback of the future?

THE PAST FORMS the future, without regard to life.

It was hard to say why this phrase made Fenia Xenopoulou happy or, if happy was perhaps too strong a word, then at least cheerful. Fridsch had called, he had called at last and told her that for the time being a switch to another Directorate-General was highly unlikely. The Commission had only recently been reshuffled and right now the president was expecting his officials – especially those at management level – to first prove themselves in their posts. It was far too early to consider changes and switches. But, Fridsch said, to underscore the consolatory aspect of his message, and it was a particularly emphatic "but", followed by a brief pause – and Xeno thought of butter, of *Last Tango in Paris*, then of butterflies, she felt butterflies in her stomach, or at least this was the association she had – and Fridsch said "but" again, then explained that she was on Queneau's radar as well as that of other very influential and high-ranking officials, there was recognition of her work, her past achievements, serious recognition, and what mattered now was not what she wanted, but that she remain visible and kept getting noticed. Xeno listened, she wasn't disappointed, it was O.K., yes, yes, it was O.K. and then . . . she couldn't remember what he'd said after that, how he'd moved on to this, but all of a sudden he came out with the phrase: "The past forms the future, without regard to life." These words stuck in her head, she thought about them for a while after her telephone conversation, translated them into her mother tongue and realised that it wasn't just international treaties and laws that depended on the tiniest nuances of every single word in the translation, but even such a personal . . . a personal what? A phrase. Simply a phrase. About life. *Her* life. A life-phrase as clear as a legal paragraph, but which in Greek, as she realised in astonishment, required interpretations that made the phrase hopelessly confused . . . What term should you use to translate *the past*? In Greek neither *parelthón* nor *istória* is coterminous with *in the past*, which also implies *history* somehow. Everything that has happened? Happened to whom? Individual history, i.e., what has been experienced, biography? Or general history, world history? The English language leaves all this open, and yet one senses there is greater precision. In the Greek translation these questions must be clarified, as a result of which everything becomes less clear and somehow narrower, a matter of interpretation. Does the past have a definite beginning and a definite end, or is it uncertain when it began and if it has ended? Does it repeat itself or was it – is it – unique? This is what the construction of the Greek verb depended on – in English it was in the present tense, but for the translation one might have to choose the aorist or the imperfect or perfect, depending on how one defines what the past did or had done. And it amused her that what the English phrase boiled down to was precisely this: that her background stood in contrast to her life – perhaps this conclusion was the translation of, or at least a valid interpretation of "The past forms the future, without regard to life."

She called for Martin Susman. He came into her office and stood there indecisively. Fenia smiled. He was bewildered; he had never seen her like this before. Greeting him with a smile. Putting on a friendly face. He could only misinterpret this. Had she been so taken by his paper? He hadn't expected that, he'd already regretted having written and sent the document in a feverish and thus unrestrained state. On the other hand . . .

It was the suit. Martin's cheap, grey, knackered suit. A man with even a limited sense of elegance, Fenia thought, would never buy a suit like that. But nor would a man who didn't care about being elegant, or harbour any pretension to elegance. With casual indifference he would wear something functional yet comfortable, but never ever a mouse costume like that. Fenia looked at Martin and imagined him in a clothes shop, in the – for him – inappropriately named "Gentlemen's" department, dismissing several suits on the rail then suddenly pointing to this grey outfit and saying, I'd like to try that one on.

Please sit down, Martin.

She found it so funny. The idea of him trying on this suit in the changing rooms, staring at himself in the mirror and thinking, Yes! It's perfect! Wiggling about in front of the mirror and then saying to the sales assistant, I'll keep it on!

She had to stop herself from laughing.

Martin felt a sense of uneasy happiness. A confusing feeling.

You've read my paper? he said.

Yes, of course, she said. She couldn't stop thinking about his appearance. Smiling, she shot glances at his suit like needles into a voodoo doll. He always wore a grey suit like this, she'd never seen him look any different. She imagined him needing a new suit. The only one in which he would recognise himself in the mirror would be exactly the same grey suit. In all the others he would think, That's not me. Habit doesn't provide security, it makes you insecure. About everything else. Pinstripes: too formal. Blue: maybe for the evening, but not for daytime. A lighter-coloured material: too dandyish. No pattern, no fashionable cut was appropriate for work; the office isn't a catwalk, after all. Fenia pictured the sales assistant trying to offer him alternatives. No, no, Martin would begin to sweat, panic even, the grey suit is O.K., he'd say, I'll stick with the grey one, that's me. The man in the grey suit.

Fenia Xenopoulou looked at the printout of Martin's draft on the desk in front of her, she stroked the paper with her fingertip, back and forth and back and forth, then looked up at Martin and said, Auschwitz! What were you thinking? I have to admit, I was shocked when I read it. I thought you were . . . wait! Here: Auschwitz as the birthplace of the European Commission. It says it right here! It's insane. What's wrong with you, Martin? Are you ill?

With his hand he wiped the sweat from his brow into his hair and said, I was sick for a few days, yes. I caught a cold in . . . I caught a cold on my trip. But I'm feeling better now.

Good. But can you explain this to me? We're looking for an idea we can, or rather *must* put at the heart of our jubilee celebrations. I thought we were agreed: a jubilee is an occasion, but not an idea in itself. So how can we get people to see that the Commission is necessary, more than that . . . how shall I put it? That we're *sexy*, that we've *got* something – she cleared her throat – yes, that people are glad we exist. That they have expectations of us. That there's something which connects us. Do you understand? That would be the idea. And you come up with Auschwitz.

Half an hour earlier, when he was smoking in Bohumil's office, Martin Susman would have been happy if Xeno had told him his suggestion was utter nonsense, let's bin it and forget about it. Although he had feared this reaction, he had also been anticipating it. Rather a brief humiliation now, he had thought, than all that work, which would no doubt lead to a whole host of rejections and complications in the office. But the way in which Xeno was now treating him, this armour-plated woman with a smile that initially had surprised him, but which in fact looked like it had been Photoshopped onto her face, this insipid artificiality he was sitting opposite, sweating, he couldn't accept this . . .

But I explained in my paper why we have to take Auschwitz as our starting point. O.K., it was just a few keywords, I thought —

So explain it to me again, Martin.

She stood up, she was wearing a black skirt with a red zip running diagonally across it. As if someone had crossed out her womb! Martin thought. And yet furnished it with a mechanism that allowed it to be opened in a flash!

Coffee? She had her own Nespresso machine on a little side table. Milk? Sugar? Martin shook his head. She sat down at her desk, held her cup in both hands. It occurred to Martin that this was exactly how he had clutched his coffee in Auschwitz, to warm his numbed fingers.

Martin coughed. Sorry, he said, then added, But this is the essence of the Commission, it's what it says in the articles of association, declarations of intent and side letters! O.K., it sounds rather abstract, but it's perfectly clear, too: the Commission is a supranational rather than international institution, which means it doesn't mediate between nations but stands above them and represents the common interests of the Union and its citizens. It doesn't seek compromises between nations, it aims to overcome the classic national conflicts and disaccords in a post-national, i.e. collective development. It's about what connects the citizens of this continent, not what divides them. Monnet wrote —

Who?

Jean Monnet. He wrote: National interests are abstract, the commonality of Europeans is concrete.

Fenia saw she had a new e-mail. Yes, and? she said. National, supranational, this was hair splitting as far as she was concerned: she was a Cypriot, but her national identity was Greek. The e-mail was from Fridsch. Opening it she said, What has all this got to do with Auschwitz?

What the Commission is, or what it ought to be, Martin said, was only conceivable after Auschwitz. An institution that makes the individual states gradually relinquish national sovereignty and . . .

When? Where? Fenia typed. (Fridsch had asked whether she had the time and the inclination to go to dinner with him.)

Auschwitz! Martin said. The victims came from all over Europe, they all wore the same striped clothing, they all lived in the shadow of the same death, and all of them, those that survived, had the same desire: a guarantee that human rights would be respected, a guarantee that would be binding for ever more. Nothing in history has brought together the diverse identities, mentalities and cultures of Europe, the religions, the different so-called races and former hostile ideologies, nothing has created such a fundamental solidarity of all people as did the experience of Auschwitz. The nations, the national identities – all that was obsolete, whether you were a Spaniard or a Pole, Italian or Czech, Austrian, German or Hungarian, it was obsolete – religion, background, all of it was subsumed in a common desire: the wish to survive, the wish for a life in dignity and freedom.

Italian? (Fridsch)

O.K.! (Fenia)

The experience and the consensus that this crime must never be repeated were what made the project of European unity possible in the first place. We wouldn't be here without it! And that's why Auschwitz —

Fenia looked at Martin and said, But —

That is the idea! The overcoming of national sentiment. And we are the guardians of this idea! And our witnesses are the survivors of Auschwitz! The survivors are not only the witnesses of the crimes committed in the camps, they are also the witnesses of the idea that arose out of those crimes, the idea that, as has been proved, we *do* have something in common and —

Pasta Divina, 16 rue de la Montagne. Eight o'clock? (Fridsch)

O.K.! (Fenia).

Xeno seemed to be have become thoughtful, and so Martin went on: The guarantee of a life with dignity, happiness, human rights, that's been an aspiration since Auschwitz, hasn't it? Surely everyone understands that. We have to make clear that we are the institution representing this aspiration. The guardians of this eternal covenant. Never again – that is Europe! We are the moral of history!

Fenia stared at him in astonishment. How animated this sweaty, grey man had become all of a sudden.

People died for this, their death was a crime and each individual death was senseless, but what they gave rise to remains. Ultimately this is what they died for, and it will endure for ever!

Even though Xeno wasn't fully aware of this at that moment, it sounded like an echo from the deep, dark depths of her pre-history; it sounded like death from undying love.

She looked at Martin. Now she seemed very serious, very pensive. Martin wondered whether he might have convinced her, even though he hadn't yet finished with his argument.

Fenia had never thought about herself much, and when she did, her mind focused on opportunities and goals rather than states of mind and feelings. Well-being – for her this was the ideal state of emotionlessness in a very broad sense, and that meant not being troubled by moods. She regarded emotions as moods.

Have you got any cigarettes?

Yes, of course, Martin said, surprised.

Fenia stood up, opened the window and said, Would you give me one?

I didn't know you smoked.

Sometimes. Very rarely. Just one.

They stood close together in the narrow recess of the open window and smoked. Martin expected her to say something, he sensed that she wanted to say something, but she just puffed away with the pinched face of the amateur smoker. It was ice-cold and finally Martin said, It's our last opportunity!

She looked at him in astonishment. How dreadfully cold it was by the open window, Martin thought, they would have to huddle together to keep each other warm . . . He gave a start and tried to edge away from her, and then she said, I'm sorry?

There are fewer and fewer of them. Very soon there won't be any camp survivors left. Do you see? We have to put them at the very centre of our jubilee celebrations. That is the idea: they are testimony to the horrific crimes that nationalism precipitated in the old Europe, and at the same time they are testimony to all that we have in common, which became so profoundly evident as a result of the camps, which . . .

It was so damned cold by the open window.

. . . and the Commission represents our common values with regard to human dignity and the law, and so . . .

Martin tossed the cigarette out of the window and took a step backwards. Fenia flicked her cigarette out too and closed the window.

Do we know how many are still alive?

I don't. All I know is that barely a dozen were there for the anniversary of the liberation of Auschwitz, and I reckon all of them were between eighty-five and ninety-five. Apparently more than two hundred came a few years back.

Good. So find out how many are still alive. Then we need to discuss how we're going to do it in practice, how we're going to put them at the centre of our celebrations. All of them, or . . . do you know what I'm picturing? Thousands —

There can't be that many!

No, wait! If we invite them all with their families and descendants, children, grandchildren, great-grandchildren, that will probably add up to thousands, and then, how should I put it? – she made an expansive gesture – then we'll declare that all of us are symbolically their children, and we'll declare our children to be their grandchildren and —

I don't know for sure, but I think that most descendants of Auschwitz survivors live outside Europe.

Yes. But. Does that change anything? Perhaps it does. So . . .

She thought for a moment and then said, The other points in your paper are O.K., let's leave them as they are for now. The usual things that need to be thought of for a celebration like this one. But what we need, and quickly, are facts and figures. How many are still alive, and how many of them live in Europe?

Once again she paused to think. Martin wondered whether he ought to sit down again, but Fenia herself made no move to do so. She stood at the widow, gazing outside. Eventually she said, Perhaps one would suffice. Essentially we only need a symbolic figure, for a united Europe, for our common values, for the ambitions of our work here.

First she wants thousands, then only one. How should he proceed from here? He looked at her. She looked down and brushed the ash from her blouse.

*

When Professor Erhart came for the first meeting of the "New Pact for Europe" Reflection Group, he was the only one with a brief-case. That was so odd. It struck him straight away and he sensed that the others registered it too; whether with amusement or mere surprise, at any rate they noticed.

He was the last to arrive because he had got lost on the way there. The meeting was in the Résidence Palace behind the European Council building on rue de la Loi, a place that to all intents and purposes was impossible to miss; you came out of Schuman Metro station and there it was in front of you. Beside the European Council building there was, however, a construction site and in front of it a closed-off pavement, with barriers and temporary concrete bollards. Reckoning that he needed to circumnavigate the entire construction site to get behind the Council building, Alois Erhart continued down rue de la Loi, but could see no oppor-tunity to turn left and find his way into a parallel street that would take him to the rear of the Council building. Then he saw the entrance to Maelbeek Metro station, which meant he had walked an entire stop from Schuman. The diversion couldn't be that long! He saw no other option but to continue uncertainly a short way down the street until finally he turned into a side street to the left, rue de Trèves, then left again, rue Jacques de Lalaing. He read the names as if the very fact of these streets having names at all might afford him comfort. He stopped, took the map of Brussels from his briefcase and worked out that if he continued on Jacques de Lalaing he would arrive at chaussée d'Etterbeek, which ran beneath rue de la Loi, without any opportunity – or at least none that was marked on the map – of coming up behind the Council building. So he turned and retraced his steps all the way. Once back at the construction site he noticed a small and discreet gap between barriers and yellow hoardings that led to the Résidence Palace.

When he entered the building he had no idea where to go, of course. In the middle of the foyer was a desk where two exceptionally friendly girls gave out information. No, they didn't know where in the building the European Policy Centre was located. They had never heard of the think tank "New Pact for Europe". Was there a name? Professor Erhart gave them his name, one of the girls typed it into her computer and said with a friendly smile that she was sorry, very sorry, but nobody with that name was in the building. But that's my name, the professor said, I thought you meant . . . O.K., I'd like to . . . one moment! He had printed out the e-mail with all the details of the first meeting, and now opened his briefcase and took out the sheet of paper. Here, he said, Mr Pinto, European Policy Centre, first meeting of the "New Pact for Europe" Reflection Group, you see! Max Kohnstamm Room, 4th floor —

Oh, the girl said, say no more! Fourth floor! The lift is over there on your right.

So, he was the last to arrive. But not excessively late. If he hadn't got lost he would have been excessively early. Usually he was the first to arrive, for fear of being late.

He had carried his briefcase in his left hand the whole time because of the pain he still felt in his right arm. Now he also felt a tugging pain in his left. He lifted the briefcase and pressed it to his chest, his arms crossed. He was trying to relieve the strain on his arms, but it looked as if he were using his briefcase as a shield, as if he were bracing himself. Such was the picture he presented as he entered the room.

A man came up to him, beaming.

Herr Erhart?

Yes.

The professor from Austria!

From Vienna, yes.

I'm António Oliveira Pinto, the head of our Reflection Group. Delighted to meet you, the man said. He spoke perfect German.

I'm so sorry I'm late, the building site . . .

Yes, the man said with a laugh, Europe is a confusing building site. And that's why we're here, it's our job to discuss what we're actually building.

I'm not an architect, and —

Ha ha! Viennese sarcasm, I presume? Very good. Right, I suggest you help yourself to some refreshments and we'll begin the round of introductions in the meeting room in twenty minutes. Not an architect – ha ha, very good!

Alois Erhart stood there, briefcase against his chest, and looked around. A buffet had been laid out, men and women stood at cocktail tables, the members of the think tank, eating with plastic forks from paper plates, chatting and glancing in his direction, or not chatting, smiling and glancing in his direction.

Alois Erhart took the briefcase in his left hand again, to free up his right in order to hold a plate . . . But how was he going to serve himself pasta salad or roast beef? Clamping the briefcase under his right arm, he grabbed a plate with his left hand and tried to scoop some pasta from the dish with his right. The briefcase dropped. As he bent to pick it up, the pasta salad he'd shovelled onto his plate slid off onto the floor. He put the briefcase down, it tipped over. It made him feel strangely nervous to see the briefcase lying there, so he took it and leaned it against the wall. Now he felt uneasy about being so far away from his briefcase while he was helping himself from the buffet. He put the plate down, fetched the briefcase again and wedged it between his feet while he served himself. Now he had to make his way to the cocktail tables. The plate in his right hand and a glass of apple juice in his left, he attempted to somehow manoeuvre the briefcase between his feet by taking small, shuffling steps, almost tripping in the process. He gave the briefcase a gentle kick, took a step, nudged it again with his foot, trying to push it to the nearest table. By now he – or his briefcase – was the centre of attention, and Professor Erhart saw that nobody else in the room had one. A few were carrying rucksacks, standing assuredly with their humps and free hands; the others had wheelie cases beside them, which they casually rested a hand on. And there he was, the old man with his schoolbag.

It was indeed his schoolbag. He had got it very late, only in senior school. There had been no money before then. Or his father thought it pointless to fork out for a briefcase when he had so many sports bags in stock. These were made of cloth, a sort of duffel bag you closed with a cord which then formed a loop that served as a handle. It was little more than a glorified gym bag and the young Alois felt ashamed that his father, a shopkeeper and thus a businessman, forced him to go to the middle-class grammar school in Amerlingstrasse with this strange sack that no other pupil had. When eventually he was given a real briefcase he was delighted. It was leather and stitched by hand. His father had bought it at Weinberger's, a "manufacturer of fine leatherware" a little further down Mariahilfer Strasse, at a handsome discount after he had given a generous discount on ski equipment for the bag-maker's son.

Alois was so proud of his leather briefcase that he kept it beside his bed when he went to sleep, so he could see it straight away on waking up. He loved the sound the clasps made, gleaming nickel that locked with a resounding click as he packed his bag for the school day. From time to time he would treat the briefcase with a type of grease to prevent the leather from cracking. There was a strap you could tie into loops for carrying on your back, but Alois never used it; he preferred to carry the briefcase in his hand like an adult, and at some point the strap got lost.

Then more modern schoolbags appeared, brightly coloured and with garish patterns, and made from some artificial material. Alois felt a combination of revulsion and pity whenever he saw children trudging to school with these ridiculous Snoopy and Batman boxes on their backs. His leather briefcase had accompanied him all his life. The leather was now a bit softer and had developed an attractive matt patina. And in it he kept everything he needed for an occasion like this: a plastic sleeve containing two sheets of paper with keywords for the five-minute introductory statement that he, like everyone else, was to give at the opening session; a plastic sleeve with the printouts of e-mails he had received from Mr Pinto in preparation for this meeting; a folder with his paper on the reform of the Union, which he intended to deliver as soon as he had the opportunity; a notepad and a pencil case. He wondered what the others kept in their bulging rucksacks and wheelie cases.

He had his first friendly exchange at one of the cocktail tables. Oh, so you're Professor Erhart? Pleased to meet you. Very pleased. Delighted. My name is, my name is, yes and my name is. Him. Her. Him. Delighted to meet you. A French man started talking to him. Professor Erhart's school French was not good enough to understand his dialect . . . until he realised that the Frenchman was speaking English. He concentrated on his pasta salad. Then António Pinto clapped his hands a few times and called out, Ladies and Gentlemen, may I ask you please . . .? Thank you, let's get started.

Professor Erhart very soon sensed that he was out of place here, and that his cause had no chance in this company. They were all so similar. Only he was different. He had been informed that the think tank would meet six times this year, for two days on each occasion, at the end of which they would deliver to the president of the Commission a paper with the findings of their analyses, and suggestions for resolving the crisis and consolidating the Union. Alois Erhart had been amazed that they had only twelve days, and these spread throughout an entire year, to develop a plan for solving the European crisis. But he had viewed this invitation as an opportunity to inject his ideas into the system.

They were now all sitting in a circle in the Max Kohnstamm Room. Erhart took from his briefcase the sheets of paper for his introductory statement, everyone else took laptops or tablets from their rucksacks or wheelie cases, and António Pinto said with the broad, beaming smile of a man who has just enjoyed the happiest moment of his life, Once again, welcome, there was a crashing sound, the woman next to Erhart ducked, a man leaped to his feet, another's laptop slid from his knees . . . What was that? A bird had flown into the window, yes, it must have been a bird. One man who claimed to have seen it said it had been a large, black bird. Everyone got up, crowded around the window and indeed you could see a speck of blood with a feather sticking to it.

How peculiar it was that Alois Erhart, such a conservative man at heart, would play the tragic revolutionary within this group.

If Inspector Émile Brunfaut had not been on enforced leave, he wouldn't have taken the time to visit the doctor. And then maybe he would never have tried to solve the puzzle of the "Atlas murder".

Now he lay with bare torso and unfastened trousers on the examination table, struck by the uneasy realisation that fear was creeping over him, a silent, paralysing fear. Breathe in deeply! Breathe out! A fear that took his breath away. It was strange that Brunfaut had never before considered his own mortality, even though he had regularly come face to face with corpses. But it was after all he who lived and had the job of ensuring those responsible for the deaths received a just punishment. As a rule this meant "life imprisonment", which even when a killer was released early sounded like the incalculable eternity of a life whose end nobody could know.

Dangerous manhunts, exchanges of fire and suchlike were what you saw on television, but not in his work, and if it ever did happen there were special teams to take care of it. In all his years of service, however, he had never come across anything like that, he had never been in a situation in which he'd had to confront the fear of death. But now, in the presence of this doctor, not a pathologist or forensic scientist, just a perfectly normal practising doctor who had just examined him, pushing a bit here, tapping a bit there, he . . .

Brunfaut buttoned up his shirt while the doctor wrote out a referral to a clinic for a precise diagnosis of the symptoms, and he . . .

He couldn't help thinking of death. His own. Without any vanity. The doctor had a suspicion. He knew something. And in the clinic they would confirm what the doctor knew or suspected. The illness he would die of. All of a sudden Brunfaut was in no doubt that he was watching his death sentence being drawn up. He perceived this moment as unreal, at the same time perceiving himself as real in a dramatic way he had never experienced before. Nobody is so out of this world and yet so at one with themselves as the person who is suddenly lost in an impenetrable fog. Panic and the survival instinct tear the body to shreds, the head becomes hot, the chest cold and numb. The doctor tapped away at his keyboard most unrhythmically, staring repeatedly at the monitor with raised eyebrows, tap tap tap pause click pause tap tap pause, then a drumroll followed by an interval like the sound of a desperate heart plugged in to an amplifier. And Brunfaut, as if he were translating practice sentences into a foreign language, gradually formulated questions in his head, slowly and uncertainly: How react, how will, I? react when the results, when I have the results, black on white? Rise up and fight? Will I want to fight? Will I collapse, give up? Lie to myself, be lied to, hope, madly? Will I feel self-pity . . . or desire, will I still be able to feel desire, learn to feel desire, for the last pleasures? Will I be angry, or, or will I able to be affectionate? Affectionate to whom?

The doctor cleared his throat and Brunfaut couldn't help smiling. There were times when being ill was idyllic, paradise. Very briefly, for a second at most, an image flashed inside his head: him snuggled up in a soft duvet, off school, his mother so affectionate, her hand on his hot forehead, so considerate, making tea and then cooking his favourite dinner to build him up. Dozing, dreaming, reading. The sweet experience of love in the form of sympathy and concern. And the certainty that everything would turn out fine. Everything was fine . . .

The doctor was on the telephone . . . Tomorrow morning is no go? . . . I understand . . . How about 1.00 p.m.? . . . *D'accord!* Many thanks!

That's tomorrow at 1.00 p.m. in Europe Hospital St Michel, the doctor said, nil by mouth in the morning if you can. Here's the referral letter. The diagnosis, that's to say the necessary tests might take three days. If it's any longer you'll definitely be able to go home for the weekend. The senior consultant, Dr Drumont, will take that decision. I've just spoken to him. You're in the best possible hands.

And then something bizarre happened to Émile Brunfaut: the fear released. This was what he actually felt, and then thought: release.

Now he saw the death sentence or, let's say, the acknowledgement of his mortality as a dispensation to act. He had to do what had to be done. Police officers on leave were forbidden from carrying out investigations on their own initiative. But what punishment could he now fear? To die knowing he had not acted, that would be the only punishment he should fear, that would be the most agonising death. Was he being melodramatic? History is nothing more than an oscillation between pathos and banality. And the mortal is pushed one way, then the other.

Inspector Brunfaut stood up and peered at the doctor with an expression his grandfather used to wear. The famous resistance fighter, after whom a street in Brussels had been named. His grandfather's expression that had frightened him as a child. When he, little Émile, had lain in bed with the sage tea his mother had made, with a slight temperature, a runny nose and sore throat – being ill was idyllic, his paradise – his grandfather had stood over him, staring down and saying, There's no such thing as being ill. You're not ill until you keel over. And then you're dead. And his mother coming into the room with the tea, exclaiming, What are you talking about? Leave the child in peace! Why are you scaring him? Brunfaut took the referral letter, thanked the doctor and left. In his mind he looked down at the child he had been, the child was terrified, the child was frightened. He was not.

Now he was in the resistance. So long as he didn't keel over. *La loi, la liberté!*

He walked slowly into the city centre with time to kill. It was an hour until he was due to meet his friend, Philippe Gaultier, in Restaurant Ogenblik in the Galeries Royales by Grande Place.

He bought some chocolates at Neuhaus . . .

These ones here, please, a small box of nine!

Nine of "*le désir*"? *D'accord*. Would you like them gift-wrapped?

Yes, please.

The lady is going to love these. I think "*le désir*" is our best chocolate!

Which lady? I'm giving them to myself.

Oh.

Brunfaut looked at the sales assistant and suddenly felt sorry for her. And sorry for himself. He had shattered an idyllic vision, even if merely the fiction of a sales scenario. Why was he so careless? It was something he couldn't allow himself any longer: carelessness. He paid, took the artistically wrapped little box and said, I've changed my mind. I do want to give these chocolates to a woman after all – a woman whose smile enchanted me today.

And he handed the box to the sales assistant.

He ran out.

Everything is fine, he thought with exclamation and question marks, so long as shame burns brighter than the fear of death.

Now he was at L'Ogenblik only a quarter of an hour too early. He drank a glass of champagne while waiting for Philippe.

Philippe was head of the Brussels police I.T. centre, fifteen years younger than Brunfaut and, despite the age difference, his best friend. The men were united not least by the fact that both were "wearers of the wet scarf", the name they gave themselves as R.S.C. Anderlecht fans who barely missed a home fixture. So many tears had been shed into their football scarves that they would never be dry again. As they discovered over a beer after work one evening, both were of the conviction that following the bribery scandal – prior to the U.E.F.A. Cup semi-final return leg against Nottingham Forest, the referee had been offered 27,000 pounds sterling – a signal ought to have been given, a signal for a new beginning. Even a merely symbolic one would have sufficed, a minor alteration to the club's name to emphasise that from this point onwards it was starting afresh and no longer had anything to do with bribery and corruption. R.S.C. Anderlecht – what sort of name change? Lose the "R", Émile Brunfaut had said, just to give a signal.

But why the "R"?

Le Roi, la Loi, la Liberté! What can we do without? *Le Roi!*

They laughed. Before long they also discovered that they held similar political views on the Belgian system, this torn-apart country that shouldn't be hopelessly stitched together by a king, but by the common legal entity of a republic. But both men had applauded the king's decision not to appoint a government at the time Belgium held the E.U. presidency, to prevent necessary European policy decisions from being blocked by domestic coalition squabbles. Never, Philippe said, had Belgium functioned more smoothly than during this period without a government.

They made their pilgrimage to the Constant Vanden Stock Stadium in Anderlecht, wept into their scarves and ribbed each other. Philippe went on and on about how he'd seen Franky Vercauteren play, how the team could do with someone like that now, a brilliant finisher. Oh, you haven't got a clue, Émile had said, he – several years older – had seen Paul van Himst. Vercauteren was a lame duck compared to van Himst.

Did everything use to be better? Nothing was better, it was just that everything was so different.

Yes, of course! Different! But wasn't it better too? Anderlecht used to be a Jewish district. It was the secret centre of Brussels because of the club and the cafés and shops. Now it's a Muslim district, the Jews are gone and nobody that I know would ever think of coming here to a café, especially not with a woman – they're not even allowed to go into cafés in Muslim areas.

You know Gerrit Beers from C.S.I., don't you? He's moved to Anderlecht, he says the apartments are cheaper there, everything's more easy-going and he's a smoker. Nobody gives a toss about the smoking ban here. He can get a first-rate coffee and the men with their shishas don't mind if he lights a cigarette.

Like in Molenbeek.

Yes. Times change. And when the club vacates the ground here and moves to the new King Badouin Stadium, it'll still be called Anderlecht, but it won't be playing in Anderlecht anymore. And you're saying everything used to be better. And today you're complaining that Anderlecht isn't what it was twenty years ago.

Come on, they weren't that bad today. 2–1 against Leuven isn't the worst.

Three years earlier Philippe had asked Émile to be his best man. One year later Philippe became a father and Émile the godfather of little Joëlle. Now he was more than a friend – he was family.

Émile Brunfaut finished his glass of champagne and ordered another. Philippe was just the person he needed right now: a brilliant computer scientist as well as a thoroughly trustworthy and loyal friend. He hoped. No, he was sure of it.

His second glass arrived, he took a sip and then Philippe was standing beside him. The rest of one's life begins with champagne and ends with herbal tea! his friend said. So? How did it go at the doctor's?

They embraced and Philippe sat down.

And I'd also like to know if you've arrested and convicted it yet.

It? What? Who?

The pig, of course. Haven't you seen the papers?

Oh, the pig. I have a lead. We've secured some genetic material. Tomorrow you're going to have to compare its D.N.A. with that of every pig registered in the Europol database.

Philippe laughed. You know I'm always at your disposal.

That's precisely what I wanted to talk to you about.

They talked and ate and drank. The food used to be better, don't you think? Yes. But nothing's changed here at all. Apart from the food, that is. How so? We ate the roast lamb here ten years ago. Yes, but it used to be better. Well, perhaps, but apart from that . . . anyway nothing else has changed. Maybe I ought to have gone for the grilled sea bass with asparagus risotto. Asparagus in winter? It's from Thailand, says so on the menu. Asparagus from Thailand? Stop it! We've always eaten the lamb here, it's fine. I don't know, it tastes of corpse, it never occurred to me before that roast lamb was a corpse. Oh, come on, what's wrong with you? It's O.K. Yes, it's O.K.

Brunfaut said that the doctor had referred him to Europe Hospital, and that they were checking him out tomorrow.

Did he give any indications?

No. All he said was that it needed more detailed examination.

He just wants to be certain. It's a good thing. Then at least you'll have clarity. So I wouldn't worry.

Yes, maybe. Maybe you're right. In any case, I'm not out of action.

Meaning?

You know I was relieved of the Atlas case and given enforced leave?

Yes.

Do you know why?

I thought that's what you were going to tell me.

But I don't know.

You don't *know*? They didn't explain why?

No.

I need another glass of wine.

Listen, Philippe, all the data relating to the Atlas case have been deleted. I was at the crime scene, C.S.I. were there, I did the initial questioning – none of that exists anymore. All the files, protocols and documents have vanished without trace, the murder has vanished as if the corpse I saw with my own eyes never existed. When I got back to my computer, everything had gone, as if it had been hoovered up. Someone hacked in, probably not just into my computer, but into the entire system. And the public prosecutor is playing along. I'd like to know why.

I don't blame you.

You've got to help me.

The waiter cleared the table, Philippe clicked his fingers and pointed to where Émile's plate had been, saying, The corpse has disappeared!

Don't joke! I'm sorry about what I said earlier. But I'm being quite serious: the case has disappeared into thin air, and if there's anyone who might be able to trace how that happened and who did it, then it's you. You head up I.T., you're in charge of the police's entire computer system. You have to find the loophole.

How could I justify doing that? I can't officially embark on a search like that without a valid reason. Especially if it's against the public prosecutor's orders.

Do you know what the public prosecutor's orders are? No. So there. You don't need a reason, you just need to do it.

It's too complicated to explain how access to the central repository works, how many security mechanisms are built in and how much paperwork is needed to take even just two of maybe twenty steps.

You don't have to do it officially, I mean, my question is not whether you think you'd get authorisation, but whether you could do it.

It would be against the law.

Listen, Philippe, a murder is a criminal offence that the public prosecutor's office is legally obliged to prosecute. If the public prosecutor's office fails to do this, however, and instead covers up the crime, then the law has been broken by the state itself, and those who employ illegal means to solve the crime are the champions of the law. If you help me and we're successful, then we will be the ones who have complied with the law.

Alright then. I'll start off by trying it from your login. Give me your password. If anything gets out, then you've been playing around with your computer on leave, O.K.?

O.K.

Mousse au chocolat?

Definitely. Why change the habits of a lifetime, today of all days? How's Joëlle?

Matek knew there was no chance of going underground without trace. By now they would know that he hadn't boarded the plane for Istanbul. They would surely consider the possibility that he had flown to Poland, even though they'd cancelled his ticket, and for them it was child's play to find him on the passenger list for a flight to Kraków. So when he arrived in Kraków he could assume that they were only one step behind him.

He had already learned this during his basic training, as Żołnierz Chrystusa: don't try to cover your tracks – it's impossible. Don't try to cover your tracks – nothing gives your pursuer more confidence than coming across traces you have tried to efface. So if you can't avoid leaving them, produce more of them! Lots of traces, conflicting traces! While they're being weighed up, you'll get a head start. And if they have to come back on themselves having been on the wrong track, you'll have increased your head start.

Of course he knew that they knew that he knew this, but they would still have to follow up the traces he produced, whether they were suspicious of them or not.

He calculated that it would take him three days to find out what had gone wrong in Brussels, and why they then wanted to send him to Istanbul, contrary to the original plan. Three days' head start – that was feasible, that was routine, and then he'd consider his next steps.

When he arrived at Kraków airport he went to the information desk and had them put out an announcement for him. Would Mateusz Oświecki please go to the Kraków Pastuszak express shuttle counter. Mateusz Oświecki! Your driver is waiting for you at the Pastuszak express shuttle counter!

He knew that passenger announcements called over the P.A. system were stored for forty-eight hours. He went to the shuttle service counter. He had booked his transfer into the city online from Brussels airport. If they hacked into his mailbox they would have only two clues. He paid by credit card. Clue three. He was driven to Hotel Europejski, ulica Lubicz.

By tomorrow lunchtime they would know what he would not have been able to keep hidden: that he had arrived in Kraków. The following day they would know where in Kraków he had gone. By handing them the address on a silver platter he would be able to put them on the wrong track and have them chasing their tails for the three days he needed. He checked into the hotel and asked the receptionist to find out when the first train to Warsaw left in the morning. She tapped away at her computer, shook her head and said, Do you really want the first train? It leaves at 4.52 and —

That's far too early!

The next one leaves at 5.41, arriving at —

The one after that, please!

Then there are trains at 6.31 and 7.47 and —

The 6.31! When does that get in?

At 8.54, and the 7.47 gets in at 10.00.

That's too late. 8.54 would be perfect. Tell me again, it's at 6 . . .?

Six thirty-one. From Kraków Główny.

Excellent. Could you please purchase an online ticket for me and print it out? Here's my credit card. And I'll pay for my room up front too. That'll save me time in the morning.

Bardzo zadowolony, panie Oświecki.

Matek took his rucksack up to the room and wrote a letter on the hotel's writing paper, which he put in an envelope along with his credit card. He stuck down the envelope, addressed it, and left the hotel. Tomorrow afternoon they would have six clues that pieced together logically that he had arrived in Kraków and gone on to Warsaw the very next morning. But he would stay in Kraków. Until they realised this, he would have some time.

He walked to Starowiślna, where he remembered there was one of those dodgy shops that sold used mobiles. The shop still existed. He bought a primitive old Nokia and a 100-zloty prepaid card. Matek watched the boy force open the phone with a bent paperclip and insert the card, he watched him as if he were an odious and yet pitiable animal in a terrarium. Everything about this boy was a cry for help as well as a demonstration of defiance and disdain. His grotesque haircut, shaved at the sides, and long and artfully dishevelled on top, the thick blue-black strands styled with gel. He wore a red T-shirt with a big fat middle finger on the front. He had a wolf's hook tattoo on his right upper arm, beneath it a kneeling naked woman in chains. But more striking than this childish swagger was his left forearm. It was evident that the boy self-harmed, a whole array of red lines, more or less newly scabbed-over cuts probably made with a razor blade. Matek remembered this from the seminary. He knew that rush of pain-relieving endorphins, that explosive feeling only when you cause yourself pain, when you divert the pain with a razor blade from your soul to your skin. Endorphins and adrenaline, they were the key. He had heard that women experience this sensation in the stress and pain of childbirth. God had arranged it thus. In the seminary, cutting and scarification on the arms and belly were widespread, and sometimes – when inflicted by mutual arrange-ment – on the back, rarely on the genitals.

The boy forced the parts of the mobile together until they shut with a snap, then pressed a few buttons, looked at the display and said, *Dopasować!*

Dziękuję, Marek said. He paid the eighty zloty for the telephone and one hundred for the card, and then hesitated, as if something had suddenly occurred to him. Looking pensively in his wallet he said, I've got one more question, you might be able to help . . . He took out a hundred-euro note and placed it on the counter, his hand on top.

Do you by any chance know anyone who's going to Warsaw?

The boy looked at Matek's hand on the banknote.

I'd have to ask around. What's this about, a car share?

No. A letter. I need someone to take it for me.

Matek placed another hundred-euro note on the counter.

What's wrong with a post office?

The post offices have been closed for half an hour. And the letter is urgent.

My brother might be planning to go tomorrow. He's got a girl-friend in Warsaw. I'll have to ask him.

Matek added another fifty.

The letter has to be there by ten o'clock at the latest.

He won't mind getting there a bit earlier than planned.

He'll have to leave very early. Half past six at the latest.

He'll want petrol money too.

Wasn't he going anyway, to see his girlfriend?

Matek lifted his hand from the banknotes, took the letter from his inside jacket pocket and placed it on top of the money.

I'll be back here at ten tomorrow morning. If I've received confirmation by text – he held up the Nokia – that the letter has arrived, you'll get the same again. That'll give him enough petrol money, he'll be able to visit his ladyfriend twenty times more and take her out for the evening. If their relationship lasts that long.

She's faithful.

Good. Faithfulness is always good. The address is on the envelope.

Matek wandered down Starowiślna towards the city centre, to Rynek Główny, the main market. The beauty and magnificence of this vast mediaeval square moved him every time he came to Kraków. It was lined with grand buildings, the strict symmetry broken only by St Mary's Basilica. With its two towers it took a step forwards, as it were, from the façades on this side of the square, standing at an angle, brazen, proud, soaring above everything else, its two towers of differing heights. The reason for this was recounted in ancient legends, which Matek knew, of course, but he regarded them as heathen insolence. For him there could be only one possible reason for this break in symmetry and harmony: not even when constructing the house of God could man presume to create something perfect, for God alone and his plan of creation are perfect. There can be no perfection from the hand of man that may rank alongside God's perfection, not even in the belief that such an aspiration would honour Him in the highest glory. St Mary's Basilica, which stood diagonally to the market, thereby metaphorically standing on the toes of people going about their business there, drew itself up high to reach for the stars, with one tower too short, the other closer to the firmament, a representation of human ambition that grows but falls short of perfection – for Matek this church was the most apposite expression of the relationship between man and God. All very different from Notre-Dame. A year ago Matek had an assignment in Paris. Of course he wanted to see the cathedral of Notre-Dame and of course he was at first impressed when he stood before it. But . . . what? Then it dawned on him. This overbearing, in effect puffed-up mediocrity, signifying a belief that geometric rules adjusted to bombastic dimensions can reflect the divine harmony of the universe . . . it annoyed him, he found it blasphemous. And this was probably why God had looked on with cold indifference as the heretical philosopher Abélard had fornicated with the canon's niece Héloïse on the altar of this cathedral. Matek had listened to a guide telling this story to a group of English tourists who were giggling uncontrollably: And here on this altar, ladies and gentlemen, the young philosophy scholar Pierre Abélard deflowered his great love, Héloïse, the niece of the canon of this cathedral. A story told and sung time and time again, Abélard and Héloïse, this here was the altar of their love! The pope decided to have Abélard castrated, which Matek considered right and just, verging on lenient, but not even this punishment, which as the guide explained was actually served, could in Matek's eyes undo the fact that this conceited house of God had been desecrated, and remained so. He had sensed it. How different St Mary's Basilica was here in Kraków. He looked up, it was now 7.00 p.m. and, as on every hour, the trumpeter in the tower began to play the Przerwny Hejnał: a signal to warn of advancing enemies, which is interrupted. In commemoration of the trumpeter who was hit in the throat with an arrow during the Tartar attack of 1241, it was only played to the last note he was able to blow before he fell.

Matek peered up at the eastern tower, where the trumpeter ought to be standing at a window, but he couldn't see him and then the Hejnał stopped.

He didn't go into the church; he couldn't pray in the endless tumult of tourists taking photographs. He turned, crossed the square and passed the Cloth Hall; he could never tire of looking at it, but he knew that he shouldn't look too closely. The shops with their beautiful old portals sold postcards showing those beautiful old shops before they sold postcards and souvenirs. The restaurants advertised "Traditional Polish Cuisine" and upheld no traditions save that of processing tourists as rapidly as possible. Beside the church where the large state bookshop used to be was now the flagship store of the fashion chain Zara. In the former textile shops tourists could buy souvenirs of old Jewish Kraków, postcards of old photographs and C.D.s of Klezmer music, but also tasteless, Nazi-style caricatures of Jews, such as woodcarvings of the greedy Jew holding a money bag or a gold coin.

He left the square and turned into Grodzka. There on the corner he used to buy the sweet rice bread he loved so much, now the place was called "Quality Burger". He walked down to the end of Grodzka, on and on, he walked down Stradomska, on and on, his rhythmic footsteps and regular breathing were now his prayer, on and on until he came to Paulińska, he knew a small restaurant there, the Kuchnia Adama, where he fancied a bite to eat. Here you found the best *bigos* in the whole city, and even though there were at least a hundred more or less official recipes for this stew, for Matek this was the only authentic one, just a hop and a skip off the tourist trail. It must never be served freshly cooked, it wasn't really good until it had been reheated for several days in succession. At

Adam's the *bigos* pot stood on the cooker for at least a week. This allowed the pork belly to release all its fat to the cabbage, the aroma of the hot red paprika to develop fully, the cubes of meat to become wonderfully tender. And yet these words are just a drone and the rhymes of songs sung about Adam's *bigos* pure coincidence – only the stomach can understand *bigos*.

Matek ate in silence, of course he did, he was alone, but even when he was alone he ate as if still prohibited from talking during meals. A short, almost inaudibly muttered prayer, with head bowed, then eat in silence. That evening, however, so many thoughts filled his head, like a babble of voices. He heard his mother who, in an attempt to protect him, had destroyed his faith in being cared for and protected by giving him away, abandoning him to the dungeons of an underground where the blissful, steaming cooking of a loving and smiling mother no longer existed. In front of him the *bigos* steamed, and he could hear himself spouting heroic fantasies as he sat with his mother to eat *bigos* or *gołąbki* – where had he picked these up, these legends he recounted with great excitement while his mother listened smiling, and saying, Don't forget to eat! And at the time he had no idea that beneath her skirt she had a gun, his dead father's pistol. Where was his father? While she held him in her arms there was no understanding of this, but then her arms released him, she delivered him into the hands of the holy men who were also called father, and now he had brothers in a dungeon from which, after years of asceticism, he emerged as Żołnierz Chrystusa to defend a homeland he had never been to. Who had ever been there? Not his grandfather, not his father, and he himself had been driven away just as he was about to enter, through a back entrance, through the door that his mother had suddenly slammed shut. And he heard the voice of the pater prior, explaining sympathetically and with a smile dripping with grease, like this *bigos*, that he, Mateusz, was not destined for the priesthood, but for the Soldiers of Christ. He was obedient, he had always been obedient, first because he had confidence in the world, and then because he was schooled in the purpose and wisdom of obedience, and now he was sitting on the edge of a trap. Why, he did not know, but he had no doubt that they had laid a trap for him. He heard his mother, he heard the pater prior, he heard voices, indistinct, unintelligible, of people he didn't know, but speaking about him like a figure on a chess-board. *Silentium!* he cried, and once more, *Silentium!* He shouted it silently, only in his head. He wished to eat in silence. Taking a deep breath, he straightened his back and looked over at the waitress, who was standing by the "no smoking" sign, puffing on a cigarette.

He walked back to the hotel, did his toning exercises, then lay down to sleep.

When he left the hotel at 6.00 a.m. the following morning the sightseeing buses were already waiting outside: "Auschwitz. Best price!"

He went to the Kazimierz district, ate a hearty breakfast at Rubinstein, then called Wojciech, his old friend from his seminary days, who the brothers in Poznań had given the apostolic name of Szymon, the mason. Now he was pater of the Augustinian monastery attached to the church of St Catherine's in Kraków. Matek knew his daily routine, the convent Mass must be over by now, which meant he would be contactable until Terce.

Mateusz, my brother! Are you in Kraków? How are you?

Yes, I'm in Kraków. I'm fine. I have such fond memories of us walking through the monastery gardens and talking. We need to talk.

The gardens, yes. We've leased them as parking spaces. It's sad, but good business. The renovation of the church swallows unbelievable sums of money. Yes, let's talk, after None?

I've got a rucksack with me.

You're very welcome to stay.

Matek glanced about him. Nobody was looking in his direction. He pushed his sleeve up a little, wiped the knife on his napkin and gently scored his left forearm. The damn knife was blunt – typical restaurant cutlery. He tilted it slightly, drew the blade across his skin and then again, increasing the pressure. Finally his skin opened a crack, blood seeped out, he closed his eyes and put the knife down.

At 9.30 a.m. he got the text message: "I'll happily pass on your regards!"

So, Brother Tomasz in Warsaw had received the letter. Tomasz would go to lunch and pay with Matek's credit card. Then he would buy a suitcase at the large luggage store on Potockich, and later purchase a train ticket to Budapest at the station, again using the card. They would find all this out. Tomasz would then cut up the card and throw it away. Matek estimated that he had seventy-two hours' head start until they had followed up all the traces.

He went to the toilets and ran cold water over his arm until he felt it turn numb, then he left. He went back to the mobile shop on Starowiślna, the boy was wearing the same T-shirt. Matek put the money on the counter.

It was an unusually warm and sunny day for the time of year.

He strolled through the city, down ulica Józefa. Coming the other way were tour groups behind boards or pennants hoisted into the air. He turned left into ulica Bożego Ciała, there was the church of Corpus Christi, the first Catholic church after the Jewish quarter. He went inside, the morning Mass had just ended, people were getting up from the pews and making for the exit. Matek stood there like a rock in the surf, people streaming past him on either side and then out, until he turned and left the church with them, as if part of a group, back to Józefa he went, an entrance door was open, giving a view of a beautiful, hidden inner courtyard behind a dilapidated passage full of rubbish bags, a tourist stopped to take pictures on his smartphone, "This way please!" called a foreign guide, ". . . would be a perfect hideaway!" a woman said, a man laughed, "You cannot escape", the group moved on to St Catherine's, gardens behind wrought-iron gates, parking spaces in the garden, a young man broke into a run, ran over to a woman, they embraced, wandered hand in hand along the blind, silent façade of the monastery, past the square with the Millennium Altar that consisted of a group of seven large bronze figures, larger-than-life saints, churchmen, a German woman stood before them and said, "Hey look, this one's got to be the Polish pope!" A man said, "Yes, that's Wojtyła!" Another: "No, it says Św. Stanisław (1030–79)". Priests walked past, turned into Augustiańska, then came two women with heavy bags as if chasing after the priests, they had already disappeared around the corner, the tourist group had moved on and the millennium statues stared from dead eyes onto an empty square.

The Union was threatening to break apart. It was suffering its biggest crisis since its foundation. Florian Susman had supported this project for many years out of a deep conviction, and of course he would have been prepared to shoulder responsibility too. You don't moan, you accept responsibility – this had been his father's credo. Anybody who builds up a business takes risks. How can you assess and calculate them responsibly? Florian remembered the time his parents had sat at the dinner table long after the meal was finished, looking grave as they weighed up the opportunities and risks associated with credit-financed investment in a licensed in-house slaughter facility. The debt could be their downfall, but to shy away from this step could spell the downfall of the farm too. There was an opportunity with risk attached, but there was no opportunity to "play it safe". His parents sat there doing their sums, they came up with objections and immediately found arguments to dismiss these objections, they put their misgivings on one side of the scales and their hopes on the other, no, their misgivings about the misgivings. Florian listened. It was unusual that his parents hadn't sent him up to bed, maybe his father thought the heir to the throne ought to listen to all of this, while Martin, the younger son, lay on the sofa reading until he fell asleep and was eventually carried to bed by their mother – no, it wasn't as tender as that, he was shoved into bed.

Gods, Graves and Scholars. Florian was amazed to remember the title of the book that his brother had read many times over, while he, Florian, just sat there listening to his parents talk about what they could and had to take responsibility for. Back then. Those long evenings.

Florian drove slowly. There was plenty of time. He didn't have to be in Budapest until the evening; it was early afternoon and he was only twenty kilometres from Nickelsdorf, twenty kilometres from the Austrian–Hungarian border. He drove as if in a trance, with cruise control, music playing softly on the car radio, a local station with folk hits interspersed with advertisements: "I'd so love to be a truffle pig," a voice squawked, whereupon a resounding voice said, "Nonsense, little piggy, don't you think our potatoes taste much better? Yes, farmer, oink. You're my little potato piggy. Does that mean I'm special? Yes, you sure are."

Florian switched off the radio.

Back when his father, a small-scale pig farmer, expanded the barely profitable farm into a pig enterprise and slaughterhouse, he also got involved in lobbying. Soon he was accepting positions in professional associations and in the Austrian Farmers' Association. We can't just wait and see what they'll do for us, we need do something ourselves, he said. Participating in discussions was all very well, but he couldn't improve conditions in the sector, and he certainly wasn't able to halt the fall in prices. And so he took a chance on volume to combat the ever-dwindling profit margins. The extra investment increased their debts, but it increased turnover too. And this enhanced his father's status on the committees. Florian wondered whether this ever more irritable and querulous man had in some quiet moment asked himself if there was a way back to that point at which necessity and freedom were in balance, where effort and hard work were rewarded with satisfaction and security. Probably not. Some ways go in only one direction, with no opportunity to turn off. Like this motorway he was gliding along, and if anything were to come towards him on this carriageway it could only be ghosts, danger.

Florian had to step into his father's shoes quite suddenly. Assume responsibility. And he found that the shoes were too small. Which is unusual for the sons of strong fathers. But very soon he realised that to save what his father had built up he would need larger shoes, several sizes larger. Austria had joined the E.U. and it took the national lobby groups a long time to recognise that they were in a trap. They defended their domestic market, which now existed only in the minds of some elderly officials, and ensconced themselves in a system of subsidies that did not lead to fair prices but, with an increasing administrative burden, to a dependence on handouts. There wasn't even a guarantee in the medium term for these, nor was there any plan in place for what would happen after the expiry of the transition arrangements that had been agreed upon during the course of the accession negotiations. He recalled a session in the Austrian chamber of commerce in Vienna, focusing on strategies for pig producers. He was young at the time, and still quite insecure. His father's shoes were pinching him. He was perplexed by how the old officials reacted when he asked questions – as if he weren't asking questions but questioning everything, particularly them, the lords of a sunken world, the princes of Atlantis.

Although he was naive, he grasped the key lesson: he needed bigger shoes, because given the new conditions in Europe he wasn't going to get any further with Austria's national lobby groups. He became involved with the Union of European Pig Producers, the E.P.P. And now he had been its president for a year.

Florian was overtaken by a police car, its blue lights flashing and siren wailing, with another one right behind it, and then an ambulance.

Once a year the E.P.P. representatives met in a European city for a three-day general assembly, at which they appointed a new president or agreed to keep the incumbent in office. They swapped experiences, discussed the contradictions between European rules and national regulations, drew up lists of demands for European governments and the Commission, visited local farms and each year there was a central theme – this time it was "European Foreign Trade in Pigs".

This year's event was being hosted by the Hungarian delegation, which had caused uproar in the Union of European Pig Producers, and even organised resistance in the course of preparations for the conference. There were statutory and political reasons for this. According to the statutes of the E.P.P., a representative of the host country must sit on the board of the union. At that moment, however, Hungary was politically ostracised because its government had ruthlessly expropriated European pig breeders who had invested in Hungary and acquired an interest in Hungarian farms after the collapse of communism. Until now they had simply ignored the note they had received from the European Commission requesting them to explain this breach of European law and setting them a deadline to reverse these illegal measures. A grouping was formed calling for the boycott of Hungary. It consisted principally of Dutch and Germans demanding that the annual conference take place in a different city – Madrid was proposed, given that Serrano and Iberico sows were very much in the ascendant. The Austrians, Italians and Romanians, however, took the view that the conference really should be held in Hungary to give a clear signal that the E.P.P. itself was willing to defend the interests of its Hungarian members.

It began to rain. Florian Susman glanced at his satnav: only ten kilometres to the border. More sirens wailed and another ambulance raced past.

As president, Florian had had his work cut out trying to prevent the E.P.P. from falling apart, and engineering a compromise between the two camps. The compromise was brittle, in effect consisting of statements of intent which were to be discussed only now at the conference. All the same, it *was* a compromise and the conference *was* taking place in Budapest as planned. As host, the Hungarian delegation had voiced its willingness to add its signature to a protest note to the Hungarian government. He would wait to see whether they followed through on this, for the larger Hungarian pig producers had benefited from the renationalisation of the farms. On the other hand, they now found themselves undercapitalised and the export of Hungarian Mangalica pigs had dropped by almost 25 per cent. But that was the central topic of this year's conference.

Florian Susman had no concerns that he might be voted out as president. After all, he had succeeded in achieving this interim compromise – a fact that was widely acknowledged – and so far no rival candidate had put themselves forward.

More sirens and blue lights. There was a flickering in the rear-view mirror, a flash in the now somewhat misted windscreen. He switched on the fan, two police cars sped past.

He was certain that he would be re-endorsed as president, but he wondered whether this was in fact what he wanted. He was no longer naive. On the contrary, he was in danger of becoming the type of pragmatist he had always loathed: someone who only ever did what was possible, but was never able to implement what was necessary. He was heading for an abyss; he could try to put the brakes on, but he couldn't change course.

In truth there was no real solution to the division within the E.P.P., or at least he couldn't see one. The aim of this Budapest conference was to work together with Hungary against the European Commission, because the latter wasn't capable of negotiating – or not willing to negotiate – a higher export quota with China for pigs. At the same time they would be working with the European Commission against Hungary, because the latter was in breach of E.U. law.

If the Union of European Pig Producers was going to fall apart, what point was there in taking on the responsibility? How absurd it was to want none of this but to take on the responsibility anyway. For what? Just to act as a puppet for people with common interests who formed a community, only to wage relentless conflicts of interest within that community until the common interest was no more.

He saw people up ahead on the motorway. Pedestrians! Ghostly figures were marching towards him. Men, women and children bowed beneath the hoods of raincoats or with plastic bags over their heads, some with blankets around their shoulders, some carrying bags, others wheeling cases, the windscreen wipers moved back and forth, like hands trying to rub this image out, wipe it away, then he heard his satnav say, "Please turn around at the first available opportunity!" That was insane! He was on a motorway, the satnav was telling him to turn around and pedestrians were heading towards him. He put on his hazard lights, slowed to a walking pace, then saw more blue lights, police cars on the hard shoulder, police officers waving glow sticks. He stopped. More and more people emerged from the grey wall of rain into the beam of his headlights. There were so many of them. Dozens. Hundreds.

David de Vriend had never found that being especially friendly had helped him in life – or rather, in his *after*life – let alone bailed him out. Nor did he expect friendliness. Politeness, yes. Politeness was civilisation. Propriety. This he would, in fact he *wanted* to stick with. But why, if he said "Pleased to meet you," should he behave as if he really were pleased?

He had been able to show feelings, but only if they were genuine. Love, that selflessness which brings out the best in one, and gratitude, such an inner and existential gratitude that it even replaces one's lost faith in God. And he had learned to conceal feelings, fear, or the feeling of emptiness, feelings he could never be rid of, but was able to hide away. Meanwhile he had learned to be mistrustful so subtly that his wariness functioned in a discreet, illuminating way, like a night-vision device. But friendliness, especially an instantaneous friendliness towards strangers, was for him mere hamming it up by character actors, as grotesque as a glass eye striving to look friendly.

As he left his room he said *Goedemiddag*, nodding politely to the man unlocking the door to the neighbouring room. *Bonjour*, the man said, immediately taking two steps towards him. The beam from the ceiling light caught his snow-white hair, illuminating it like a halo. *Bonjour, Monsieur.*

David de Vriend nodded again and was about to hurry on his way, but instead looked – just for a second, yet this was still too long – in wonder at the man lit up by the ceiling spot. He wore a raincoat with a moiré pattern, which switched between light green and beige at the slightest movement. His face shone as if he had just applied a cream.

Bonjour, Monsieur, permettez-moi de me présenter, the man said and gave his name: Romain Boulanger. He offered de Vriend his hand, beaming as if this were the happiest moment of his life.

De Vriend shook his hand formally, told the man his name and then said *Aangenaam*, before correcting himself: *Enchanté!* All perfectly polite, but it threatened to develop into an irritatingly friendly conversation.

Oh, he spoke French.

He ought to have said, Not very well, I'm afraid, then apologised and left, but instead he said, *Oui, Monsieur.* Many Flemings spoke passable French and David de Vriend spoke it perfectly. After escaping from the train on which he was being deported he had been hidden for two years, between the ages of fourteen and sixteen, by a Walloon family in Villers-la-Ville, until someone informed on him just before the end of the war. At the time, French had been his second mother tongue, the language of his surrogate parents, and the language of love in an existential sense. He was immediately nauseated by the exaggerated way in which this stranger – what was his name again? – said, *Quel bonheur* and then again, *Quel bonheur*, what luck, then babbled away that he was the new resident, he'd moved in that day, how nice to meet his neighbour straight away, he hoped they would have good neighbourly relations, at any rate this was a splendid start, and what luck that Monsieur de Vriend spoke French, he'd already noted that some residents only spoke Flemish, including some of the staff, that had unsettled him at first, that there were staff in the Maison Hanssens who weren't French speakers, not competent ones at any rate, like the carer who had run through the house rules with him, a Madame Godelieve, that was an unpronounceable name, Godelieve.

Yes, Monsieur, do you know her? Well, he hadn't understood what she was saying, but thankfully he had arranged it so that he was now looked after by Madame Joséphine . . .

What luck!

Monsieur Boulanger's coat kept changing colour.

Yes, Monsieur, very nice, very helpful, but – he pulled a mischievous face and raised his index finger – you mustn't ever call her "nurse", it was true that they weren't in a hospital here, even if she went around wearing a cap, did he know her?

David de Vriend nodded.

At any rate, he was delighted to have such a nice neighbour. Had he been here long? He must, he absolutely must tell him all about it here and give him some tips, maybe at dinner or later over a glass of wine.

David de Vriend could not bring himself willingly to agree to this suggestion, to say yes, of course, I'd love to, he was hunting for a polite answer that didn't commit him to anything, at the same time he was distracted by the fact that this man's face reminded him of someone, but he couldn't say who. Monsieur Boulanger took a small step forwards, thereby moving out of the direct beam of the spotlight, his hair and face at once stopped shining and turned grey, and he said, Oh, but I'm detaining you! Had he really said "*arrêter*"? Please excuse me! I shan't detain you any longer! See you later!

When De Vriend walked into the dining room he noted there was no table where he could sit alone. He was about to turn around and go to Le Rustique – in the meantime he had sorted out his discount there – but he was immobilised by Madame Joséphine. There we are, she said, so loudly that he flinched, then she pushed him energetically to a table at which the professor was sitting, who "we", as Madame Joséphine said, had already met, haven't we, Monsieur de Vriend, when we had that little mishap with the fish bone, didn't we, but there's no danger of that today, because we've got a delicious *waterzooi*, alright? Professor, may I sit your acquaintance, Monsieur de Vriend, beside you?

How was he, did he feel happy in the home, did he have any family who came to visit? Politely but curtly, David de Vriend answered the questions with which the professor – what was his name again? – was trying to make conversation. Then came a moment of silence while they ate their starter – a fennel and orange salad – and de Vriend wondered whether it would be impolite to ask the professor his name yet again, i.e. admit that he'd already forgotten it, whereas the professor had addressed him directly. He thought it would be more proper to ask rather than attempt to cover up his inattentiveness, which would be tedious and ultimately embarrassing.

The professor did not appear in the least annoyed, in fact he was happy to venture the information. His name was Gerrit Rensenbrink, he said, fumbling in his wallet and taking out a business card. He pushed away his plate and placed the card in front of him. Professor at the University of Leuven, he said, now with a biro in his hand with which he crossed out "Katholieke Universiteit". He was retired. Head of the research centre for political history, he said, crossing out the corresponding line on the card. His main field of research had been the history of nationalism, in particular the history of collaboration in Belgium and the Netherlands during the Second World War. What was he crossing out now? His e-mail address and telephone number. These didn't exist anymore, he said.

There you are, he said, pushing the card towards David de Vriend. At that moment there was a crash: Monsieur Boulanger slamming the door too energetically behind him. David de Vriend looked up, Romain Boulanger raised his hands apologetically and said, *Pardon, Messieurdames*, looked around, noticed de Vriend and hurried smiling over to his table.

Puis-je me joindre à vous? he said, How marvellous that we can continue our conversation so soon.

He sat down, nodded to Professor Rensenbrink – it was more of a seated bow than a nod – and said, I'm the new boy, so to speak. May I introduce myself? My name is . . .

As he chattered on, de Vriend felt terribly tired. The starter plates were cleared away and dishes of *waterzooi* arrived. There was a rattling and clattering followed by a sudden silence – Professor Rensenbrink apologised that he didn't speak French.

Oh! And Monsieur Boulanger didn't speak Flemish.

De Vriend had always liked *waterzooi*, or at least he'd never had a problem with it, occasionally you were served *waterzooi*, in the school canteen there had been *waterzooi* from time to time and he had always eaten what he was given. Of course, he would go for *coq au vin* if ordering chicken in a restaurant, but he would never dream of making a fuss, if it was *waterzooi* then *waterzooi* it was and he was grateful. He glanced at the chunks of meat, looked up, Professor Rensenbrink and Monsieur Boulanger were staring at him. In desperation? Helplessly? But it had nothing to do with the *waterzooi*, which smelled funny, de Vriend thought. Was that a spice he wasn't familiar with, or was it the smell of decay, already?

Vous devez m'aider! You have to help me, Monsieur de Vriend! The *monsieur* doesn't speak French, would you be so kind as to translate? Nodding again to Rensenbrink, Boulanger said, *Mon nom est Romain Boulanger . . .*

His name is Romain Boulanger . . .

Ik begrip dat . . .

J'étais journaliste jusqu'à récemment chez Le Soir . . . He'd been retired for ten years, but still wrote articles now and again, you couldn't just give it all up, the gentlemen knew how it was, surely, you couldn't wave goodbye to your life from one day to the next, obviously they weren't letting him write anything important these days, but he was grateful they let him write at all, and it was fun, for example, the story of the phantom pig, maybe you heard about it, the pig that . . . well anyway . . . He paused and jerked his head to signal that de Vriend should kindly translate for Professor Rensenbrink.

Alors, de Vriend said, *il a dit qu'il était un journaliste. Retraité.*

But he's still writing. About a pig.

Boulanger looked at him in astonishment, hesitated, de Vriend said, *c'est tout*, and Boulanger continued, Yes, if he had a vineyard he'd look after it with passion, or at least a house with a garden, perhaps he'd just prune roses and read. All he'd had, however, was an apartment, a nice, large apartment in Ixelles, but what was there to do there, then his wife died and he felt constricted by everything, the apartment, it was a big apartment, but he'd felt cramped, after his wife's death he couldn't possibly have a daily routine there, a continuation of his daily routine, all he could do was shuffle from one wall to another, and he wasn't able to manage it any more . . .

What did he say?

Manage it, it all got too much for him, and at the same time not enough, could the gentlemen understand this, at any rate it wasn't his life any longer —

Wat heeft hij gezegd?

Taking a deep breath, David de Vriend repeated what Boulanger had said and when he noted Professor Rensenbrink's surprise he added that it was understandable. That after the death of his wife, Monsieur Boulanger —

Oui, Monsieur, Boulanger said, but you . . . I thought . . .

At that moment de Vriend felt an anxiety in his chest that made him breathless. He felt hot too, it was burning shame, he realised that . . .

He hadn't translated what Monsieur Boulanger had said in French, he had just repeated it.

He lowered his head, stared at the chunks of meat on his plate, got to his feet and walked away, out of the dining room. The door closed with a bang.

Seven

How can you not believe in the future
if you are aware of mortality?

THE DAYS GOT warmer, unusually warm for the time of year. When people met in the corridors, canteen or lift they now made witty remarks about global warming.

We in Brussels are the clear winners in this development!

Something else for them to get at us for: another privilege for the Brussels bureaucrats!

You've got me to thank for the warm weather. I've only ever used aerosol deodorants!

We're shooting ourselves in the feet with these climate regulations!

Everyone ignores them anyway – we'll soon be growing palm trees here in Brussels, you'll see!

But this was the Ark, not the Directorate-General for Climate Policy, and in truth nobody was laughing at these banal jokes; it was just that the sun had been shining for several days in this rainy city, and at a chilly time of year. The sun was reflected on people's radiant faces, it shone from their eyes, it glinted in windows and gleamed on the metal of the street traffic.

Following his meeting with Xeno, Martin Susman had fleshed out his paper for the Jubilee Project. She had added a few written comments and now he had to revise the document and develop it further, so it could form the basis of an Inter-Service Consultation. That was the next step. He had promised to deliver the paper by the end of the week, but there were still some unanswered questions, or one major unanswered question, at least. He needed to resolve the issue as rapidly as possible with Bohumil, who had been tasked with addressing it. He went to his office and asked him whether he fancied a spot of lunch.

In this weather we could wander down to place Jourdan. How about Brasserie L'Esprit? I think you can even sit outside there.

Great idea! Shall I call and reserve a table?

Please do. I'll go and fetch my jacket.

Tractors were coming down rue Joseph II.

Is this a farmers' demo?

What?

Farmers' demo! Martin yelled.

Bohumil shrugged.

A long convoy of tractors. People stood on the trailers of some of them, shouting something that was drowned out by the noise of the engines, horns and whistles.

The side streets were blocked off by police cars parked sideways.

Martin and Bohumil made for rond-point Schuman. It was impossible to talk. They could see more tractors chugging down rue Archimède and avenue de Cortenbergh, tractors carrying loads of manure, between them groups of people marching with pitchforks and scythes. It looked menacing and yet from a completely different era, fury in traditional costume. At rond-point Schuman, between the Commission and Council buildings, and all the way down rue de la Loi stood tractors, manure was unloaded, banners unfurled, it stank of diesel, black clouds of exhaust fumes hung in the sunlight, a young woman stood on a trailer, topless, brandishing a *tricolore*, Martin stopped to watch, police waved him on – *Continuez s'il vous plaît, ga verder alsjeblieft* – guiding pedestrians through the barriers, they came to rue Froissart, where it was quieter, and they walked on in silence to place Jourdan.

In the brasserie, or rather, outside the brasserie, because you could sit outside, Martin and Bohumil lit cigarettes, glanced at the menu and ordered the dish of the day – *waterzooi de la mer* – and some white wine and water. Bohumil blew smoke rings into the air and said, It's like being on holiday, don't you think? I'm already worried about going home.

Going home? What do you mean?

I have to go home on Friday. My sister's getting married on Saturday.

The waitress brought the wine, Bohumil took a sip and said, And it's going to be horrendous. She's marrying Květoslav Hanke. The name will mean nothing to you, but he's quite well known in Prague. In fact he's notorious. He is . . . how do you say it in English? We call it *křikloun*. Yes, a thug. A fairly radical Úsvit member of parliament – they're our nationalist party, die-hard opponents of the E.U., of course. It's completely mad, isn't it? Here I am, working for the European Commission, and my brother-in-law is working to destroy the E.U.

Seriously? Don't tell me you're their witness?

No, of course not. My sister still has some sensitivity. For the time being, at least. It was obvious that she wouldn't even think of asking me. I gave her a pretty hard time when she told me about her sweetheart. I first found out about their relationship from the television. I look at the Czech news on the internet from time to time. And there he was, in a report about a charity event. Charity! These murderers organise charity events for poor criminals! When he came on the screen, this member of parliament, a voice said, Accompanied by his charming new girlfriend – and what do I see? My sister! I called her at once and confronted her. All she said was, Men!

Men!

Yes, she thinks political differences are just a male quirk. Women are responsible for love, and men for idiotic conflicts.

That's your sister?

Lunch was served, Bohumil put his spoon into the dish and shovelled around as if trying to turn everything upside down. Shaking his head, he said, Can you picture the wedding? The reception? Prague's entire fascist scene will be there, and Květoslav has sold the photo rights to *Blesk* . . .

To who?

Blesk. It's a newspaper. The name means lightning. A tabloid.

Lightning? Clearly the opposite of enlightenment.

Bohumil made an agonised expression.

I wouldn't go, Martin said.

It's my sister. And our mother said that if I don't go she'll kill herself.

I wouldn't go, Martin repeated. He was shocked. He liked Bohumil and thought he knew him. He would never have imagined that his happy-go-lucky colleague, who had just been blinking blissfully into the sun, could have such an existential problem. He thought that he . . .

Bohumil said something, all Martin understood was "pre-war era", had he really said "pre-war era"? At that point Martin's mobile rang and he answered, said, I'm in a meeting, I'll call you back, and asked Bohumil, I'm sorry, what did you say?

Bohumil took a mouthful of *waterzooi*, then suddenly pushed the dish away and said, Actually, I don't really like it!

What?

I'm no historian, he said, but for me it was always history, in the past somehow, you know? The Stone Age, and this chapter of the Stone Age was called the pre-war era: the time when radical political conflict ran straight through families, one joined the fascists, the other joined the communists and so on. Did I not pay enough attention at school? But that's how I remember it, that's how it was told to me: in the past, in darker times, political hatred ran right through families. What kind of nightmare is that? Why should I have these dark times in my family now, *now*? My father *isn't* coming to the wedding, by the way.

And that's not a reason for your mother to kill herself?

No, on the contrary. She'd be happy if *he* killed himself. They've separated, they're going to court.

Martin had wanted to discuss an important matter with Bohumil, relating to the Jubilee Project, but he decided to put it off until they were back in the office. Now he sensed that he – *he!* – needed to cheer *him* up! Raising his glass he said, I can offer you some consolation. Think of Herman Van Rompuy!

Bohumil looked at him blankly.

Just imagine: Van Rompuy was president of the European Council, effectively president of the European Union, while his sister is chair of the Belgian Maoists and his brother a Belgian nationalist M.P., an intransigent Flemish separatist. I read in the paper that the family meets only once a year: at Christmas!

Bohumil, who was just taking a sip of wine, proposed a toast: To Christmas! The European president, the nationalist and the Maoist!

And they sing "Silent Night"!

"Silent Night"! Ha ha! Is that true?

Yes, supposedly. So I read. It was in *De Morgen*.

Bohumil laughed and said, Let's have another glass!

By the time they left the restaurant the demonstration had dispersed, they walked across Schuman, through barriers and past heaps of manure that were being shovelled onto municipal cleaning carts. It stank. The sun was laughing.

On the way back to the office Bohumil was quiet and thoughtful. In the lift he said, I'm going to cancel my flight on Friday. I won't go to the wedding. I don't want to be in the same photo as Květoslav Hanka and then end up in *Blesk*.

What about your mother?

I'll tell her I'll come at Christmas.

He punched Martin on the arm and said with a grin, Silent Night!

Half an hour later, Martin, Bohumil and Kassándra were sitting in the conference room for an update to the preliminary work on the Jubilee Project. In one of her notes on Martin's paper Xeno had remarked that they needed to determine how many victims of the Holocaust were still alive. Is there a central register of survivors of concentration and extermination camps? How many today live in Europe, how many in Israel, the U.S. or elsewhere? Is there an institution representing survivors that we can partner with for organising the event?

They needed to find out in order to decide whether they could in fact invite all the Holocaust survivors to Brussels, or just a group that would be properly representative.

It was a real surprise, Bohumil said. Of course we expected

there to be a central register of Holocaust survivors. But we couldn't find one.

Kassándra: None of the institutions we asked for information from replied. Yad Vashem, for example. No response. When we tried again we did eventually get a reply, but even that wasn't a proper one – look, they said they'd forwarded the e-mail to the relevant member of staff. After that, nothing again for several days. I wrote back asking them to give me the name and e-mail address of this member of staff, so I could contact them directly. No reply. Nothing yet. Then the Wiesenthal Center in Los Angeles: no reply. When we followed up we were informed that it wasn't the job of the Wiesenthal Center to document the victims of the Shoah. All they had was a list of the Nazi war criminals who were still alive, it was published on their website, but they had no register of living victims of the Shoah. We should get in touch with Yad Vashem. We forwarded the e-mail to Yad Vashem, with another request for information – no response. We wrote to all the memorial sites, Auschwitz, Bergen-Belsen, Buchenwald, Mauthausen and so on ... In fact the only reply we got was from Mauthausen.

What did they say?

Here: they only had a list of the survivors of Mauthausen itself, but even that was incomplete, because of the chaos that followed the liberation in May 1945. The survivors had been able to leave immediately, and had turned to different authorities and institutions for help and documents. No information was collected centrally. Only a small proportion of the incomplete personal data held by the Mauthausen memorial service was up to date, and not even that was guaranteed to be correct. The people they had addresses for were invited every year to the commemoration of the liberation. Those who fail to respond to the invitation for several years might be dead, but equally they could have moved.

The director of Mauthausen referred us – surprise, surprise! – to Yad Vashem, but also to Steven Spielberg's Shoah Foundation. An interesting lead! And they attached the text of the Mauthausen Oath, to remind us, that's to say the Commission, that the Treaties of Rome refer to it. The director wrote . . . hold on a sec, I've got it here: the slogan "Auschwitz: never again" was problematic because it set one camp above the rest, i.e. ultimately it put the camps in a kind of ranking, but the Mauthausen Oath was universal, and for that very reason was there at the beginning of the project of European unity, even though you never hear about this anymore.

Martin nodded. This is exactly why we . . . he paused, then said, We're using Auschwitz as a symbol, but basically he's understood our idea. So, did you write to Spielberg?

I did.

No response?

Actually, yes. Short and sweet. They said they had only one list of survivors, those who had been willing to tell their life stories as testimonies on camera. But they didn't know how many Shoah victims were alive overall, nor did they even know how many of their eyewitnesses were still alive now. The recordings had been made with people who had got in touch themselves. The archive was freely accessible. For more details we should contact —

Yad Vashem.

Exactly. Which means we know nothing at all.

That's so odd, Martin said. It's quite mad. The Nazis registered every individual deported to concentration camps: their name, personal details, date of birth, profession, last address, numbering everyone consecutively, those murdered were crossed neatly off the lists . . . and after the liberation everything vanishes into thin air —

Nazi bureaucracy!

Not just Nazi bureaucracy! They should have registered them all so that —

No, Bohumil said. Many couldn't or didn't want to return to the countries they'd been deported from. Nobody was interested in another list of "displaced persons". They were given medical assistance, and then those that could leave were allowed to go.

I can't believe that, Martin said. Are you telling me that Yad Vashem has traced the names of all the people who were murdered in the camps, but isn't interested in those that survived? I can't believe that. The list must exist, but somebody seems to want to keep it secret.

Come on, Martin, Kassándra said, there's no conspiracy here. What would be the point in that? There are plenty of reasons why we don't have the total number of survivors. They weren't able to leave behind an address when they left the camps after liberation, because obviously they didn't have an address yet. And when they started rebuilding their lives somewhere, why would they write to their former concentration camp with a change of address? Come on, Martin, camp survivors aren't alumni! O.K., some got in touch with the memorial sites, made themselves available as eyewitnesses to talk about their experiences, some came to the liberation commemorations, some came decades later with their grandchildren – that was their triumph over Hitler – but others wanted nothing more to do with it. Some died very soon after the liberation, so they were survivors but then died of natural causes right after the war, some felt ashamed and didn't want their names put on file again, some remained silent because they realised that nobody wanted to hear their story, not even in Israel would anyone listen to them, the embarrassing Jew from the slaughterhouse, how could all that have been recorded and systemised?

So we've got a problem, Bohumil said. The list that Xeno wants doesn't exist. It's pointless trying to fathom the reason why. And there's no simple solution to the problem. What is this really about? The narrative of the European Commission. You say it came about as a response to the Holocaust, it must never happen again, we guarantee peace and the rule of law. O.K., but to attest to this we don't need a complete list of those victims who are still living. Are you going to have them muster in rue de la Loi? And count them?

Stop it! Shut up!

There are those Holocaust survivors we do know of, Kassándra said. We could make a list and see which of them would like to —

Have you asked Eurostat?

Why would we have done that?

Please, Bohumil, Martin said. We have a European statistics authority. They've got stats on everything. They know everything. They know how many eggs were laid in Europe today. So they'll know how many Holocaust survivors are still alive in Europe. Kassándra, please make the request and we'll talk again when we've got the answer.

Kassándra wrote "Eurostat" on her notepad and looked at Martin: I'm not being funny, but why do you want a number, statistical information about people who themselves were turned into numbers?

She undid the button on the sleeve of her blouse, pushed up the sleeve, wrote 171185 on her forearm and held it out to Martin.

What . . .? What's that?

My date of birth, Kassándra said.

Martin Susman often worked until seven o'clock or half past, so he didn't have a bad conscience when he left the office at half past four that day. There was nothing urgent left to do, and any routine matters that might still crop up in the next hour or so could be dealt with tomorrow morning. He had nothing to eat at home, but he wasn't hungry. He decided to stop for a beer on the way to the Metro, at the James Joyce pub on rue Archimède. Tanks were making their way down the street. He went on a bit further, to Charlemagne, but there too, and in rue de la Loi, military vehicles were on the move, their greenish-brown lacquered steel appearing to consume the evening sun. Soldiers patrolled, police officers diverted cars and directed pedestrians into narrow corridors between barriers, which led to the Metro station. Direct access to the Council building was closed off.

The scene reminded Martin of a film he'd once seen, *Z* or *Missing*, or of television documentaries. He rarely watched T.V. But whenever he channel surfed on sleepless nights, he always ended up on historical documentaries. History interested him more than stories, and he was especially fascinated by historical footage, old weekly newsreels and amateur films dug out and used in documentaries, while a sonorous voice talked momentously of a bygone era. These were the pictures he had in his head: the tanks in Wenceslas Square after the crushing of the Prague Spring; the armoured vehicles driving through the streets of Santiago de Chile after the Pinochet putsch; the military presence on the streets of Athens after the Obrist putsch; shaky, amateur Super 8 films and black-and-white scenes from old television news bulletins. To Martin it was as if this historical material were being projected onto the street he was walking down, creating a virtual reality for which he lacked the console. The tanks moved through the car-free streets like giant beetles, the few pedestrians squeezed themselves past houses and railings, and were swallowed up in the entrance to the Metro.

Martin was not scared; he remembered there was a Council

summit of European heads of state and government. These were the accompanying security measures. He went into the James Joyce pub, where men stood chatting in suits, their ties loosened. It was happy hour.

On his way home he bought a six pack of Jupiler at the shop on the corner of rue Sainte-Catherine.

Goedenavond.

Bonsoir, Monsieur.

Au revoir!

Tot ziens.

Once home he took off his trousers, they were tight on him, he was putting on weight. He hated himself for it, but he made no resolutions; in Brussels you counted the time in kilos rather than years. In his shirt and underpants he smoked a cigarette at the open window, then sat in the armchair by the fireplace where the old books were lined up and lit the candle. Why? Because it was there. He drank beer and watched insects flutter into the room through the open window, seek the light of the candle, fly into the flame and burn to death.

For him this was the proof that there was no God, no purpose to creation. For what was the purpose of creating a species that only becomes active at night, but then looks for the light, only to burn to a crisp in it? What use are these creatures, what contribution to the purported or hoped-for harmony of nature do they make? Maybe they have reproduced beforehand, set progeny into the world which, like them, will spend all day in a slumber somewhere before emerging at the onset of night and seeking the light they have slept through, only to end their lives because of some grotesque death drive. The flight to death begins at twilight. They cling to windows where there is light, as if the glass offered sustenance, they buzz around lamps and lanterns, as if so close to the light there were something to find apart from being blinded, and on discovering a candle or an open fire they meet their fate, instant death into which they plunge, into the darkness from which they came.

On the spur of the moment, Inspector Brunfaut got out at Schuman station instead of continuing on to Merode. Between these two Metro stops lay the Parc du Cinquantenaire, commonly known as "Jubilee Park", where he was now going to take a pleasant stroll on this beautifully sunny day. He prescribed himself this walk, eaten up by the cold fear that had assailed him on the underground, fear of the tube they would insert into him in hospital. He had plenty of time; in his anxiety he had left home far too early.

The Justus Lipsius exit was closed and he was carried along by the throng to the Berlaymont exit, where there was a crush because the up escalator wasn't working. People diverted to the stairs, but kept coming to a standstill and had to move to the side to make room for the passengers coming down. At the same time they were jostled by those coming up behind them with their wheelie cases and rucksacks. Brunfaut clutched his small travel bag to his body, he heard yelling reverberating from the exit, shrill whistling, a few passengers climbing the stairs turned around, more and more people were now heading down. Brunfaut had no idea what was happening, but he let himself be moved along and swam with the flow of the crowd back to the platform. A train pulled in, Brunfaut got on and went one more stop to Merode.

Right beside the Metro exit on avenue des Celtes was Brasserie La Terrasse. This was where he intended to fill the time until his appointment, over a beer. The terrace had plenty of custom, but there was a free table and although the brasserie was on a busy main road, Émile Brunfaut felt as if he were in a peaceful oasis behind a wall of green plants. Peace. To be able to think in peace. What? About what? He ought to make a life decision. It sounded so melodramatic: a life decision. And just then he felt overwhelmed. Although it had been a little while now since he'd been dismissed – not formally, but effectively dismissed from his life – it still felt so "sudden" to him. Strange how long "sudden" could last.

At the same time he wondered what point there would be in making a life decision just because he had this notion in his head, and he didn't even know ...

The waiter. Brunfaut ordered a beer.

Would he like anything to eat?

No, he said. He just wanted a beer.

... and he didn't even know how much time he had left to live.

The waiter brought his beer, put the bill next to it and a note that said: "Reserved 12.30". He asked Brunfaut to pay immediately. 12.30, that was in ten minutes. The waiter must be looking to free up the table again, for somebody who wanted to order food as well.

Brunfaut had always been a formidable man. But now it was if he had been anaesthetised. How small and woolly he felt as he looked up at the waiter.

He got to his feet, took a deep breath and puffed himself up. You ought to have told me straight away that this table was reserved! I have no wish to guzzle my beer in such a hurry! You shove this "Reserved" note under my nose after I order. I find that cynical and humiliating. Goodbye!

But ... Monsieur! You can't ... Wait! You can't just go! You have to pay for your beer.

Why? I'm not going to drink it.

Then I'll have to call the police.

Here's my I.D. I've come right on cue!

Oh! Excuse me, Inspector! Of course you can stay at this table for as long as you like. I'll change the reservation, Inspector!

I don't want it anymore!

This was no more than a brief fantasy which, childish as it was, only served to humiliate him further. In reality he paid, said, No problem, I have to go in ten minutes anyway. I've got an appointment and —

And what? He left an excessively large tip.

He spent a few minutes staring into the distance, looked at the beer, how could he have forgotten that . . .? He got up and left, without having taken a single sip.

Émile Brunfaut crossed avenue des Celtes and walked up rue de Linthout. He had forgotten the number but walked on, imagining he would recognise the hospital anyway.

He didn't. He walked far too far. At some point this dawned on him and he turned back. Instead of arriving too early, he almost managed to get there late. He was sweating. He would give the worst possible impression on admission and during the initial consultation.

There! Now he could see it! The Europe Hospital. From the outside it looked like a neo-Gothic cathedral, which was why he'd walked right past it. Who expects a hospital to look like a historic house of God?

He went in and found himself in a space station. White plastic surfaces, aluminium, bluish light, bright strip-lighting on the floor to guide patients to the different departments. Brunfaut was surprised that the people wandering about or sitting there weren't floating weightlessly in mid-air. On the other hand, this was a perfectly ordinary hospital reception. Everything washable and gleaming clinically. It only looked like the set from a sci-fi movie because the space was entered via the façade of a Gothic cathedral.

Brunfaut stood at the information board. The first word his eyes alighted on was "Psychiatry". Only after that did he see "Internal Medicine". He followed the blue strip of light along the floor.

Arrival, admission, allocation of room, initial doctor's consultation with anamnesis. Then Dr Drumont explained which examinations he thought were necessary and said they should be able to complete them all over the course of two days. He would schedule them accordingly. He was sure they would find a diagnosis for Brunfaut's complaints. Had the inspector fasted? Yes, Brunfaut said. He hadn't eaten or drunk anything today. Excellent, the doctor said, we can take a blood sample immediately, then. Nurse Anna will take care of that. She'll come to your room. And I will arrange for you to have a little refreshment straight afterwards.

The nurse who brought tea and waffles with strawberries after the blood sample also asked Brunfaut what he would like for dinner.

From your chart I can see that you haven't yet – she looked at him – been put on any special diet. So it's normal food for you. You can have meat or the vegetarian option.

Staring at the plate with the two waffles and three strawberries, Brunfaut said, both please, Madame.

What do you mean, both?

I assume the meat dish comes with vegetables on the side?

It's *boulettes sauce lapin*.

With?

Mashed potatoes and carrots.

There you go, that's vegetarian. I'll have the *boulettes*, which means I'll have both.

Brunfaut was frightened. He had never before felt this degree of fear. But something inside him baulked at it, almost forcing him to behave as if he took none of it seriously. The nurse left. On his bed lay his pyjamas, like a disembodied corpse. His dressing gown hung limply from a hook beside the bed – this was him after his disappearance. He didn't undress and get into bed yet. He ate a waffle, took a sip of tea and smiled when he caught himself listening with baited breath, then opening the door and glancing left and right to check whether the coast was clear. He left the room and took the lift down to reception to go for a beer in the canteen.

No alcohol in the hospital canteen. So he stepped out of the space-age world, through the neo-Gothic façade and into the open air, walked a short way in the stream of people who weren't thinking about death, found a café and ordered a beer.

A small beer, Monsieur?

A large one, please.

He sat with a view of a pharmacy.

Sweating, he wiped his brow with his handkerchief. Did he have a temperature? No, it was just a hot day. The sun beat down through the gap between two umbrellas and onto his back and neck. He shifted his chair slightly to one side and took off his coat.

His mobile rang. Philippe.

Listen he said, I've got something for you. Not on the phone. The picture isn't clear yet, but there are some very interesting – how shall I put it? – symptoms. I don't know if I can keep on with this, it's very risky. We need to have a chat. Could we meet tomorrow?

I'm in hospital, Brunfaut said. I'm being checked out, remember? Tomorrow I've got a series of tests, but —

How's it going? What's the doctor said?

The same as you: interesting symptoms, but the overall picture isn't clear. Can you do tomorrow evening?

Early evening. Half past six, seven.

Good. Come and visit me in the Europe Hospital, rue de Linthout. If you're coming by Metro, it's Merode station.

D'accord. See you tomorrow.

Émile Brunfaut was in a room with two beds, but fortunately the second was unoccupied, which meant he could make a number of calls that evening without annoying anyone or feeling obliged to leave the room. He could switch on the T.V. on the wall above the table, and switch it off again without having to come to any agreement with anyone. There was an interview with the chief of police, who was rejecting accusations that they had failed to act, catching a pig was no simple matter if you didn't know when and where it was going to strike next. Did he really say "strike"? Brunfaut wondered. Then the journalist asked, What did he mean by "strike"? What he meant was appearing out of the blue and unnerving passers-by, although . . . Brunfaut turned the television off in irritation. Because he was alone in the room, he could be as unsettled as he liked in a very unsettling night, tossing from side to side, getting up time and again, taking a sip of water in the bathroom, going to the loo, flushing – the flush was so loud it made him jump – he could curse when he crashed into the edge of the bed on his way back, he could snore and fart without having to lie their tensely, worrying about being discreet.

But this silver lining in his cloud was gone the following day. Early in the morning he was taken for an E.C.G. and when he got back to his room there was a man in the second bed, leaning against the fold-up head rest. He was very frail and very pale, almost translucent, his thin blond hair in a severe parting. He wore pinstripe pyjamas! Dark-blue silk, the delicate stripes in orange. His legs were crossed, and on them he balanced a laptop.

The term "ventricular extrasystoles" was still pounding inside Brunfaut's head, wrapped in the cardiologist's reassuring words as if in cotton wool. And now there was this man in his room, greeting him with such glee, apparently delighted to have a room-mate. Brunfaut, now standing between the beds, nodded to the man again and noticed that a crest was embroidered on the chest of his pyjamas, a light-blue snake – what . . .? Offering Brunfaut his hand, the man introduced himself as Maurice Géronnez.

Pleased to meet you. Brunfaut said his own name and bowed – in fact he merely bent forwards to get a better look at the crest. The snake was a stylised "S", beside which was written Solvay and beneath that, Brussels School of Economics. Brunfaut was taken aback. He possessed a scarf and T-shirt from R.S.C. Anderlecht and as a joke he'd bought a romper suit in the Anderlecht colours from the fan shop for his goddaughter Joëlle on her christening, but he had never seen or heard of anyone wearing university pyjamas.

Of course Monsieur Géronnez wanted to swap medical histories without delay. Brunfaut said tersely that he was just here for a full medical examination, a precautionary measure.

Well, Géronnez said, they'll find something, they always do, after the age of fifty you can bet your life that they'll find something; if the doctors don't find anything wrong with a man over fifty then I start asking myself what they've been studying. Then you need to change hospitals. But don't worry, you're in good hands here, the Europe is the best of the lot, here they always find something. With me it's my spleen. Isn't that strange? The spleen, of all things. Now you're going to ask me, Why is that strange? Tell me, what does the spleen do, what's its job? You see! You don't know, do you? Nobody does, ask your friends, acquaintances, ask anybody on the street. The liver, yes! The heart, that anyway! The lungs, the kidneys, you don't have to have studied medicine to know what those organs do, what their function is. But the spleen? Tell me what the job of the spleen is. You see, it's so strange! The spleen leads a shadowy existence. And yet none of the other organs we think we know about and regard as so important could function in the long term if it weren't for the spleen. The spleen controls all the other organs, it knows everything, it checks them all the time. It fends off disease in the other organs, removes damaging particles from the blood, stores white corpuscles that it releases as required, deploying them like a rapid reaction force, you might say. The heart doesn't notice if the liver has a problem, or conversely, the kidneys try to do their job whether the lungs are working properly or not, but the spleen, the spleen notices everything about everything and responds to everything. And the other organs are aware of everything the spleen does. It is the great communicator, and at the same time the secret service that nobody notices. Why does nobody notice the spleen? Because for the most part it doesn't stand out. The spleen is the organ that rarely has problems of its own. It solves other organs' problems, it fends off their illnesses wherever possible, but is rarely sick itself. Do you know what I think? I think there's something in this theory of psychosomatics. That's my suspicion. You can eat as healthily as you like, but if, metaphorically speaking, you've always got a lot on your plate, you can develop stomach trouble. Do you understand what I mean?

Yes, it's common knowledge.

You see? And in my case it's the spleen. No coincidence there. Professionally I'm a spleen, in a manner of speaking, and some time ago I realised I couldn't go on any longer, I couldn't accept what my job was and . . .

What? What are you professionally? I mean, a spleen isn't a profession. Brunfaut groaned.

I work for the European Commission, Géronnez said, in the E.C.F.I.N., that's the Directorate-General for Economic and Financial Affairs. I'm responsible for communication. Between the various organs I am, as it were, the communicator who stands in the shadows. I have to pull together and coordinate what everybody is working on and, crucially, draft the speeches that the commissioner gives to present this to the outside world. Now, picture an organism where the lungs are badly damaged by chain-smoking, the liver by excess alcohol, the stomach by chemicals in foods and you have to detoxify all this, as well as write the speeches with which the mouth will announce that everything is absolutely fine, in so far as the greatest efforts are being undertaken to ensure the organism functions as well as possible, you might save on nail-cutting, for example, by amputating all the fingers. I couldn't go on anymore, Monsieur Brunfaut. My problems began three years ago because I couldn't function any longer. Then on my desk appeared the study that Webster University and the University of Portsmouth carried out in conjunction with Vienna University of Economics and Business – just wait for this!

He tapped the keyboard of his laptop. Here! I saved it. The Impact of Fiscal Austerity on Suicide Mortality. This is dreadful, a long-term study on the relationship between fiscal austerity programmes in Greece, Ireland, Portugal and Spain and the growth in suicide rates in these countries. I don't want to bore you with figures and statistics, but let me just give you an idea: when Greece embarked on its austerity programme, the suicide rate increased by 1.4 per cent in the first year. It doesn't sound much, a low figure, but don't forget these are *people*, and now listen to this: in the third year the graph makes a steep upward curve and now we have a figure that means we have to start talking about an epidemic, and 91.2 per cent of the suicides are people over sixty whose pensions and health insurance were either cut or simply withdrawn, then in the fourth year the proportion of those over the age of forty increases in the suicide statistics, the majority of them single and long-term unemployed. In the fifth year the reduction in the unemployment figure is consistent with a marginal difference of 0.8 per cent in the number of suicide cases that year. But now, conversely – he typed something – we have Ireland. My commissioner's favourite example. There, economic growth has taken another leap forward! The model country! But what does this study show us? No drop in a suicide rate that had risen dramatically in earlier years. The study shows that the economic upturn didn't reach those places where the safety net had been destroyed previously. Do you understand?

The man's delicate nostrils vibrated.

I have to admit, I was furious when I read that. I wrote a paper for the commissioner, for the Commission's Wednesday conference, I remember beginning with the words "We are murderers" and making a few points that he, the commissioner, must propose for the Commission to honour its task of protecting European citizens. I sent a copy to the director-general, who's responsible for the economy of the Member States . . . at any rate, since then I've felt unwell. It's my spleen, it can't manage the detoxification anymore and . . .

At that moment a nurse appeared. Monsieur Brunfaut? I'm here to take you for your sonography.

Brunfaut excused himself and followed her. A speech writer who wouldn't stop speaking – it was all a bit much. Even though he had to concede that, deep down, this man was a brother-in-arms.

The bruise on Professor Erhart's forearm sustained when he fell against the radiator in the hotel had turned into a substantial dark-blue patch. It looked like a poorly executed tattoo of the map of Europe.

After the "Reflection Group" meeting Professor Erhart had not gone to dinner with the others, but instead had taken the Metro back to Sainte-Catherine. Now he was sitting at a table outside Brasserie Van Gogh, right beside the church. Passing it on the way from the Metro station to his hotel, he had spotted the oysters, lobster and prawns arranged on ice, and spontaneously sat down, as a treat. As a comfort. In defiance. After the humiliating scene at the meeting earlier.

Although it was now evening, it was still so warm that Professor Erhart took off his jacket and hung it over the back of his chair. Then he saw his involuntary tattoo. It startled him. He touched it gingerly with his fingertips, moaned softly, but it wasn't the pain, at least not the one in his arm; it was his despair, the burning of his soul.

In the think-tank meeting he had behaved like one of the anti-authoritarian students he had encountered many years ago as a professor. Even though he'd been better at dealing with them than most of his colleagues, because he had the ability to recognise talented young people and take seriously the ideas that impassioned them, he fully realised that such behaviour was unbecoming in an individual such as himself. Could he be called an unconventional professor? Not in this day and age, when everything unconventional was acknowledged only if it could also come across as mainstream. His behaviour was merely stupid, and scandalous. It would have been better to keep shtum for as long as possible, pipe up with a few brief statements until he had tested the water, diplomatically speaking. But what he'd had to listen to was such utter tosh . . . So what? You can respond to nonsense calmly and soberly too. If, for example, an expert were to postulate the theory that – metaphorically speaking – the problem in question was obesity and the best way to combat this obesity would be to eat more, to force the body to excrete more, the increased volume of excrement leading to weight loss, and so on, you wouldn't *necessarily* have to shout out that the expert was an idiot. It wouldn't be hard to do things differently. Really? On the contrary. It had spooked him that from the opening of their session there had been consensus that Europe's crisis could be solved only with those very methods which had brought it on in the first place. More of the same. Had this or that strategy failed? Then it couldn't have been implemented systematically enough! Keep on going systematically! More of the same! Had the problems not merely been exacerbated by this or that decision? Only temporarily! Don't allow any let-up in these endeavours! More of the same! It had driven him potty.

He ordered a dozen oysters followed by half a lobster. With a Chablis.

We only have Chablis by the bottle, Sir. By the glass you can have our house wine, a Sauvignon.

Then bring me a bottle of Chablis.

Gently he kept stroking the blue patch on his arm with the tips of his fingers.

The oysters. Swallowing one after the other, he wondered why he'd thought he might enjoy it. Eating oysters. The taste of oysters didn't remind him of a single happy moment in his life. So they couldn't make him happy. The best thing about the lobster was that there wasn't much of it. He had no patience for the claws. He wasn't hungry. He had simply wanted to spoil himself. He'd already drunk half the bottle of wine. In the square a man was playing German songs from the thirties on an accordion. Erhart knew them; his parents had owned the records. And then he found something he did enjoy: licking his fingers before dipping them into the bowl of warm water with lemon.

Best of all was when one of the German economists, right in the middle of the heated debate conducted in English, had said in German to Erhart: "Show some restraint!" Restraint! Him! In a discussion that was dumb beyond all restraint. A Greek financial expert had described in painstaking detail how the Greek budget deficit had come about, explaining with the authority of a man who had taken himself to safety in Oxford that things couldn't work without further swingeing cuts to the Greek welfare system. An Italian political scientist – of all people – agreed at once and underlined the necessity of abiding by the stability criteria. He gesticulated as he spoke, drawing figures-of-eight in the air with his index fingers, as if conducting a children's choir. The French philosopher – to begin with Erhart had thought it exciting that a philosopher had been invited to the think tank – insisted that the Franco-German axis be strengthened again, a demand that even their colleague from Estonia agreed with. The only minor difference of opinion emerged between the two Germans who couldn't agree on whether Germany should exercise her claim to leadership in Europe "with greater confidence" or "with greater humility". This is how the meeting had progressed, leaving Erhart to wonder what had happened to these people that after years of study and striving for professorships and positions of responsibility, all they knew was how to formulate the well-honed experience of years and years as a desideratum for future policy. I don't need a think tank for that, Erhart had heckled, all I need is a tabloid!

Then things had kicked off until one of the Germans, who was unknown beyond the walls of the Department of Economic Sciences at Aachen University, said to Erhart in German, "Show some restraint!"

A British professor of cultural sciences at Cambridge University said that the fundament of unified Europe was Christianity, and today we were seeing this single unifying factor disappearing both at a socio-political level and from individual behaviour.

At that point Professor Erhart had leaped to his feet and —

No, he said, he didn't want any dessert. He finished his bottle of wine, paid and left. He had been prepared for everything, but not everything in caricature. He was in contact with colleagues in various countries with whom he could hold productive discussions, there were plenty of initiatives, foundations and N.G.O.s who, he could assume, understood what Europe was about. He corresponded with them, followed their blogs. But far too little seeped into the consciousness of the general public. And thus he had placed great hope in this "New Pact" think tank, which had a direct link to the president of the European Commission. So close to power. Evidently, however, the only thing so close to power was a bubble, as vacuous as a soap bubble, and yet indestructible – if you stuck a needle in it didn't burst; it only floated buoyantly upwards. He tripped. Almost. He steadied himself. Brussels cobbles. People sat on the terraces of cafés, blinking in the setting sun. A juggler kept four, six, eight, *eight!* balls in the air. The accordion player. Erhart tossed a coin into his hat and he played "*Junge, komm bald wieder!*" Tourists took photographs with selfie sticks outside the church. Erhart crossed the square, but rather than go back to his hotel he turned into rue Sainte-Catherine. He wandered aimlessly, glancing occasionally into shop windows, but all he ever saw was his pallid face with the large black-rimmed spectacles and the white hair that stood up from his head as if he'd been electrified. Entering rue des Poissoniers he noticed a coffee house on the corner, Café Kafka. How apt, he thought, and went in for a glass of wine. Now he was well and truly tiddly. He had always liked a drink, but usually to celebrate, not out of frustration. He had only ordered the bottle of Chablis because he'd heard somewhere that you drink Chablis with oysters. His wife had known things like that. Trudi. If she were still alive he would call her and she'd say, You've got to do better tomorrow. You have a vision. Don't insult the others! Just try to explain to them your vision.

He paid and moved on. Crossing boulevard Anspach he noticed an old shopfront to his left, which looked like an elegant jeweller's, and made for it – why? He didn't need any jewellery. Trudi was dead. And she had never cared for it anyway. It was pure veneer. The sign above the shop read: "mystical bodies". He peered in through the window. Needles and pins with tiny stones at one end, drawings – what was this? Eventually he realised that this was where you could get piercings and tattoos.

He went in. A young man was sitting at a large, empty desk, the sort you might imagine would grace the office of a president.

Erhart greeted him and said he would like a tattoo. He found the situation so surreal, and yet as vivid as an intense dream. He had thought that tattoo artists were themselves always tattooed from head to toe, but this boy didn't have one, at least not one that was visible.

You want . . .

Yes, Erhart said, taking off his jacket and stretching out his arm

233

towards the boy. I want twelve five-pointed stars here, on this . . . on this blue patch.

That's a bruise.

Yes.

And you want me to tattoo stars on it?

Yes, please.

Why?

Don't you think it looks like Europe?

What?

Look! This here is the Iberian peninsula, and this little protrusion is quite clearly the boot, don't you think?

Italy?

Yes. And where it frays there, that's Greece. Surely you can see that.

With a bit of imagination, yes. But the proportions aren't right, it's, no, that's not Europe, it's a distorted picture. Whatever, it's going to heal – at least for your sake I hope it will.

In this mark I see Europe. And now I want the stars to go with it. How much would it cost?

No. I'm not going to do it. The blood vessels are damaged, capillaries burst, I'm not going to stick a needle in there, I can't really see what I'm doing. I wouldn't touch your arm. And in a few weeks' time it'll have vanished anyway. So you'd have the stars, but not the reason for having them.

So no stars for a vanishing Europe?

Sorry, man, I'm not doing it.

Nobody in the Ark could have imagined the violent storm the Jubilee Project would unleash in the Commission, even though the storm had announced itself in precisely the way major storms do: with an eerie silence.

To begin with, Eurostat had delivered the goods. Their answer was thorough, full of figures, but not helpful.

Statists! Bohumil had said in German to Martin with a shrug.

You mean statisticians!

Yes.

Purged of its tables of figures, its formulae and graphics, what Eurostat was saying left Martin so astounded that he read the paper three times over, then stared at it in disbelief for an hour. Essentially what the Eurostat expert had written meant that, in all statistics-based projections, the individual was a confounding variable, Martin thought. You could read the information thus: with his unfathomable will, God ultimately renders all available statistical data relating to human beings obsolete.

They knew how many ninety-year-old men and women were alive in Europe today. And they knew that the gap in life expectancy between women and men closed as people got older. These days, ninety-year-old women still had an average of four years left to live, men another three and three-quarters. The number of Holocaust survivors in 1945 could only be estimated. There were no figures relating to the ratio of men to women. But assuming that the differing life expectancies of men and women aligned as people got older, any projection of the life expectancy of Holocaust survivors without any differentiation between the sexes, to find out how many might still be alive today, must fail because life expectancy differed between countries and the distribution of survivors amongst these countries was unknown. It makes a difference whether a Holocaust survivor lives in Germany, Poland, Russia, Israel or the U.S.A. It was also necessary to take into account whether the individual was well off or lived below the poverty threshold. In 2005 (see note) an Israeli demographer estimated that 40 per cent of Holocaust survivors were living at or below the poverty threshold. These people had undoubtedly been dealt the worst hands, tempting one to assume that none of them were still alive today, although this could not be proved because another statistic suggested the opposite: people who have suffered long periods of hunger in their youth had a greater life expectancy, and in old age too were better able to brace themselves physically against deprivation than those who had never experienced such a physiological pressure to adapt. It should be noted, however, that not only Holocaust survivors, but large sections of the civilian population suffered epidemic hunger in areas affected by, or occupied during, the war, which was why no formula existed for exclusively calculating the life expectancy and probable numbers of Holocaust survivors still living today.

Now the Eurostat expert returned to the aforementioned life expectancy of ninety-year-olds today: "If we start with the assumption that the youngest of the Holocaust survivors still alive was born in 1929 – for they had to be at least sixteen years of age for admission into a camp; anyone younger was sent straight to the gas chambers – then, on the basis of life expectancy statistics, we know that there must be a certain number of survivors. But even if we knew the precise figure, we would not be able to say whether the statistic applies to them, i.e. whether they correspond to the statistical mean. All of them must be over ninety, which means that theoretically they have an average life expectancy of between three and three-quarters and four years. It is possible, however, that within a year 100 per cent of the unknown total of survivors will be dead or all 100 per cent could still be alive. Both are within the deviation range." Then came the sentence which now danced before Martin's eyes, as if it were printed in capital letters: "THIS IS NO LONGER STATISTICS, IT IS DESTINY!"

Martin forwarded the Eurostat information to Xeno with some

accompanying remarks. He suggested leaving open for the time being the question of whether they should put as many Holocaust survivors as possible (so far as they could be accounted for) at the centre of the Jubilee celebrations or just a small, representative group (individuals from different countries), or even a single representative. What was crucial at this initial stage was to win general acceptance for the idea; the Jubilee should be perceived as an opportunity to show the wider European public that the Commission was not merely the "guardian of the treaties of the Union" (as it said on the Commission's website), but more importantly the guardian of the greater and broader vow that a breach of European civilisation such as Auschwitz would never occur again. This "eternity clause", Martin wrote, had to be presented as the actual beating heart of the Commission to make it not only an abstract "bureaucracy", but a "moral authority". The presentation of the final testimonials of the Holocaust could forge the necessary emotional connection of the public to the Commission's work. Ultimately the Commission's poor profile was down to the fact that it was seen as the apparatus of a mere economic community, which stood for an economic policy that was being rejected by ever greater numbers of people. Now there needed to be a permanent reminder of the fundamental European idea, in the words of Jean Monnet: "All our efforts are the lessons of our historical experience: nationalism leads to racism and war, and with dire logic to Auschwitz."

For this reason the first Commission president, Walter Hallstein from Germany, gave his inaugural speech in Auschwitz. Later this idea was taken up by Commission presidents Jacques Delors and Roman Prodi. The new president, too, spoke at Auschwitz at the liberation commemoration on 27 January and declared that "the economic integration of nations is not an end in itself merely to generate economic growth, but a prerequisite for the more profound purpose of the European project: to thwart in the future national wilfulness and ultimately nationalism, which leads to resentment and aggression against others, to the division of Europe and ultimately to Auschwitz."

Martin concluded his e-mail to Xeno with the strong recommendation that the project should not be financed by the E.U. budget, but that the money should come exclusively from the coffers of the Commission itself. This would avoid the need for any agreement with the Council or Parliament (involving predictably lengthy negotiations and what would turn out to be unproductive compromises) and in the end the image boost would be exclusively to the benefit of the Commission.

Xeno informed Mrs Atkinson and asked for her consent that the project should be financed exclusively from the Commission's budget. Mrs Atkinson had other worries, however. A few days earlier a rumour had been doing the rounds on social media that the Commission, bribed by lobbyists for the big pharmaceuticals, was planning to impose a ban on homeopathy. Within a day, one and a half million e-mails of protest had come in from all over Europe, almost crashing the Commission's server. The German tabloid newspaper, *BILD*, published the false report as its lead story, the headline – tempered by a question mark – in huge letters: "Bonkers Brussels Bureaucrats?" The *Sun*, *Kronenzeitung*, *Blesk*, *A Hola*, even *El País*, *France Soir* and – although not on the cover – *Libération* reported the story too. Each of these hysterical articles concluded with an appeal to protest to the Commission against the corporations and their lobbyists. Mrs Atkinson sat at her desk, wringing her hands in despair. Her long, slender fingers were cold and blue. She kneaded, pressed and massaged them as she pondered how she might counter this nonsense effectively. A press release with an emphatic denial had been printed only by the *Neue Zürcher Zeitung*, and this had led to another shitstorm on social media: everyone knew which major pharmaceutical companies had their headquarters in Switzerland. Mrs Atkinson wondered why newspapers that could hardly be described as anti-capitalist rags were appealing with such relish for a campaign against the big corporations, gunning especially for the European Commission, which itself was locked in battle against the un-bridled power of large corporations. After all, only recently the Commission had dished out fines to Microsoft and Amazon that totalled more than a billion euros.

Mrs Atkinson was an economist by training, not a specialist in communications, even though this was now her field of work. She had applied for the job to improve the Commission's image; she had planned an offensive, but had been on the back foot ever since. The Commission president had asked to see her about this hom-eopathy story: did she have a plan, how could the damage to the Commission's reputation be curtailed and its achievements better communicated?

Yes, of course.

And when would they be able to see the fruits of this plan?

For the time being she couldn't say.

To err on the side of caution he would only call a plan a plan if there was the realistic likelihood of a desired outcome which could be verified rapidly.

Yes, Sir.

She kneaded her hands. She couldn't take Fenia Xenopoulou's idea any further just now. But she was grateful for her commitment and would certainly be able to help in the medium or longer term.

"I agree to the financing from the Commission budget," she wrote back, "but I would like a precise costing and a tally of the necessary resources, including staff. Go ahead!"

Now Xeno gave Martin the O.K. Please prepare a "note" by tomorrow for the Inter-Service Consultation. With the anticipated level of funding required, a schedule, all necessary resources, including staff, and the desired contribution from other Directorates-General.

Afterwards she dutifully searched amongst the papers on her desk, the side table and on the shelf for the novel she hadn't picked up for at least three weeks – the president's favourite. At last she had been given an appointment by his office; the timing was good. Now she had something she could show him: a project with which she would place culture, the wallflower within the Commission, at the centre of public awareness. Anybody who could pull this off – and surely the president would realise this – ought to secure a better position in the Commission. And ideally in the D.-G. TRADE, where she could work alongside Fridsch. On the other hand was it such a good idea to work so closely with the man she . . . what? She hesitated even to think of the word "love". And first he would have to learn to overcome a certain professional distance. During their recent dinner at the Italian restaurant he had been polite and friendly in the way you were with acquaintances or valued colleagues, but when they slept together afterwards he had ended up weeping. It's just sweat, he'd said, wiping the tears from his face, but she was certain they had been tears of happiness and emotion.

She found the book. Although she knew what she had to discuss with the president, it wouldn't hurt to get in the mood by reading his favourite novel.

She leafed through the pages at random, then began to read . . . and gasped in shock when she encountered this sentence: "Once she called a cosmetician so she could try out different types of make-up for the time when she would be lying in a coffin, mourned by her weeping lover." What shocked Xeno was that she could picture herself in this situation right now: lying in a coffin, immaculately made-up, with a smile that can be conjured only by the thought of one's lover as one enters eternity. And Fridsch . . .

Eight

"Get in trouble, good trouble!"

BLUE LIGHTS WERE flashing all around the Pietà, and above it an emergency helicopter circled. More and more people, men and women, young, old, children, poured onto the scene, some stopped in horror and stared, but most began to run, they ran towards the police officers who stood in a row across the carriageway, their arms outstretched. Stop! Stay where you are! The police tried to prevent people moving forwards and closed off the motorway to allow the emergency helicopter to land, but the swelling mass charged at them and past them as well as past the police cars parked across the lanes. These people didn't understand the situation, they couldn't see the injured, didn't care about the wrecked cars, all they could think about was that the authorities were trying to stop them and send them back, perhaps they thought the emergency helicopter was a police or military chopper, a forlorn yet threatening gesture by the Austrian border police who couldn't stop them, they had already crossed the Hungarian–Austrian border, they had come this far, they wanted to head on to Germany, nothing was going to stop them now.

Journalists were already there too, filming and taking photographs and getting in the way. And the image of the Pietà in the midst of all this chaos would speed around the world: the woman in black with a headscarf, sitting on a suitcase, the man in a business suit lying across her lap. On her face the rain like tears. She supported his head with her right hand, her left was stretched upwards, her head thrown back, she gazed at the sky and in the photograph it appeared as if the woman in the headscarf were levelling a desperate accusation at heaven. She looked up at the helicopter.

This woman had been the first to realise that the man needed to be stabilised.

Pulling her suitcase behind her, she had heard the crash, the bang, something that sounded like an explosion. Without understanding anything, she had seen people scatter before her, leap to the side, screaming, and all of a sudden she was standing beside the wreck, hanging from which was a groaning man.

The man was Florian Susman.

People had been walking towards him on the motorway, police cars with flashing lights and sirens had driven past and stopped a short distance beyond. By that stage he had been driving at a crawl, and then he put his foot fully on the brake and stopped the car. He switched on the hazard lights. He had seen a policeman approaching, brandishing a glowstick. The policeman was perhaps no more than twenty metres away when he screamed, screamed in a way that for a split second – which was also a moment of eternity – Florian saw nothing but this screaming, through the wet windscreen he saw the policeman's gaping mouth as if in close-up, zoomed in and grotesquely distorted. The policeman dived to one side.

Later, Florian was unable to remember the crash, the violent collision, the aggressive sound of crunching metal, the bang of exploding tyres, only one very fleeting moment in which he felt – with an astonishment greater than the shock and the pain – like a prisoner in a confined capsule being hurled about by an incredible force. Jammed in, he saw himself careening along past blurred images, an incoherent film, strangely without any sound.

He first regained consciousness, but only briefly, in the hospital when his clothes were cut from his body with a large pair of scissors. He opened his eyes, the scissors were moving up his torso, cleaving his polo shirt, as if he were being opened up, he saw a face above his, heard the words: Do you understand? Can you understand me?

He said something about pigs, the pigs, it was incomprehensible, then he passed out.

A taxi driver from the Burgenland, who had raced to the border crossing at Nickelsdorf several times already that day to bring refugees to the Westbahnhof in Vienna, from where they could travel on by train to Munich, had been in a hurry to collect his next fare. It was good, fast money – those poor bastards didn't bat an eyelid at paying three times the usual fare. In his rush, his greed, his frenzy, he hadn't noticed that the traffic in front of him had come to a standstill, and so without even touching the brakes he ploughed straight into Florian Susman's car.

The woman, who with the help of her son carefully lifted Florian from the wreck, laid him in her lap and held his head still, she was his salvation. Florian had a broken vertebra, but the delicate extrication and stabilisation had prevented damage to his spinal cord – otherwise he would have been paralysed. Florian realised this only when Martin came to the hospital with the papers that carried the Pietà photograph. You're on the front page!

Because of this photograph the Christian Occident, fearful of the inrush of Muslims, was touched to the core for one historic second. The Muslim woman who had saved Florian was a Madonna.

How might things have turned out differently if Florian hadn't had the accident? Had Martin Susman stayed in Brussels rather than flying straight to Vienna to be with his brother, he might have been able to prevent, or at least keep in check the turmoil that his

Jubilee paper unleashed. But while Martin looked after his brother, conflicts and arguments broke out in the European Commission back in Brussels, escalating very rapidly and in such a way as to render any rational solution impossible. There wasn't even the option of a compromise. Who was to blame for this uproar, who had come up with this mad idea? Mrs Atkinson? Xeno? Martin.

But if everybody is merely doing their duty, can there be culprits? And what is "duty"? Abiding by the bureaucratic rules, the stipulated procedures? Or defending interests to which one is beholden, or feels beholden? Everything is ground between the big wheels above and the little wheels below, and in the end nothing has happened, even if the crashing and crunching of the milling process causes jumpiness and agitation to begin with. And yet before Martin's departure for Vienna, he and Xeno had been confident that the Jubilee Project would now smoothly run its course. They had interpreted the calm before the storm as the absence of objections, as silent acquiescence. And they felt reassured and protected by the encouragement and protection from "the very top".

Xeno had at last had her meeting with the Commission president, two days before the Inter-Service Meeting she had called on account of the Jubilee Project. Well, not actually with the president himself, but with his private secretary. Even this was an honour, an acknowledgement of her work and an unmistakable show of interest in her as an individual, for officials of Xeno's status were usually granted a meeting with a staff member from the president's office at best. Was this privilege perhaps the result of an intervention by Fridsch, who had strongly recommended her for higher accolades? Then again, hadn't she expected even more than this, a meeting with the president himself? Wasn't that why she had prepared so meticulously for him, studying his biography, his likes and dislikes, even reading his favourite book? But she must have realised when, after she had been promised a meeting ("What's it about?", "We'll try our best!"), they kept putting her off until finally Fridsch said, A meeting with the president is merely a meeting with someone from his office! Especially if you're from Culture.

He smiled.

Imagine, he said, that the president doesn't really exist. That there haven't been any presidents since Jacques Delors! Only puppets. The strings are being pulled by the office. Every word the president utters is being spoken by his ventriloquists. Everything he says has long been decided and whenever he signs something his hand is guided. Have you seen the president on television, when he meets heads of state? How he pulls on the tie of one and gives another a little nudge? These are the only snippets of improvisation, the only autonomy he can permit himself, his personal note in this mechanism of power, so to speak – his ironic game: he, who is hanging by so many threads, pokes fun at it all by pulling and nudging as if he were the puppet master himself. So, Fridsch had said, you will get your meeting with the president, but don't expect a meeting with the puppet himself.

Thus Xeno was sitting face to face with the Commission president's private secretary, Romolo Strozzi, whose full name, as she had gleaned from his Wikipedia entry, was Romolo Augusto Massimo Strozzi, the last and childless descendant of an ancient noble Italian family. Various anecdotes about him and his unconventional manner were doing the rounds of the European institutions. He was known as a "colourful figure", and to her astonishment Xeno realised that this might be literally true: Strozzi wore a blue suit, a yellow handkerchief in the breast pocket and a red waistcoat that both emphasised his stomach and contained it. He wasn't fat, just plump enough to demonstrate that he was no ascetic, a fact reinforced by the signal red of his waistcoat. Strozzi was an anomaly at this level of power, which was dominated by the "Énarques", graduates of those elite schools such as the École Nationale d'Administration, slim men in discreet, not-too-expensive suits (ascetic in every respect) capable of negotiating for hours on end and all night long too. They appeared to need barely any food and as good as no sleep, they got by with few words, few gestures, they avoided sugaring their souls with the sweetness of empathy, they didn't need a public arena (for them the metabolism within power was enough), they eschewed the outside gloss. In their lives and work there was no ornament; everything was as clear as it was invisible. Xeno was able to pass professional judgement on this type of man, having learned how to, having been prepared for it in her elite schools and having come across them throughout her career to date. Now she sat opposite this Baroque Italian count, who stuck out his red paunch at her and spoke with expansive gestures like an operetta conductor, his signet ring dancing before her eyes. It wasn't ridiculous, it was thoroughly awe-inspiring and impressive, and anything else from a man in his position was inconceivable. Nevertheless, Xeno was bewildered by his manner and found it difficult to cope with. Not only did he speak perfect Italian, German, English and French, but he opened the conversation, licking his lips with relish, in Ancient Greek. When Xeno just stared at him blankly, he apologised: his modern Greek was so rudimentary, unfortunately, that it would pain her to hear it. And he was always forgetting that Ancient Greek was as foreign a language to Greeks as Swahili.

Ἐν ἀρχῇ ἦν ὁ λόγος, he said, then added, Ἀλλ ὁ λόγος ἦν ἁμαρτοεπής. In the beginning was the word. But the word was wrong. *Je suis désolé*, he said with a chuckle.

Xeno felt intimidated by this jaunty assault. She had done her homework on Conte Strozzi in order to be able to gauge him, to avoid being caught off guard and to deliver the right responses in their negotiations as swiftly as possible. But only now – too late – did she grasp what it really meant, all that she had heard and read about him: the Strozzis had been elevated to the nobility centuries back, by Holy Roman Emperor Frederick II, and they were related by blood and marriage to the Austrian, German and Czech aristocracy. Romolo Strozzi's grandfather had been a war criminal as commander of a unit of the Italian 9th Army which carried out mass shootings in Montenegro in 1941 and 1942. In 1964, however, his father, a graduate of the diplomatic academy, became the youngest member of the negotiating team that prepared for the Italian government the European Community Merger Treaty, which led to the establishment of the European Council and Commission. His Austrian great-uncle, Nikolaus Graf Khevenhüller, was a fanatical National Socialist who became deputy Gauleiter of Carinthia in January 1945, but then vanished to Spain at the beginning of May that year, where until his death in 1967 he lived undisturbed as "advisor" to the Spanish secret police with an honorarium from Generalissimo Franco. By contrast his great-aunt Marion (née von Tirpitz) married the German resistance fighter Ulrich Hesse, became a local politician for the Social Democrats in Hannover and secretary of the Association of the Victims of National Socialism.

This family history was probably the reason for the most famous quotation attributed to Romolo Strozzi: "*L'Europe, c'est moi!*"

It was without doubt a fascinating family history, but it puzzled Xeno too. It was entirely alien to her that all this could have a continuing influence and put its stamp on a person's biography. She had a notion of family in which ancestors were people you only knew about because of the existence of photography, and even then you knew little more than their names. In essence they were people who probably hadn't lived much differently from her own parents, people who stuck together and helped each other, prisoners of their circumstances, that was how it must have been, for no stories existed about them, they didn't give rise to any, just now and again a special case cropped up like Uncle Kostas – the one with the undying love – and then, in the end, the complete break: like hers – she had left everything behind. When Xeno finished reading the detailed Wikipedia entry about Romolo Strozzi, she wasn't particularly impressed by this man's origins and family. For her that was all window dressing – even though Strozzi was private secretary to the Commission president, the entry made it sound as if his main job was that of being a descendant, and Xeno found this insane. But another nugget of information had surprised and impressed her: at the 1980 Summer Olympics, Romolo Strozzi had won a fencing medal – bronze – in the individual sabre.

Did you know that? She had asked Fridsch.

Yes, he'd said, I heard. Those were the Moscow games. They say that Strozzi benefited from the fact that lots of countries – I don't know how many – boycotted the games in protest at the Soviet invasion of Afghanistan. So a number of world-class fencers weren't there.

But he qualified, he fenced and he won a medal.

Yes, he did. And do you know what's interesting? Queneau told me this one time: the Italians didn't boycott the games, but they competed under the Olympic flag – the five rings on a white background – rather than their national one. And to honour the victorious Italian athletes they played "Ode to Joy" instead of the national anthem. At the time the Strozzi family was said to have had substantial influence over the Italian Olympic committee's decision.

Xeno looked at Strozzi, the signet ring danced before her eyes and all she could think about this man with the red paunch was: an Olympic medal in fencing! She knew nothing about the sport. Why should she? Strozzi had won his medal for the sabre. That wasn't the foil. Had Xeno known the difference she could have better gauged how their conversation would go.

She had expected him to come straight to the point, without beating about the bush. Men like him have little time. He would ask Xeno directly what he could do for her, then either show or feign an interest, and she would have to present her case with great speed and precision to ensure his reaction would tend towards "being interested". But to her astonishment he said, Do you know what interests me? And I'd like to hear your opinion on this. What do you think about the burkini ban? I'm asking you as a woman. I'd really like to know what you've got to say. Do you think men like the mayor of Nice should be allowed to determine what women wear or, more accurately in this case, what they should take off? A woman has to take off her clothes, is that our Christian culture? Yes? What do *you* think? You wouldn't believe how many requests we've had for the Commission to take a position on this.

Xeno was speechless.

Strozzi smiled. Perhaps it's an unfair question, he said. My personal opinion is that the burkini protects women from skin cancer.

Xeno didn't know if Strozzi was seriously expecting her to —

But calls for a ban are growing louder by the day, he said. On what basis could we implement that? A war on fanaticism and orthodoxy? There is no policy that obliges us to go in that direction. Thank goodness. We could turn out the light in Europe and shut up shop. Because we'd have to ban the kaftan and the shtreimel too, and —

The what?

The shtreimel. It's the huge round felt hat that Orthodox Jews wear.

But there is a difference, Xeno said, her voice almost non-existent.

Of course there's a difference. There are differences in all things that are similar. And all things that differ from each other are also alike! Let me tell you something: we'd even have to ban business suits. In this building I'm surrounded by men in business suits. They're like a uniform. They all look identical. It's frightening. And believe you me, all these men are orthodox and fanatics in their own way. So would you say that they should take off their suits?

Xeno looked at Strozzi in disbelief. He laughed, leaned back and opened his arms wide. Then he bent forwards, still smiling, but languorously now, with a profoundly curious expression, and said, But I don't wish to waste your precious time. Tell me straight out what I can do for you.

The fact that Strozzi said he didn't want to waste her time was more than an ironic reversal of the situation; it was a classic *doublé* as a fencer would say. Xeno couldn't break through his guard because she didn't even know what a guard was. She had no idea how fencing can shape a man. Which was why she, who always prepared so thoroughly for every situation, was not at all prepared for Strozzi. Pre-empting the opponent's clear intention, dodging and tricking, setting up the feints, *doublé*, feint thrust, feint cut and then the hit after a sudden, unexpected lunge. And before the opponent knows it, the whole thing is over, you shake hands with a show of respect and the greatest deference. Before she knew it

Xeno was being shown to the lift by an intern and escorted to the foyer of the Berlaymont. She stepped out into the light of a virtually exploding sun and walked back, as if numbed, to her office in rue Joseph II. What had just happened?

Strozzi had already rattled Xeno with his unexpected overture in Ancient Greek, before catching her entirely off-guard by switching to French. She had accepted the challenge, even though she felt unsure in French; she would rather have spoken English, which they were both fluent in. Strozzi must have known this, he had been briefed down to the last detail. Conversing in French, Strozzi was able to move more freely and elegantly than she was, and dominate the bout at will. And the burkini story – was he serious? He can't have been – it was the perfect deception. Xeno was so dumbfounded that she was no longer alert, she had lost her concentration. And now, on the way back to the office, she couldn't be sure what the repercussions of the conversation would be. On the contrary, she kept telling herself that in the end she had put in a good performance; she kept reinterpreting the key moments of the meeting in her head as if playing a film clip, winding it back and playing it again until she was convinced: yes, it had been a triumph! She might have shown weakness, but ultimately it had been a victory!

She had known that he had known that her principal aim was to secure a transfer to a different Directorate-General. For this had been the original reason given for the meeting. It was also the reason it had taken so long to get one. That was not how things were done; without an intervention she would never have been granted the meeting. And she hadn't even touched on the topic. She had presented the Jubilee Project. She thought it the perfect strategy. She would showcase the significance and merits of the Commission and improve its public image. It had been her idea, she had the vision and she could pull it off. In due course it would be evident that she deserved a more important position in this institution. That didn't need to be articulated any more overtly for the time being; all she needed now was the president's approval and formal support. If he were to express his wish that this Jubilee celebration take place, there would be no going back. Everybody would have to pull together. Xeno had handed Strozzi Martin's paper and explained the idea in a nutshell, placing particular emphasis on the fact that this was about the Commission rather than "the E.U.", it was about stripping the Commission of its image as an institution of unworldly bureaucrats and presenting it as guardian of the lessons of history and of human rights. For this reason too it was important that funding for the project came exclusively from the Commission's budget, and of course what it needed most of all was the president's support. Surely the project must be in the president's interest, particularly now, when the Commission was suffering from a serious image problem. She pictured the Jubilee celebrations being opened with a keynote speech from the president and —

D'accord, Strozzi had said, *d'accord*. I don't believe I'm overstretching the elasticity of my authority if I —

Pardon?

I believe, he said with a smile, that I have the authority to grant you my approval straight away, without need for consultation. The president supports this idea and will give a speech at the opening ceremony. I'll have a protocol of our conversation with the approval drawn up immediately and you will receive it today.

This was Xeno's triumph. She had got what she wanted. This is what she was telling herself when, having arrived back at 70, rue Joseph II, she fetched a coffee from the canteen. With her coffee she made for a table in the courtyard where she joined two salamanders, and suddenly she felt a warm affection for Conte Strozzi, yes, business suits ought to be banned, she asked whether anybody had a cigarette, this was the moment for one of the very occasional cigarettes, and the salamanders recoiled as if she had asked for arsenic or opium. Martin and Bohumil stepped into the courtyard with their coffee cups, Xeno waved them over and said, Good news! The Jubilee Project now has the president's full backing. Have either of you got a cigarette for me?

She was nagged by a feeling of unease, which she pushed to the back of her mind. What she was suppressing were the comments Strozzi had made at the end of their conversation, about the planning for the project: Oh yes, I'll look into how we might involve the Member States.

The Member States? You mean the Council? Xeno had said. Why? We agreed that the project is the Commission's baby.

Yes, absolutely. But the Member States founded the Commission.

Bien sûr.

This was precisely the point at which Xeno was not alert. This "*bien sûr*" opened up her guard. She didn't notice the sabre cut. And that was the end of it. With her "*bien sûr*" she now had around her neck those institutions that Martin, with good reason, had recommended ought to be kept out of it: the European Council and European Parliament. Instead of everyone pulling together, from now on there would be an almighty tangle; rather than the common interest prevailing, many different interests would be brought to the fore. Only a few days later Xeno, who had been so keen to demonstrate her *visibilité*, now wanted to become invisible, to offload everything onto Martin – who just happened to be sitting at his brother's bedside at Lorenz Böhler Hospital in Vienna.

*

But first there was the Inter-Service meeting. This too ran incredibly smoothly. Most of the directorates-general didn't turn up. For anybody in the Commission wishing to advance a project, a general lack of interest in it came as a great relief. It meant that you didn't have to grapple with endless opinions, counter-opinions, unproductive suggestions and petty criticism, but could make rapid and immediate progress and get to a stage from which there was no turning back. And now everybody had been informed.

Somebody *did* turn up from the D.-G. COMM (Communications), of course. After all, the idea for the project had originated with Mrs Atkinson, with whom Xeno was in regular contact. A representative came from the D.-G. HOME (Migration and Internal Affairs), which was to prove most fruitful as Holocaust commemoration was one of their fields of activity; it meant they could bring useful skills and contacts to the project. A young man came from the D.-G. TRADE. This had been arranged by Fridsch, who was evidently interested in Xeno's project; the young man himself just made the odd note and nodded occasionally. It came as a surprise that somebody turned up from the D.-G. JUST (Justice and Consumer Affairs). As it transpired, this was because the JUST official responsible for cooperation with the E.A.C. (Culture) was the grandson of French Holocaust survivors. Martin had immediately taken an interest: were his grandparents still alive? No, unfortunately not: they had been dead for more than thirty years.

No-one here from AGRI? Martin said ironically at the beginning of the meeting.

The D.-G. AGRI (Agriculture) was the ministry that commanded the biggest budget, comparable to a state within a state, with fierce interest-driven politics, but notorious for its lukewarm engagement with the interests of other directorates-general. The official from COMM said, The farmers only assume responsibility when grass has grown over the issue.

Not only were there no objections in the meeting to a major campaign to boost the Commission's image, but nobody questioned the idea of putting Auschwitz survivors at the heart of the Commission's jubilee either. The news that the project had the president's unqualified backing ensured that Martin's paper was accepted in toto and only a few practical and organisational details were discussed: schedule, financing and necessary resources, including staff. After one and a half hours the meeting was over and everything seemed to be definitively on track.

Friday afternoon. On the way home Martin Susman had stopped off at the cheese shop on Vieux Marché to buy a baguette, a bottle of white Sancerre and a small selection of cheeses. The sales assistant, a young man whose own mouth watered at everything he sliced and packed with such relish, had also talked him into buying a fig mustard from Ticino, a new addition to their range. You won't believe this, but it's even better than the *moutarde aux figues* from Burgundy, he said, ecstatically and audibly kissing the tips of his fingers. And fig mustard is an absolute must with goat's cheese, he said, but of course you know that. But this time you really have to take the one from Ticino.

Alright then, this time I'll take the one from Ticino, said Martin, who had never bought fig mustard from this shop before.

Once home Martin arranged the cheeses on a plate and put the plate on the table together with the mustard. Cheese with mustard? He tore off a piece of the baguette, it tasted like cotton wool. It was sticky and hot, he took off his shoes and trousers and opened a window. The wine wasn't chilled. He put the bottle in the freezer, took a Jupiler from the fridge, stood by the open window and looked down at the square. He drank beer from the bottle, smoked a cigarette, looked out of the window at the hustle and bustle down below, the ash fell from his cigarette, the cheese melted and ran on the plate.

The view from his window reminded Martin of a children's book he had adored and spent ages poring over time and again, even before he had learned to read. It was called *The City*, a large-format search-and-find book with colourful, detailed scenes. His mother had never had the time to look at the book with him and he couldn't remember who he'd been given it by, but it must have been a present because his parents would never have bought it for him. Sometimes Florian, his elder brother, would sit on his bed and they'd gaze at the book together, just as he was staring out at the square now – Where is the flower lady?

There!

Where is the policeman!

There!

Where is the postman?

There!

Where is the fire engine?

There!

Where is the fountain?

There!

Where is the vegetable stall?

There!

Where is the man with the shorts and camera?

There!

Where is the woman with the shopping bag?

There!

Where are the soldiers with the machine guns?

There, there, there, there and there!

*

His smartphone rang and Martin looked at the display. He didn't recognise the number, but he took the call anyway.

And so standing there in his underpants with a bottle of beer, looking aghast at "the city", he learned that his brother was in hospital.

When Alois Erhart was twelve years old he became a member of M.A.C., Mariahilf Athletics Club, a small but dynamic sporting association in their district of Vienna. In Erhart's recollection this had been his father's wish rather than his own, and there hadn't been any discussion: of course Alois had to become a member of the "club". Otherwise what would people say? Is the son of the sports shop owner unsporty? The world was a smaller place back then, people thought in terms of their local district identity. If you lived in Vienna's 6th district you knew as much as you possibly could about who, what, how and why, from Laimgrube over to Magdalenengrund and down through Gumpendorf to the Linke Wienzeile. Alois Erhart could remember his father raving about a wedding that had taken place in St Ägyd parish church on Gumpendorfer Platz: "That was the loveliest wedding Mariahilf has ever seen!" Mariahilf! Not Vienna! You were a "Mariahilfer", and if you walked down Mariahilfer Strasse and crossed Babenberger Strasse into the first district, you were "going into town". In Café Kafka people prattled on about only having seen the "laddie", the son of "Sport-Erhart", with books, never a ball. And all of a sudden Alois was a member of the "club". He had to choose a "section". Floor gymnastics was not an option as it was for women. Apparatus work was utterly alien to him – he was already terrified of it at school and on the horizontal bar he couldn't even manage an upward circle forwards. On the other hand he found the gymnastics instructor at M.A.C. to be a friendly and amusing man:

Jakab Görgey, a '56 refugee from Hungary who called himself "Gym Jim", welcomed him with a beguiling Hungarian accent: "The gym's a nice place of ours, for nasty folk don't play on bars." But no – no parallel bars, no horizontal bar, no horse! M.A.C. was renowned for its boxing section, having produced the Austrian champion in three weight divisions. The boxing trainer, Toni Marchandt, tweaked Alois's upper arm, croaked something incomprehensible in a hoarse voice and looked at him so contemptuously that Alois was confirmed in his belief that boxing wasn't a sport but a behavioural problem amongst madmen. He was willing to sign up for the football section – he knew the rules and boys discussed football at school, so he would be able to talk about it with more authority – and he reckoned he would be able just to trot up and down a bit without standing out, because there were always others who *really* wanted the ball.

The ball.

One day after training, which had been a mud fight in the pouring rain on the Denzel-Wiese, the coach, Herr Horak, gave Alois the club ball to take home. At the time they were still playing with a hand-stitched leather ball, a so-called "genuine" ball, an object of value with which club members distinguished themselves from street boys who played in the park with "Fetzenlaberl", balls cobbled together from scraps of fabric, or cheap plastic balls and better-quality balloons.

This time it was Alois' turn to undertake the ball care, which meant cleaning the ball of all mud, dung and rain, "work" dubbin into the little cracks and tears in the leather and then, when the leather was nicely "greased", rub and polish the ball with a soft cloth "as if it were a pair of shoes you put on for an audience with the emperor."

Alois Erhart smiled to himself. Actually, he thought, he had learned something back then which he couldn't possibly have understood: how persistent the continuing influence of history is, even in the most banal matters.

Perhaps Herr Horak had felt a pedagogical impulse and believed he could effect more engagement and identification with the club in Alois by allocating him this task. Perhaps Herr Horak had noticed that Alois had already lost all enthusiasm for attending the club, having been driven too hard during training, and then sitting on the substitute bench during the actual games, but acting as a walking advertisement for his father's shop; he alone had the latest football boots with removable studs, available from "Sport-Erhart".

So Alois took the ball home and was to bring it back the following Sunday for the game against Ottakring. One of the most important fixtures of the season, because there was a particular rivalry between Mariahilf and Ottakring: the Mariahilfer would scornfully refer to the Ottakringer as "the Bavarians", or even "the Teutons". There were historical reasons for this which nobody could quite remember. Supposedly Ottakring had been founded as a Viennese suburb by Bavarian immigrants. This legend somehow merged with the widespread hatred at the time of the "Piefkes", the Germans who were of course to blame for all misery of the war, the post-war and the occupation period. It was grotesque, but it ratcheted up the emotions which ran high enough anyway, on account of the traditional rivalry between the inner districts and outer ones, those beyond the "Gürtel".

The Ottakringer came. And the Mariahilfer had no ball.

It was in Alois' bedroom, in the dark corner beside his wardrobe. Alois hadn't turned up to the game. Having decided to quit the club he had forgotten the ball and hadn't brought it back.

One can imagine the chit-chat in Café Kafka in Capistrangasse on the Monday. Erhart's father was only able to rectify the scandal by donating to the club a brand-new "genuine" ball as well as kit for the entire team. And he took his son to task.

Alois Erhart sat on a bench in Brussels cemetery, head back, eyes closed and a smile on his face. Why was he remembering all this now?

Reliability, his father had said, is the be-all and end-all in life. Do what you want, but make that an iron law. You need to be reliable towards two sets of people: those you love and those you need.

I don't love Herr Horak, Alois said.

His father looked at him in silence.

And I don't need him, either.

Are you sure? Are you sure you'll never need him? Nor any of your teammates?

Alois looked at his father in silence.

Right. Have you understood? Repeat what I said to you.

I must be reliable.

Towards whom?

Those I love and those I need.

No, my son, we've moved beyond that. So then, towards whom?

Alois looked at his father in silence.

You must always be reliable. As a matter of principle. Towards those you love – that's obvious. But towards everybody else too, because you never know who you might need and who might do you harm. So then?

I must always be reliable.

If you make a promise what must you do?

Keep it.

If you take on a task what must you do?

Ful . . . ful . . .

Yes, fulfil it.

If somebody expects something of you and you don't make it clear from the outset that you can't do it, nor do you have any good reasons for not wanting to do it, what must you do?

Alois looked at his father.

Correct: do it! Never again do I want to be accused in Café Kafka of not being able to raise my son properly, do you understand?

Yes, Father.

Why was Alois Erhart thinking of all this now, half-moved and half-amused, as he sat on a bench in Brussels cemetery, watching and waiting.

He was angry because he'd flown back to Brussels for the second "New Pact for Europe" meeting. He was angry when he booked the flight, angry when he packed his case, angry in the taxi to the airport, furious with himself in the aeroplane, aggressive to the young lady with her honeyed voice at reception as he checked into Hotel Atlas, because the whole thing was getting on his nerves terribly, this self-important wheeling of suitcases around Brussels, this crucial hurrying to meetings, this answering of cliché with cliché, the whispering transformation of no ideas into a Babylonian gibberish – all of it was pointless as far as he was concerned, utterly pointless, it was wasted time. He wanted to roll the ball into the corner and forget.

But he had said yes. He was part of this team. Moreover, he had agreed to give the keynote speech to open the second consultation round. He had taken on this task. The ball was with him. That was why he had come. He was reliable.

He smiled.

He couldn't help it. This reliability was deeply ingrained and had taken him far. From Mariahilf around the world and to himself. Compared to that, what was the disappointment he'd felt at the first meeting of the think tank? Compared to that, what was the petty contempt he felt – yes, he, the philanthropist, had to concede that it *was* contempt – towards the other members of the group?

Could he generalise in this way? Claim that they were all contemptible? At the very least he should assign them degrees of contemptibility and degrees of efficiency. Professor Erhart divided the members of the think tank into three categories. First there were the conceited. Fundamentally they were all conceited, even he was in a way, so he needed to be more specific: the nothing-but-conceited. For them the think tank was hugely important – precisely because they were members. And that very fact exhausted the importance of the think tank, because it was all about them feeling their own importance and radiating this to the others. Erhart knew these types, he knew the way they purred self-importantly at home, at their university or other institutes where they worked: "By the way, I have to go to Brussels tomorrow. I'm in the Commission president's Advisory Group, remember!" For them this was the elixir of life: the impact on their immediate professional environment, the pride at having made it so far that they no longer had to listen, but could always lend an ear. They were easily enthralled – by themselves – when they spoke, rhetorical exhibitions of sheer bliss at being able to be part of the conversation. They never came up with a single original idea, nor could they comprehend or acknowledge any idea that hadn't already been cross-referenced hundreds of times by people of their ilk, and backed up by footnotes. In essence they were harmless. But was that really true? They were the people who could produce a majority when it came to decision-making and resolutions.

Then there were the idealists. Weren't they all idealists to a certain extent, including Erhart? But their ideals were different. What appeared to one as an ideal state of affairs – having, for example, a far greater income than other people because one had merited this in a meritocracy – contradicted another's ideal of distributive justice. Erhart had discussed such banalities in his first semester of economics. Deep down you could only call someone an idealist if they didn't actually benefit from being one. The nothing-but-idealists. To begin with they were allies against the conceited, but the alliance very quickly crumbled because there was always some aspect, some detail that contradicted their selfless ideals. They were so selfless that "to be able to look in the mirror" and see themselves they needed something that only they possessed. Which was them. When it came to voting and decision-making, suddenly they were no longer uncompromising, concerned as they were with preventing greater evils by agreeing to lesser ones. For the most part, however, the nothing-but-idealists were irrelevant for obtaining a majority as they were too few in number. Usually the nothing-but-conceited were enough to secure a majority. It was striking, however, that the idealists often voted with the conceited. They must believe the familiar, the self-evident to be less dangerous, the lesser evil compared to the vague, the uncertain, which their conscience would not permit them to embrace. What nonsense! Conscience–nonsense: Erhart apologised to himself for this silly play on words, even though it wasn't bad. He smiled. At any rate the deception was astoundingly effective: the certain, the realistic, these always appeared with tables and statistics, boxes and arrows – oh, the realistic things you could do with these! – then more boxes and arrows, sheet after sheet on the flipchart filled with boxes and arrows drawn with different-coloured markers, even the movement required to flip a sheet like that over the flipchart frame, there was something magnificent, something dynamic about it, and whoosh! New boxes on a new sheet, connected by arrows . . . The only problem was that the world didn't work like that, nor any alternative world and surely not the world hereafter either. But for the idealists you only had to draw one box, write one of their ideals inside this box, sketch a few arrows from the box up to the president, then a few arrows from below to this box, while calling out, Demand-driven, bottom-up, not top-down, and there in the tangle of arrows and connecting lines you had a net in which the idealists were trapped.

Those in the third group were smiling. Like the conceited, they smiled knowingly, but knowing better and having the last laugh – thereby laughing the longest – whenever the idealists had merely prevented the worst. These were the lobbyists. But some distinctions needed to be made here too. Wasn't he, Professor Alois Erhart, a lobbyist himself? The lobbyist for an idea? The lobbyist for certain interests, even though these – in his opinion – were for the common benefit? These lobbyists didn't have an idea like his; they couldn't even conceive that it might exist. The community, common interests – that was something they had to sell. Buy and sell, that was their world, and perhaps they even believed that this was where the only common interest lay. In such Advisory Groups they didn't represent large corporations, but the foundations of corporations. One mustn't disparage all the things they promoted, financed, supported, one ought not even to moan about their investing in mere cultural alibis, every so often all of it was of substantial benefit to society, and Professor Erhart wasn't trying to dispute that, he was an old hand not just as an economist, but also in acquiring external funding for his university. What made him mad about this think tank, however, and drove him to despair, was that the lobbyists hijacked every discussion and always came out with the same mantra: We need more growth! Whatever subject they were discussing, it always led to the same question: How do we create more growth? In-growing toenails were a problem with growth, Erhart once interjected, reaping nothing but blank looks, but the general loss of faith in European institutions was a consequence of poor growth, the menacing threat of right-wing populism – clearly if there were more growth there would be no growth in right-wing populism. And how could we generate more growth? Through greater liberalisation, of course. Instead of the Union stipulating common rules, each Member State ought to axe as many rules as possible for itself. Although there would never be a real union, there would be growth, and this would be best for the Union. It was already perfectly clear that in the end the "New Pact for Europe" group would deliver a paper to the Commission president in which the recommendation would be: We need to ensure more growth. The president would thank them politely, praise the group's important work, and then put the paper to one side without reading it, for he wouldn't have to read the paper to be able to say in his next keynote speech or interview: We need to ensure more growth!

Erhart knew that these lobbyists weren't complete cynics, not all of them. They really did believe what they were saying, first because they didn't know any different, and second because they'd learned to earn their money this way. Their mantra was well paid, everything else was less well paid or not at all. That was their experience at least. You couldn't criticise somebody for aspiring to prosperity, not even for aspiring to wealth, but you could condemn them for being venal. And they were. Objectively. With their ignorance of ideas that didn't fit the formula they were paid to defend. When they talked of the future they talked rather of a frictionless extension of the present. They couldn't understand this because they believed the future consisted of trends that prevailed for evermore. At the last session one lobbyist said, The trend is now clearly heading in the direction XY – we need to ensure that we are prepared for this development! Erhart replied, At the end of the 1920s the trend was clearly heading in the direction of fascism. Was it right to prepare for this development, or was it not perhaps better to offer resistance?

The conceited were stunned, the lobbyists grinned and the idealists – stupidly – just nodded, but then they bailed out anyway because what Erhart went on to say contained details they could not follow.

Yes, Erhart had been naive. His publications over the past few years had led him to be invited into this circle. But he had overestimated it. He had actually believed that through his ongoing work with the Advisory Group – in the president's antechamber, as it were – he would gradually be able to exert influence over the political elites and make a difference. Work on schemes that were relevant to saving the European Union. And then the ball would be in the court of Europe's political leadership.

But that was not how things played out, a fact he realised all too soon.

He would, however, stick with his keynote speech. He had promised. Even though the hopelessness of the whole situation was driving him crazy. He had committed himself, he was reliable. And he also owed it to his teacher, Armand Moens, whose grave he was now looking down on. He had arrived in Brussels around noon and the meeting with his keynote speech didn't begin until 6.00 p.m. To fill the time he had decided to take another trip to Brussels cemetery and visit the grave of his teacher, who he would cite at the beginning of his speech: "The twentieth century ought to have been the transition of the nineteenth-century national economy to a twenty-first-century economy for mankind. This was thwarted in such a horrific and criminal way that afterwards the desire returned with greater urgency, but only in the minds of a small political elite, whose successors soon no longer understood the criminal energy of nationalism and the consequences that had already been drawn from this experience."

Having taken the decision to leave the club after this, he had completely rewritten his paper. He no longer saw any reason to spend a year very patiently attempting to make it from the substitutes' bench onto the pitch. He would never get into the game. This had been his mistake: to believe he could join in with the others while also changing the rules. That didn't work. Never, ever would he win over a single person from this circle – it was as unlikely as being able to bring an assembly line to a halt by patiently carrying out your repetitive hand movements while every day telling your colleagues that you had a different notion of useful work. He would merely fulfil his duty and deliver his keynote speech. He had drafted a radical paper – for this audience it was totally insane. Just for once he had possession of the ball. And this time he had made sure that the ball was going to get its grease.

Are you talking to the dead too?

Professor Erhart looked up and saw an old man whose light-blue eyes contrasted strangely with his black, bushy eyebrows, lending the man both a radiant and sinister air. He had very little hair, but it was still black, and it looked as if it had been daubed onto his stooped head with ink. He was wearing a fine suit that was slightly too large and too warm for this hot day. The man had said, *Praat U ook al met de doden?* Professor Erhart hadn't understood.

He couldn't speak Flemish and he knew that if as a German speaker you thought you'd understood something, you were invariably wrong. Should he say in English that he didn't understand? "*Kannitverstan*" came to mind, but before he could utter it the old man repeated the sentence in French. Erhart's French was poor; he had spent a year as a visiting lecturer at the Panthéon-Sorbonne Paris I, giving lectures in English and endeavouring to learn French in this time, but he soon learned that it was better to say he wasn't fluent in the language.

He was able, however, to put together this sentence: "The dead do not answer."

As Erhart knew, the problem with a foreign language – if it wasn't at least your stepmother tongue – was that you only ever said what you knew, not what you wanted to say. The difference was the no-man's-land between the world's borders. What he had actually wanted to say was, "The dead have already given their answers before the living come up with the questions." But his French didn't stretch that far.

The old man smiled. Might he sit down?

Of course, please do.

David de Vriend sat and said, There are too few benches here! This is the only one until the – he made an expansive gesture with his hand – until the war heroes.

He wheezed and took a few deep breaths. Even walking was a real effort. De Vriend had in fact planned to spend the afternoon in his room, the blinds closed, until the worst of the heat had passed. But in the dark room he had soon lost all sense of time.

He couldn't remember how long he'd been sitting there brooding. He became thirsty.

He opened the fridge and took out the notepad.

This was the pad on which he'd written down the names of survivors as he remembered them, because over the years he'd had sporadic contact with them or from time to time he had heard or read something about them. There were nine names on the list. Five were crossed out. He looked at the list in astonishment and realised that he would have to cross out another: Gustave Jakubowicz. After the liberation of Auschwitz this man had studied law in Brussels and Paris and had become a top human-rights lawyer. For the past few years – he had been retired for a long while – he had represented refugees scheduled for deportation. De Vriend had read the news of his death in the newspaper. He looked for his biro. Pulling the blind right up he was amazed to see how brightly the sun was shining on the cemetery, the green of the treetops, the white of the gravel paths, the silvery-grey of the stones – everything seemed to be gleaming.

Then he had decided to go outside.

Alois Erhart thought that the wheezing old man who had sat beside him on the bench needed some company and wanted to chat, so he felt uncomfortable sitting there in silence. War heroes? What did he mean? On the other side of the cemetery there was no doubt a section for those who had fallen in the war. What should he say? He groped for words. Yes, Monsieur, he said eventually, very few benches. And then: Do you come here to visit relatives who – he didn't know the French for "fell", how did you say "fell"? Sure, he could say "died", he knew "die" in French – but the man was already saying, No, I come here to stroll. This cemetery is our exercise ground.

"Our?"

I live in the retirement home over there. The Maison Hanssens. That's all.

*

Now another man walked past and Erhart's first impulse was to say hello because he thought he knew him, he looked familiar, but where from? Who was he? Yes, now he remembered, it was the inspector with the huge potbelly who had questioned him at the hotel on his first visit to Brussels. The inspector passed by at a lively pace without looking at them; he had lost weight, Erhart thought.

Professor Erhart looked at his watch. It was time to leave, freshen up at the hotel and go to his meeting.

Feeling out of breath, Inspector Brunfaut slackened his pace. His shirt stuck to his sweaty back and belly, he took off his jacket. He had underestimated the length of the avenue that led to the soldiers' graves. By the victims of the Second World War was a memorial, "*Le Mur des Fusillés*", unmissable, opposite which stood a park bench. Philippe had told him to meet there. Brunfaut was late, even though on the telephone Philippe had urged him to be punctual; somebody was joining them, and they had very little time to spare.

Who?

You'll see. I can't say over the phone.

It's about . . .

Yes, exactly!

Why there?

It's what . . . my friend wanted. And we'll be able to talk in peace. Very few visitors come to the monuments, only politicians commemorating the end of the war. And that date has been and gone. So it'll just be us and a few withered wreaths.

Brunfaut checked the time: he was almost fifteen minutes late. He began to run. He pictured himself from an outsider's perspective and thought he must cut an excruciatingly awkward figure with his frantic jogging – it was no longer a walk, but he hadn't broken into a run either. He slowed down again, wiping the sweat from his face with a sodden handkerchief. Why was it so hot? This was Brussels, not the Congo!

Finally he saw before him the squares of white crosses. And there! That must be the memorial Philippe was talking about.

He saw it perfectly clearly, and yet had the impression he wasn't getting any closer. It was a nightmare.

It had been weeks since Philippe visited him in hospital to report his discoveries about the Atlas case with the means at his disposal. Or, more accurately, about the disappearance of the Atlas case.

Our I.T. department isn't bad, Philippe had explained, we can do quite a bit and I interpreted the boundaries of legality most freely. But don't forget: we are the Brussels police, so we're never using state-of-the-art technology. The whole thing is complicated by a web of security levels – how can I explain it? O.K., very roughly it's like this. If there's a piece of information, or rather the suggestion of some information, which, let's say, it's in the interest of the French secret service to keep entirely secret, then our Sureté de l'État might gain access, but not our police force. If you try to hack it, then of course an alarm goes off at their end. Now just imagine that they see the attempted hack has come from the police. And then there's Europol. The police forces of the European Member States are supposed to cooperate and exchange intelligence. But the problem is that the exchange doesn't work. Obviously every country wants to find out everything the others know, but none wants to proffer anything themselves. They turn up with their constitutions – "sorry, but our national constitution doesn't allow us to do this or that" – which means nothing happens, each snippet of information becomes like a needle in a haystack. There's always somebody who knows where the needle is, but who knows where this person is who knows it? And so we have two haystacks. No, we have hundreds of haystacks and in two of them there is one needle we're looking for. But if we succeed in finding either needle, that means we've found the safe containing the thing we want. Now we have to crack the safe. And if we manage that, the first thing we find when we open the safe is another one with an even more complicated combination. Do you follow me? Let me give you a concrete example from our work. Whenever there has been a terror attack, all the pieces of information necessary to prevent the attack have been present at every different security level and behind each locked safe door. But these pieces of information have not been put together. Something we occasionally hear about in the newspapers. And then somewhere in Europe a minister of the interior is forced to resign. But that doesn't change the system one iota. By the same token, if intelligence manages to prevent a terror attack but there's a glitch in the process, then it's not remotely in the interest of the secret services to have this appear in the newspapers either, and then the case disappears. One dead person in a hotel is not the same as thirty dead after a bomb at the airport. It can be covered up. It must be covered up. The intelligence agencies don't want investigations and inquiries to be launched, let alone public discussion of why a policeman should bump off a tourist in a hotel room. And so we come to the Atlas case. I can't prove it, but I'm 100 per cent sure that it's an intelligence agency story. The Sureté? No. And not the S.G.R.S. either. This story is bigger. Much bigger. We began by reconstructing your hard drive. You can recover everything that's been stored on a computer and then deleted. Unless the documents are deleted from the central server rather than the P.C. Well, that's basic stuff. Anyway, it's how we proceeded.

Not only do you have to find weak points where you can get into other systems, you must do it in such a way that the attack can't be traced back. While we were working our way around the Belgian system this was relatively easy. I mean, I'm sort of familiar with it, I know how our people tick and I also know where they have to skimp, what limitations and obstacles they're working with. And listen to this, typically Belgian: the security police really have invested highly in file encryption and security measures to protect against external attacks. But what they forgot was to protect their recycle bin. Everything that's deleted centrally goes into a central recycle bin, which is perfectly logical. Maybe they've also got a backup copy somewhere, which obviously I won't be able to access. But it's in the recycle bin too, and I *can* rummage through that. Isn't it funny? Their thinking is that an external hacker will be interested in their secret documents, but what they can't imagine is someone sifting through the recycle bin. Anyway, that's how we went about it. Somewhere there must be a weak point where we can get at more information, not just what was deleted and covered up, but who wanted this to happen and why. Don't look like that. I'll tell you right now – what I believe, because I can't prove a thing. We did actually find a weak spot. It's impossible for us to hack intelligence agencies' computers, it would be like trying to open a safe with a toothpick. But we can detect the network they form and, if I've interpreted all the clues correctly, then N.A.T.O. is right at the heart of this. Yes. N.A.T.O. But wait! Listen to this: the system does have a weak spot after all, and that's the computer belonging to the Archdiocese of Poznań. Yes, Poznań. What do you mean, what's that? It's the oldest Roman Catholic diocese in Poland. A few scraps of information from intelligence services converge there, but a far greater volume of information goes out from Poznań to N.A.T.O. and collaborating intelligence services. Got your attention now, haven't I? You know that Armin de Boor is helping me, don't you? Well, when Armin and I hit on this we looked at each other in disbelief and Armin couldn't help laughing. This is crazy, he said, quick, type in the access code! It's a word, just one word. Yes, I said, but which one? We have to try to decrypt the keychain. He laughed and said, Don't you see? They think simply, try "Judas". It's got to be a word that a Catholic padre finds apt. But it wasn't "Judas". Wait, Armin said, maybe Judas is spelled differently in Polish. He opened some translation software and we found out that Judas is written Judasz in Polish. But it wasn't that either. Armin fetched some beer from the fridge, we had a drink and all of a sudden he said, Of course! Of course it's not Judas. They don't want to betray anything, they want to know everything. He typed something into the translation software, then entered the password – and the portal opened. The password was "*Bozeoko*": the eye of God.

The eye of God?

Yes.

The Catholic Church?

The Archdiocese of Poznań, yes.

Émile Brunfaut moaned.

What's wrong? Philippe said.

My spleen, Brunfaut said.

The fact that the cover-up of the murder in Hotel Atlas didn't just go back to a Belgian public prosecutor, but involved N.A.T.O. somehow, meant the case really was "too big" for Émile Brunfaut. Let's forget it, he had said to Philippe. I can't forget it, Philippe had said, but I won't do any more.

We're going to leave it alone now, Émile said.

Yes, we're going to leave it alone! When are you getting out of hospital? Next Sunday at three we're playing against Bruges.

We've got to be there.

We will be there!

In the weeks that followed, Émile Brunfaut focused on his health. This meant that whenever he smoked he did it with a bad conscience, and only rarely drank his Duvel followed by glass after glass of his beloved rosé. He did, however, axe the Mort Subite altogether, and he cut off all visible fat from whatever he was eating and pushed it to the side of his plate. He eyed his *frites* suspiciously before "just having a taste" and eating only two-thirds of the portion, and the *moules* were practically all protein. He did walk more than before, although after three weeks he went back to his old habits, interpreting the feeling of liberation and the pleasure he experienced as clear symptoms of his recovery. He reported for work again and was given back his police badge, his computer and a mountain of bureaucratic work. There were more reports than dead bodies and that was fine by Inspector Brunfaut, who was calmly cheerful about it. Maigret popped into his office and engaged in some abstruse small talk to see if Brunfaut really had forgotten the murder in Hotel Atlas. But how can you see if someone has forgotten something without reminding them of it? The inspector was so amused by Maigret's naivety that he saw it as definitive proof that he was back to his old self. No, he wasn't going to go near the case anymore.

Except he couldn't entirely leave it alone.

N.A.T.O., though – that was too much for him to handle. And in any case he wouldn't have known how to embark on an investigation like this, no matter how circumspectly. He did, however, have the name of the victim, his three names in fact, for three different passports had been found in the hotel room. As soon as he had been assigned the case, Brunfaut had jotted these names down in his notebook. And that hadn't vanished – you couldn't delete a notebook. Also on his mind was the question of what the Catholic Church or one of its dioceses might have to do with the case. He got no further with the names; none of the three was on a police database nor even on a civilian register anywhere in Europe. Which could only mean that all three passports were forged. For Brunfaut and the means at his disposal, this represented a dead end. And what about the involvement of the Archdiocese of Poznań? In the notes he made he kept writing VAT as an abbreviation for Vatican, because he couldn't imagine a Catholic bishopric cooperating with intelligence services without the Vatican's knowledge. He could only speculate. So he hadn't lied when he emphasised to Philippe and, more importantly, Maigret that he was leaving the case alone. After all, he was merely staring at empty boxes like a complex Sudoku puzzle he couldn't solve.

He was all the more surprised, therefore, when out of the blue Philippe told him to come to the cemetery to discuss the matter. He must have been tacitly fishing around the case too and now had something on the end of his line.

When Brunfaut eventually got to the Mur des Fusillés he looked around for the bench where Philippe and "his friend" were supposed to be waiting. But there was no bench. Not in front of this huge monument "AUX VICTIMES INNOCENTES DE LA FURIE TEUTONNE". Behind it, perhaps, on the other side? Or to the side? Or had Philippe meant another bench? He saw the field with the endless white crosses. Not that he'd never seen a military cemetery before, but for the first time he was shocked that he . . . that he found it beautiful. He stood there, took some deep breaths and found this large, hedge-lined square with its identical white crosses beautiful. After all the grave mounds, grave slabs, gravestones, crypts, mausoleums, chapels with which the dead or their descendants sought to outdo everyone else, after all the statues of weeping putti, weeping angels, weeping mothers, in granite, in marble, in bronze and in stainless steel, after all the sprawling, creeping, climbing plants, after all the restlessness in the field of eternal rest, here it was peaceful at least. Sheer optical peace. He found it beautiful in a radically aesthetic sense, as if this part of the cemetery were an installation, the project of an artist working with the stylistic idiom of peace, liberated from any meaning. Each time he took a step to the left or a step to the right new views emerged, new lines, diagonals, alignments. How clever, he thought: alignments. Changing alignments, but the perspective was always pointing in the same direction, to eternity. Eternity was everywhere, as was – ultimately – the liberation from sense and meaning. In order to honour these destinies every distinct destiny was extinguished; in commemoration of the sacrifices made they had sacrificed the idea that each individual life was unique and irrecoverable. There was only form, symmetry, harmony. Integration into an aesthetic picture. In death there was no resistance at all. Brunfaut was horrified because he, the sweating, panting, stinking creature, found this beautiful. Not good. Beautiful.

But where was Philippe? Standing next to the memorial, Brunfaut looked about him. All of a sudden he saw a pig break through a hedge and begin to root amongst the white crosses. The pig! It kept sticking its snout into the ground, boring down, scraping with its hooves. It backed into a cross, making it crooked, the pig kept digging and rooting, and the cross slowly began to tip over. Inspector Brunfaut, who throughout the course of his professional career had never encountered armed men, but had trained for such a scenario in simulation exercises, felt an unfamiliar fear and helplessness in the presence of this animal. He didn't know what to

do. His rational side told him to approach the pig as if to appre-
hend it. How ridiculous! His instinct was to run away. A policeman
run away from a pig? Whatever Brunfaut actually did at that
moment – later he was unable to remember – whether he took one
or two steps forwards, or retreated a couple of steps, or both, an
indecisive back-and-forth, the pig raised its head, made a terrible
sound and scurried away, an animalistic force, in a dead straight
line diagonally across the field of harmonious symmetry. With a
groan, Brunfaut realised that he was on his backside. He was sitting on the path, one hand clutching his damp handkerchief, the
other digging into the gravel. His palms were grazed and he could
feel a stabbing from his coccyx up to his back. And the wind blew
across the graves.

Back in the hotel Professor Erhart took a shower, then put on a
fresh shirt and a light suit of blue linen. He looked in the mirror:
European blue. He smiled to himself. Pure coincidence! He
decided against a tie.

Then he took the folder with his speech from his briefcase.
The buckle straps were cracked and he made a mental note to rub
in some dubbin when he got home. Beside the bed was a chair,
essentially just a seat, not padded, covered with red Nappa leather.
Erhart sat down and put his feet on the bed.

It was uncomfortable and claustrophobic. With difficulty he
heaved himself out of this half egg and sat on the bed. He wanted
to go through his speech one more time before leaving for the
meeting. He had written it in English, and although his English
was excellent after visiting professorships many years earlier at the
London School of Economics and the University of Chicago, he'd
had it checked over by an English professor friend of his.

Are you really going to give this speech?

Yes.

What I'd give to be there!

Erhart quietly recited his speech at the speed he intended to deliver it, and timed it on his smartphone. Seventeen minutes. Two minutes too long. But what did that matter; his life was at stake. That was melodramatic. He wondered what was wrong with him. He felt as if he had fallen out of time. He sat on the bed, the pages of his lecture on his lap, and stared at the gloomy brown wallpaper of the hotel room. Why were they now coming into his head, these foreign words, words foreign to him. With a pang of emotion he recalled words his mother had explained to him when he'd read them in a book and hadn't understood: improvident, behove, apothecary, asunder, game . . .

Mama, it says here: The poachers slipped into the forest under cover of darkness in search of some game. I don't understand.

You know what poachers are! People who hunt illegally.

Yes, I know that, but: in search of some game. Does that mean they were going to play something at night in the forest?

No, game are the wild animals that are hunted and eaten.

He had sat there for a long time, astonished and unsettled that killing could be some kind of game.

Professor Erhart pulled himself together and set off for the meeting.

Nine

La fin, un prolongement du présent –
nous-mêmes une condition préalable du passé.

THE **PIG WAS** captured by one of the Sheraton Brussels Hotel's security cameras on place Charles Rogier, a short sequence showing the pig entering the frame slowly, its head raised, as if it were out for a pleasant stroll and breathing in the early summer air, one passer-by leaps to the side, others stop in amazement, some take out their mobile phones to film the pig and then it is already out of the picture. This video was uploaded to YouTube with the title "*Aankomst van een afgevaardigde op de conferentie van de dieren*" by a user calling themselves Zinneke. There was an enquiry at the Sheraton to discover which of the security personnel, who had access to the saved footage from the security cameras, this Zinneke was. The hotel manager was concerned about the damage to the hotel's reputation if a video of a pig running free outside the Sheraton went viral. But there was no damage; on the contrary. The film was shared on Facebook and before long had been viewed 30,000 times. *Metro* was now able to publish a photograph of the pig, after which more images were leaked to the paper from the Carrefour security cameras in chaussée de Louvain, the post office in avenue de la Brabançonne and the Austrian embassy in rue Kortenberg. All the images were so blurred or shaky that Professor Kurt van der Koot, who had now secured a regular column in *Metro*, was unable to say with absolute certainty if it was the same pig or a different one. A horde of pigs, he thought, would make people feel uneasy, whereas they'd be touched by the thought of a lone pig wandering through Brussels – it would stir in them an almost childish fondness for animals, it was the stuff of legend. And so, only five days after the publication of the first video on YouTube, he launched a campaign in *Metro*: "Brussels has a pig! What should we call it?" Suggestions to be sent to the editor within the next three weeks. Professor van der Koot bridged the intervening time with his series "The pig as a universal metaphor". In daily articles he wrote about the range of things the pig had been made to act as symbol for: good and evil, fortune and disaster, sentimental love, contempt and deep-seated hatred, eroticism and wickedness. It was the only animal which as a metaphor covered the entire breadth of human emotions and philosophies, from the pig in clover to the filthy pig, from being "piggy in the middle" to "a greedy piglet". He even ventured into the political realm and discussed the concepts of the "Jewish pig" and "Nazi swine", before moving on to the pig as forbidden meat in some religions and the much-loved Babe, Peppa Pig and the Three Little Pigs. His series became a huge success, not least thanks to its illustrations: photographs of cute little pigs, facsimiles of old caricatures depicting emperors, generals and presidents as pigs, reproductions of paintings showing the pig in art (an illustration by Tomi Ungerer showing a mother sow reading her piglets a fairy tale: "Once upon a time there was a butcher . . ."), figurines and trinkets, from piggy banks to pig cooks, from the hunted to the hunter, and photographs of everyday objects: van der Koot himself had learned to his astonishment that there was barely an item of everyday use that had not at some point assumed the form of a pig: beer tankards, salt cellars, slippers, caps, even toasters . . .

The editorial team appointed a jury of prominent figures who were to compile a longlist from the submissions, and then a short-list from which they would select the winning name. On the jury were: the folk singer Barthold Gabalier; the actress Sandra Vallée; the professional footballer and champion goalie from the Jupiler Pro League, Jaap Mulder; the widow of the former mayor of Brussels, Daniela Collier; the cartoonist Roger Lafarge, who had been under police protection ever since his Muhammad caricatures; the writer and Brussels chronicler, Geert van Istendael; the two-star chef Kim King, *maître de cuisine* in "Le Cochon d'Or"; and the artist Wim Delvoye, known for tattooing his pictures on pigs. Chairman and spokesman of the jury was, of course, none other than university professor Kurt van der Koot.

Romolo Strozzi was virtually unflappable. Things that might take other people by surprise elicited from him no more than a wry smile. What could possibly astound the man to whom nothing was unfamiliar? Personally he'd had a rich and varied life, and what he hadn't encountered himself had been passed down to him by his family and forefathers as a treasure trove of experience. Besides, he was extremely well read. And in the field he cultivated professionally he knew every grain, every stone and every weed. He'd had to smirk discreetly when that Fenia Xenopoulou had quoted the president's favourite book out of the blue, trying hard to be casual, but there was no doubt it was a deliberate tactic. It showed that she had prepared with a considerable degree of neur-otic energy. But it had failed to take him off-guard. He knew people would try everything possible, but her attack had missed its target. Did she really think that he would go and tell the president: By the way, this Madame Xenopoulou's favourite novel is the same as yours, Monsieur le Président? Did she really believe that this would give her an advantage?

He sat down at a table outside Café Franklin on the corner of rue Franklin and rue Archimède, on the shaded Archimède side. It was a hot day and he fancied a cigarette while he waited for Attila Hidekuti, chief of protocol of the president of the European Council. He needed an informal chat about Madame Xenopoulou and her *soi-disant* Jubilee Project.

All of a sudden there was a huge pig standing before him. A person in a grotesque full-body, pink-polyester pig costume, holding a stick to which a placard was affixed. The pig leaned the placard against the wall of the café, sat at the neighbouring table and removed his head – that's to say, his pig's head – to reveal a red face dripping with sweat, wet blond hair sticking to his scalp. The man was roughly Strozzi's age. He wiped his face several times with his pink polyester sleeve and said to the waitress, who had just appeared with Strozzi's coffee, A beer, please!

Are you shocked? I don't blame you, he said, turning to Strozzi. Please don't scoff, I've been unemployed for months. It's difficult at my age. In the end I stood outside the stock market on boulevard Anspach with a sign that said: "I'll take any work!" Then I got this job. Carrying a placard around. Wandering the streets of the European Quarter in a pig costume. Advertising, he said, wiping his face again.

Strozzi turned to read the sign:

Van Kampen's the Butcher
Finest meat!
Best sausages!
Telephone to order
(Please note our new number . . .)

Lots of people laugh. Some ask, how can you do it? Why is it so hard to imagine what people will do for money these days? Do you think it's any fun, wearing this costume in this heat?

Strozzi took out his wallet, the waitress brought the man's beer, smiled and asked him, Anything with that? Corn on the cob, perhaps?

Strozzi put a five-euro note on the table and left. On the other side of the street he texted Attila: Not in Franklin! I'm in Kitty O'Shea's, blvd Charlemagne.

He stood in his socks and underpants on the small balcony, carefully brushing his suit. On these warm, dry days the gravel paths in the cemetery were very dusty; each step between the rows of the dead threw up dust that crept up his trouser legs and got caught in the fibres of his jacket. David de Vriend treated his clothes with great care. When he had returned to life, after the liberation, he had set great store by good suits tailored from top-quality material. Although he had never enjoyed a large income as a teacher, eventually he earned enough to order bespoke suits rather than buying them off the peg. He brushed and thought of bread. Why was he thinking of bread? He brushed carefully and patiently, he was happy with the clothes brush he'd bought forty years earlier at "Walter Witte", the shop for "Everyday Goods" on boulevard Anspach. Monsieur Witte himself had recommended this brush, Top quality, Monsieur de Vriend, this brush will outlive you, the very best clothes brush, German horsehair, inserted by hand into the oak head. De Vriend faltered briefly: German . . . what? Horsehair? before suddenly realising that he cared more about the quality of everyday goods than the ghosts of the past. He bought this German brush which would outlive him, which was innocent, as were perhaps the hands that had crafted it. As he brushed his suit the telephone rang in his bedroom. He heard the sound but didn't register it was for him. The ringtone was unfamiliar and he wasn't expecting a call. Time and again it is said that nobody who survived a concentration or extermination camp could ever throw away a piece of bread. He had read it again just now in the paper. The daughter of Gustave Jakubowicz had mentioned it in an interview for *De Morgen*, after the death of her father, the famous human rights lawyer: As children we were often made to eat hard bread. We wouldn't get a fresh loaf until the old one was finished, our father couldn't throw bread away, he just couldn't. De Vriend brushed. Gustave, oh Gustave! The telephone rang again. Gustave had loved top-quality suits and fresh baguette in restaurant bread baskets. No more threadbare clothes, good, thick fabrics! Nothing off the peg, certainly nothing striped, and no cap, nothing covering the head! Anybody who'd been in a camp knew what no cap meant. It meant death. And so afterwards it meant life. Freedom. The very best fabrics and an uncovered head. De Vriend brushed expertly, he stood on the balcony in his underpants, one leg of his suit trousers pulled over his left arm, rhythmically brushing the material, immersed in this movement like a violin player. Somewhere a telephone started ringing again. He had four men's suits. For the winter, two of thick tweed, one Harris in herringbone and a slightly softer salt-and-pepper Donegal suit. For the transitional periods of the year he had a midnight-blue pure new wool suit and a lighter, but nonetheless pleasantly warm charcoal one of mohair. He didn't have a summer suit. He had frozen too much in his life and for him summer was another transitional period too. He didn't mind a hot day and the grey mohair he was now brushing was so wonderfully light. How long had he had it? Many years, it must be many years now.

He felt a hand grab him firmly on the upper arm, the hand jerked him back, almost making him drop his brush. Well, what

292

are we doing out here? Madame Joséphine shouted. We can't stand out on the balcony naked, can we now, Monsieur de Vriend? Alright?

He looked at her, she was still squeezing his arm and talking far too loudly: We're going to go inside and put some clothes on now, aren't we?

He wasn't deaf. The only reason he hadn't understood her immediately was because she was shouting her head off.

Didn't you hear the telephone? she screamed. Right then, let's go inside, shall we, come on, look, there you go, there's your shirt, we're going to put that on now and . . . my, my it's sodden, you really must have been sweating, we'll have to put a fresh one on, won't we, come on, let's fetch a fresh one. Alright?

She pulled open his wardrobe, peered in, reached inside and de Vriend said, No! He didn't want that, he wasn't going to allow someone to just open his locker and rummage around . . . but she was already saying, that's a lovely shirt, such a lovely white shirt, let's put that on, shall we?

Madame Joséphine took the brush from his hand and placed it on the small table. De Vriend's suit trousers had slid from his arm and were lying on the floor. As she helped him into his shirt she spotted the number tattooed on his arm again, hastily threaded the arm into the sleeve and was about to say, Well done! but thought better of it.

She picked up the trousers from the floor and handed them to him. Without a word. He put them on. Without a word. He buttoned up his shirt, fastened his belt. She looked around, saw that his shoes were beside the bed; he saw where she was looking, went over to the bed, sat down and slipped on his shoes. He looked at her, she looked at him, then he bent down and tied his laces. He sat up, looked at her. She nodded.

Madame Joséphine was a seasoned carer. She had seen a lot in her twenty years of service. During her training she had taken a psychology course and only a couple of years ago she had completed her most advanced training course. She was the more surprised of the two when suddenly she said, Auschwitz?

He nodded.

He wanted to get up but couldn't. He stayed sitting on the bed.

She thought she had gone too far. So she went one step further: What was it like? Do you want to talk about it?

She sensed an asphyxiating horror. Because she had asked this question.

De Vriend sat on the bed, looked at her, then said, We stood for roll call. We stood for roll call. That's all.

After Madame Joséphine had left the room, de Vriend stayed where he was for a while, then got up, wandered around the room, eyes peeled and . . . there was his brush.

Slowly he got undressed, picked up the brush, put his arm into one of the trouser legs, stood naked on the balcony and began to brush.

Private Secretary Strozzi knew, of course, that the president of the Commission would never declare his opposition to an initiative designed to polish the Commission's image and prestige. This was why he had assured Fenia Xenopoulou of the president's support straight away. *Carte blanche*. But Strozzi also knew that this peculiar project would throw up more problems than it would benefit the Commission. The whole idea of the Jubilee Project was madness, and even if you could provide perfectly sound justification for it, as Fenia Xenopoulou undoubtedly had done, in a political sense it was anything but auspicious. And so the *carte blanche* had been a feint, a favourite ploy of the old swashbuckling bureaucrat Strozzi: if you wanted to kill off an idea, first you had to agree with it and offer your full support, upon which everyone happily dropped their guard. The best thing about this was that often you didn't have to make the decisive strike yourself. It was an old fencing joke: if you can induce your opponent to commit hara-kiri you no longer need to attack, but watch out that they don't collapse wheezing into your arms. And with Fenia Xenopoulou the ruse had worked once again: buoyed by his support she had carelessly agreed to his suggestion that the representatives of the countries which had founded the Commission should be informed of this new Commission project. What could she have offered by way of an objection? In any case he had already got to his feet, a signal that their conversation was at an end. She wouldn't be able to claim later that he had stabbed her in the back. On the contrary, the bout had been fair and square. Now all he had to do was make sure she didn't collapse into his arms and stain his waistcoat with her blood. And for that he needed a little chat with his friend Attila, the chief of protocol of the Council president.

It was a crazy venue for such a conversation: two senior officials with ice tea in Kitty O'Shea's, the Irish pub behind the Berlaymont building, sitting at a table sticky with spilled beer, surrounded by bellowing Guinness drinkers and darts players.

At least we won't be overheard here, Attila Hidekuti said in his charming "Hunglish" – Änglish with ä Hún-gä-ri-an äcc-ent.

Strozzi smiled. For some years now he had maintained an excellent dialogue with Attila and they'd resolved many issues in detailed consultation with each other. Whenever there was a clash between the Commission and the Council – a frequent occurrence – or if the Commission president wanted something from the Council president – not a rare one – then Strozzi preferred to talk to Hidekuti than to the Council president's private secretary, Lars Ekelöf, that hardcore Lutheran from Sweden who by definition found the Baroque Italian count rather sinister. Conversely, a scornful Strozzi had once said of Ekelöf, On contentious issues it is impossible to reach an agreement with a man who feels morally superior at every turn and thus regards any compromise as a betrayal of his morals! And with an ironic smile he had added, The reason why Ekelhöf can never be lured out from his cover is that he's nothing *but* cover, he is cover personified. If you could get behind it you would find nothing apart from a fleeting aroma: the dissipation of self-righteousness.

The opposition between north and south ran precisely between these two men who worked north and south of rue de la Loi in Brussels.

And we Hun-gä-rians are grrr-ound to pów-der bet-wéen you! (Hidekuti)

Now Hidekuti was watching the darts players standing uncomfortably close to him. The darts fly low in here, he said.

One of them said hello, Hidekuti returned the greeting with a nod, shifted his chair to the side, then another player raised his glass and toasted Hidekuti and Strozzi.

Come on, let's sit over there, Strozzi said, and then: They're the Brits. British E.N.D.s. Since the start of the Brexit negotiations, all some of them have done is come here for the beer and darts in preparation for their return home. I prefer this lot to the other Brits who soldier on, with Brexit not yet signed and sealed, yet all they're actually doing is diligently obstructing our work.

Is this why you asked me here? Are you having problems with officials in my department?

No, Strozzi said, then he told him about the Jubilee Project.

Hidekuti realised at once the turmoil the project would cause.

It wasn't so much that the Commission was planning a solo effort against the other European institutions, or at least without including them, even though this in itself was highly problematic. No, it was this idea of parading witnesses whose biographies and destinies were supposed to show that nationalism had led to the most heinous crimes in human history, and for this reason it was the Commission's moral duty to work for the overthrow of the nation state. To infer from the trite "Auschwitz: never again" the need to "overthrow nationalism and ultimately overthrow the nation state" and to try to sell this to the public as the moral imperative and political mission of the European Union was something the heads of state and government could never accept.

We have experts for everything, Hidekuti said. We can make it rain and we can see to it that the Commission stands out in the rain.

I know, Strozzi said. That's why I'm telling you all this.

"Auschwitz: never again" is right and proper.

Yes.

You could say it in a sermon every Sunday.

Yes. So it's never forgotten. Never forget, this needs to be said over and over again.

Exactly, but it's not a political programme.

Morality has never been a political programme.

Especially when morality produces conflict.

Exactly. The Council could never agree to the "overthrow of the nation state". That would mean war. Against the Commission. And people in every country revolting against Europe.

Exactly.

So?

I understand what you're saying. We will put the lid on this prrró-ject before it even sees the light of day.

Strozzi knew he could rely on his friend Attila.

And Attila Hidekuti made an excellent job of it. It wasn't a big job: a signature, a telephone call, basically a click of the fingers. This got the ball rolling, which hit the next ball and so on to produce a momentum, and very soon nobody could remember who had actually started it, but the energy was transmitted from ball to ball until the final one rolled out of play, into the void, into a black hole. That was the aim. That was Hidekuti's job. Even the individual who triggers such a process ends up being just another one of those balls, which knocks into another, basically no more than a marble or a grain, invisible by the end, an atom – the fissile nucleus of intangible political energy. The Hungarian foreign minister was already on the telephone the following day to his "esteemed colleague and dear friend" the Austrian foreign minister, informing him that under the pretext of jubilee celebrations the Commission was planning to trigger a process that would lead to the abolition of the European nation states.

You know what it means, dear friend, when the E.U. decrees that Austria isn't a nation, he said sanctimoniously. No, you couldn't call it sanctimoniously, for the nation really was his sanctum. Only his own nation though, the Hungarian one. He didn't really care whether Austria was a nation or an occupational accident of history, quite rightly pruned back in its megalomania to a mini state of mixed-bloods, although "in private", as he liked to say, he tended towards the latter. But he knew he had an ally if he "scratched the balls" of his neighbour's nationalism, as he put it to the Hungarian prime minister.

Around 86 billion neurons were communicating, and within milliseconds complex electrical processes occurred in thousands of cells, semiochemicals did their job and the synapses were working. In short, the Austrian foreign minister was thinking. And within the twinkling of an eye – or a few anyway – he had weighed up the alternatives and come to a decision. Option one was to do nothing for the time being until the Commission went public with its project, then enter the ring as the defender of the Austrian nation against "the E.U.". At first his synapses glowed with relish, but what was this? Now they began to flash red. He had already done the anti-E.U. crowd a service with his statements on European refugee policy; taking a step further into the arena of outright rejection of the European idea (thank goodness this was so unclear anyway) would not only unsettle "the economy", but position him close to the party of right-wing hooligans, who with their "Austria First" nationalism were garnering ever greater support. He didn't want to be the monkey on the shoulder of the organ-grinder, he wanted to be popular without the whiff of populism, which meant that if nation and nationalism were to become a major public topic of discussion, he was undoubtedly holding a bad hand. Thus option two: he had to stop this project. If he were able to prevent a debate about the pros and cons of the nation state, he could on every issue appear as the representative of Austrian interests, of the interests of the national voters and also as a European – he would be the organ-grinder.

He thanked his dear friend, his Hungarian colleague, "of course" promising harmonised cooperation, then drummed up his staff and allocated the tasks. Everyone hurried zealously out of his office apart from the press officer who cleared his throat. He reminded the minister that they still had to fill out the questionnaire.

What questionnaire?

For *Madonna*, the women's magazine. Where we had that photoshoot last week.

Oh, yes. Well, fill it out, then.

But I'd like to run through it with you, Minister. The personal questions, such as your favourite book.

What do you suggest?

It's traditional in Austria for politicians to mention *The Man without Qualities*. You can't really opt for a lesser work. And living authors are strictly taboo. People don't want living authors.

Alright then, let's be good Austrians. *The Man without Qualities*. Kreisky loved that book as far as I recall.

And Sinowatz, Klima and Gusenbauer.

Only socialists?

No, Mock and Khol too, even Molterer.

Well then, I can't go for anything lesser.

Next one: Who's your favourite character in literature?

What's up with this magazine? Do they only have literature graduates working there?

No, Minister. It's just these two questions, then we get onto music and food.

O.K. My favourite character. What's the chap from *The Man without Qualities* called?

Ulrich. But I wouldn't recommend him. As it says: without qualities. I Googled him, he's got incest issues. I recommend Arnheim.

Who's that?

He's perfect for you, Minister. He's described as a "great man", a politician and an intellectual. And he has a deep Platonic love relationship.

Seriously?

In *The Man without Qualities*.

Fantastic!

*

The following day the Polish government instructed Polish officials in the various ministries to pull the plug on this European Commission "campaign", which was an attack on the pride of the Polish nation. In particular the D.-G. COMM needed to be reminded that Auschwitz extermination camp was a German crime and therefore a purely German problem. The Federal Republic of Germany was cordially invited to dismantle the German extermination camp on Polish soil and exhibit it as a museum in Germany. In any case a culture of commemorating crimes committed on Polish soil by occupying powers would be an inappropriate moral canopy over an economic community.

On the desk of the president of the European Council there arrived a note from the Austrian foreign minister, which made unequivocally clear that the Republic of Austria was both for and against the project: she supported the European Commission's initiative, but could not give her approval to the plan in its current form. In the name of the Austrian government, the foreign ministry unreservedly backed the European Commission's initiative to "market Europe better to its citizens". In Austria, however, the notion that a Polish camp where thousands upon thousands of Austrians died should now be a reason for questioning the existence of the Austrian nation was unmarketable.

The ambassador of the Permanent Representation of the Czech Republic to the European Union relayed a note of protest that was worded more sharply: The Czech government would not permit the European Union to plan a campaign of so-called "coming to terms with the past" by which Czechia would once again be wiped off the map. There was no mandate for this, nor could there be one.

A few hours later there came a similar-sounding communiqué from the Permanent Representation of the Slovak Republic.

Attila Hidekuti smiled. As expected, the little countries had been the quickest to offer their resistance when their national . . . what? identity? honour? or even their right to exist? had been questioned. He could rely on that. He could work with that. Now the big and crucial question was how would Germany react? What about France? Britain was out of the game, even though she was still hanging around on the pitch. Hidekuti thought it possible that the United Kingdom would instruct its Brussels officials to support the project and push for it, announce it publicly, only to exploit it domestically as further proof of the necessity of Brexit. Britain, Hidekuti thought, could be used as further leverage against the Ark and the D.-G. COMM to stop the project at all costs, before it became public.

Lars Ekelöf was markedly composed when he came into Hidekuti's office. He had so internalised the need to behave *comme il faut* anywhere and at any time that only fleetingly had he felt the urge to storm in there and scream, "What the hell is this crap?" But he would not allow himself to indulge in uncontrolled emotions and filthy language. Never. Naturally he suspected that Hidekuti somehow had his finger in the pie of these peculiar protests that were arriving at the president's office from the foreign ministries and embassies of some Member States. Because this Hungarian hussar with a permanent mischievous sparkle in his eyes and that wobbly grin above his double chin always had his finger in the pie. Ekelöf couldn't prove it, but he suspected that Hidekuti had a habit of inventing problems he then solved, to show off to the president. And he, Ekelöf, the private secretary, was left out of the loop every time. Taking a deep breath, he entered and said, I've got a little problem and I'm sure you can help me.

And Hidekuti could.

A particularly driven individual in the Commission is throwing their weight around, Hidekuti explained. But I've already had a word with the president. For the time being we'll wait and see. The matter is bound to throttle itself.

Lars Ekelöf was not the sort of man to hang around watching something "throttle itself" – another excruciating choice of words from the chief of protocol. Ekelöf pursued the matter, the immediate consequence of which was that Mrs Atkinson was assailed with problems.

Hidekuti smiled. Everything was going to plan.

He who loves freedom and loves the truth forgets how to love, his grandfather had once said. Émile Brunfaut, a schoolboy at the time, had been shocked without understanding precisely why. He had thought long and hard about this phrase, just as he might about a puzzle that really bothered him, and this was no doubt why he had remembered it. Brunfaut could still see his grandfather before him when he uttered this phrase. He remembered his furrowed, sullen face, which the young Émile had completely misunderstood, believing it to be the expression of an intimidating self-righteousness and lack of empathy – if only he had known these words back then. His grandfather would have told him about his time in the resistance – what else? – and explained that mistrust, deep mistrust was a sort of life insurance, not a good one, but perhaps the only one. You could to some degree protect yourself and those dearest to you only if you shared as little as possible with them, not trusting even those you loved. Brave, wonderful men and women have been betrayed by friends, brothers, fathers and even by their own children: by people they loved. Love didn't guarantee freedom, and it offered no protection.

Only later, when his grandfather was long dead, did Brunfaut begin to understand the phrase. It was when he became a policeman. When he learned to become mistrustful in principle, not to believe anything he was told, to regard all appearance as disguise and initially to treat each rapid, honest explanation as an attempt at a cover-up. But he had sworn not to let this colour his private life; in no way would he allow it to encroach upon his relationships with the people he loved.

Of course, you don't think about a resolution like this every day of your life. But now Brunfaut did have cause to think about it, and he prided himself on how well he'd done: he loved those people closest to him with affection and without mistrust, he loved freedom without fear, and with an unwavering confidence he loved the truth, whether this truth be openness towards his loved ones, the results of police investigations and inquiries, or even – why not? – the objectives of the liberal press.

At the same time, however, he had to admit – and this thought shocked and confounded him – that perhaps none of this was true any longer. Did he love? Really? Ought he not now to concede that he *had* loved?

He couldn't love unconditionally anymore. At a stroke he had forgotten how. Could that be true?

The episode at the cemetery. It had rattled him. And it wasn't the pig which had shocked him and left him in such disarray, no, it was rather the fact that afterwards he had wandered about with torn trousers, backache and lacerated hands for a good half hour and still hadn't found Philippe, let alone his "friend" who, after all, had been the reason for their meeting there in the first place. Eventually he had sat down on a bench and called Philippe several times, but it went straight to voicemail. And then an old man had appeared, sat beside him and said, Are you talking to the dead too?

The whole thing was horrific and Brunfaut fled the entire length of the avenue, running properly now, past his grandfather's grave, panting all the way to the exit and his car. With a hellish stabbing in his side, as if a huge question mark were slicing like a sickle into the warp and weft of his soul, a pain that sat deeper than the cuts, a pain that he was able to put a name to only when he was back home and in the bath. What really hurt him was the sudden, profound mistrust, or to put it more accurately: the loss of trust.

Even his professional mistrust as a policeman had been founded on a basic sense of trust: trust in the rule of law. Yes, there had often been political interventions – whenever people of influence were entangled in scandals, for example – but essentially that was childish; it might obstruct the wheels of justice, but not eliminate the law for good, and certainly not when it came to criminal offences such as murder. The cover-up in the Atlas case, however, had shaken his trust more than he cared to admit. The question now was how to deal with it. Like his grandfather? Or like Philippe? And this was what he found so painful: he no longer trusted Philippe. His best friend, the father of his goddaughter Joëlle. All of a sudden he saw him in a bad light. Everything he had told him was hazy, about N.A.T.O. and the Vatican, spine-chilling stories calculated to make him leave the case well alone, and, out of the blue, here he was with new information, the precise content of which was unknown, an informer would explain at the cemetery – but neither he nor the mysterious informer had turned up and now he couldn't be contacted by phone either.

Brunfaut nudged the plastic duck that bobbed on the water between his knees and wondered whether Philippe might have been given this as an assignment, first to convince him that any further inquiries were pointless and would only put him in danger, and then, using the informer story, to check whether he had left the case alone or was still nosily dabbling in it.

The bath did him good. It didn't relieve his pain, but it relaxed him. Now he sensed he was thinking clearly, but what he was thinking unnerved him. He made waves, the duck danced stoically on the water, knocked into his tummy, turned around and bobbed between his knees, he nudged it and it gave a little hop before rocking in the water again.

Brunfaut had never liked the public prosecutor. He respected him, yes, but loathed him at the same time. A man who identified himself so blindly with the state that he confused the most powerful and influential individuals in the state with the state itself and thus – only in exceptional cases, of course, and for the benefit of the state – was even prepared to bend the law, which the state was supposed to uphold. But did Brunfaut have to love the man to understand him? No. Whenever he made an appearance it was clear that certain interests were at stake. And these interests were clear. Basically it was always truthful and this truth needed no bond of trust or love. Oh, Philippe! Brunfaut slapped the water. I trusted you. Have you betrayed me?

As the water turned cold and Brunfaut wondered whether the whole thing might not just be an unfortunate coincidence and he had got the wrong end of the stick. Perhaps his suspicion was wrong and Philippe was still the loyal friend he could love and trust.

But mistrust had taken root in his heart; it was there and he couldn't simply opt to dismiss it.

The duck had been a shampoo container: "No tears guaranteed". As a child he had loved this duck and after it was empty had always held on to it, through every house move and every change in his circumstances. At the base of its tail was a screw cap where the shampoo had come out.

With both his feet Brunfaut pushed the duck under the water. When he took his feet away the duck bounced back up, bobbed and swam.

It couldn't sink. It would always be on top. He could rely on that. Brunfaut unscrewed the cap, held the duck below the surface, now it began to fill with water. He laid his arms on the rim of the bath, spread his legs and watched the duck slowly go under.

Once again Professor Erhart had arrived almost too late. As usual he took the Metro and got out at Schuman, but the Justus Lipsius exit was closed. So he took the Berlaymont exit, which meant he was not only on the wrong side of rue de la Loi, but also below the street in the strange hollow where the Berlaymont building stood. When he had walked around the boundary wall of the hollow and up to street level he realised it was impossible to cross rue de la Loi. Barriers had been erected along the pavement, behind which army vehicles were parked. Military police impatiently waved on the people coming up from the Metro. Keep going! Don't stop!

I've got to get over there, Erhart said. I need to —

Keep going! Move along!

He would have been better off going up to the rond-point Schuman to get to the Justus Lipsius side from there, but Erhart interpreted the policeman's waving to mean that he should go in the other direction, which was exactly where he had got lost the last time. He strode along rapidly, his arms swinging, carrying in his right hand his old briefcase which at this hectic pace kept knocking against his kneecap or into the back of his knee. He had to go as far as Maelbeek before he was able to cross the road. The next time, he thought, he wouldn't take the Metro as far as Schuman, but get out at Maelbeek station instead. If there ever was a next time. After the keynote speech he was scheduled to deliver in ten minutes. He ran all the way back to the construction site beside the Julius Lipsius building and looked for the passageway between the temporary metal fencing and plywood hoardings, the corridor to the Résidence Palace where the meeting was taking place. Everything had changed since the last time; only the chaos seemed unaltered. He turned to the left, then took a few steps to the right, but all he saw were wire railings, behind him the military vehicles, in front of him the barriers – he felt like a cornered animal. Panting, he pressed his briefcase to his chest, the briefcase with the lecture that at its heart was a speech about freedom. About liberation. At the very least a speech about self-liberation.

Erhart was the last to arrive. He wasn't in fact late, but the last one nonetheless. Now everyone's here, Mr Pinto crowed. Would you like a cup of coffee before we begin? Some water? Yes, please, Erhart said. He looked around, nodded here, nodded there and his greetings were returned. How perfect they all were. Not even the tiniest particle of street dust on their shoes – did they all know another way in? Hadn't they had to cross the building site? No crumpled trousers or jackets, not even the minutest patch of sweat on any shirt. How had they all got here? It was so sticky outside that you didn't need to run around the barriers as he had; even walking slowly would bring on a sweat.

Are you ready, Professor? Mr Pinto said.

Professor Erhart was ready. Always. He had been prepared and on call all his life. Times may change, but all that really happens is that the loose bits flake off from what is timeless. He finished his coffee and nodded.

The first time he was invited to a conference, as a very green university assistant, he had bought himself a new suit especially for the occasion. He had been permitted to give a paper at the European Forum in Alpbach, a mountain village in the Tyrolean Alps, where every year the elite of the business world, well-known academics from different disciplines and successful artists met to exchange ideas. His professor, Dr Schneider, had arranged this invitation to encourage Erhart, or at least to keep him interested, and he had already written a few articles which Schneider had then published under his own name. Erhart had felt honoured and flattered, and only later did he realise how the prospect of an honour such as this could beguile him into absurd submissiveness: it wasn't to be a public lecture, but rather a short paper to a working group. All the same, he would be there in Alpbach and, if he was keen, would come into contact with eminent and influential people. He was anxious, therefore, to make the best impression. Hence the new suit, his first three-piece, and new shoes. He smeared leather grease onto the shoes he had never worn and polished them. And there he was, standing in a room where coffee and quark pastries were being served. The new shoes pinched his feet and it felt as though he had come in disguise; it wasn't actually him wearing this new outfit.

He watched Sir Karl Popper gaze down at the bowed backs of Austrian politicians and officials, who suddenly flew up and swarmed around the American secretary of state at that moment making his entrance, so they might bow even deeper and catch his cigar ash in their cupped hands.

And then Erhart caught sight of him: Armand Moens.

Erhart's first conference. And Armand Moens' last public appearance before his death a few weeks later. The only meeting between the teacher and the pupil, between God and His apostle, as Erhart might even have put it at the time. And they ended up speaking about clothes.

Erhart was surprised by how little interest this man showed in his appearance. He wore threadbare cords, a grey pullover with stains (coffee?) down the front and a cheap, blue, nylon jacket.

Erhart went over to Moens to introduce himself and to pay his respects to this esteemed academic.

Moens was old and ill. He was at the end. Erhart immediately regretted having approached him. He would have liked to discuss Moens' book, *The End of the National Economy and the Economic System of a Post-National Republic*, but when Erhart came face to face with the old man, he realised at once that this would no longer be possible. The yellowed face with brown blotches, the watery eyes, the lips moistened with spittle . . . then a student appeared with one of Moens' books and asked for a signature. Erhart could hardly bear to see how long it took Moens to shakily write his name. He didn't remember what he said then, all he knew was that, rather than respond to it, Moens said simply, Everybody here looks like they're in fancy dress.

Erhart: I'm sorry?

Can't you see? All these people in the suits they wear in Vienna, Paris and Oxford – he was struggling to speak – these, these costumes, here, in front of the Swiss pine and the whole Alpine aesthetic . . . fancy dress! They look like they're in fancy dress! And the others who've come in their loden and traditional outfits, because it's the Tyrol. They thought, let's put on traditional Alpine garb because it's the Tyrol. They really look like they're in fancy dress! Look! Nothing but people fancy dress. An academic carnival!

Erhart didn't know what to reply; eventually he said, We should never disguise ourselves!

And Armand Moens said in a strikingly loud and gruff voice: No!

*

Back in Vienna, at the institute, Alois Erhart wrote on a piece of notepaper:

"NO!"
Armand Moens

. . . and pinned it to the wall by his desk. He knew it was childish, but it also wasn't. It was a little electrical impulse. "No!" was never wrong. What, never? No!

He buttoned up his crumpled jacket to hide the sweat marks on his shirt and followed Mr Pinto into the room where he would deliver his keynote speech.

When Kassándra Mercouri cycled in to the office that day, as she did most days, she met Bohumil on rue d'Arenberg. Kassándra was excited, impatient, she had a lot to say, she wanted to talk about her weekend, she was proud of what she had found out, it was amazing, and so important. But instead she said, What's up, what's wrong with you?

The ever cheerful, exuberant, childishly reckless cyclist Bohumil was pedalling along in silence, his face pinched. He didn't take a "You're in the way!" sticker from his bag when a car was parked in the cycle lane. She had always been worried when he carried out this risky manoeuvre, but now she was worried because he wasn't doing it.

What's wrong? Tell me!

I spent the weekend at home. In Prague.

Kassándra had to fall back behind Bohumil to cycle past a car that was double parked, while a bus thundered past them to the left. When she caught up with him again, Bohumil said nothing.

So you were in Prague. Visiting family? *Allons!* What happened?

La famille est la mort de la raison!

Bohumil!

Nothing out of the ordinary. No surprises. Or let's say: Why am I surprised that it surprised me. I was with my parents. *Eh bien!* Parents are parents. Then I'd planned to meet my sister for dinner in U Zavěšenýho, duck with red cabbage as always. She didn't want to come!

Your sister didn't want to meet up with you?

Not in the restaurant, just the two of us. She wanted me to go to hers.

But that's nice, isn't it?

No. She knows how much I love the duck at U Zavěšenýho. It's what we always used to do! We'd meet there, eat and tell each other everything, all our news, all our secrets, all the rumours. No, I didn't want to go to hers. She got married recently and . . .

Do you know her husband? So you were invited for dinner with both of them?

You didn't come to our wedding! she said. Of course I know why, she said. So now you're going to come over to ours and shake my husband's hand. I'll cook duck. But you're going to shake my husband's hand. In our house.

So what's the problem?

The door of a car parked ahead of them swung open. Bohumil braked so abruptly that he almost flew over the handlebars. Kassándra wrenched her bike to the left and then immediately right again, in the process almost colliding with a delivery van. She stopped and dismounted. Her heart was thumping, it pounded against her chest and temples. Bohumil yelled at the driver of the parked car. The man apologised profusely, Bohumil pushed his bicycle past the car to Kassándra, let it fall to the ground, then perched on the bonnet of another car and wept.

Kassándra sat next to him, put her arm around his shoulder and said, Nothing happened. Nothing happened. Everything's alright.

Nothing is alright!

The driver of the car stood there, ashen-faced. With a wave of her hand, Kassándra gestured to him to go.

Nothing is alright, Bohumil said again, wiping his eyes with the back of his hand. So I went there, to my sister's house. She wanted me to shake her husband's hand. And then he refused. I offered him my hand and he refused to shake it. Ignored it. He looked at me with his fat, self-satisfied face, his hands in his trouser pockets, and said, *Y smrade zasranej!*

What?

Tu es un crétin d'idiot!

Non! Ce n'est pas vrai!

It is! I'd been bought by corporations, he said, in return for an exorbitant salary I was betraying the national interests of the Czech Republic, I was a parasite on the nation and so on. All that in the hallway of their house. Next to the coat hooks.

So what did you say? What did you do?

Bohumil laughed, sniffed and said, What did I do? Took my hand back. And then I said to my sister, If we go on chatting too long in the hallway the duck will burn. And she said, There isn't any duck. We just wanted to get things straight.

Kassándra squeezed him, pulled him to her bosom, stroked his head. It was ridiculous: she was stroking his cycling helmet.

All of a sudden a man was standing there, bellowing at them. The owner of the car they were sitting on. Bohumil looked up, took a sticker from his shoulder bag, slowly and deliberately

313

peeled off the back and slapped the sticker on the man's forehead. The man staggered backwards, Bohumil picked up his bike and said to Kassándra, Come on! We have to get to work!

Kassándra was amazed at how quickly she was back in the saddle, and now they were pedalling hard and in silence. It wasn't until they got to avenue des Arts that Bohumil said, My sister is five years younger than me. When she was at school I used to do her homework. Nobody said she was stupid or lazy. She was the princess. Now she's pregnant with the child of a fascist. And nobody in the family is batting an eyelid. He's nice to the relatives, sings old folk songs in a tuneful voice, he's quite a handsome chap, he earns well and he's not a communist. That's what counts in my country these days.

Kassándra didn't know how to respond. Only when they had arrived, locked up their bikes and were on their way to the lift did she say, I should tell you about my weekend too.

Two salamanders were standing by the lift. They greeted Kassándra and Bohumil with effusive politeness, the lift door opened and one of the salamanders said, It's the third floor, isn't it?

Yes, Kassándra said, the salamander pressed buttons three and six and asked cheerfully, Did you have a nice weekend?

My weekend was crap, Bohumil said.

Kassándra felt a frisson, a cheeky, crazy urge, and to her surprise said, Yes, and Monday's been crap so far too!

Oh!

The lift floated upwards, it was very slow, cruelly slow given the situation. Bohumil said, And this lift is crap too.

Kassándra giggled. To herself.

At the third floor Bohumil and Kassándra got out.

Bonne journée!

Bonne journée!

Bohumil laughed. Kassándra said, I'm glad to see you laughing again. Now I want to tell you about my weekend. You and Xeno. It's important. And you'll be surprised.

Fenia Xenopoulou was already at her desk with a cup of coffee from the canteen. The forecast was for another oppressively hot day, the window was open, and already now, at eight o'clock in the morning, the air was warm, but Fenia Xenopoulou seemed to be freezing. She clutched her coffee with both hands as if trying to warm herself. But perhaps that was habit. She wasn't cold, or if she was, then only emotionally. She had a hangover. Not a physical hangover, but a moral one. She had spent the night with Fridsch and to begin with hadn't been able to tell him that . . . in the end she had – much too late, when it was no longer the right moment – made the suggestion that . . . and he . . . dozing off . . . and she . . . holding her coffee with both hands and feeling ashamed that then she . . . she had held the pillow over his face and . . . she just wanted to see if he was capable of any more emotion, or are men incapable of emotion when all the protein has gone? He thrashed about, knocked her away, screamed, and she burst into tears . . . well, then he took her in his arms and . . .

Kassándra came into the room, why was she so wired? We need to talk, have you got a moment, it's important, for the Jubilee Project, oh, you've got coffee, good idea, I'll get one too and tell Bohumil, is it O.K. to meet back here in ten?

Have you got a cigarette?

No, I don't smoke. If you want to smoke we'd better go to Bohumil's office, he disabled that thing on the ceiling, you can smoke in his room without the alarm going off.

A quarter of an hour later they were sitting in Bohumil's office, Kassándra had fetched coffee for everybody. For the first time in public Xeno smoked three cigarettes, one after the other, while Kassándra talked about the Dossin barracks in Mechelen.

Kassándra loved going places by train at the weekends. She adored the fact that "from Brussels everything is so close", as she liked to put it – her Europe: you were in Paris in less than ninety minutes, in London in two and a half hours, and in Cologne or Amsterdam in less than two. Sometimes she left early on Sunday morning and came back that evening, sometimes she left on Saturday and spent the night away. She would visit museums and galleries, meet friends in bistros and occasionally treat herself to a nice little number from a boutique. That weekend, however, she had taken a regional train rather than the Thalys and gone to Mechelen, only thirty kilometres away, less than half an hour from Brussels.

In *Le Soir* she had read an obituary of Gustave Jakubowicz, the famous Brussels lawyer who had also played an important role in the history of the European Court of Human Rights. The man was a legend, highly active until recently, until he had died at the age of almost ninety. What had particularly caught Kassándra's attention was the line about the obituary's author: "Jean Nebenzahl, academic staff member at the Documentation Centre on the Holocaust and Human Rights in Mechelen". During the Nazi occupation the Dossin barracks had been the S.S.'s transit camp in Belgium, from where Jews, Roma and resistance fighters were deported to Auschwitz. Kassándra was aware that the barracks were now a museum, but she didn't know that there was a research centre too, an academic institution that was methodically examining the history of deportations to Auschwitz. She wrote an e-mail to Jean Nebenzahl, who replied promptly. He would be very happy to meet Kassándra on Sunday, show her around the exhibition and answer any questions she might have as best he could.

Kassándra was a dedicated official. She went to Mechelen and met Jean Nebenzahl because she thought it might be of interest to the Jubilee Project. It would never have occurred to her to put in for overtime for these hours, or even to wait for her excursion to be "approved as a work trip" for which she could claim expenses afterwards. It interested her, it was a Sunday outing which would give her the opportunity to see something new, learn something, and if it proved helpful for their project, then so much the better.

Jean Nebenzahl was a dedicated academic. Of course he would make himself available on a Sunday, "outside his working hours", if someone from the European Commission came to Mechelen because they had taken an interest in his work. It was becoming ever more difficult to interest people in the work being carried out at this research centre, let alone to secure funding for it. He was touched, therefore, by the curiosity shown by this European official whom he'd Googled at once: area of activity – photographs.

You don't need to thank me, he said, I mean, I'm not some sort of soulless bureaucrat, even if I do sit at Eggert Reeder's desk in this building. Who was he? He was the head of the German military administration in Belgium, he organised the deportation of more than thirty thousand Jews to Auschwitz. After the war he was sentenced to twelve years imprisonment and was then pardoned by Konrad Adenauer. All he did was sit at a desk. He wasn't responsible for the murder of Jews in Auschwitz. He just wrote their names on lists during his office hours so they could be delivered to the slaughterhouse in an organised fashion. He never worked overtime, he was definitely not a fanatic. After his pardon he received a civil servant's pension in the Federal Republic of Germany. And today I sit at his desk and work with these lists.

Jean Nebenzahl was a good-looking man, around Kassándra's age, and physically a very similar type to her: not thin. Kassándra didn't trust gaunt men; they tended to be ascetics – rigid and joyless. But Jean wasn't fat either. Kassándra found fat men shapeless, unattractive and lacking self-control, but one ought not to generalise, so Kassándra suspected that most fat men, or at least many of them, had let themselves go. Jean was simply a man, tall, strong . . . and yet soft, that was how she regarded what he himself would have described as "a bit too snug". And she was entranced by his brown eyes and curly black hair.

Why should we be interested in the fact that you've fallen in love? Xeno said.

There were only two chairs in Bohumil's office: the desk chair and a visitor's chair. Bohumil had offered his desk chair to Xeno, but she preferred to stand. With irritation writ across her face she looked down at Kassándra, who was sitting on the visitor's chair. Kassándra leaped up. Don't you understand? I thought I spelled it out clearly enough! They. Have. Got. The. Lists! In Mechelen! The archive of the S.S. intelligence agency responsible for the deportations is preserved in its entirety. We've been corresponding with the entire world while all the time it's been here under our very noses. Thirty minutes away by train! Now I know how many Auschwitz survivors are still living and I've even got their names.

How many are there?

Sixteen, Kassándra said.

Sixty?

Sixteen!

Sixteen? Worldwide?

If they were on the deportation lists and later were registered as survivors, i.e. if there's some sort of record of them and they're known, then yes.

Are there contact addresses?

Jean said not all of them are up to date. With some there's been no regular contact. But basically, yes.

And in what – how shall I put it? – state? I mean, how is their health . . . I mean, could they travel, and appear in public?

Five are known to make regular appearances in schools or as part of other history eyewitness programmes.

Five?

Yes. And one is a special case. A certain David de Vriend. And he lives here in Brussels. Jean said that if he understood our project correctly then this de Vriend would be our ideal eyewitness.

Why?

Not only is he one of the last Auschwitz survivors, he's also the last living Jew from the legendary 20th deportation train to Auschwitz. This was the only deportation train that was ambushed by resistance fighters and stopped out in the open. They used pliers to cut the wire that secured the locks on the cattle-wagon doors, slid them open and called to the Jews to jump out and escape. Anybody who jumped got fifty francs and the address of a secure place to stay. Most of them were frightened, scared of being shot by the Germans if they tried to escape. They stayed on the train which, after a brief exchange of fire between the resistance fighters and S.S. guards, continued on its way. All those who didn't jump went straight to the gas chamber on arrival at Auschwitz. But de Vriend was one of those who jumped.

But you said he was in Auschwitz.

The escape happened in April 1943. He was taken to a family in a village – he can't remember the name – who claimed he was a nephew from Brussels. He was very young at the time and seriously traumatised: his parents had stayed on the train. He could have waited for the end of the war with the family who had taken him in, but he wanted to fight, perhaps to liberate his parents?

In June 1944 he joined the resistance group *"Europe libre"* as its youngest member, this was the group around Richard Brunfaut, you might have heard of him – you'll know rue Brunfaut at least. The group was legendary for its daredevil missions, but also because it differed politically from all the other resistance groups: it was the only one that was committed to a free Europe – as its name suggested – rather than just a free Belgium. After the war, after the victory over the Nazis, they wanted the abolition of the Belgian monarchy and the establishment of a European Republic. Until the end of their lives, Brunfaut and his comrades involved themselves in the struggle against the fascist regimes in Spain and Portugal too, against Franco and Salazar, who curiously the victorious powers had forgotten after liberating Europe. Anyway, in August 1944 David de Vriend was betrayed, arrested and deported to Auschwitz. He wasn't sent to the gas chamber because he was young and strong. He survived the months until liberation. After the war he became a teacher. He didn't just make the occasional appearance in schools as a historical eyewitness like many other survivors, he wanted to become a teacher so that every day he could be looking after the next generation. He didn't want to be an eyewitness, he wanted to be an educator. If we're going to stick with Martin's idea – and we do, after all, have the president's consent – then this man must be at the very centre of our celebrations. He's got everything: a victim of racism, a resistance fighter, a victim of collaboration and betrayal, a witness of the extermination camp, a visionary of a post-national Europe founded on human rights, history and the lessons from history all rolled into one, in the person of this teacher.

Very nice, Xeno said. What rousing intensity. There's just one small problem.

*

Madame Joséphine was worried about de Vriend. She was a fair woman who liked to treat all her "charges", as she called them, as equally as possible, whether she found them nice, unpleasant or even repellent, whether they were communicative or gruff, friendly or aggressive. Joséphine believed that they all had good reasons for being the way they were here, biographical reasons that manifested themselves explicitly in this place, when they understood that in the Maison Hanssens they had nothing to do but doze their way to the end of their lives, even if they did behave as if they were guests in a spa hotel.

All the people she looked after were at the end of their life, but not yet finished with it. This was Joséphine's experience, her insight. Every day she tried to imagine what this meant. For each individual person. In this respect they were all the same, and in their sameness she no longer differentiated between low-maintenance and more troublesome charges, friendly and unfriendly ones. David de Vriend had never shown the need to communicate with her more than was necessary. And if he thanked her for something it sounded more like a dismissal than a manifestation of gratitude. De Vriend wasn't, therefore, one of those charges you couldn't help loving and who you wanted to spoil extravagantly with your attention. And yet Joséphine felt that she had a particular responsibility for Monsieur de Vriend. Was this because of the number on his arm? She wondered about this and at the same time wouldn't allow herself to entertain the thought. She was fair, equally considerate to them all. Life had played its game with each of them.

And so, with the best of intentions, she stormed into de Vriend's room with two newspapers and shouted, You never come —

De Vriend sat in the armchair wearing only his underpants.

I haven't seen you in the common room for days, Joséphine

bellowed, where the newspapers are. But we have to read the papers, don't we, Monsieur de Vriend? Or don't we want to know what's going on in the world? No, no, we *do* want to know, we want to remain cu-ri-ous, don't we, Monsieur de Vriend? What do you prefer, Monsieur de Vriend? *Le Soir* or *De Morgen*? I think you're a *De Morgen* reader, aren't you? Now we're going to read and give our little grey cells a bit of training, alright? De Vriend's apathy naturally got on Joséphine's nerves, but she nonetheless tried to encourage him to remain alert, communicative, before he faded away altogether.

De Vriend picked up the paper, looked at it, then leafed through it slowly until suddenly he bent forwards and stared.

Shall we read an article together? Are you interested in . . .

De Vriend stood up, walked across the room, back and forth, looking, searching. Madame Joséphine stared at him in astonish-ment. What are you looking for?

My notepad. Haven't you seen? The death notices. I have to cross out a name, yet another name from my list.

Ten

Gdy wszystko było na próżno,
nawet najpiękniejsze wspomnienie nas nie pocieszy.
I jak tu szukać usprawiedliwienia?

É MILE BRUNFAUT STOOD naked in the bathroom with his back to the mirror, trying to peer over his shoulder to establish whether there was a bruise or a wound in the area of his coccyx or sacrum. Initially the bath had relaxed him, but the longer he sat in the tub the more intense the pain above his buttocks had become, unquestionably a result of his fall.

His cervical vertebrae clicked and crunched, but he couldn't turn his head far enough to see the small of his back. Now the pain in his coccyx was joined by muscle tension in his neck. Brunfaut knew, of course, that his body couldn't be as supple, flexible and elastic as a Russian gymnast's, but the fact that he was so stiff depressed him. "To avoid getting rusty", his colleague Jules Meunier had regularly done Yoga exercises in police headquarters. He had even performed the odd headstand during the longer meetings. How ridiculous Brunfaut had found it! But so quirky, on the other hand, that it was almost endearing. Jules had probably been right. Brunfaut was certain that Jules could turn his head and look at his back and coccyx in the mirror without feeling any tension or pain at all. Oh Jules! How elastic and flexible you were when the Atlas case was taken from me and I had to go. You were able to turn your back on me just like that, without any tension or pain!

Brunfaut was trying to massage his neck – it was all very stiff back there – when the telephone rang. He ran from the bathroom to the bedroom where he had undressed, but his mobile wasn't there. He ran into the sitting room and there it was, on the desk. He picked it up and froze. It was Philippe.

Listen, Brunfaut said, we're not going to discuss this over the phone. Yes, I do want you to explain. Of course. Let's meet . . . where? Café Kafka? Where's that? Rue des Poissonniers? Corner of rue Antoine Dansaert. O.K. In an hour and a half. *D'accord.*

When Brunfaut got to the café there was no sign of Philippe. He was a good quarter of an hour early, so it didn't necessarily mean anything, but all the same he had a queasy feeling that Philippe was playing some sort of a game and was going to stand him up again.

Stand him up? Well, it was better than sitting down – Émile Brunfaut could barely sit at all. The pain in his coccyx was excruciating. Sitting was only bearable if he shifted his weight onto one half of his pelvis. But how long could he do that for? He stood up and went to the bar. In agony he kept shifting his weight from one leg to the other, drank his beer down in one, ordered another and a jenever to go with it. He checked the time. He certainly wasn't going to wait half or three-quarters of an hour for Philippe, who might not turn up anyway. He'd wait ten minutes at most. He knocked back the schnapps, picked up his beer glass and went outside. How hot it was. He couldn't recall a spring or early summer in Brussels ever having been so hot, so oppressive, so brutal. The tarmac, the cobblestones, the walls of buildings stored the heat and radiated it. Not even the occasional gust of wind brought relief; it merely slammed the heat into your face like a crushing blow. And right now there was a most peculiar, unnatural-looking light, it was just before sunset, but here in the depths of the street you couldn't see the sun itself, only yellowish-pink shafts of light that – Brunfaut looked up – appeared to coat the sky with a toxic varnish.

Émile Brunfaut was a poetic soul. He just didn't know it because he read few books. And no poetry at all. Of all the poems he had learned at school – and there weren't many – only one had stayed in his memory: "À une passante", because at the time the line "*Un éclair . . . puis la nuit! – Fugitive beauté*" had strangely moved him. Later, when he was a police inspector, he used to pep up his team when they were groping around in the dark with his own version of the line: *La nuit . . . puis l'éclair! – Le fugitive est visible.* As far as he was concerned, this had been the only poetic success of his life. But he underestimated himself. Now he was painfully moved by this light and he sensed it as a metaphor – unquestionably a poetic act. The bad light. All of a sudden everything appeared in a bad light. The familiar assumed a toxic coating and – he was looking at the building on the corner opposite the street sign: "Poissonniers" – there was a fishy shimmer.

He would have liked to hang around longer in this light, in this atmosphere – not that he found it pleasant, but . . . actually, yes, he did. He found it atmospheric. Atmosphere, atmospheric, yes, that was it. It was the light of his mental pain, but he could not bear the physical pain. He finished his beer and was about to go back inside and pay when all of a sudden there was Philippe, embracing him – why so cheerfully, and why was he squeezing him so tightly?

Brunfaut groaned briefly and withdrew from the embrace. What's wrong? Philippe said. Are you in pain?

Why did Brunfaut find the expression of concern in his friend's face so exaggerated? How could Philippe think that he would fall for this charade? But if it weren't a charade, then how could he believe that his best friend might be capable of engineering one?

He was so furious he was on the verge of stamping his foot to check that the ground wasn't shifting and wouldn't fall from under him. Yes, he was in pain, he said, he fell at the cemetery. At the *cemetery*. Did that ring a bell? He took a deep breath. We had an appointment, didn't we? You weren't there. I'm sure you've got an explanation.

My God, what made you fall? Did you injure yourself?

What if I say it was because I didn't see you, but I did see a ghost?

Philippe was about to say something, but instead shook his head, then pointed at Brunfaut's empty glass and said, Let's go inside, we need a drink.

It was the time of day when the café filled up quickly. Now there was no table free, but Émile Brunfaut said that he couldn't down sit anyway.

I went arse over tit. At our meeting point in the cemetery. My coccyx, it's sheer agony.

He made a sign to the man behind the bar: two beers!

I won't be able to stand for much longer either, so let's not beat about the bush. What happened? Why weren't you there? What's the deal with this mysterious friend we were supposed to meet? Is he the old boy who asked me if I was talking to the dead? Are you going to tell me that this was some kind of code for me to identify him? And why couldn't I get you on the phone? Please, Philippe, give me some explanation. And I beg you, explain it in a way that I can understand.

You're not going to believe this, Philippe said, but —

Their beer arrived.

Émile Brunfaut raised his glass and said, *Santé!* So, I'm not going to believe it? Go on.

Listen, Philippe said. There's a very simple explanation. The problem is, even though it's very logical, it's not very believable.

You'll manage to make me believe you.

I don't believe I will. I've never seen you so mistrustful, you're turning into your grandfather, you've got to be careful, it's this mistrust that destroys trust. Anyway, I'll tell you the story as quickly as I can so you can get straight back to bed. By the way, Joëlle says hi and asks when you're going to come and see us again. I'll tell her she's got be patient because you're poorly. Right, the whole thing began when I got a letter. We'd already drawn a line under the matter, hadn't we? You know what I mean. And then this letter arrived. I'll say it again: a letter. Not an e-mail, not some electronic message. I almost missed it because all I ever do with the contents of my mailbox is tip them straight into the bin. Nothing but flyers, right? Anyway, the author of this letter, who called themselves "Nobody", said that they'd traced me back.

Traced you back?

Yes. When I was trying to make some headway in finding out how the Atlas case could have been wiped from your computer, I must have found my way at least into the periphery of a system that was – let's word it carefully – involved. I just don't know exactly. Anyway, someone there noticed that I was trying to hack in. And if this really is a big deal, then "Nobody" will have worked out pretty quickly that it was me. What my name is, where I live, everything. They can do all this. So Nobody wrote me a letter and explained why they'd chosen this medium to establish contact: a good old letter sent by snail-mail is the only form of communication that can't be stored somewhere, read by others, analysed and used against you. What used to be called a "dead drop", a safe place for secret messages is now your everyday mailbox. Well, you know Léo Aubry from the laboratory. A good guy. Always helpful. And absolutely trustworthy, wouldn't you agree? Exactly. I gave him the letter. The paper: bog-standard, the top-selling brand, you can get

500 sheets of it for four euros in every discount store. The printer: so far as he could conclude from the ink, a simple Canon, the best-selling printer in Belgium. And not the slightest trace of D.N.A. on the paper, nor anything else that might provide a clue to the sender.

O.K. But what did the letter say?

That I'd really stuck my neck out. That there was no way this could have been agreed with my superiors at work. I must be a lone warrior working outside my job. He was too.

He? What made you think that Nobody is a man?

Good question. I assumed it.

I see. What else?

He – I'm convinced it's a man – wrote that he wasn't the type of whistleblower who was prepared to wreck his own life, but he sympathised with everyone who looked for cracks for the truth to seep through.

Those were his words?

Yes. And he offered me his help. If I was interested in corresponding with him I should avoid making any further attempts to penetrate into the system, because he could no longer guarantee that the alert I had triggered could be kept hidden. He would supply me with the information I needed. If I agreed to this I should enter the following search into Google at a specific time the next day: "Hopi Indians rain dance".

Hopi what? What on earth are you talking about? That's crazy!

No, it's not crazy. Obviously this Nobody is able to see what I do at my computer. If I entered his search and then then clicked on one of the websites that came up, he'd know I was accepting his proposal without it showing up in the system at all.

And so you did it?

Yes.

I need another beer.

Me too. And do you know what happened next? I entered the words "Hopi Indian rain dance" and Google immediately came up with "System theory and new social movements. Identity problems in the risk society."

I don't understand.

There is nothing to understand. It's the title of a book and in this book there's obviously a chapter about Hopi Indians and rain dances. For whatever reason. And I clicked it.

And?

Two days later came the next letter.

How did you reply?

By means of Google searches at specific times. The keywords were my answer or my questions. He was obviously somewhere where he could monitor who was searching what on Google.

How often did you . . . I mean, how long did this go on?

Three weeks? Maybe four.

And you didn't say a word about it to me? We went to see Anderlecht against Mechelen, we wept into our scarves, how could they have beaten us 2:0? Then we had at least five beers and talked about everything under the sun, but you didn't say a thing about this Nobody. It must have . . . it must have been at that time.

It was, but first I wanted to be sure it was for real. It could just as easily have been a nutter.

But it wasn't a nutter.

No, or, I don't know. He gave me interesting and credible information. Like the dossier on the cooperation between the Vatican and the Western intelligence services. I read it, it was bewildering, fantastical even, but at the same time entirely logical and understandable too. They were pieces of a puzzle that fitted together perfectly. Look, no secret service in the world has the resources – neither the financial means nor the personnel – to develop a network of agents stretching across the globe in a way which can keep up with the current state of globalisation. Nowadays they have their agents in the hotspots. But who trusts them, who gives them information? Only those who are already cooperating with the governments of these intelligence services. Which means that what these agents report back doesn't really differ from what the ambassador reports back home. And anyway, where will the next hotspot be? What will catch fire tomorrow while millions are invested in the work of perhaps thirty agents sitting in the spas of the few hotels still up and running in crisis zones? And twenty of those thirty are with the C.I.A., all in the same place treading on each other's toes, whereas elsewhere they've got nobody. And that's supposed to be the most powerful intelligence service in the world. Right then, here's a simple question: Who, on the other hand, has got an agent in every backwater? The Vatican. Why? In every backwater there's a priest. Who gets wind of the most secret of secrets in every corner of the planet? The priest, not least via the confessional. And even if they don't have everything covered, their information yield is many times greater than the best-equipped secret service could ever muster. And that, my friend, is why the intelligence services compete for the Vatican's favour, for cooperation and information exchange with the Church. It was like that during the Cold War and now it's not even a secret any more. Now there's a different enemy. These days it's no longer godless communism, these days the enemy is called Islam.

But . . . hang on! A Muslim isn't going to go to a priest and confess that he's carried out a terror attack or is planning one. That's crazy.

No, of course not. But good Christians might tell their priest if they notice anything suspicious about the new tenants who've moved into the neighbouring apartment, for example, or the block next door or opposite. They might sit at their windows with binoculars and peer into the buildings on the other side of the street. Is inquisitiveness a sin? Surely not our kind of inquisitiveness. But just as we usually file reports on what we've been investigating, the Christian confesses. And that's why the partnerships established between the intelligence services and the Vatican during the Cold War still exist.

Do you really believe that? Brunfaut said.

Philippe hesitated, then laughed. I'm not a religious man. I don't believe. And you can believe what you want now. I'll give you the facts. How's the coccyx coping, by the way?

Another beer and another jenever and it'll be fine.

Good. I'll try to keep up. So this Nobody has now hinted that with the sanction of the intelligence services the Church operates some kind of death squad that simply bumps off suspected terrorists or so-called hate preachers. That is to say, people who are suspected of planning an act of terror, but who the democratic state has insufficient evidence against to detain legally. And so we come to the Atlas case. Holy warriors carry out the job and the secret services support them by making the case disappear into thin air. Nobody sent me a list of fourteen murder cases in Europe from the past year, none of which made it into the newspapers.

Did you check them out?

Yes. I couldn't find even the slightest hint of any of the cases on his list. Which means either they didn't happen, or the cover-up was so immaculate that it left no clues whatsoever.

We're getting into conspiracy-theory territory here.

No, we're not. Because if you were to look for clues relating to the Atlas case you wouldn't find a scrap of evidence either. Nothing. Absolutely nothing. But we know it happened. And what we need isn't proof of the fourteen murders on the list, but an explanation for the murder in Hotel Atlas. I must say, Nobody's explanation sounds damned logical to me! *Santé!*

Something was troubling Brunfaut. And his experience as a policeman told him that if something about a cover story troubled you, then in all likelihood there really was something fishy about it.

I don't understand why you didn't let me know and keep me posted, he said.

But I did, Philippe said. I mean, I know you. I knew I had to offer you more than a story like that. You need facts. I wanted to meet Nobody. And so the only search entries I made at the time agreed were variations on the word "meeting". Three days later came another letter: Meet at the cemetery, I'll let you know the details.

So finally you get your meeting with this ghost, and then you don't turn up?

What do you mean? I *was* there. Of course I was. I have no idea where you were. Maybe by the wrong memorial, maybe at the wrong time, I don't know. At any rate, I was there. And I sat on a bench, waiting for Nobody and you. Then my mobile rang. I picked up and a voice said, Monsieur Philippe Gaultier? Yes, I said. Are you sitting on the bench we agreed as our meeting point? he said. Realising who it was, I said, Yes. Stand up, please, he said. What? Why? I said. Please stand up, he said. I stood up and he said, Please turn around and tell me what you can see. I thought that was ludicrous and said, Listen, I don't want to play games. No games, he said. What can you see? A tree, I said, then thought how ridiculous that was, what sort of an answer was that? And behind it? he said. Graves, I said. Soldiers' graves. White crosses. Very good, he said. And behind those? Nothing, I said, just a vast field of white crosses. Look up, then, he said. What do you see now?

Nothing, I said, I don't know what you want me to say. I want you to tell me what you see, he said. Nothing, I said, trees, sky. And between the trees and sky? Beyond the cemetery? he said. Yes, two large buildings, I said, like two giant blocks of Emmental. Exactly, he said, do you know what that is? N.A.T.O., I said. Correct, he said. And now you have all the information I'm able to give you. Work with it or give up! Ciao!

You were at the cemetery when you got this telephone call?

Yes. I waited another three-quarters of an hour for you, and then I left.

But why did you switch off your phone? I called you several times because I couldn't find you, and —

After that there was a problem with my mobile – I couldn't receive or make calls. And as soon as it started working again I rang you. Which is why we're sitting here now.

What a marvellous story this was, Brunfaut thought. So exciting. He wouldn't have thought Philippe capable of it. But he didn't believe a single word. And he felt dreadfully hurt.

The pain's getting worse, he said. Forgive me, I've got to go home. He saw that Philippe hadn't touched his schnapps. Émile picked up the glass, downed its contents and said, *À bientôt, mon ami!* Then he hobbled out. He realised he was limping, he didn't want that, so he tried to walk upright, without any visible injury, but without success. He hobbled out of Café Kafka with the violent urge to scream.

They had known that same day that Matek had flown to Kraków rather than Istanbul. And three days later they knew that all the clues leading to Warsaw the following day were a false trail he had laid deliberately. Matek had no confirmation of this, but he assumed it was the case. And he also knew that if he didn't leave after three days he would put Pater Szymon, his close friend from his seminary days, in a moral dilemma. Szymon had given him refuge in the Augustinian monastery in the belief that Matek needed a period of retreat and contemplation. Szymon was absolutely loyal, Matek knew that he could rely on him, but he also knew Szymon would never be able to understand that Matek was in fact hiding in the monastery from the Church authorities. They knew his contacts, so Szymon would certainly appear in their sights from day four. And it was equally clear which side Szymon would come down on in the conflict between loyal friendship and the vow of obedience he had taken as a priest. Matek had used the three days for meditation, to ponder his situation and recharge his batteries. But now he had to leave. He had two options. First, he could keep on the move, staying in cheap hotels that weren't so fussy about registration and I.D. papers. He wouldn't use bank cards or credit cards, and wherever he could he'd avoid C.C.T.V. cameras in public places. He was a submarine, invisible and unlocatable. On the other hand, he had no possibility of finding out what had gone wrong in Brussels, in Hotel Atlas, and what they were now planning for him. And his cash would last another week at most. A week as a submarine would not improve his situation, nor would he be any the wiser at the end of it. His second option was to enter the lion's den! He had to find out what had happened and what was in store for him. And there was only one place he could do that: Poznań. If he went to ground, they wouldn't expect that he would turn up at H.Q. It was dangerous. But if it went badly he could show humility and argue that he had in fact come home of his own accord.

As he left he embraced Szymon and said, Thank you, Brother. Then giving both his hands a squeeze he added, May God protect you!

Szymon smiled: May God protect you too! And ... have a good trip to Poznań!

Very little fazed Matek. He was constantly on his guard, he calculated all the possibilities and was, or so he thought, prepared for every eventuality in every situation. He had the cold blood of a man who was a fourth-generation soldier. But he hadn't counted on this. "Have a good trip to Poznań!" – it hit him like a blow that briefly stunned him. He took a deep breath, put down his rucksack and said, You know ...

Szymon nodded.

... that I'm going to Poznań? But I didn't tell you.

You're expected there. And you have nothing to fear.

What do you know, Brother Szymon? And why didn't you tell me anything?

You didn't ask. You participated in the spiritual exercises, the common prayer, the observation of silence. You came to the meals, apart from in the evening, and kept quiet at all times, not only during the prescribed silence. Otherwise you spent hours in the chapel, kneeling before "Our Lady of Consolation". If a brother asks me something, I give information, but you didn't ask.

But you gave information?

Yes.

They asked about me?

Szymon nodded.

Matek looked at the floor, then slowly raised his head. He saw Szymon's black habit, the black leather belt, the black mozzetta from the collar of which a grey neck emerged, on which Szymon's grey face sat beneath the black hood. Matek lowered his eyes again, looked at his own hands, which were grey too, he let them fall by his sides and they disappeared in the greyish-black above the black stone floor in this gloomy antechamber. Now Matek looked

Szymon directly in the eye. Szymon's lips were red. As if he'd bitten them and drawn blood. I'm going to ask you now, Matek said. What do you know? What can you tell me?

You had a mission. I don't know what it was. It went slightly wrong. I don't know how. It wasn't your fault. You are expected. You have nothing to fear. That is what I was to say to you if you asked.

Matek looked at Szymon, nodded, took his head in his hands, pulled him towards him and pressed his mouth onto Szymon's blood-red lips. The blood-red, the only glow in the room, which at this very moment was outer space and at the same time just an airlock out into the world.

Then he stepped out of the monastery into the open air, into the perilous, into the imperilled open air.

After days in the silent gloom behind thick walls, the harsh light struck him like a thunderbolt.

The D.-G. AGRI hadn't responded to the Inter-Service consultation about the Jubilee Project and hadn't sent anybody to the meeting. No-one in that directorate-general was interested in the planning of jubilees and ceremonies, particularly if the celebrations weren't focusing on showcasing the achievements of European agricultural policy. And AGRI was even less interested if the D.-G. COMM was delegating the preparations for the celebrations to Culture, that "ark in a dry dock", as George Morland had once called it. Every mountain knows that you can't really make a mountain out of a molehill.

And now it was that very same George Morland from AGRI who, after preliminary spanners in the works from the Council, had begun to weave threads in the Commission that would become the rope around the neck of the project.

Like most of the British officials, George Morland wasn't especially liked in the Commission. The British – even the president
had once said this – only accepted one binding rule: that fundamentally they were an exception. In truth the British were always
suspected of neglecting the interests of the Community for the
benefit of London's interests. In many instances the suspicion was
justified. But in others it was more complicated: whether one liked
it not, the United Kingdom was indeed a special case. The British
Crown held possessions that legally were not part of the United
Kingdom, such as the Isle of Man and the Channel Islands, which
represented an intractable problem when it came to the development of a European tax policy: the tax havens of a Member State
to which there was legally no access. The Queen was formally the
head of the Commonwealth States, which necessarily led to legal
nit-picking, for example in all trade deals concluded by the E.U.
with non-E.U. states. Had this exceptional situation not been
taken into consideration each time with the implementation of
special regulations, then Australia, for example, would all of a
sudden have become part of the European internal market. With
Britain it had been complicated from the outset, but there were
definitely Brits who became Europeans in Brussels. And George
Morland had to be given credit, not only for having learned a few
scraps of French during his years in the Commission, but also for
his significant contribution to European policy. In his role within
AGRI he had always been a passionate defender and supporter of
small-scale agriculture. Even if he was principally motivated by
the desire to see the English countryside cultivated by traditional
methods, rather than destroyed by enormous agro-industrial
complexes and monocultures, it was also in the interests of Europe
generally. And in this regard Morland, with his upper-class breed-
ing, would not be bribed by agro-industries, multinational seed

companies or their lobbyists. He – or his family – had a considerable landholding in the East Riding of Yorkshire, leased out to several small farmers. Morland knew the difficulties they faced as well as their successes. Defending their concerns against the radical intensification of agriculture was a classic case of self-interest that served the common good. The only monoculture he found acceptable was the golf course.

Thus Morland was a very ambivalent case. He knew he wasn't popular, but that had little to do with his work in the Commission. He had suffered already in his youth, first as a schoolboy, then as a student at Oxford. He cut an unfortunate and at first glance comical figure, and despite his every effort he lacked charm. His round pink face, his flat nose, his thick red hair that he could tame only by means of a crew cut, his short, stocky frame – as a child he had spent many a night sobbing into his pillow because of the nasty names that had been flung at him. But his background had protected him from a worse fate than taunting. Like a kind of psychological self-defence, it had ultimately made him haughty, but also especially ambitious. He learned how to earn respect through the posts he held during his career, although he was, with his ironic smile, thoroughly old school: Morland ensured that if in doubt, anybody who didn't have a high regard for him should fear him.

Now is the winter of our discontent / Made glorious summer by this sun of Brussels.

But the sun was being eclipsed. He was an E.N.D., an *Expert National Détaché*, and his time in Brussels was running out. And in all the chaos of the negotiations around Great Britain's exit from the Union he'd made a grave error that had critically damaged his reputation back home. The Germans had indeed concluded a bilateral trade agreement with China, opening up the Chinese market for their pig production. Pigs! He had failed to take this seriously; he had been heavily involved in boycotting all attempts to bring about a treaty between the Union and China, trying to defend privileges for the United Kingdom, and he hadn't been able to see the consequences. That Kai-Uwe Frigge had been right after all! The turbulence on the London Stock Market had been considerable and had accelerated the transfer of important funds to Frankfurt. All because of pigs! It had left Morland stunned. He simply couldn't understand the vast economic significance of China's intention to import the offal from pigs too. In times of hunger the Irish had bought pigs' trotters for a few pence and cooked them for hours – wretched food in times of extreme poverty – while butchers in London had given away pigs' ears to regular customers for their dogs. And the pig's head . . . well, he'd once stuck his penis into the mouth of a dead pig to be accepted as a member of the Bullingdon Club, the exclusive student society at Oxford for the offspring of "better" families. This initiation ritual had been his final humiliation, mitigated by intoxication and the cheering of other members. Afterwards he merely earned respect. Pig may contain traces of Tories. Yes, ha ha! How they were laughing now, the Germans! They were selling offal for the price of fillet, but Britain wasn't getting a slice of it and soon the U.K. would be out altogether.

It was crazy, totally irrational, but this pig story was a major reason why George Morland now shifted to a policy of radical obstruction. If Britain was suffering the damage, then at least it ought to be able to mock the party that inflicted the damage. And now every failure by the Commission was strengthening the U.K.'s position in the forthcoming negotiations. If the Commission, allegedly under the patronage of the president, was preparing a P.R. campaign, then it must fail. If the Commission had a poor image, it was a good thing. For Britain.

Morland leaned back in his chair and filed his fingernails. Why were they tearing, splitting and breaking all of a sudden? He pondered as he filed away, occasionally blowing the nail dust from his chest.

And dear Mrs Atkinson! Morland smiled. It might not be a matter of national – and certainly not of European – significance, but it would be a nice footnote in the history of his political endeavours if this frigid woman with her muff were damaged in the collapse of the Jubilee Project. It was only because of the female quota that she had landed that job, which he had aspired to and for which he had initially been regarded as the favourite. George Morland would never admit it, it wasn't exactly what he would call "an objective necessity", but the mere thought that he might be able to bring about Mrs Atkinson's downfall pleased him greatly.

Assuming he had analysed the situation correctly, he had a clear idea of what now had to be done. A few lunch dates with important colleagues from other directorates-general, preferably in Martin's, which with its lovely garden kept the smokers amongst them happy and much more relaxed, open. There he would serve up bespoke arguments to unnerve them and turn them against the project.

Morland changed files. After the coarse, now came the fine.

To begin with it would have a certain momentum of its own – gossip, rumours – and then the anxiety would have to be guided carefully in a particular direction, so as to create the need for a Council working group to thrash out the problem and solve it.

"Solve the problem." George Morland was conservative in relation to this phrasing too. Over the past few years an astonishing language shift had taken place within the Commission and nobody had noticed, or at least nobody had commented on it, let alone questioned it. Whereas people used to talk of "solving a problem", now they said: "bringing a solution to the problem". Whereas it used to be "making a decision", now it was "effecting a decision". Instead of "analysing something", that thing now "underwent an analysis". Arrangements that once were "made" were now "facilitated". You could compile an entire lexicon of the new "Comitology-Speak", and it was astonishing how in this Babylon certain linguistic trends immediately caught on in all languages. George Morland was sensitive enough to recognise this. Although he was no expert in semiotics, hermeneutics or linguistics, he nonetheless had the sure feeling that this development was a sign, had a significance that was symptomatic of the state of the Commission, of its helplessness, its paralysis. "Facilitating" was clearly different, more defensive than "making". These formulations betrayed the fact that it was no longer about the destination, only the journey. That was broadly how he saw it. But he wouldn't accept it. He insisted on the good old "solving a problem" and in this instance it was straightforward: kill the project, kill Mrs Atkinson.

He picked up the soft nail brush, to remove any tiny particles of nail dust that might still be in evidence, then fetched the colourless nail polish from his desk drawer. As he cheerfully varnished his nails he thought, with just a touch of derision, of Mrs Atkinson hiding her cold fingers with their chewed nails in her muff.

And only two weeks later, above any suspicion, he was able to join in the general chorus of those calling for the creation a Council working group under the aegis of the C.A.C. ("Cultural Affairs Committee").

Mrs Atkinson knew at once that this was the end of the project she hadn't at all been in favour of herself. It had been Culture's initiative. Externally the project was entirely associated with that

Xenopoulou woman, who had been throwing her weight around. For her part, Xeno wasn't so sure; she felt that if there was need for further discussion, then Martin should deal with it. After all, the project had been Martin Susman's idea. And she had assigned all the organisational work to him.

And Martin wasn't there.

Where the Maison Hanssens retirement home now stood there had once been a gravestone manufacturer's. Piet Hanssens, a fourth-generation stonemason, had no children, nor was he able to find anybody who wanted to take over the business and keep it running. When, at the age of seventy-three, his silicosis forced him to give up work and embark on a degrading odyssey through hospitals and care homes, he left his house, the workshop and the grounds to the Ville de Bruxelles, on condition that the city or Brussels region build a dignified retirement home on the land. Then he passed away. The financially strapped city accepted the legacy, but it was years before the old gravestone manufacturer's could finally be converted and extended into a modern "Centre of Excellence for Geriatric Care" with the help of E.U. money from the European Fund for Regional Development and the European Social Fund. The former workshop now housed the dining room while the home's library and common room were in the former showroom. Apart from that, nothing remained of the original structure; nothing recalled the history of this place any longer.

Well, almost nothing. Next to the library there was a side entrance, an emergency exit in fact, and behind it a dozen blank gravestones stood on a patch of grass, display pieces left over from the old manufacturer's. It wasn't clear if these stones had simply been forgotten or deliberately left there as a reminder of the place's past. Nobody save the caretaker, Monsieur Hugo, who also mowed the grass around the house, normally got a glimpse of them.

But then David de Vriend discovered the gravestones. Wanting to leave the home – he couldn't remember why – he had momentarily become confused when he stepped out of the lift on the ground floor, what did he want, where was he planning to go, out, he went left instead of right to the front door, now found himself beside the emergency exit, pushed the large red bar that opened it, and in front of him were the gravestones that he stared at in astonishment – he hadn't gone to the cemetery, he'd just wanted a bite to eat. He noticed that there were no names on these headstones – a cemetery of the anonymous? Thousands, hundreds of thousands of people no longer had a name when they were forced to die, the names of millions of people were extinguished before they were sent to their deaths, they had been turned into numbers, but innumerable, and here – he looked and began to count – there were only: two, three, four, five . . . A carer grabbed him by the arm; de Vriend had set off the alarm by opening the emergency exit.

What are you doing here? Did you want to go out? Yes? That's the wrong door. Come on, I'll take you . . . Where do you want to go?

Now de Vriend said assertively that he wanted to go for something to eat.

In the dining room?

No! Outside, in the restaurant, in the – he pointed – in the, there! Next door.

Soon afterwards he was sitting in Le Rustique, the waitress brought him a glass of red wine and he felt ashamed. This was another moment of clarity. And clarity meant shame. He wondered why . . .

Of course he knew why . . .

And he became angry. He didn't want to . . .

It was unbearably hot. De Vriend took off his jacket, rolled up his sleeves and wiped the sweat from his brow with his handkerchief. He couldn't think. It was too loud. At the neighbouring table the large, chattering family, the shrieking children. Irritated, he looked over and smiled. It was a reflex. He had always smiled when he saw children. Out of delight, sympathy or just politeness.

He noticed a girl looking at him inquisitively. How old might she be? Eight, perhaps. Their eyes met. She came over to his table.

Please don't! he thought

Cool! she said, pointing to the number tattooed on de Vriend's arm. Is that real?

Yes, he said and put his jacket back on.

Cool! she said and showed him a transfer on her forearm.

Four Chinese characters.

But this isn't real, she said. I'm not allowed a real one.

Do you know what it means? de Vriend said. No? But you like it? Yes?

He tapped the characters.

The first one: All

The second: People

The third: Are

The fourth: Swine

. . .

I got it wrong he said and tapped

the first one: Old

and the fourth: Silent.

*

Prof. Alois Erhart followed António Oliveira Pinto into the meeting room. He saw the members of the Reflection Group sitting in a semi-circle around the chair from which he was to talk. A semi-circle of laptops and tablets, behind them lowered eyes, gazing at the screens, and he heard the soft, rapid clicking of keyboards.

Erhart stood there and eventually took his seat. The eyes began to focus on him.

So this was to be no more than a discussion? It was deceptive. This was the stage for his execution, more like, the end of his life in the world of experts. But hadn't this been what Erhart was aiming at? What does one say when awaiting an execution? Last words. This is how far it's come, he thought, this was precisely what he'd been driving at for ages: last words.

How cheerfully Mr Pinto greeted all those present! Only the Greek professor who taught at Oxford was still typing something frantically on his laptop, it must be something vitally important and urgent, or at least it was a demonstration of importance and urgency. With a smile Erhart said to him, Are you ready? Can we begin?

Last words. This was a story that went right back to Erhart's first academic publication, an article which appeared in the quarterly *Journal of Economic Research of the University of Vienna* when he had still been a research assistant. In it he had written about Armand Moens' theory of post-national economics, underpinning it with new statistical data on the development of global trade. Brimming with pride, Erhart had sent a copy of his piece to Armand Moens, who, to Erhart's amazement, promptly replied. Alois Erhart had brought Moens' letter with him today, an excerpt of which would form part of the short lecture he now gave.

Erhart began with the Armand Moens quote: "The twentieth century ought to have been the transition of the nineteenth-century national economy to a twenty-first-century economy for mankind. This was thwarted in such a horrific and criminal way that afterwards the desire returned with greater urgency, but only in the minds of a small political elite, whose successors soon no longer understood the criminal energy of nationalism and the consequences that had already been drawn from this experience."

A few people tapped away at their laptops. Erhart didn't know if they were taking notes or answering e-mails. Nor did he care. He had another thirteen to fifteen minutes, he had time, his moment was still to come.

Erhart gave a very brief outline of global economic development up to the First World War and, citing a few figures, the drastic setback caused by nationalism and fascism, and he saw that in the fifth minute of his speech some of his audience were already bored. Nothing bored them as much as a reminder of fascism and nationalism. It was a dark chapter, the book containing that chapter was closed and a new one had been opened long ago, this bookkeeping is fantastic now, apart from in a few sluggish countries where action needs to be taken, that is our job, we disapprove of chapters in old books, we are the new bookkeepers.

Just one example, Erhart said, of the caesura in the years 1914 to 1945: if global trade over the next few years follows the same linear trend as that of the past twenty years – and we cannot take this for granted – then in 2020 it will reach the same volume of global trade as in 1913. This means that we are only just creeping up to the level of globalisation in the pre-war era.

That's nonsense! That can't be true!

They were waking up! Oh, if only they knew that they were nowhere near awake yet!

Why do you say "nonsense"? This is verified statistical data, Erhart said. I just wanted to remind you, I'm surprised you didn't know it.

Then Erhart came out with three further Moens quotations as evidence for his argument that the development of the transnational economy required new democratic institutions, which must supersede the national parliaments. O.K., he had really condensed all this, but Erhart didn't have much time left and he wanted to move on to the shock.

He took a deep breath, then said, And now I'd like to tell you a little story. I've cited Armand Moens a few times in this paper. You swallowed that. Maybe you thought, O.K., Moens might not be mainstream, but these are quotations from a noted economist, and you, ladies and gentlemen, you cite others in your work and your discussions, you cite the names who now are mainstream. You don't look for the truth, because you consider the mainstream to be the latest truth. Wait! Wait! I'm not saying that I know what the truth is. All I am saying is that we have to ask ourselves this question. And I say that we're not necessarily going to get any closer if we let ourselves be guided by the zeitgeist, by the current powerful interests of the few, for whom the majority of mankind is just an item of depreciation in their bookkeeping. Anyway, what I wanted to tell you is that in my first academic publication I examined Armand Moens' theory. Full of pride I sent him my article. I didn't expect him to reply, but he did. I would like to read you a passage from his letter. Dear Herr Erhart etc., etc., etc . . . yes, here it is: What you have done is most flattering and testimony to your considerable talent. You have cited my work favourably while adhering to all the citation regulations. You have produced a perfect first publication, according to the rules of our business. But imagine you were to die now and this publication were all that remained of you. Would you still be satisfied with it? Do you not have any ideas, any visions that go far beyond what you have cited? Is this article really what you wanted to tell the world, what only you could say? Will it continue to have an impact if you never have the opportunity to say anything else?

I say: NO!

NO in capital letters, Erhart said.

And now let me tell you something else, he continued. If, as you say in your accompanying letter, you regard yourself as my pupil, then the first thing you need to learn is this: whenever you say anything publicly, whenever you publish anything, you must always bear in mind the possibility that these could be your last words. Take your next lecture – imagine you knew you had to die immediately afterwards. What would you say then? One last time you have the opportunity to say something, one last time, it's a matter of life and death. What would it be? I'm sure you'd say something different from what you've written in this article. And if not, then you shouldn't have written it at all. Do you understand what I'm getting at? There are countless words with which one can affirm one's life, secure an academic post and defend it, words that end up in collected works and commemorative publications, and I'm not saying that all of them are wrong or unnecessary, but what we urgently need are words with the existential weight of last words, words that won't lie dormant in some archive but will wake people up, maybe even people who are not yet born. So, my dear Herr Erhart, send me another text. I'd very much like to know what you would write if that was your last chance to say something. And then I shall tell you whether it's worth your while publishing anything else.

Erhart looked up. He didn't tell them that after having read this letter he was unable to write anything for weeks, until he found out that Armand Moens had died. He could sense that a peculiar atmosphere prevailed in room, which he wasn't able to gauge. António Pinto called out, Many thanks for this interesting . . . um . . . stimulus, Professor Erhart. Now would anybody —

Just a moment, please, Erhart said, I haven't finished.

So sorry, Pinto said, there are still some last words, so to speak. Please go on, Professor!

I have tried to show, Erhart said, that we need something completely new, a post-national democracy, so that we can construct a world in which national economies no longer exist. There are two problems with my thesis, which I shall defend to my dying day. The first is that not even you, the elite of international economists, members of numerous think tanks and advisory committees in E.U. countries, can conceive of this, can accept this idea. All of you still think in terms of national budgets and national democracies. As if there were no common market and no common currency, as if there were no freedom of movement for finance streams and value chains. You actually believe that something will improve within Europe if the Greek budget, i.e. a national budget, is restructured in a way that brings about the collapse of the health system, the education system and the pensions system in Greece. Then everything is fine as far as you're concerned. Do you know what your problem is? You're cats inside a box and there is no certainty that you even exist. You and your theories are only presumed to be real. Such an assumption allows calculations to be made, and because these calculations are possible, this is taken as immediate proof that the calculations reflect reality and that this is the only way it can be. No, wait! You can get all get up in a minute, there are a few things I'd still like to say. O.K., I acknowledge that you are experts of the status quo. Nobody understands it more intimately than you do, nobody has more insider knowledge than you! But you have no idea of history, and you have no vision of the future. Am I right? Wait, Professor Stephanides, I have a question. If you had lived in the era of Ancient Greece when they kept slaves and you had been asked whether you could imagine a world without slaves, you would have said: No. Never, ever. You would have said that a slave-owning society was the prerequisite for democracy, would you not? No, no, Professor Matthews, please wait. Please. I am trying to picture you in Manchester at the time of Manchester Capitalism. If you had been asked back then what needed to be done to secure Manchester's future, you would have said, Under no circumstances must we give in to these unions; they're demanding an eight-hour day instead of fourteen, a ban on child labour and they even want retirement and disability pensions – that would totally undermine the attractiveness of Manchester as a place to do business . . . and what about now, Professor Matthews? Does Manchester still exist? Oh, and you can wipe that arrogant smile off your face, Herr Mosebach. The radicalism with which you defend German interests today suggests that, had you been born in an earlier era, you would have ended up a defendant at the Nuremberg Trials. And you don't even know it. But please don't tremble, dear Mosebach. People like you are always pardoned, for any expert witness can see that you're not a bad man, you're just blinded. You are a fellow traveller. And this is the problem with all of you. You're all fellow travellers. You are outraged when somebody tells you this today, but you are precisely the people who, when there is a catastrophe tomorrow and perhaps even a trial, will say in your defence that you were only fellow travellers, tiny cogs in the system. So now I ask you, do you have any clue what we're discussing here? We're discussing the future development of the European Union – a post-national community, born of the realisation of the historical error that you consider again to be "normal": this is how the world is, this is how people are, they want to define themselves by means of their affiliation to a nation, they want to define who belongs to their nation and who the others are, they want to feel better than the others and if they're afraid of them they want to smash their skulls in, this is perfectly normal, this is how people are, the main thing is that the national budget falls within the framework of the agreed criteria.

Thank you, many thanks, Professor Erhart, António Pinto said, now are there any questions —

Please, Mr Pinto, I'm not finished yet. A couple more minutes, please.

Erhart's briefcase had slipped from his lap to the floor, along with the text of his lecture. For most of the time he'd been speaking off the cuff, his lecture had strayed off course, but he was determined to get to what he wanted to say, the crux of his radical intervention. Just a couple more minutes for my summary. No, for my vision. Really the last words. O.K.? O.K.! Right, I'll start by summing up. Competing national states are not a Union, even if they share a common market. Competing national states in the Union block both European policy and national policy. So what needs to be done now? Further progress towards a social union, a fiscal union, i.e. the creation of parameters which will turn the Europe of competing communities into a Europe of sovereign citizens all enjoying the same rights. This was the idea, after all, this was what the founding fathers of the European unification project dreamed of – because of their experiences. But none of this is achievable so long as national consciousness continues to be fuelled in the face of all historical experience, and so long as nationalism remains largely unrivalled as an ideology with which citizens can identify. How can we make people on this continent more aware that they are European citizens? Many small measures are possible. For example, all national passports could be replaced by a European one. A European Union passport in which the holder's birthplace is noted, but not their nationality. I believe that this alone would stir something in the consciousness of that generation growing up with such a passport. And it wouldn't cost a cent.

Erhart could see that the idealists in the group were rocking their heads from side to side, but at least they were prepared to contemplate the idea.

But this is not enough, he continued. We also need – and we need this most of all – a symbol for our cohesion, it needs to be a concrete project a collective effort which emphasises what we have in common; we need something that belongs to everybody and binds them together as citizens of the European Union, because collectively it was the citizens of Europe who wanted and created this, rather than merely inheriting it. The first great, bold, conscious cultural achievement of post-national history, and it must be both of political significance and powerful psychological symbolism. What am I getting at?

Erhart could see that some in the room now seemed intrigued as to what would come next. Taking a deep breath, he said, The European Union must build a capital city, it must give itself a new, planned, ideal capital city.

Professor Stephanides smiled: The discussion as to which city in Europe should enjoy the status as capital of the Union is dead. That's water under the bridge. It was a sensible decision not to award this title to a single city, not even to Brussels, but to distribute the European institutions amongst different cities in different countries.

You have misunderstood me, Professor Stephanides. I'm not saying that a city ought to be awarded the title of capital. I am convinced that this would only fan the flames of nationalism in the individual countries, whose citizens would feel that their lives were being controlled remotely by this capital, which was also the capital of another nation. This, of course, is the problem with Brussels too, even though at first I deemed Brussels to be a sensible choice as E.U. capital: the capital city of a failed nation state, the capital of a country with three official languages. No, what I meant was that Europe must have a new capital city. A new city built by the European Union, rather than the old capital of an empire or country in which the Union is merely a tenant.

So where do you want to build this city? In which no-man's-land? In the geographical centre of the continent? The richest and most powerful nation in Europe can't even build an airport for its capital city, and you're dreaming of a whole new city? With a faint smile on his lips, Mosebach shook his head.

Do you mean a sort of European Brasilia? As a thought experiment I think it's interesting, said Milana Eliste, the Estonian political scientist who taught in Bologna.

You can't build this city in a no-man's-land, of course, Erhart said. There isn't any no-man's-land left in Europe, not a single square metre that doesn't have history. And this is precisely why the European capital must be built in a place whose history was decisive for the idea of European unification, a history that our Europe wishes to overcome, but nonetheless must never forget. It must be a place where the history remains tangible and alive, even when the last individual who experienced or survived it has died. A place as the eternal beacon for future policy in Europe.

Erhart scanned his audience. Was there anyone here who suspected what was coming? Milana smiled and looked at him inquisitively. Stephanides was peering at the window with pointed boredom. Mosebach typed something on his laptop. Pinto looked at his watch. But ten seconds later they were all staring at Erhart, their mouths agape. Speechless. Thirteen seconds later Erhart, the esteemed professor emeritus, was history as a member of the think tank "New Pact for Europe".

And this is why the Union must build its capital city in Auschwitz, he said. Auschwitz is where the new European capital must come into being, planned and erected as a city of the future, and at the same time the city that can never forget. "Auschwitz: never again" is the foundation stone upon which the project of European unification was built. And it is also a promise for the future, for all time. We must build this future as a tangible, functioning centre. Do you have the courage to entertain this idea? This would be a concrete outcome of our Reflection Group: a recommendation to the Commission president to launch an architectural competition for the planning and construction of a European capital in Auschwitz.

Alois Erhart set the suitcase on his bed in Hotel Atlas so he could start packing. His face felt hot; he thought he had a temperature. What he had just been through burned inside him. He pulled the curtains to one side and looked out of the window, down onto the square. Slow motion, he thought. Down below was hustle and bustle in slow motion. When the heat was oppressive everything moved very slowly, as if the movements were all part of a collective movement with a collective destination, the arrival at which must be delayed for as long as possible.

Erhart had learned that the project of European unification was based on the understanding that nationalism and racism had led to Auschwitz and must never be repeated. This "Never again!"

accounted for everything else, the Member States' surrender of sovereignty to supranational institutions and the conscious creation of a transnational, integrated economy. It also accounted for the most significant work of Armand Moens, who as an economist began to think about how the post-national economy should be organised politically. It was a question to which Professor Erhart had dedicated his academic life too. His life, the life of his teacher, contemporary history, the maintenance of social peace, the future of the continent – all this was based on two words: "Never again!" That was how Erhart saw it. "Never again!" is a promise to eternity, an assertion that claims eternal validity. The last people to have survived what must never be repeated were dying. What then? Did eternity, too, have an expiry date? Now the responsibility had been assumed by a generation which, in their political sermons at least, still felt duty-bound to voice this "Never again!" as a muttered warning. But what then? When the last person had died who could bear witness to the shock from which Europe had wanted to reinvent itself, then for those living now Auschwitz would have receded as far as the Punic Wars.

Whenever Alois Erhart needed a powerful, objective reason to explain his pain and submit himself defencelessly to it, he would think in such grand political, historical and philosophical terms. For this pain was world weariness, and for that no remedy existed.

Pragmatists like his father knew about remedies. In 1942, Erhart's father received a call-up to the OrPo – Ordnungspolizei, batallion 326 – which was being transferred to Posen to carry out the shooting of Jews under the heading: "Combatting partisans". To carry out the shooting of Jews. Alois Erhart found this drafting order in a folder in the drawer of his father's desk after he died. His father had already joined the Nazi Party before the annexation of Austria, after which he became the outfitter of sports and field equipment for the Vienna division of the League of German Girls, the Hitler Youth and the Gymnastics Association. Deemed essential to the war effort, this was how he was able to avoid being conscripted for so long. When he had to close the shop, his call-up became inevitable. Thanks to his good contacts and the services he had rendered, however, he was not sent to the front, but joined a police battalion behind the lines.

His father was in Posen / Poznań during the war? Was he, Alois Erhart, born in the shop storeroom while his father, a "policeman" in Poland, was executing Jews? Why had he never talked about it afterwards? For a long time Erhart had studied these documents in disbelief and eventually he questioned his mother. She was already suffering from dementia when his father died, and she followed him to the grave a few months afterwards. At that point, however, she was still alive and Erhart tried to stir her memory, but she just stared at him and laughed abruptly. Poland? she said, and began to sing. *Sto lat, sto lat*, she sang emphatically and joyfully. Alois didn't understand a word, he shook her by the shoulders and shouted, Mother! Mother! What are you singing? Erhart tried to memorise the words even though he couldn't understand them, but he remembered *Sto lat* and *Jeszcze raz* because his mother sang them over and over again. He ran to the lavatory and wrote them down, phonetically, roughly how they sounded. Then he went back to his mother, who was sitting there still, staring dreamily and saying nothing.

The following day Erhart asked one of his colleagues in the department of Slavonic languages. She said that the words he'd jotted down meant "one hundred years" and "again". And she thought Erhart's mother might have been singing an old Polish folk song. At any rate, *Sto lat* was a drinking toast too. Was this of any help?

No.

How did his mother know a Polish folk song? What had his father done in Poznań? And why was his mother, whose memory was shot, singing "Again! Again! Again!"?

Alois Erhart packed his suitcase, lost in thought and memories. He paused. Why was he packing? He wasn't flying back until the day after tomorrow, the room in Hotel Atlas was booked for another two nights and already paid for. The "New Pact" think tank was due to meet again tomorrow. Just because he no longer wanted to be a part of it, didn't want to show his face again, he didn't have to leave straight away. In any case he couldn't change his flight. Another day in Brussels, then.

He sat at the desk and opened his laptop with the intention of making some notes of the session from memory, summarising the reactions of the group's members. One by one, according to the categories he had sorted them into. He began with his Estonian colleague and typed "Eliste", but before he could write another word he saw that the autocorrect function had improved this to "Elites".

Oh well, he thought, shutting his laptop.

Matek took the 11.04 intercity from Kraków Główny to Poznań Główny, a journey that should have taken just under five hours and twenty minutes. It was over for him in less than three. Soon after Łódź the driver put on the emergency brake, hurling Matek, who had just got up to go to the loo, down the aisle of the carriage, against the back of a seat and then into the door, where he crashed to the ground. He tried to get to his feet but couldn't support himself, his right arm was at an unnatural angle, his legs wouldn't obey him, he couldn't draw them up and get onto his knees, there was a problem with his stomach, as if something had burst behind his navel, as if a powerful energy had been released that was now flowing red-hot through his guts, he heard whimpering, there must be other people injured, he tried to stand but could only raise his head slightly before letting it drop again. Somebody bent over him, said something, it was a woman's voice that inspired confidence in Matek, gave him a sense of security, he closed his eyes. He saw a small boy running across a field, flying a kite. Other children were running behind the boy, they wanted to snatch the kite from him, but the boy was quicker, and the quicker he ran the higher the kite rose, the line unravelling so fast from the reel that it tore and cut into his palms, now men with pistols and rifles appeared, they shot at the kite, but the large cross covered with red-and-white fabric flew so high that the bullets couldn't reach it, his hands bled, the blood dripped onto the field, the kite flew ever higher into the sky, he saw his mother standing to one side, laughing and clapping, and the boy let go, the kite flew up into the sun, to where the sun no longer dazzled, but turned deep red and finally black.

The following day newspapers across Europe carried reports of the rail accident. A man had committed suicide by throwing himself onto the tracks between Łódź and Zgierz, in front of the intercity train to Poznań. Rail traffic was blocked on this stretch for more than three hours.

It was an unusual report. This was a relatively minor, local accident, and there was a consensus in the media to keep such incidents out of the news, to deter copycats. But there was a simple reason why this one got coverage, even outside Poland: the victim, given that he was dead, was of general interest. The man who had thrown himself in front of the train was eighty-year-old Adam Goldfarb.

After 1942, next to the Łódź ghetto there was also a young person's concentration camp where Jewish children were incarcerated from the age of two. And Adam Goldfarb was the last survivor of this children's concentration camp in Łódź. Had been the last survivor. The motive of this "warning voice", as the paper said, was unknown.

Eleven

Something cannot fall apart
without there having been connections.

THE FIRST MEETING of the Council working group on the European Commission's Jubilee Project took place on the very day the Belgian newspapers, as well as some French and German ones, wrote about the scandal caused by the new exhibition in the Musées royaux de Beaux-Arts in Brussels. Like so many major scandals, this one had started small. Following the opening of the exhibition "Art in the sidings – forgotten works of modernism", a trickle of short, rather conventional and uninspired reports had initially appeared in the local media. When a collective exhibition displays works by forgotten artists, even the normally ambitious critic finds it hard to criticise the selection and complain that one or other artist who ought to have been included in this exhibition has been forgotten. For the exhibition is about forgotten artists only, and any critic claiming that a name or two is missing from amongst these forgotten individuals, also forgotten by the exhibition curator, would fall into a trap: they would be recalling a forgotten artist only to add them to the list of the forgotten. This gave rise to an art-history conundrum of infinite complexity: is there art that is significant in a particular era, but which is then rightly forgotten? Evidently. But why? We do not forget the era, so why do we forget examples of its art? Is there textbook forgotten art, does a prototypical forgotten artist exist?

To what extent does a forgotten artist deserve the verdict "forgotten" if a critic remembers them, and to what extent are they then not forgotten or all the more forgotten if the critic merely criticises the fact that they have been forgotten from the list of forgotten artists?

For this reason the exhibition was not a great success amongst the critics – the general thrust of opinion was that these were works of art that ultimately hadn't penetrated the market. But they weren't failures, for all the exhibited artworks had at some point after 1945 been purchased by the royal museums, which meant that at a particular time they must have been judged differently, as outstanding within the context of their peers, or at least as the works of promising young artists. Some critics, therefore, explored with greater or lesser originality the following question: How can something be regarded as important only to be forgotten so soon afterwards?

Thomas Hebbelinck, the exhibition's curator, revealed in an interview with *De Standaard* the puzzlingly banal reason for this exhibition: The royal museums were preparing a major Francis Bacon exhibition. The sums demanded by other institutions as insurance for their loans devoured such a large proportion of the budget that to plug the gap it had been necessary to stage an exhibition which cost nothing, i.e. featuring artworks from their own depository. This had given rise to the idea of displaying purchases by artists who were forgotten, an idea which he himself found exciting and worthy of discussion. For the question of what we forget and why we forget, and whether exhibited works perhaps show a collective desire for suppression, was of fundamental importance.

And that was that as far as the exhibition and the media were concerned . . . or so it seemed.

366

But then a long and razor-sharp essay appeared in *De Morgen* by Geert van Istendael, the renowned Brussels intellectual whose most recent mention in the media was as a member of the "Brussels seeks a name for its pig" jury. He opened a completely new front in the debate, which was half-heartedly defended for a day and then no more. He didn't discuss the forgotten art itself, but Hebbelinck's curation. The exhibition was entitled "Art in the sidings". Railway tracks had been laid out through the large exhibition hall, and at the end of them stood a buffer which, as van Istendael wrote, was probably intended to signify "the end of the line". Visitors were led down the left-hand side of the tracks, while the artworks – sculptures, paintings and drawings – were on the right.

Geert van Istendael began his essay with the words: "Although this exhibition provides much food for thought, there is one tiny but important detail missing: above the entrance to the exhibition the phrase 'Art sets you free.'"

And he posited the question of whether the museum, or the curator of this exhibition, believed that the relationship between successful and failed art could be compared to the selection on the ramp at Auschwitz. To the left, life; to the right, death. Presenting art that had failed to penetrate the art market as a mass of works being sent to their death at the end of a railway line – for how else were the tracks and buffer to be interpreted? – while visitors to the left were being told that they were classed as survivors, wasn't only making light of Auschwitz, it also emphasised the stupidity and inappropriateness of the idea that there always had to be a reference to Auschwitz. Moreover, van Istendael continued, the question arose as to "What is more outrageous? Equating Jews to bad art, or regarding the art market as a sort of Josef Mengele? Either way, this exhibition is an outrage and hopefully the last of its kind. For from now on the cudgel of fascism is a papier-mâché prop, crafted from the sodden catalogue of a poorly curated exhibition of cardboard cut-outs that call themselves artists."

That hit home. All of a sudden the exhibition, which newspaper arts pages had covered only half-heartedly, became a scandal that was flogged to death in comment pieces and editorials.

Even the grand old man of the bourgeois Belgian press, Tom Koorman, former editor-in-chief of *De Financieel-Economische Tijd* and now retired for more than ten years, made a return to his old paper with a comment piece: this exhibition was a crime, because it equated no crime with the greatest crime of all. The free world had the freedom to forget too, and the free market, including the art market, did not define itself by the worship of ashes.

This vacuous and at the very least unfortunate phrase "worship of ashes" in relation to Auschwitz led to further ill-tempered responses, even though Koorman certainly hadn't meant it in the way it was interpreted. But nor had Hebbelinck, the curator, intended any of the things he was accused of in the comment pieces and reviews. At any rate, on the day that the Council working group met, there wasn't a newspaper in which the "misappropriation of Auschwitz" did not feature.

Right at the start of the meeting George Morland said, This is off the record, please, but if the exhibition, which undoubtedly has a certain affinity with COMM's idea, were already part of the planned jubilee, I would not exactly call it a boost to the Commission's image.

When Mrs Atkinson read the protocol of the meeting she knew that she could . . . well, forget the project in its current form. Now there were only two options. First, shift the project definitively onto the Ark and thus let it fail. This would create barely any rumblings within the Commission, because nobody ever expected anything illuminating from the Ark. What had her colleague, Jean-Philippe Dupont, recently said about it? *"J'adore les lucioles, vraiment, elles sont magnifiques. Mais quand je veux travailler, elles ne me donnent simplement pas assez de lumière!"*

Second, she could focus on the basic idea of the Jubilee Project as a way to improve the Commission's image, but divorce herself from the content that had been dreamed up by the Ark. That, after all, had been one of the working group's suggestions: "Why the Jews? Why not sport?"

Yes, she thought. Why not indeed? Sport, which brought nations together – they could work with that in accordance with article 165, paragraph 1, Treaty on the Functioning of the European Union, as noted here in the protocol. Sport also fell under the Directorate-General of Education and Culture, so she could continue to work with Mrs Xenopoulou, and they could still count on the president's inherent support for the Jubilee Project. This was in the protocol too. A solo effort by the Commission was firmly rejected, however, as it would invalidate the point of the project, which was to boost the image of the Commission. All they agreed was that the project should be financed exclusively from the Commission's budget, although this would be hard to accept if the Council and Parliament were on the bandwagon and kept voicing all their objections during the planning. And could one expect Culture to discard its original idea, while being forced to implement a totally different one, but with no prospect of an exclusive image boost?

Grace Atkinson kneaded her fingers. She was doing well on Brussels cuisine; she had already put on eight pounds and was amazed that even the circulation in her hands and feet seemed to have improved. And no hint any longer of that pallor, of the face that used to be as white as paper. Now her cheeks were red like the portraits of Sir Thomas Lawrence, the queen's favourite painter. This might also be a consequence of the odd little glass of champagne – or prosecco, she didn't want to exaggerate – that she drank. In her experience a little glass, a tiny little one, two at most, stirred her imagination, made her more open-minded but also more resolute. It was merely out of habit that she still kneaded her fingers.

She kneaded and pondered. The first thing she had to do was to find out Fenia Xenopoulou's reaction to the protocol of the working group meeting.

Ought she to write her an e-mail and suggest a meeting to discuss how they could adapt the objections expressed?

No, nonsense. There was nothing to adapt. And an e-mail like that would already be tantamount to distancing themselves conclusively from the idea the Ark had proposed.

Grace Atkinson felt bad. She was a loyal woman and had honestly appreciated the commitment shown by Fenia Xenopoulou. Loyalty and fairness – for these weren't mere phrases, but principles anchored deep in her soul, human skills with which one went one's way with dignity and a definite ambition for success. She had got caught up in something where professional and human survival were perhaps dependent on other parameters, and she didn't know if this was connected to the fact that people with very different cultural backgrounds had to work together here, or if large bureaucratic systems fundamentally produced such contradictions. She had previously worked on committees at the University of London, then in the private office of the British foreign secretary. In both cases these had been slim, albeit not transparent structures. Essentially everything had happened behind closed doors – the famous padded doors were metaphor and reality in one. But here, here she was constantly under observation and all e-mails were saved and assigned to a folder, which after a certain time was sent to Florence, to the Archive of the European Union, where historians sat and poked about in them. If the foreign secretary's private office in London had to reach a decision, the discussion lasted half an hour at most, including all the rituals and small talk at the beginning and end. People there had the same background, they were of comparable stock, which meant they had also been to the same schools, spoke the same language with the same accent by which they recognised each other, they all had spouses from the same social class, between 80 and 90 per cent of their biographical details were identical and on the whole they'd had exactly the same experiences. Was there a problem? Within twenty minutes these white, Anglican graduates of elite schools had reached an agreement. Outsiders speaking in this circle sounded as if they were having a conversation with themselves. But here in Brussels? Around the table there were always people with different languages and of different cultural backgrounds, many from working-class or artisan families too, especially from the eastern countries, with very different experiences, and everything that Grace Atkinson was used to resolving in twenty minutes here took hours, days, weeks.

She found it fascinating. She had to admit that the decisions which the elite coteries in the U.K. were able to reach so swiftly didn't usually correspond to the interests of the majority of the British population, no matter who was in government. Here it was the other way around. There were so many endlessly painstaking compromises that nobody, no matter where, could understand that their interests were somehow represented in these compromises. It was more complicated, but more exciting too, although sometimes she thought there ought to be scope for a touch of authoritarian intervention, with the right to issue directives and intervene and . . .

Mrs Atkinson swallowed. She was shocked by the thought. Not an e-mail. She would have considered it unfair to distance herself from Fenia Xenopoulou on record. Totally unfair. She poured herself another glass of prosecco and decided to give Fenia Xenopoulou a call.

When Fridsch rang and asked whether she was free for lunch, Xeno thought he wanted to talk about the upheaval the Jubilee Project had triggered. It was in her interest, he said, some information he urgently needed to pass on, and he had suggested lunch in the Rosticceria Fiorentina, rue Archimède. O.K., she said, see you there in an hour.

Xeno wasn't naive. But now, reading the protocol of the Council working group, she wondered how she could have been so surprised by forces that she, with all her experience, ought to have envisaged and anticipated. And why she suddenly found the little games that were being played repugnant, even though they were routine. She'd seen all this for years, hadn't she? The general approval of an idea, followed by so many objections and suggested changes that nothing remained of the original idea.

In the novel that Xeno had read, the president's favourite novel, there was a bit where the emperor promises his mistress that with all his power, which after all comes directly from the gods, he will make the age-old human dream of flying come true. If he could achieve this miracle, it would not only consolidate his rule, it would also unleash his people's belief in what they were capable of, thereby increasing the happiness and prosperity of his realm. He summoned the most important philosophers, priests and scientists to work on a solution to this task, but efforts very soon failed because all these wise men couldn't agree on which bird was the right one from which to wrest the secret of flying. They couldn't see the flying, only the differences between the birds.

What puzzled Xeno in particular was the reaction of the Germans. The protocol began in very routine fashion with a "general approval of the proposal by COMM and the E.A.C. to organise a jubilee celebration for the anniversary of the founding of the European Commission, with the aim of improving the Commission's image (PT, IT, DE, FR, HU, BG, SI, AT, FR, UK, NL, HR, LV, SE, DK, EE, CR, EL, ES, LU). BG underlined its particular interest in this initiative, which would occur during the period of its presidency.

And to begin with it went on like this, polite expressions of agreement, until the first objections emerge: "Approval of the budget proposal, but Member States (IT, DE, FI, EE, CR, HU, SI, HR, FR) demanded a binding commitment that even in the event of costs overrunning, the financing of the project should proceed exclusively from the Commission's administrative budget, without burdening the general budget. Council and Parliament would not agree to that. Nevertheless, the Member States (DE, IT, FR, HU, PL) insisted on the Council and Parliament being involved in determining the content of the project."

This by itself was pretty steep. But Xeno was flabbergasted when she read the objections to the substance of the project, especially from Germany: "DE queried the idea of Auschwitz as the fundament of European unity and stressed that the Muslims in Europe must not be excluded from the venture of European integration. (Agreement: UK, HU, PL, AT, HR, CR)."

Xeno regarded herself as hard-nosed. Over the course of her time at the Commission she'd had plenty of experience of resistance, obstruction and bureaucratic hurdles. And even though of late she had become more uncertain about her future career, she had always been able to rely on her ability to anticipate resistance, which meant she was prepared for it accordingly. But this objection by Germany – Germany! – and the list of states in agreement left her utterly speechless. She had not expected the Germans to express concerns about Muslims, and then for those very countries which in their domestic politics advocated the most robust defence of the "Christian West" to come out in agreement. And then Hungary voicing its fear that the endorsement of a wider European public might not be forthcoming if, at the heart of commemorations supposedly designed to forge an identification with the Commission, they put the crime against the Jews, without reminding people that the Jews were now inflicting on the Palestinians precisely what had been inflicted on them in the past. For this objection they were applauded by the left-wing M.E.P.s (from DE, GR, ES, PT, IT). And Hungary also wished to remind people that in the coming year they would be chairing the International Holocaust Remembrance Alliance (I.H.R.A.) and therefore organising a raft of commemorations anyway. Then the Italians chipped in: "IT suggestion to hold the jubilee celebrations in Rome, in memory of the Treaties of Rome. Official function in the Palazzo Montecitorio with the presidents of the Parliament, Council, Commission, Economic and Social Committee, Central Bank and Committee of the Regions, and . . ." – Xeno found this addendum especially perfidious – ". . . thus they can agree on a joint ceremonial declaration (Agreement: UK, DE, HU, CR, LV, AT)". For the first time Xeno wondered why people without even a knowledge of the basics kept having a say in the decision-making process. "In memory of the Treaties of Rome" – the Commission had its origins in the Treaty of Paris, not the Treaties of Rome, while its current iteration had its genesis in The Hague Summit. But nobody in the working group had said anything to counter the Italians' suggestion that the celebrations take place in Rome? Not even the French, who always knew better! No-one knew anything anymore. How could people forget so much and yet talk so much! Seen that way, the Italians' additional proposal was in fact quite touching: "To be followed by a people's festival in the centre of Rome."

Xeno found the proposal forwarded by the Poles with the words "Why the Jews? Why not sport?" so outrageous that she literally as well as mentally shook her head. If they went along with the huge support for this idea, the project would remain with her department because the Ark was responsible for European sport, but it had even less expertise and capacity in this area than in culture. The national populist parties were small beer compared to the nationalism of Member States' sports associations.

At that moment Kassándra came into the room to say that she had managed to get David de Vriend's most recent address from the registry offices: place du Vieux Marché-aux-Grains in Sainte-Catherine. But the building had just been pulled down.

Who is David . . . what?

But we discussed this. He would be ideal for our project. And there's no official record of his having passed away, which means he's probably in an old people's home. We can find that out too.

Passed away? Xeno said, feeling very tired. No official record? Thank you.

She checked the time. I've got to go, she said. Lunchtime meeting!

Fridsch was already there when Xeno arrived at Rosti. He was sitting at an outside table in the blazing sunshine, as if the street were a stage and the sun a spotlight now directed at him. This thought crossed her mind as she glimpsed him from a distance and then approached, also wondering for the first time about the word spot-light: spot-light!

She couldn't work out whether he had spotted her too. Fridsch was wearing mirror sunglasses – ghastly, Xeno thought. She hated mirror sunglasses; you couldn't see the eyes. For Xeno this was the direst of all disguises, even worse than the niqab and burka, which at least allowed you to see the eyes, the window into the soul, as people said. These shades also reminded her of men she'd been frightened of in her childhood. The ones her father had warned her about. Anyone who wears sunglasses like that, who doesn't show their eyes, has a dark secret. And who has secrets? The secret police, of course. That's why it has its name. It betrays people who then go to prison, or murders them outright, her father had said, putting a protective arm around her shoulders and pressing her to him.

Knowing Fridsch as she did, he would have bought these sunglasses at the flea market, but if he was wearing them now, then she had to entertain the possibility that mirror glasses were back in fashion.

He leaped up to greet her. Because she couldn't see his eyes, for the first time she became acutely aware of the hairs in his nose. They protruded from his nostrils like spiders' legs. At the same time she saw her own gaze in his glasses. She hated nasal hair. She shaved her armpits, her legs and trimmed her pubic hair, whereas this man wasn't even able to snip away these stupid little hairs from his nostrils.

What was wrong with her? Fridsch asked the question too: What's up?

Trouble —

Is the sun —

— with the project.

— dazzling you? We —

— Yes.

— could go inside. I —

— Yes?

— reserved tables both inside and outside.

He was so thoughtful. And inside he'd also take off his sunglasses, Xeno thought.

Forget the project! We'll discuss it in a sec, Fridsch said, holding open the door to the restaurant to let her enter first, then staring at her, fondling her with his eyes – with the pride of a man who had conquered this woman, and was at the same time moved by the fact that this pride filled him with feelings of tenderness. Tender tenderness. Was that a tautology? Surely there were grades of it. The tenderest tenderness! As if he were placing a hand on the belly of a pregnant woman – but what on earth was he thinking? He wasn't thinking anything, not in words, but if you could input your feelings into a programme that would translate them into words then roughly these words would come out.

Fridsch had combed his hair into a severe parting, signalling a pedantry and propriety that irritated Xeno. What wasn't irritating her at the moment? When they had sat down, Fridsch took off his sunglasses and leaned across the table towards Xeno. She ran her hand through his hair, ruining his parting, then laughed – a touch too falsely perhaps – and said, That's better! You look five years younger.

Is that what I want? Five years ago I wasn't as happy as I am now!

This response left her speechless. The woman who owned the restaurant arrived with the menus and took their drinks order: water for Fridsch, wine for Xeno.

Now you have everything you need to preach and drink, the

owner said. Xeno nodded politely; she hadn't understood as the owner spoke Bavarian. She was an Italian, from Milan, but before coming to Brussels she'd run a restaurant in Munich for years, and that's where she had learned her German. And she knew Fridsch was German.

She came to Brussels because of a man, she says "feller" when she talks about him, he was very good looking, "quite the beau", but "not in a good way" as it turned out, in short, he didn't live up to "what it said on the packet". Fridsch loved this restaurant and knew all the stories.

Not long ago she had announced closing time by playing the Internationale, Fridsch said, a few guests were quite taken aback. Do you know why? Homesickness for Milan, she said.

Xeno looked at him blankly.

Fridsch laughed. Her father, he said, was an ardent fan of Internazionale Milan, that's the famous football club in Milan. And when the club got to the European Cup Final against Real Madrid he travelled to Vienna.

Why Vienna?

Because that's where the final took place. Inter Milan against Real Madrid. Before the match the Austrian military band was supposed to play the anthems of both clubs.

Why the military band?

I don't know. It's just how it was. Do you think the Vienna Philharmonic are going to play on a football pitch? Anyway, the band starts with the Real Madrid anthem. Then it's time for the Milan song. But by mistake the band had been given the score to the Internationale rather than the club's anthem. So all of a sudden the communist Internationale struck up. And some of the Italian players actually sang along: "Stand up, damned of the Earth!" I've no idea what the Italian translation is. Playing for Madrid was

Ferenc Puskás, probably the best footballer in the world at the time. A Hungarian who in 1956 had fled the Soviet tanks in Budapest. He was so perturbed when he heard the communist anthem prior to the game that afterwards all he did was stray from one end of the pitch to the other in shock, which was why Inter Milan won 3:1 against the favourites, Real Madrid. And that's why, in memory of this triumph, her father kept playing the Internationale at home, and so she . . .

Fridsch could see that Xeno wasn't in the least interested. But he was so buoyant, so happy, his heart so full of emotion that he just kept talking. The owner arrived with the drinks. They hadn't yet glanced at the menu and simply ordered the set lunch.

Anyway, Fridsch said, what I wanted to tell you is important. Listen, your Jubilee Project —

Have you read the protocol of the working group?

Of course.

What's so important then?

Nothing —

She interrupted him, somewhat too loudly, and people at the neighbouring tables looked over: What are you saying? Nothing is important, and that's so important that you've summoned me here to tell me?

No, just listen! What I wanted to say was that there's nothing more you can do for the project now. It's dead. For a while it will go on as a typical Commission zombie, lurching through a few departments and authorities, before being buried once and for all. What you have to do now is put some distance between you and the project. Let the Sherpas take it to the gravediggers. You can't defend the idea, it'll never work. You're out of the game. COMM wanted a jubilee celebration, the president says he would support a good idea, the Council working group says there isn't a good idea, or it makes other bad suggestions, none of which have a chance because they're merely alibi suggestions, do you understand? If anyone still believes they can reap any personal benefit from this, then let them. But if someone's going to fail miserably with it, this won't be you. O.K.? You're out of the game, because you – here it comes . . . Fridsch was about to mimic a fanfare to herald his revelation when the owner arrived with the salad and said something in Bavarian that sounded like "garden".

Because you, Fridsch continued, you're going to be somewhere else altogether by then. A nice little career move, maybe to TRADE or HOME.

What are you talking about?

Wasn't that what you wanted? And I've discovered how to work it. Listen! You're a Cypriot, aren't you?

Yes, you know that already.

But was Cyprus a member of the E.U. when you came to Brussels?

No. I —

You came on a Greek ticket.

Yes, I'm Greek.

So what is it now? Greek or Cypriot?

Why are you laughing? Are you making fun of me? What's so funny? I'm a Greek Cypriot.

Let's take this nice and slowly, Fridsch said. Greece is a member of the European Union. The Republic of Cyprus is now a member too. But back then, before Cyprus became a member, you, a Cypriot, came here as a Greek.

Yes, that was the opportunity I had. As a Greek Cypriot I could get a Greek passport and —

And now you've got a completely different opportunity. Because the Republic of Cyprus has also been a member of the

Union for several years. A small island. Half of a small island, in fact. With fewer than a million inhabitants, a country with roughly the same population as Frankfurt. That's bizarre, isn't it? And what do the people there do? Are they tourist guides? Diving instructors? Olive farmers? I don't know. But there's one thing I do know . . .

Xeno looked at him, his beaming eyes, he was working towards a climax, she didn't know yet what, she found something about this disagreeable, like a very subtle insult she couldn't yet understand. Now she wouldn't have minded if he put his mirror shades back on.

Your tiny Republic of Cyprus can't fill its quota of officials at all levels of the hierarchy, it can't occupy all the posts to which Cypriots are entitled. Too few of its people are qualified. Now do you understand what I'm getting at?

This was the important thing you had to tell me?

Yes. Isn't it wonderful? So logical. So simple. You get yourself a Cypriot passport and with your C.V. you'll get a directorship at once.

But someone would have to go.

The Brits are going. Others are retiring. In a month's time one of our directorships in TRADE will become free. And another in HOME. And if the Cypriots, who occupy only 50 per cent of the posts allotted to them, can suggest someone —

But I passed the *concours*, I haven't been on a national ticket for ages.

Even better! The Republic of Cyprus will be delighted to be able to place one of its citizens, such an experienced and permanent official, in a position of responsibility within the Commission.

And all I've got to do is . . . get a new passport?

Yes. Which you can, of course, immediately.

Fridsch's eyes shone. He was surprised that Fenia showed no sign of enthusiasm.

Garden!

They said little as they ate their ravioli. Fridsch thought she needed to digest this information first. He put off the other important thing he wanted to tell her, the private matter. Feelings were so hard to comprehend, and no sooner had one put them into words than they were so uncertain again. He thought it would be better if she felt grateful towards him first.

After lunch Fenia Xenopoulou was back at her desk, answering e-mails, typing set phrases that were as routine as they were vacuous . . . and soon she got stuck. How should she react to the suggestion Fridsch had made? Now she no longer saw the screen, only images from her memory, and her fingers lay motionless on the keyboard. She leaned back. This thing with the passport, surely . . . she leaped up and opened the window. The heavy, sun-warmed air that poured into the air-conditioned room reminded her of summers in Cyprus as a child. Although the sky was just as cloudless in those days, for her it wasn't the cloud-free time she'd seen those children from moneyed families enjoy, playing games in sunny meadows and being cuddled by their parents. She saw herself reflected in the window, but only hazily, as if this image were a projection from a distant time, no, of course it wasn't, she could see how hard her mouth had become, wrinkles on either side, in her reflection they looked as if they'd been airbrushed on. It was her and yet it was a different person, it was . . . she hurried back to her desk and called Bohumil: Could you pop in to see me for a moment?

He came at once and Xeno asked him for a cigarette.

They're in my office, I'll go and fetch them, he said, then looked up at the smoke alarm. Shall I bring my ladder too, and tape that thing up?

Not necessary, she said, I'll smoke by the window.

He came back, gave her the packet and said, Keep it. There are only five left. I've got more in my office.

Thanks, that's very kind. Do you have a light?

She stood smoking by the window, staring at Bohumil in a way that made him feel uncomfortable. As if she were all at sea. And looking straight through him. Was it because of the Jubilee Project? He knew that there were problems with it, obviously, in fact he'd been expecting her to talk to him about it. But she didn't touch on the project. It was eerie. She was a hard-nosed pragmatist, but he'd never seen her so unhinged. O.K., he said, taking a step backwards. He was about to leave the room when Xeno said, Do you have a passport?

Bohumil looked at her in astonishment.

I mean, she said, what passport do you have?

She was expecting him to say, A Czech passport, of course. And she would have nodded and envied his "of course". But for a moment she was dumbstruck. I've got an Austrian passport, he said. Why do you ask?

She looked at him, holding the cigarette to her lips without taking a drag and screwing up her eyes. Then she stuck the hand with the cigarette out of the window and shook her head. Did you just say an Austrian passport?

Yes, Austrian. Why?

That's what *I'd* like to know. *Why*? You're Czech.

Yes, but I was born in Vienna. My grandparents came over in 1968, when the Russian tanks quashed the Prague Spring – you know, the Prague Spring?

Xeno nodded.

Well, my grandparents fled to Austria. With my father, who was sixteen at the time. Ten years later my father married my mother, who was also the child of Czech refugees in Vienna. By then the two of them were Austrian citizens, and so when I was born I was an Austrian citizen too. In December 1989, right after the revolution, we went back to Prague. This was my parents' triumph, the fall of communism. I was ten at the time. In 2002 I did the *concours* in Brussels. I'd studied political science in Prague, but I wanted to get out and it was a good thing I still had my Austrian passport, because Austria was already a member of the E.U., whereas the Czech Republic wasn't. That's why I'm here and – he smiled – that's why I'm a smoker and always have a packet to spare.

Xeno looked at him, her eyebrows raised.

Well, as a small child I would spend every evening with my parents in Vienna's smokiest pub, Azyl, a meeting point for exiled Czech dissidents and those who'd escaped. My parents went there every evening, they didn't have any money for babysitters so they just took me along. They'd spend hours chatting to Václav Havel when he was in Vienna, Pavel Kohout, Karel Schwarzenberg, Jaroslav Hutka and all the others. And they chain-smoked, every one of them. I would sit or sleep beside them, I was addicted to nicotine before I even smoked my first cigarette.

He laughed, but broke off when he saw Xeno's face.

And? she said.

That wasn't the end, he said – he'd understood "End?" – or maybe it was: for my father. Havel became president, Schwarzenberg foreign minister, Kohout almost got the Nobel Prize in Literature – at least that's what he said – and Hutka, who'd been a star on Radio Free Europe, toured the country with his protest songs until a generation had grown up who no longer understood them. He retired with the title "living legend". My father became education minister . . . and on the day he was sworn in he suffered a heart attack. He went down in Czech history as the "ten-minute minister".

I'm sorry.

Thanks. Me too.

At any rate, you can speak German, Xeno said.

Lausig, Bohumil said in German.

Lousily?

Yes.

But why? If you —

Because when we went back to Prague, so from the age of ten, I never spoke it again. And although I learned German at primary school in Vienna, we always spoke Czech at home. In fact there's only one thing I've retained: I can't help laughing at German loan-words in Czech. "*Pinktlich*", for example. It's a Czech word that comes from the German and means everything that's unappealing and ugly and typically German: it means pedantic, inflexible, insensitive, mercilessly thorough, self-righteous, with Prussian discipline – if someone's like that, in Czech you say that they're *pinktlich*.

He laughed. And stopped laughing at once. Xeno's poker face.

I see, she said. What about the passport? Did you ever have a problem with it?

No, why? What sort of problem? It doesn't matter which passport I have, does it? It's a European passport.

Xeno had tossed the cigarette out of the window and now took another from the packet, put it between her lips and stuck her mouth towards Bohumil. If you ignored the cigarette it looked as if she wanted to give him a kiss.

He lit her cigarette, she thanked him and turned to the window, which Bohumil took as a subtle hint that he could leave now.

He said, O.K., well, and she said nothing, she just stared out of the window. So he went. He felt as if he were leaving a morgue. Could he identify the corpse? It looked familiar, but he couldn't be sure.

What was Xeno's problem? So surprised was she by Bohumil's story it was as if she were paralysed. Cheery old Bohumil. But it wasn't that simple. She was torn. She was divided in two. She didn't understand why she should be, for in a some way his story was hers too. And yet hers was quite different. This confused her. Initially.

She had a passport that had always been her European passport, rather than a badge of her national or ethnic identity. For her it was the entry ticket into Europe's realm of freedom, free movement and the right of establishment, it was her licence to go her own way in Europe. Χαῖρε, ὦ χαῖρε, Ἐλευθερία! she had sung fervently as a schoolgirl in Cyprus on occasions when the national anthem was played: Hail, O hail, Liberty! But it would never have crossed her mind that as a Greek Cypriot she must become a Cypriot nationalist – that was totally alien to her. Why should your place of birth be more important than the ambitions you could have – indeed had to have – as a human being? Freedom, she could understand that, but Cyprus über alles? That would never have occurred to her. Which was why she hadn't been in the least surprised when she came to Greece to study and realised that they sang the same hymn here: Χαῖρε, ὦ χαῖρε, Ἐλευθερία! For her, therefore, it wasn't an affirmation of nationality, nor did she find it at all confusing that two countries should have the same hymn, a hymn that for her was simply a song about freedom – and how apt it was for her situation: Arisen from the sacred bones of the Greeks! Arising, rebirth – this implied energy, a productive force.

But surely the promise of freedom couldn't mean: wither away in your narrow world, but your thoughts are free! Look at the olive trees in the parched grove beside your house! How little they need, and yet their leaves shimmer like silver in the sunlight.

If your thoughts are free then so must your opportunities be, your deeds, your actions. She already understood this when she was twelve, dragging bottles of mineral water to the dried-up Baths of Aphrodite, for tourists from all corners of the globe. From all corners of the globe – she had learned this at school – they always came to Cyprus, because Cyprus is so close to Turkey, to Greece, to Syria and Egypt, so was always a crossroads between Europe, Asia and Africa. Cyprus wasn't a nation, this island was a tiny ship, rocking on the waves of history and the tides of nations and the wealthy who surfaced and then sank again.

When she obtained her Greek passport she would never have thought that this meant she was abandoning and betraying the country of her birth. For her the Greek passport was a travel document, from the island with a dove on its coat of arms to the continent that regarded itself as a peace project and offered her career opportunities. Now she found it totally crazy that she should relinquish this passport and exchange it for another, which could do nothing different and promised nothing different from the old one. It only demanded of her that as a Greek Cypriot she decide whether she was Greek or Cypriot. She was to swap her passport, which she had considered to be a European document, for one that was now a profession of nationality – in order to further her career in Europe. Yes, that *was* crazy. She had worked long enough in the Commission to know that the nationalists were bashing this Europe with escalating brutality, this Europe in which she wanted to go her own way, freely, with all the anger and frustration she'd brought from her narrow world and which, it struck her then, was perhaps subconsciously an anger at the constraints that forced one to say, I am . . . a Cypriot! Or a Greek. Or something else. Anybody who says, You are . . . means: Stay where you are!

Fridsch's suggestion had turned her entire life upside-down. Identity was just a piece of paper, wasn't it? Would she become a different person if she swapped this piece of paper for another? Would she become a different person if, instead of "Hail, O hail, Liberty!", she now sang "Hail, O hail, Liberty!", the anthem of the new passport, which was identical to the anthem of the old one? Yes – because she would have swapped an anthem to freedom for a national anthem, and thus the same text and same melody would assume a quite different meaning. She had been born in Cyprus a Greek, and in Greece she was a Greek, born in Cyprus. It was crazy that she was being forced to regard this identity as a dual one, requiring her to make a decision: You are schizophrenic – decide who you are!

The awful truth was that, beneath it all, she knew she was lying to herself in her ruminations. Of course she would grasp this opportunity and change passports. It took her two hours to admit this to herself. She was a pragmatist. And this was nothing more than a pragmatic decision. Why should she have such scruples? Because she had a niggling feeling that something inside her was dying. And who likes to die? The prospect of a better life thereafter, whether you're talking about God or a career, is no more than a desperate consolation.

She began an e-mail to Mrs Atkinson, then paused and closed the document. A window popped up that said, "Save as a draft?"

How happy she would be if in life it were possible to do what the computer offered: to save drafts. She clicked on "No", leaned back and thought: O.K.

It was almost 5.00 p.m. She wrote another circular e-mail to her colleagues: "Meeting re: burying Jubilee Project tomorrow, 11.00 a.m."

Martin Susman would be back by then.

She deleted "burying" then clicked "Send".

Xeno switched off her computer and left the office. She didn't want to "go home", to her small, functional apartment which was basically a place to sleep with a walk-in wardrobe. But she didn't want to stay here any longer either, at a workplace she'd already deserted with the decision she had just made. A drink somewhere? She couldn't decide. If so, then in Het Lachende Varken, the café in the street where she lived.

She walked up rue Josef II to Maelbeek Metro station. The information board on the platform said: Next train in 6 minutes.

So it really was true. A man could be transformed into a beetle.

This thought was just a tiny and yet typical symptom of the fact that strong, robust Florian Susman was all of a sudden a different man: shocked, helpless, desperate. He was not well read. His younger brother Martin had always been the one into books.

What are you reading now? Stories about Indians?

No. A man is turned into an insect, a beetle.

By a magician?

No. Just like that. Out of the blue. He wakes up and finds he's a beetle.

How weird he'd found his younger brother in those days. How could you read something like that, waste your time with such stupid books? He had been his father's son, the designated heir to the throne, idolised by his father even though he'd been treated without affection. He, who would take over the farm one day, must not be a sissy, he must never be weak or dreamy. His father didn't express emotion. If he ever showed any at all, it would be a look of approval, a nod or an awkward arm around Florian's shoulder and a brief squeeze that said, My son!

Martin was his mother's son, a dreamy child who cried a lot, read a lot and was often frightened. Then he would run to "Mama", who protected him, but she too found it hard to show affection. Life's struggles had hardened her, the debts they had incurred in the expansion of the farm into a pig enterprise and slaughterhouse had given her sleepless nights. Every muscle was tense. Those who carry weights cannot caress. Which didn't mean that she rejected him, even though she was sometimes bemused and wondered why he was as he was. She felt that he ought to toughen up, he needed a shell, and certainly he ought to show willingness to do his bit, help out with the work on the farm, no matter how inept he was. Whenever she caught him reading she would send him to the stalls. It was pointless, because by this time the pigs were being fed mechanically and the stalls were mucked out by two employees using machinery. Which meant that Martin just got in the way. Eventually he would run back to the kitchen, where she let him either help with the cooking or read. Until he had to set the table when the men came in to eat, his father, his elder brother and the two employees with their pungent odour – the men.

Transformed into a beetle? Just like that? Without a magician? What nonsense!

Can you remember, Florian said, how old we were? Fourteen and sixteen? And now he lay there like a beetle that had fallen on its back. Now he had been transformed into a helpless beetle. Suddenly. Just like that. And was waiting to be looked after. Waiting for infusions to combat the pain, waiting for food, waiting for attention. Whenever he could he read, newspapers at first, and then the books that Martin brought him. When reading became too strenuous, made his eyes tired and his arms heavy, he dozed, ruminated, dreamed. In-between times his younger brother attended to an array of matters that had arisen and needed to be dealt with, while Florian lay helpless on his back. Discussions with the ward doctor and telephone conversations with the company Florian had private supplementary insurance with. He made enquiries as to which surgeon had the best reputation, in order that he might have them carry out the complicated and dangerous operation on Florian's back. They needed to be a master of their craft . . .

A magician?

No, just a no-nonsense master of their craft, Martin said.

Martin informed the Austrian pig farmers' guild, the chamber of commerce, Florian's business partners and the chair of the European Pig Producers. At Florian's request he asked the E.P.P. for a report of the conference in Budapest and stayed in constant contact with Marlene, Florian's wife, who had to hold the fort on the farm. He organised a lawyer specialising in traffic offences and accident damage, instructing him to represent his brother against the insurance company of the taxi driver, who had been to blame for the devastating accident, and this led to a civil case to press the compensation claims for both damage and personal injury.

Florian either read or stared at the ceiling. An uncanny role reversal, just like that, suddenly, without a magician.

Now Florian had a titanium plate and twelve screws in his back, his spine had been stabilised, the spinal cord was undamaged and any danger of being paralysed had evaporated. Florian was congratulated on his lucky escape.

He lay on his back, dreaming, occasionally sighed or groaned, and he smiled when his brother whispered to him, dabbed the sweat from his brow and took his hand.

When our father died he was as old as I am now, Florian said. I was young at the time, but I could . . . my children, if I'd died now – Elisabeth is seven, Paul is five – it would be . . .

Isn't it weird that this happened to me now, at the age our father was when . . . do you know what's strange? I've never thought about death. Not even beside Father's open grave. A shovelful of earth thrown on top and . . . yes, I was in shock. But I never thought about death, only about myself. For the living, death is always the death of others.

He ruminated.

If I'd died now, I wouldn't have been able to say goodbye, he said. Just like our father wasn't able to say goodbye.

He paused, then said, Is it better if you can say goodbye? Or is it only more painful?

He thought hard.

If I'd been paralysed, would you have helped me to end it? I wouldn't have wanted to go on living. Now I think I can rely on you.

No, Martin said.

As far as possible Martin exhausted his unused holiday, carer's leave, and eventually the opportunity of unpaid leave. Spring came, balmy air flooded in through open windows, the first pollen, and the hospital room was overheated because according to the calendar it should be cooler, and the heating worked in accordance with the calendar rather than the actual weather, Florian pushed the duvet off, shouted Ow! when he had to sneeze, the physical trauma still hurt his back, he sweated then shivered in the draught from the open window, Martin had to cover him up, then Florian angrily pushed the duvet away again, the only energetic thing he could do, the beetle lying on its back.

Martin had kept a small apartment in Vienna, in the second district, a pied-à-terre for whenever he came home for a few days, but it had never been home, it was a base, a kitchenette in which he'd never made anything apart from coffee, never opened a drawer apart from the one containing the bottle opener, where from one visit to the next jam would grow mould and butter pass its use-by date. A room with a bed and table. And boxes. Eight large packing boxes. He had left them here when he gave up his former apartment because he was moving to Brussels. Now he couldn't remember what was in them. His home. He had a room on the farm too, in his parents' house, with the pigs, three hours from Vienna, that wasn't home either, what was there for him?

Some evenings when he came back from the hospital he'd go to Zum Sieg around the corner, where he got a decent goulash and on Fridays excellent fish. Once he saw a German, brought to this restaurant by a Viennese acquaintance, ask in anxious confusion, Zum Sieg? I hope this isn't a Nazi place!

The waiter, who had heard this as he passed, propped his hands on the table, bent forwards and said, Hey listen! It means victory to the working class! Got it?

Martin had to smile. It was like a wave from the ghosts of history, a shard unearthed in an archaeological dig. Later the waiter came up to him and said, I was only kidding, you know! We're called Zum Sieg because the restaurant's been around since the victory of Aspern, the victory of the Austrians over Napoleon.

One layer deeper, another shard.

One Saturday he had breakfast at the Karmelitermarkt and bumped into Felix, a friend from his student days. He wouldn't have recognised him. He was recognised, though. It's great to see you! he lied. They drank coffee, chatted and Martin braced himself for sentimentality. It worked. The old days, oh yes, the old days! And do you remember back when? Yes, back when. They blinked in the sun, drank coffee and moved on to wine. All of a sudden the sentimentality turned to weepiness. Martin told him – why *him*? Why this stranger with the biographical pretext of having been an old friend? Maybe for exactly that reason! Martin told him he was vulnerable, depressive, he was suffering from depression . . .

Depression? Come off it, Felix said with morbid joviality. Tell me one thing: Do you brush your teeth before going to bed?

Martin looked at him in astonishment. Yes, of course, he said.

Felix laughed. Then you don't have depression. If you brush your teeth you don't have depression. At most you're depressed, he said. And I know what I'm talking about! He pushed up his sleeve and showed Martin the scars on his wrist.

When was that?

Doesn't matter, Felix said. The point is, I'd stopped brushing my teeth at the time.

In the meantime Florian was recovering slowly but surely. He didn't want to read anymore. He took part in life again. And this was strange: at the same time he began in some way to make peace with his life.

He learned that a new president had been elected at the annual conference of the European Pig Producers in Budapest. He had been expecting that. After all, his accident on the way there meant he couldn't attend, nor inform the E.P.P. board of the reason for his absence. Of course, this could only have been misinterpreted. As if he no longer had any interest in his position, nor even in the usual handing-over of office. So he could understand that they'd elected a new president, it didn't offend him. But what did cause him great concern – more than that: sheer anger – was that a Hungarian had been elected president, the ineffable Balázs Gyöngyösi, a radical nationalist who to date had used his work and involvement in this European organisation only to gain advantage for his own large Mangalica enterprise. He tried to abuse the European Pig Producers' lobbying position to have the "Hungarian Mangalica pig" trademarked as a protected designation of origin, thereby booting out Austrian and German Mangalica breeders. Besides, time and again Gyöngyösi had drawn attention to himself with his anti-Semitic remarks. For him the E.U. was a conspiracy of world Jewry to destroy the European nations, what he called the "host peoples". All these contradictions – demanding legal protection from the E.U. for his Hungarian purebred pigs, while in principle rejecting the E.U.; running a pig enterprise, while describing his mortal enemies, the Jews, as pigs – were not only grotesque; in Florian's eyes they were scurrilous and dangerous for the Union. It had thus been his intention to put forward a motion to have Balász Gyöngyösi expelled from the E.P.P. And now this individual was the new E.P.P. president. How was that possible?

Hungarian pig farmers and slaughterhouses were very well represented at the Budapest conference. Allegedly Gyöngyösi had bussed dozens of them in. His rival candidate was a Spaniard, Juan Antonio Jiménez, who Florian didn't know. The Germans and Dutch had apparently abstained, whereas the delegates from the smaller countries had united behind the Hungarian, and this was sufficient to outvote the French, Italians and Spaniards.

Later Florian found out the reason for this. The Germans had indeed negotiated a bilateral trade agreement with China to the point where they were ready to sign, as had the Dutch. As far as they were concerned, the union of European Pig Producers and the question of who should be its president was now . . .

. . . irrelevant! Florian exclaimed. Pardon my French, but they don't give a toss anymore!

He lay there motionless, staring at the ceiling, but Martin sensed that inside him a roaring animal was leaping against the bars of its cage.

Days later there came an e-mail from Gabor Szabó, the only Hungarian colleague Florian was still in contact with. Martin read it aloud. Hungarian pig producers were involved in bilateral negotiations with China. The delegation, led by Balász Gyöngyösi, was now in Beijing. "Just picture this. A welcome reception with food and plenty of toasts, and Balász raised his glass to say how delighted and honoured he was to be there and he drank to friendly relations etc. Then he said how the Chinese government was an example to Hungary for the clarity and determination with which it represented the interests of its people, for the benefit of the people, and particular admiration was due, for example, for the resolve with which they had undertaken their crackdown against enemies of the state in Tiananmen Square. The Chinese were extremely vexed. They hadn't been expecting the Tiananmen Square massacre to be mentioned, nor were they at all interested in it. In the ensuing negotiations they might as well have read out the Budapest and Beijing telephone directories in turn. Even before he'd arrived back home, Balász was dismissed as chief delegate and president of the Syndicate of Hungarian Pig Producers."

Florian smiled, then stared at the ceiling again. He ruminated. Martin squeezed his hand. Florian withdrew it.

*

At some point Martin felt the life sucked out of him by his brother, as if he had been a vampire. Was this a sign that everything had now returned to how it was, or almost? Florian could now lie on his side occasionally, get up for a short time and take a few steps.

I've got to go back to Brussels.

I'll never forget all you've done for me.

I've got a flight next Monday. I'll help you move to the rehab clinic over the weekend.

Thanks.

What are you going to do then? When you come out?

This is it.

What?

What I'll be doing. Nothing.

I mean when you're out.

What I just said. The E.U. is paying set-aside premiums for pig farmers. You get money for each pig you don't fatten. I'll let all our employees go. I'll look out of my living-room window and watch the farm go to ruin. At some point your successors can excavate it and draw their conclusions. In the meantime I'll collect the set-aside premium.

You're not serious!

Oh yes. I'll invest the capital in Germany, buy a share in a large pig enterprise, probably Tönnies Fleisch – I've got good contacts there through the E.P.P. – and with my experience and expertise I can play a role there. Or maybe not. At any rate, I'm going to stop farming. Can you see into the future?

No.

You can't see anything?

No.

Me neither. I can't see anything anymore.

*

397

The so-called "pyjama plane" to Brussels (7.00 a.m. Monday) was fully booked, of course. All the officials and M.E.P.s who had spent the weekend in Vienna and were now returning to work, and Austrian lobbyists and representatives of associations who had meetings in the morning and were flying back that evening or the following day. As was often the case, a dedicated Austrian school-teacher was probably on board with their class too, as part of the "Young Europeans visit the European Parliament" scheme. Martin had only been able to get a seat on the afternoon flight, which was fortunate as he overslept and would have missed the early one and possibly the lunchtime one as well. He hadn't got to sleep until almost four, unable to switch off. Late that afternoon he had taken his brother to the rehabilitation clinic in Klosterneuburg, then from the Greek place on Taborstrasse he had bought three bottles of Mythos beer, some cheese and a bottle of "Drama" white wine, and a flatbread from the Turkish shop next door.

He ate, drank and stared at the packing boxes, trying to imagine what it would be like if the next time he visited his brother and family at his parents' house, there was not a pig to be seen, the stalls, the large fattening shed, the slaughterhouse, everything empty, disused, the white tiles not bloody, nor gleaming white having been sprayed with a hose and washed down by Herr Hofer, but a dusty grey, dustily dry, Herr Hofer in early retirement, all the workers dismissed, nature having found its way into the disused sheds, ivy, ferns, creepers, weeds beginning to grow on the dung left behind by the pigs before the decommissioning . . . The windows broken, waterpipes burst due to frost in the cold stalls, cracks in the walls where airborne seeds have settled, sprouted and taken root, the render devoured by every variety of plant and the walls demol-ished, creating a biotope for mice, rats, hedgehogs, ants, spiders, swifts, hornets, wild cats, and Martin drank the third Mythos and saw the roof of the fattening shed cave in, it stood before the family house, the original living quarters of the old farmhouse that over the years had twice gained another storey and been extended, and Martin opened the wine and wondered whether they would really stand at the windows or sit on the bench outside and watch the roots of weeds and rank growth and the claws of all manner of wildlife sink themselves into the foundering family history. And if the business crumbled to dust, for how much longer would his brother be able to collect his set-aside premium?

He ought to go to sleep. He brushed his teeth. He smiled to himself: a good sign. A less good sign was that he sat down at the table again afterwards, wanting to smoke another cigarette and drink another glass of wine after all. He pondered what now awaited him in Brussels. Thanks to the circular e-mails he had realised that there were problems with the Jubilee Project. And of course he'd received the protocol of the Council working group too. He had skimmed it – and had not taken it particularly seriously. Important for him was that Xeno clearly wanted to go on with the project, at least there hadn't been any "Stop!" from her. Some evenings he had sat at the computer making a note of additional thoughts relating to the project. Even though he was on leave, he wanted to have something to put forward when he came back. In any case, he hadn't known what to do some evenings after spending the afternoon with his brother in hospital.

There was one idea in particular that he had pursued. If they were to present Auschwitz survivors as living testimony to the idea of the European peace project and the historical mission of the European Commission, then it would also be logical and rational to include officials from the time of the Commission's foundation, to let them talk about the ideas, intentions and hopes with which they had set about their work. Martin was convinced that the officials from the first generation knew far more accurately what its purpose was than the current bureaucratic elite. This would be, Martin Susman thought, the second jaw of the clamp, as it were. On one side the survivors of the extermination camp as a reminder of the oath: no nationalism or racism ever again. On the other side representatives of the founding generation of the European Commission as a reminder that its precise purpose was to build supranational institutions to overcome nationalism, and ultimately the nations.

He had written Kassándra an e-mail: What do you think?

Kassándra: I'll look into it.

One week later, Kassándra: First generation of the Commission: a) dead. b) dementia. c) no dementia, but can't travel. Do you want to proceed with this idea? Poss. video messages from c)?

Martin had finished the "Drama" wine, but still didn't feel ready for bed. In the kitchen he found a bottle of grappa. Don't do it, he thought, and opened the bottle. He staggered slightly as he took the three steps from the kitchenette to the table.

Maybe, he thought, the Jubilee Project ought to be organised completely differently. They should go the whole hog. Be uncompromising. If dementia and death prevented people from giving testimony and being able to remember what it had all been about, and what it was *still* about, then let the dead and demented come forward and vouch for it. They would elicit horror and sympathy, and they might bring about catharsis. Understanding even. All of a sudden a society with dementia understands what it had wanted to be, all of a sudden a terminally ill continent remembers the medicine that had promised a cure, but which it had discontinued and forgotten. How? How could this be played out? With actors? They would have to hire actors to appear as the officials from the founding period, not famous actors already fêted for the many different roles they'd played – they would just be themselves yet again, but in a different role, stars of pluralism, for whom everything was equally valid – no, they would need old actors, idealists who had never become stars, had never been able to make the big breakthrough even though they were masters of their craft and had garnered experience that shaped themselves and their work, but meant nothing to subsequent generations for whom fame was more important than truth, as was the rhetoric of truth as a platform for fame and fame as a platform for earning money rather than as a beacon of significance and meaning. Failed actors wouldn't even have to act this, they were what the dead founding fathers would demonstrate if they could be fetched up onto a stage tomorrow: inalienable respect for the ideals of their youth, despair at their failures and at their being forgotten, a longing for rediscovery and being remembered and the gravitas of an idea more beautiful than all the debris beneath which they were buried. Were there eighty- or ninety-year-old failed actors who weren't gaga and who could still learn their lines? These would be the authentic representatives of the founding era of Europe.

Martin drank schnapps out of his tooth mug.

He saw it in his mind like a film: the march of the dead, on a large screen, through all the streets and alleys, converging on the Berlaymont building, a demonstration of suppressed history, a torch of the founding fathers of the European project of unification. Then came the coffin. What sort of coffin? Who was inside? The last Jew, obviously, the last Jew to have survived an extermination camp. And who, in fateful coincidence, had died on the very day of a major anniversary of the Commission! The jubilee would have an ostentatious procession, a solemn funeral, bigger even than a state funeral, the first supranational, European Union funeral, the Commission president renewing the oath beside the coffin: "Nationalism, racism, Auschwitz: never again!" And following the death of the very last eyewitness, eternity would be extended, the line drawn under everything would be crossed and once again history would be more than a pendulum whose oscillations put people into a vacant trance. Now dark clouds appeared in Martin's film, in a dramatic spectacle of the firmament, as extraordinary as an eclipse, the clouds veiled the sun, veiled all light, with breathtaking speed, in fast motion – here the film faltered briefly because Martin got caught on the phrase "fast motion", he smoked, stared into the distance and thought: fast motion. Then the clouds gathered more thickly, the sky turned ever darker, a storm whipped up, tearing the hats from peoples' heads, he saw hats swirling through the air, darker and darker and . . .

Unconsciousness. It wasn't sleep. At some point around four in the morning Martin fell into unconsciousness.

He took a taxi to the airport, almost nodding off during the journey. He dozed on the flight. He swallowed aspirin like Smarties. At Brussels airport he took the bus from level 0 to the European Quarter, from where he walked the short distance to Maelbeek Metro station because the Berlaymont exit was closed again. He wanted to go home. Never before had he felt so intensely that his Brussels apartment was home. On the platform he looked at the display board: Next train in 4 minutes.

Professor Erhart had to check out of Hotel Atlas at 11.00 a.m., which was too early to go straight to the airport. He walked slowly across the Vieux Marché aux Grains, pulling his case behind him, which hopped and leaped over the cobbles as if Brussels were trying to be rid of him. What should he do to fill the time? Go for a bite to eat? Yes. But he'd had breakfast very late and wasn't hungry.

He made for Sainte-Catherine Metro station. What to do? It was unbearably hot and he began to sweat. In the paper he'd read about the "Forgotten works of modernism" exhibition and the heated arguments it had unleashed. Maybe he ought to go and see it? He couldn't make up his mind. When he arrived at the church of Sainte-Catherine he spontaneously went in. He had the time. It would be cooler inside. He had passed this church so many times before, but had gone in only once, on his first evening in Brussels, to escape a downpour. In fact the church looked like a cathedral. Maybe it was of historical or artistic interest.

No sooner had he entered than he wondered what he was looking for here. People sat praying in the pews, tourists held up smartphones or tablets and took photos, flashes kept lighting up the interior, while in the side chapels the flames of the votive candles quivered. He never visited churches in Vienna, so why should he go into one in Brussels? When he was twelve years old he had been on a tour of St Stephen's Cathedral with his class. Not for religious reasons, but for the history of his home city. And at fifteen he had gone to Midnight Mass with his grandmother, who when she heard death knocking at the door had discovered her faith at the last minute. But only after she had slipped him twenty schillings. Since that day he had never been back inside a church. He was glad that he hadn't been brought up to be religious; he was content with the inherent atheism of his parents, even though much later – far too late – he discovered that they had been staunch National Socialists and therefore anticlerical.

He walked up the left-hand aisle and was approached by a man in black dress and a dog collar: *Est-ce que vous l'aimez aussi?*

Pardon?

The black Madonna!

Following the man's eyes, Erhart noticed the Madonna statue.

A miracle! You can see it, can't you?

What do you mean? Her face? Because it's black?

No. Take a look at her hand. Do you see? The thumb was chipped off. Back during the Reformation the Protestants desecrated the church and threw that statue into the canal. Do you see the break? And now count the fingers! There you are! Do you see? Five fingers! The Catholics recovered the Madonna, returned it to the church and erected it again. And although one of her fingers had been chipped off, she had five fingers again! A miracle! Do you see?

With a beaming smile he crossed himself.

Could it be, Erhart said, that she had six fingers before?

The man in black looked at him, then turned and walked away.

Professor Erhart left the church and walked on to the Metro station. From Gare Centrale he could take a train to the airport. But he would be there far too early, and to kill time would wander listlessly through the duty-free shops, eat a poor sandwich, drink a beer, then another out of boredom, then wander around again, buy a coffee, sit somewhere and wait. Eventually, because time simply refused to pass, he would buy some Belgian chocolates, because Belgian chocolates were what you brought home, although he had nobody he could or wanted to give them to, Trudi had liked chocolates, sometimes he used to bring her one of those Milka rolls with the blue tassel, in the early days on their dates, later as a little gift when he came home from the university and when there was still that shop on Grillparzerstrasse, around the corner from the Institute, Bonbon Kaiser, run by old Herr Kaiser who would say things like, "Please give my regards to your wife, Herr Professor", when Erhart was still an assistant, and he had been delighted to see Trudi's delight, but he himself wasn't that fussed about chocolate, so why buy some now? When he was last at Brussels airport he had bought a box of chocolates from Neuhaus just to kill time. It lay around in the kitchen at home for weeks, in fact it was still there somewhere. He didn't get out at Gare Centrale but continued on to Maelbeek; he knew of an Italian restaurant somewhere close to the station, where he'd been one time after a "New Pact" meeting. It was friendly and unfussy, and the food was so good that you could enjoy it even if you weren't hungry. He found the Osteria Agricola Toscana again, and while waiting for his food, and then as he ate and drank his wine, he contemplated his future. Or at least that was his intention, but it wasn't so simple. The only certainty he could have about his immediate future was that everything he was eating and drinking now would be metabolised and, once he was back in Vienna, egested. He urged himself to think less banal thoughts. It wasn't so simple. He was enjoying the food, but it felt like a waste. Such good food just for him, and he was unable to celebrate it with anyone. The wine was excellent. He thought about his future. He thought that he might as well start pondering whether there was life after death. Yes indeed, he thought, it was called posterity. Could he leave something behind that might have a lasting influence? A testament? He thought that he might still have enough time to write a book. Could you plan and write a book in such a way as to make it a testament and establish a legacy that future generations might actually make use of? An autobiography, perhaps? He could write an autobiography cataloguing his experiences and thoughts, so that one day it would be possible to remember what might have been and what rumbled on, as yet unresolved. In Armand Moens' autobiography he had read: "History is not only the account of what happened, but also a continual assessment of the reasons why things could not have happened more rationally." This would have to be the epigraph of his own book, he thought, ordering an espresso and the bill. Rather than writing an autobiography that recounted his modest life, he wanted to set out what had *not* happened. The non-happenings of his time. And time was now short. He had to get to the airport. He paid for the entire bottle of wine.

He became fretful, he had lost track of the time.

Should he go to the rond-point Schuman and take the bus to the airport? Or head back to the Metro, three stations to Gare Centrale and take the train? He thought the train would be quicker. He ran with his hopping suitcase to Maelbeek station, stumbled down the escalator, noticing too late that it was out of order, looked anxiously up at the display board: Next train in 2 minutes.

David de Vriend heard someone shout "Stay!", he put his hands over his ears, but heard it boom even more resoundingly in his head, this "Stay!", as if it were being tossed from side to side inside his skull, echo following echo, "Stay!", and he knew he had to go. Straight away. No more deliberation, just a decision. Out of here and away at once.

He didn't even close the door behind him. He didn't bump into anyone. In the stairwell, in the foyer downstairs, over in the dining room, in the library, it was quiet everywhere, not a soul to be seen. Most of the residents slept after lunch, or went for walks, either down rue de l'Arbre Unique to the stream with the weeping willows, where they would feed the birds, or through the cemetery to the bench, a short rest, then back for tea. The carers were now having their coffee break in the staff room, swapping notes about their problem cases.

De Vriend left Maison Hanssens as though it were a world without people. Or a railway wagon with corpses. "You're leaping to your doom!" – those had been the last words. He had to get away, as fast as possible. But where to?

It had been a decision that had left him no time to weigh up the pros and cons. Out! Break free and out!

He went to the cemetery gate, but not into the cemetery; he had an address he needed to get to.

When he had leaped from the train a young man had slipped him an envelope containing a safe address and fifty francs. It all happened so quickly. After an exchange of fire the train started moving again, but he saw it all so slowly, the train pulling away, the open sliding door of the cattle wagon like a black hole, behind it his parents and little brother, it was as if this image were edging forwards centimetre by centimetre, gunshots and a stamping and gasping, the clatter, now faster and faster, as iron hit iron, a shove, the man shoved him again and shouted, Run! Go and find the address – he pointed to the envelope he had just handed him – in there! And the train picked up speed, the black hole, behind which his family were huddled, was gone, another black hole trundled past, and another, and he turned and saw people running across the fields, how many were they, a hundred? Here and there he saw individuals collapse or crumple, hit in the back by bullets, and he threw himself on the ground, rolled down the railway embankment and lay flat until the train had passed, S.S. men were shooting from it at the escapees. Only then did he run away.

On the field in front of him he saw people who had thrown themselves to the ground and were now getting up. He ran past people who lay there and would never get up again. He ran into the night. He had an address.

He didn't know the way. A bus came, stopped beside the cemetery gate.

Bus number 4 – this meant nothing to de Vriend. He got on. The bus drove off. Took him away. He left everything behind. Upon arrival in Auschwitz his parents and brother were sent straight to the gas chamber. He couldn't have saved them even if he hadn't leaped from the train, if he'd stayed with them. And there had been no time to discuss it: Shall we jump or not jump? What can we expect in the first scenario and what in the second? He had jumped. He had survived. His father, that small accounting clerk, that weak, delicate man with the sad, dark eyes, who was able to contribute nothing more to the workings of the world than his ruthless propriety, his trust in the auditing process, the affected pride that was in fact his defiance against the times, against the ironic, condescending smiles of those greater and more flexible than he was. Even at home, within his own four walls, he maintained this act of absolute propriety as if the king and government were watching and nodding approvingly. And his mother, he saw her too, whenever he thought of her she had that sadly acquiescent look, both of them had those sad eyes, not because they could see what was coming, but because they believed everything would remain as it was. They hadn't been worried, they had merely settled into the worries that they considered to be their life, rather than cobblestones on the way to their death. Only once had de Vriend heard her shout, yell even: Stay! If he had stayed he would have ended up in the gas chamber like them. He hadn't saved them, and he couldn't have. Is that guilt?

He had an address.

Strangers had taught him pride and resilience. They had loved him like their own child. When he was finally betrayed, there was no longer enough time to murder a strong young man through hard labour. He had been lucky. Unlucky. Lucky in his misfortune. Unlucky, lucky in his misfortune again.

He couldn't find the address. Sitting on the bus he realised that his pockets were empty. He had to remember. He had to find the way, recognise it. He groaned. He had to remember. But there was only a black hole. He looked out of the window. What flew past wasn't a memory. There was no signpost, nothing that linked to his experiences. Façades.

Now there was nothing. The doors of the bus opened and closed. Then the bus jolted its way past façades again. The doors opened and closed. That's all.

The door of the wagon was wrenched open. A voice shouted: Out! Jump out!

The bus doors opened. Stay! You're leaping to your doom!

De Vriend jumped off the bus, almost falling over. A man at the bus station steadied him.

Run! To that address there . . .

De Vriend looked around, saw people hurrying down the street, he followed them. Where was he? By a black hole. There was a fleeting moment of recognition: Maelbeek Metro station. It sounded familiar. Why? He went in, down the steps. He had to remember the way. He came onto the platform and thought, This is the way.

One more minute.

A man with a bag. A woman tapping away at her smartphone. A man with a suitcase. The train arrived. The doors opened. In the open door in front of him he saw a child holding its mother's hand. The child wrested itself free as it jumped off the train.

Then the bomb exploded.

When Madame Joséphine and Monsieur Hugo, the caretaker at Maison Hanssens, were clearing out David de Vriend's room, they found a piece of paper with a list of names.

Monsieur Hugo threw three shirts into a box and said, He didn't have much.

Madame Joséphine nodded. All the names on the list were crossed out.

Very few of them have much stuff, Hugo said. I've been working here for eight years and I'm still always surprised by how little remains of a person in the end.

Yes, Joséphine said. She sat down and stared in amazement at the piece of paper. At the bottom of the list of crossed-out names David de Vriend had written his own.

He had nice monogrammed handkerchiefs, Hugo said, chucking them into the box too.

Only David de Vriend's own name wasn't crossed out.

He had nice suits! Really top notch. The homeless shelter will be delighted. But if someone goes out begging in a suit like that they won't get a single cent. Nobody's going to help a man wearing this suit, he said, holding up de Vriend's tweed.

Joséphine wished he would shut up. She said nothing. On the table in front of her was a biro. She picked it up and held it like a knife.

What did he actually do in life? Monsieur Hugo said. Was he some sort of prominent figure? A politician or a high-ranking official? I mean, the Commission's organising his funeral.

The silent funeral of an epoch, Joséphine thought.

What I can't find, Monsieur Hugo said, is all the classic stuff: photo albums, diaries. Very unusual. He didn't have anything, not even a photo album, everybody's got one of those, he said, tossing the shoe trees into the box.

Joséphine wondered what to do with this list of names. Throw it into the box? Or in the bin? Should she cross out David de Vriend's name too? Is that what he wanted? Is that why he left the piece of paper here on the desk, along with the biro? So that she . . .

Monsieur Hugo chucked toothbrush, toothpaste, nail scissors, deodorant and razor into a plastic bag and the plastic bag into the box. We're not even going to fill the box, he said.

Such a horrific death, Joséphine thought. That de Vriend, of all people, in this attack . . . But what did she mean by "of all people"? For all of them, all of them who were in the wrong place . . . for all . . . twenty dead, one hundred and thirty seriously injured.

She folded the list of names, put it into the pocket of her white work coat, patted the pocket and thought, So long as his name isn't crossed out, so long as . . .

That's all, Monsieur Hugo said.

Epilogue

THE **EDITORIAL OFFICE** of *Metro* had been expecting the protest by animal rights campaigners. Kurt van der Koot had warned them before the start of his series. The editor-in-chief had just laughed: a protest by radicals would only strengthen the bond between reader and paper.

The only surprise was how late the protest came – weeks after an article had appeared in *Le Soir*, attacking *Metro* and its sensationalist campaign journalism.

It was a cynical article in which *Le Soir* floated the likelihood that the pig on the loose in the streets of Brussels didn't exist and that the blurry pictures from C.C.T.V. cameras were fakes. This series in *Metro*, it claimed, was yet another example of how free newspapers functioned: stirring up excitement with invented stories. The piece was illustrated with a photograph taken in Slagerij Van Kampen of two pig halves hanging on meat hooks. The caption: "The end of Brussels' pig?"

Appended to the article was an interview with Michel Moreau, the president of "Animal Welfare Belgium", who described *Metro*'s actions as the "greatest scandal since Marc Dutroux". It was outrageous and abusive, he said, to exploit a pig running through the streets for a newspaper advertising campaign, rather than trying to rescue this pig, assuming it actually existed. The city's streets were not the natural environment for a pig which, faced with challenges such as tarmac, crowds of people and road traffic, might well be in a state of stress even more agonising for the animal than being kept in the stall of a factory farm. And he appealed to the "relevant authorities" to clarify once and for all whether there was a "real, living pig", and if this were the case to officially capture the animal, have it examined by a vet and then taken to a farm where it could be kept in a species-appropriate way. "As an animal rights campaigner I am very careful with my animal metaphors, but what is happening here can only be described as a pig's ear," Moreau said.

Now *Le Soir* had its own shitstorm. Dozens of readers protested in letters and online about the comparison between animal torture and the child abuse and murder committed by Marc Dutroux. Within a few hours the interview with Michel Moreau got hundreds of angry emojis on Facebook.

The attack on *Metro* backfired and for a short time became a problem for *Le Soir*. All the same the editors at *Metro* had an even bigger problem that needed urgent solving before the public got wind of it too: The "Brussels seeks a name for its pig" competition had got completely out of hand. Readers were able to post their suggestions online or like others' suggestions, and the rankings of the various names were updated with every new suggestion or click, corresponding to how many times a name had been suggested and the number of likes. This ranking was intended to be the basis for the jury's longlist. To begin with the suggestions had been the most obvious names: Miss Piggy, Babe, Peppa Pig.

The only Brussels-related names were Varkentje Pis (17 likes) and possibly Catherine as well (21 likes), because the pig had first been sighted in Sainte-Catherine. But then something inconceivable happened. One name was suggested hundreds of times, and it made its way to the top of the rankings with thousands of likes: Muhammad. That could only have been the result of concerted action. As soon as the editorial office realised this they took the page down. Several jury members resigned, unwilling to be associated any longer with a competition that seemed to be turning into an act of aggression against Muslim citizens.

We're axing it, the editor-in-chief said. We'll keep our heads down. Soon it'll all be forgotten. By the way, Kurt, have you noticed we haven't had any new photos of the pig for two weeks? And no reports of any sightings. It's vanished. Vanished without trace.

À suivre.

ROBERT MENASSE was born in Vienna in 1954 and studied there before moving to Brazil, where he lived for six years as a professor of literature at the University of São Paulo. He is the author of several novels translated into English, including *Wings of Stone* and *Reverse Thrust*, and of a work of non-fiction, *Enraged Citizens, European Peace and Democratic Deficits: Or Why the Democracy Given to Us Must Become One We Fight for* (2016). In 2017 he was awarded the German Book Prize for *Die Hauptstadt* (*The Capital*).

JAMIE BULLOCH is the translator of Timur Vermes' *Look Who's Back*, Birgit Vanderbeke's *The Mussel Feast*, which won him the Schlegel-Tieck Prize, *Kingdom of Twilight* by Steven Uhly, and novels by F. C. Delius, Jörg Fauser, Martin Suter, Roland Schimmel-pfennig and Oliver Bottini.